12+

D0585966

# BLOWN AWAY

# BLOWN AWAY

## PATRICK CAVE

**SIMON AND SCHUSTER**

**SIMON AND SCHUSTER**
First published in Great Britain by Simon & Schuster UK Ltd, 2005
A Viacom company

1 3 5 7 9 10 8 6 4 2

Simon & Schuster UK Ltd
Africa House
64–78 Kingsway
London WC2B 6AH

A CIP catalogue record for this book is available from the British Library

ISBN 0 689 87541-X

Typeset by Rowland Phototypesetting Ltd,
Bury St Edmunds, Suffolk
Printed and bound in Great Britain by
Mackays of Chatham plc

# The Sunday Gazette

Sunday, April 6th 2023        Price: £2.40

Austerity Edition: The editors wish to apologize for the brevity of the current editions of the Gazette. Whilst endeavouring to bring our readership the main points of the news in the best tradition of the newspaper, we would point out that current rationing of paper, electricity and other essentials is limiting our product. We intend to return to our usual format as soon as possible. Until then, we thank our readers for their loyalty.

## PM PROMISES IRON RESOLVE

### 'A steady hand on the helm, in the style of Churchill'

Last night the Prime Minister, Juliet Howell, promised in a statement recorded at an unknown location, that the democratic government of Britain would continue to function for the foreseeable future. She insisted that despite the closure of the Houses of Parliament due to security concerns, contingency plans were in place and that she was ready and able to lead the country through what she called 'this darkest time'. Twice she referred to her Tory predecessor of eighty years ago, comparing her own task with that confronting Winston Churchill as war threatened to overcome Britain.

'The determination and grit of these islands has been tested before, and not found wanting,' she said; 'I would ask all the good, strong people of Britain to tighten their belts, spurn the panic-mongers amongst us, and prepare to weather the coming storm in the best tradition of our grandparents and great grandparents. I cannot say "we will fight them on the beaches" for the threat this time is more complex, coming as it does from environment, disease and perhaps, war... but still I say to you "we will never surrender". And I offer you a steady hand on the helm of government to see us through.'

## INFLUENZA GRIPS CHINA

### Worst epidemic since 1918.

The World Health Organization today confirmed that the death toll in China and neighbouring countries from a new strain of influenza has now topped the 40 million mark, making it the most severe flu pandemic of recorded history, overtaking even the 1918 outbreak. Despite the relative lack of travel worldwide at present, owing to shortage of fuel and risk of terrorist action, the WHO is warning that the new strain of flu has undoubtedly got a foothold elsewhere in the world. A spokeswoman said: 'The resources to deal with such an outbreak are just not available to us... or to the Chinese government. It is an inescapable fact that such outbreaks occur very frequently in the wake of other disasters, whether famine, war or whatever. The rigours of the First World War left a population ill-equipped to deal with such a threat, and that is similar to the situation we face now.'

## PENSIONERS DECLARE READINESS

### Emergency fails to dampen party spirit.

The nation's senior citizens this morning declared themselves ready to face the days to come with humour, courage and plenty of tea. Celebrating its twentieth anniversary, the British League of More Mature Citizens settled in for a week of party events at the Wavetop Hotel, Lyme Regis, with good cheer and considerable scepticism about the bleak future that is being painted in some quarters.

'You don't want to get in a strop, dear,' a hundred-year-old delegate said gaily, as she arrived last night, one of the BLMMC's guests of honour: 'We seen it all, we have. It's never as bad as what they say. Just make a good strong cuppa and you're laughing. There's always a way to the light at the end of the tunnel.'

## MEDITERRANEAN WARS - TOLLS RISE
### Seville falls as refugees push north.

Fighting has again been bitter and prolonged at all the major flash points along the Mediterranean. In the wastelands of Palestine and Israel, bombardment continued through the night, but without movement on either front line. Hospitals across the Middle-East continue to struggle with the flood of cases of chemical and biological poisoning, many of them children, although both sides maintain their claim that the nuclear option has not yet been exercised.

Meanwhile in southern Spain, fresh waves of refugees and soldiers have been pushing over the Straits of Gibraltar, many of them heavily armed. Some are looking for food or medical supplies or a new place to live and work, many simply wish to lay waste to the homelands of those who, as they see it, have wreaked such havoc in their own continent with their economic hunger and wastefulness. EU troops have this morning fallen back and ceded Seville and its environs to the incomers. They hope to establish a new, stronger line of defence eighty kilometres to the north.

## OTHER NEWS IN BRIEF

• Flooding: More storms and rising waters threaten large areas of East Anglia, the Thames basin, the Fens... 2 million displaced.

• Rationing: The following items have today been added to fossil fuels, electricity, medical supplies and foodstuffs in the official government rationing list – clothing (including footwear), paper products of all kinds, timber, metal products. Detailed information from the Dept. of Rationing website

• Worldwide cloning ban: UN agree international deal following latest scandal of dead, deformed and disabled babies in United States cloning experiments.

• Lottery numbers: Last night's lottery numbers were – 3 7 19 20 22 and 41. Bonus ball was 8.

*There is no standing still*
*In this high, weathered place.*

*The sweet gale tugs,*
*Like infant fingers, at the cloth*
*Where your body hides;*
*Hurries you along;*
*Beheads the flowers so that they*
*Brush your cheek;*
*Brings bitter brine*
*To blind you, and*
*Gritty, scented loam*
*To choke you.*

*Let go.*
*Be blown away.*
*Be free.*

# PROLOGUE

Dawn in the mountains.

The first iron heat gathering, shimmering in bands across hard, thirsty slopes.

Two figures standing still in a high place, eyes closed, facing the rising sun across the dragon's teeth of the Pyrenees.

After too short a while, the girl, about eight, starts to giggle, quaking silently with her sunburnt face screwed up, until the laugh bursts out. The other, a young woman, poised and careful, opens her eyes. Her face is stern, ready to reprimand the girl for her lack of concentration; but it is difficult to be strict with the little one, all smiles as she is.

'I'm sorry, Rissa,' the girl sighs, still shaky and hiccoughing with laughter. 'Je suis désolé. Really. But you know, I *did* feel the rock and the air and myself and all that.'

The woman lays a hand on her head. 'Then let's pass on to another exercise, Adeline. Some movement work. The fifth kata. Remember, slow as a breath, and with deep, deep roots. Feel those roots through your soles. As if your feet were sticky on the rock.'

The girl nods cheerfully. She knows all this.

'D'accord.'

They perform their dance, gracefully and in unison. The woman has her eyes closed again. The girl, though, is soon watching a buzzard as it rests on the hot air, combing the ground for prey.

*In a minute,* she thinks, *we will stop for breakfast. Rissa will have currant rolls for us to eat, as a surprise. And milk. And maybe a fig or two.*

She slides into the final movement, her arms stretched out, palms flat, one ahead, one behind, knees slightly bent, spine vertical. It ends with the last sighing of breath, trickling from her lips, emptying her.

The girl wiggles her bottom before the woman reopens her eyes, but keeps the pose.

She is happy. Life is an intoxicating game.

'*Yes,*' the other voice agrees, inside her, '*it is a game.*'

# PART ONE

# DOMINIC
## – day 8 –

Hey.

If anybody is out there, please scream when you hear the tone.

Bleep.

Louder dude, I can't hear you.

*Get a grip, boy. Use your initiative. Don't let the family down. Se mundumque vince.*

(That's Father. He's allowed to bypass the tone. And he never screams. And yes, he talks like that . . .)

Today the endless cold became way too much and I used my initiative and burned Kingsley's desk. Hacked it apart with tools from the craft room, like a caveman. Tore the boards off the fireplace. So now I'm set up: a fire, some candles, a heap of crap books from the library, and (downstairs) two fifty-litre cooking-oil drums full of water in case that goes too, which it will. Christ, it must be at least five degrees Celsius in here now. I'm laughing.

Can you hear me laughing?

And tonight's decision is . . . I'll give it ten more days. Then try to make for one of the old man's houses. Not Kensington, of course; maybe the Tayside bothy, except that'll be even colder. Tomorrow I'll kick my way into the Geography department and sort out some OS maps. Not that breaking and entering has the same buzz any more. I even felt funny when I saw Jessica Ward's measurements (36C-24-34) go up in smoke on Kingsley's desk leg. Seriously, though; I thought I might cry.

Will I ever check out those fabulous measurements again or hear Kingsley's Neanderthal grunts as he imagines pawing the exquisite Ward form with his sweaty mitt? These and other questions will be answered, people, next time you tune into our story.

*The Kid Who Was Left Behind*.

Or what about: *The Kid Who'd Nearly Finished the Staffroom Scotch?*

Yes, that sounds more dramatic, doesn't it? The suspense of not knowing what the hero will do when it's gone.

I could always try for Ogilvy's, or the pub. If I have the guts.

Signing off. Passing out.

# – day 9 –

OK, so boy receives message from his old man; respected, iron-balled pillock of the establishment. Message comes unsatisfactorily from spittle-flecked lips of 'Wildman' Wishart, abnormally hairy Economics teacher, whilst said WW, flies undone, throws worldly possessions into ancient Renault and then churns up the gravel and mud to join the general exodus to God-knows-where.

Marks out of ten for the developing writing style?

'Don't bother with all that,' Wishart snaps on seeing boy shouldering rucksack in preparation for trying to hitch a lift to the station. 'Your father says you're to stay. Someone will come for you.'

Boy breathes small sigh of relief, whilst flinching from the spray, and asks, 'Who will come for me? Did he say, sir? And how long am I to wait?'

Wishart catches the corner of his 'Junior' sound system on the car door and spills a shoe box of CDs across the tarmac. What's he taking those for? Will he even have enough fuel to get wherever he's going? Turns fiercely upon boy – the ferocity of fear – and growls, 'Don't be more of a fool than you must. Who can say how long? Not even your father can work miracles.'

Which seems well wide of the mark to the boy, for Father is precise and unstoppable and would no doubt be here if he chose, even with the world ending. It is more likely that Wishart in his crawling fear has screwed up the message. It is not even clear *how* the message was received, for phones and power have by then been down for three days.

5

But Father has spoken, and the boy is trained to obey. Even when he is the last of eight hundred and twenty-three staff and pupils to leave.

(Boy stops here as he knows he will soon throw up.)

Back and a bit better.

Of course the boy shares Wishart's fear, everyone's fear. The boy is crapping himself with terror. More than ever when, for the first two lonely days, the radio keeps him zeroed in on unfolding disasters. Then much more again when the radio goes down with the rest, ended mid-sentence, so that he is alone in the world.

*People are being advised this morning to avoid any ...*

That was the sentence. I'll never know what I should avoid. How can I sleep, now?

If you'd offered me the run of this place before, sure, I'd have taken it p-d-q, certainly in preference to rattling round one of Father's houses for dead weeks on end. A good laugh, climbing in and out of Orchard through the downstairs bog windows – all the doors have ancient mortises, everything-proof – eating tinned sardines and plum tomatoes by candlelight, starting the day with a few lengths in the now-unheated Olympic pool and dancing like a naked savage on the edge.

The first time, I streaked all the way back to Orchard – the long way, by the Science block – and sang the Sex Pistols as my privates bounced around, frozen to half their normal size.

*'I don't want a holiday in the sun ...'*

(Our standard encore number in The Wonderbras.)

But hey, let's not kid ourselves, the boy's little rebellion was half-hearted. All the time his mind was running after the eight hundred and twenty-two others, trying to catch just a glimpse of what they had planned. Which of them, he wondered, were silently climbing into private planes in the freezing dawn in some back-of-beyond airfield, heading for Canada or Mexico or somewhere? Which were trying to bribe their way through the choked, flu-and-TB-infested ports? Which were at home, boarding up their windows, hoping the chocolate-fat dogs would keep the looters away?

Outside there is meltdown. Inside Bede's there is silence and the boy. And although he feels forgotten, he has not yet even dared to walk to the village, because that is Outside and he is crapping himself. But today, people, he is *going* to the village, just as soon as his head is better.

Se mundumque vince.

Hey, I was wrong.

I was WRONG. I'm not alone. Can you believe that?

(And answer came there none.)

So I went to the village, right? It's four miles over the hills and five and a half by road, so I went over the hills. This is June by the way, 14 June 2023, and if these pages are being deciphered by aliens many centuries from now, then 'beep beep', guys. The ground was still stiff with frost at twleve-thirty, but I jogged it and got a good sweat going to deal with the drink. (Vitamin C, sugar, fluid, caffeine and punishing exercise. Such is the hangover lore of Pinkley, our noble head of house.) And the village – Newcombe – was a mess. A labrador had been run down and was rotting on the main road; two houses had been burned to the ground and only Mrs McCartney was still around. She's at least eighty and as poor as a church mouse and was arranging bits of polythene over her dead roses.

I hated how the village was. I'm being serious now. G-minor seven slides smoothly to D-major seven; Dom will speak seriously. Why had they done all that? Yeah, I know I told you about breaking back into Orchard and burning the furniture, but that's survival; it's sense. I've also carted out all the rotten stuff in the kitchens – took two whole days – and I even scrubbed the bogs once. I will burn the furniture in a methodical manner. I'm master of what Father would call 'a tight ship', up to a sensible point. Those people had nicked all the stuff from Ogilvy's and then crapped on the floor there. And it must have been villagers themselves. (The same lot who were runners-up in the county floral village awards three years ago.) I can't see looters bothering with Newcombe.

Isn't it mental?

But the point of the story is that I met someone else; not Mrs McCartney, but Ruth Beckett. Witchbitch.

Abrupt, mad, repeated chord: CDF#G CDF#G CDF#G CDF#G etc.

I didn't know that the Becketts were still here. How could I not know that? Nine days and not a sight of them, though they certainly knew (or *she* did) that *I* was around. I came back from Newcombe the road way, along the valley and then through the Park; and there she was, outside the lodge, chopping firewood in a black T-shirt. And of course I jumped about and flapped my arms and burbled like a prat and was so pleased to see her, and I said, 'We can help each other. If there's anything you want, food from the kitchens and stuff, or . . . anything.' I just meant I'd be happy to help because we all know what her old man's like.

But she carried on her chopping. Smack. Smack. And she said, 'Food from the kitchens? That's kind. Will you be delivering it naked?' Then she took a key from her jeans and said: 'Hey! What's this? The key to the kitchens! I think we'll manage fine.'

Her cheeks flushed red. She has such a temper, that girl. But I was angry too, especially as, obviously, she must have seen me that other morning, running from the pool. I said, 'Look, I didn't mean to suggest you couldn't manage. I just thought that with the school closed down and everything, we could, you know . . .'

*Smack, smack.*

She said spikily, 'Closed down? What makes you think that?'

8

Then she went inside with her armful of wood. I could hear her old man coughing away in there, hawking and spitting. She's always so bloody unfriendly. Every time I start to pity her, she reminds me why people give her such a hard time.

BUT ... at least the boy is not alone now. Maybe she'll even streak for *me* one day soon, if she has no other engagements. (Oh God, if only my dick hadn't been so cold!)

Who knows what she meant about the school. Most of the kids assume she's clinically mad.

# ADELINE

The pain this time was the worst yet. It felt like a spear thrown hard into her side. But it wasn't the pain she minded. It was the way her strength drained away, her breath wouldn't come, her brain became a useless, fragmented thing.

It was the loss of control.

Her left foot turned feebly on the hot, red rock as it came down, suddenly minus any guidance from above, and her slender frame went crashing down after it. The side of her head jarred and lolled in the dust. Then she was just lying there, and sweating and trying in her fog to calm the panic. She closed her eyes against the glare and the brain fragments drifted further apart, like the expanding universe.

Perhaps, already, this was dying and she need worry no more.

Unguarded, she let her thoughts drift to *before*.

*Dominic stood before her. He had patches of colour on his cheeks from his running but underneath was quite pale, from the drink no doubt. She could smell the ghost of it on him. He was very alive in the unnatural cold, solid, quivering like a hunting dog. His mess of dark curls, the few soft bristles on his jaw, his white knees where the shorts ended. She was moved by his openness, his determination. A shiver passed through her spine.*

Time passed and she did not die. Not yet.

She dozed and sweated and ached and dreamed and in time the little universe slowly imploded again and she lay knowing that she was burned from being out too long under the unforgiving sun. And the anger and fear welled up in her so that she clenched her hands in the dust.

A last tendril reached out from her wandering dreams and the anger fastened upon Ruth – Witchbitch – who had been so mean to poor Dom, teasing him and shutting her door in his face when he was alone. She hated Ruth for that, hated the mask that the girl lived behind.

Then strength and sense seeped back into her and Ruth was forgotten.

The sun was, she thought, a full ten degrees lower than when she had fallen. They must not begin to worry at Seven and send people out to search. She must arrive soon and seem unhurt. What had happened was her own business. She was not their precious thing, their talisman, as they secretly thought. How Clarissa would fuss. She must move.

She lay a moment more, putting off the return, assessing damage, testing communication with muscles, then flipped back to her feet. Nausea threatened her and the sweat broke out again on her brow, but she carefully fought these things down and set off at an easy warm-up pace, brushing the red dirt from her vest as she went, shaking her hair back into place.

The great teeth of the mountains, marching away into the sun's liquid fire, made her glad that death had not claimed her. The tears ran freely from her eyes and cleaned their paths through the grime on her cheeks. The world was too beautiful to lose. The thorny scrubland shimmered olive and white down the flanks of the ridges, holding jealously onto the thin moisture that came with the dusk. The great hawks rode the thermals and watched for rabbits. And in a month, if the monsoon did not fail, the valleys would be sudden, brief beds of emerald, swept across with white chamomile, and the streambeds would thunder with their torrents.

And, despite her decision to leave, all the people she knew or cared about were at Seven; save Dom, of course.

The original Seven, the hub of the larger settlement, was perched bravely on a fragment of plateau. The timber buildings were weathered grey and cracked from the heat and the storms. Lookout posts leaned giddily over the steep ascents to south and east, braced by bare pine struts. If you hung over the far rail you seemed to float above the valleys and could feel the heat and scent spiralling up. In the monsoon you could stand there and see only grey, beating rain in all the world.

But gradually the hard, dusty land below had been terraced and made fertile, and the greater Seven had spread, so that now, as you approached, the first stunted strips of corn were three kilometres from the cluster of short-wave antennae, solar-generating and weather-monitoring equipment at the plateau's heart. More than two thousand souls had drifted in and signed the ARK charter, fleeing from the waters or the chaos or the gods knew what. They scraped their living from the settlement, calling out to each other in Arabic, Spanish, Swahili, French, English. Or simply signing their needs with hands and faces and single words: use of the harrow, a piece of irrigation pipe, a swapping of patrol duties, half a lemon for the soup.

When Adeline reached the broken shoulder of South Peak, she took out a shard of mirror and signalled the Lookout. It was difficult to judge the angles necessary from here and would not be possible at all in summer, but after a moment an answering signal came back – *welcome home.* Then, a moment later, more flashes: *we have a visitor ... trouble?* She wondered what it might mean. Below her the valley looked peaceful enough. It couldn't be too bad, whatever it was. She picked her way

down...
and the...
was a ne...
of nothing...
smiled her re...
to the rare flash...
to her cheerily, th...

'Bonjour Missy, b...

A large, pale Arkie...
and using a flat stone t...
made knife, raised his han...
as she passed, his face seriou... a
face that she knew. One of th... new
arrivals no doubt.

She toiled up the winding stone ... the plateau, working her body hard to put colour ... her face and to show that she was in fine health. At the top she saw Sebastien waiting for her in the doorway of the lookout and the fragile moment of peace in the valley fled. She wanted a wash and some quiet to think. Not to be pestered and mooned over.

She waited for him to cross to her. Sebastien said, 'Hola! I was Lookout for this watch. Did you remember? It was *I* who signalled you.'

'Yes,' she made herself say, falsely, 'of course I remembered. Did you tell Clarissa that I've returned? Or Maman? Who is the visitor? What trouble?'

'So many questions! Like a prowling tiger. I don't know who the visitor is. She's been shut in with your sister for hours. A woman, quite old. I think she's been hurt. Your sister asked three or four times for news of you, though. I sent a message to her when I'd signalled you.'

They spoke mostly in French, although both could speak well in Spanish and she was perfect in her English, even dreaming in that language these days.

13

...ven. Sebastien was
...ore to say, but obviously
... and try to look into her eyes.
... they had been good friends, two
... on the plateau, but could not remember
... felt. She couldn't bear the way he tried to press
...ward into her private space. She wanted to make
faces at him, to cross her eyes.

She said, 'Oh well. I'd better get cleaned up, then. See
you around.'

He fidgeted about and she relented and waited a
moment to see if there was more to come from the
churning well of feelings that he seemed to carry with
him, behind the moonish grin. But he simply shrugged
and said, 'Yes, see you around,' so that was OK.

His fear of her was so irritating. She knew she was
scowling when she entered the women's quarters.
Eloise, sitting cross-legged on her bed, combing out her
ridiculous hair (again), took one look and knew to stay
silent. Everyone else was still out, down in the greater
Seven, or working in the kitchen, the operations shack,
the sparkling solar farm. Unless she were Lookout,
Adeline made sure that her own work was finished
before the midday meal, so that the afternoons could be
hers alone.

She strode through the low building and entered her
sister's office.

Clarissa was at her desk, frowning, moving papers,
while she listened to the person sitting in the other
chair, back to the door. Her eyes flicked up and met
Adeline's own and there was such a charge of love there
that the girl wanted to cry out all her fear from earlier:
but she did not. The scowl remained on her face and she
watched it, helpless, from inside.

The visitor was a hook-nosed, grey-haired woman
of sixty or more, with yellow bruising across her face

and a drying gash above her brow. She had a proud, stubborn set to her mouth. She held a beaker of water in a hand that trembled and her other hand clutched a slim cloth bag. A woollen coverlet lay draped around her shoulders, despite the heat.

'Adeline,' her sister said, more guarded again, 'I'm glad you're back. This is Frau Kästener, come to stay a while. A few days. I was . . . she was . . . very kind to me, once. Frau Kästener, my sister Adeline.'

'Ah!' The woman carefully put down the beaker and the bag, pulled herself to her feet, using the chair arms, and gave a little bow to Adeline. 'I am most delighted to make your acquaintance. You do, indeed, look remarkably like your sister did at your age. Even, may I say, the, um, *ferocity* of expression. Uncanny.' She smiled and then winced and sank back into the seat.

Adeline liked the woman instinctively, but there had been disagreement and tension in the air when she arrived. She said, 'Welcome to Seven, Frau Kästener. I'm always keen to find out about my sister's mysterious past.' And then to Clarissa herself: 'What is it? What's happened?'

But it was Frau Kästener who replied in her accented English. 'An unfortunate meeting with – what shall we call them – some very . . . *violent* types, some days ago, when we first entered the mountains. People with no love for the International Crisis Strategy Agreement. My . . . my little team, my colleagues and helpers, were unfortunately lost to me. I was able to hide. And so to come on here, presently.' She spoke matter-of-factly, almost cheerfully, but there was a bleakness in her eyes.

Clarissa shook her head. 'You can't be sure who your attackers were. The mountains are never safe. Bandits, robbers, terrorists . . .'

Looking at her sister's face with puzzlement, Adeline said, 'You're from ICSA, Frau Kästener?'

'Such as it is, my dear, yes. Such as it is. Though I fear our modest power will soon be altogether ended. The new disasters – challenges, I should say – are dissolving whatever cooperation we once had in this continent. Nation states are ignoring us. We are unwelcome, even at risk, in much sovereign territory. What can one expect? Panic is the enemy of cooperation. And there is much cause for panic, is there not?'

Again Clarissa spoke hastily. 'It's confirmed, Adeline. A thirty-four per cent increase in the rate of sea-level rise. The largest for over a century. We've had the figures from every Ark. They all match.' She gestured at the sheaf of papers before her.

*What was she avoiding? What was happening here?*

Adeline went across to the papers and studied them herself over the other's shoulder. Even in her foul mood, even whilst puzzling over the strange visitor, she was shocked. Her mind ran smoothly through the figures and she looked up in surprise. 'That will mean one city lost in France, two in Briton, two in Spain . . .'

The old woman said clearly, in her hard, precise voice, 'Thirteen in Europe, over ten years. And twenty-two per cent of remaining land becoming liable to flooding. Best guess: a possible seventeen million new refugees between the Atlantic and the Caucuses.'

The three of them were silent for a minute, thinking about what that would mean. The jostling for space, for food; the extra numbers on the move.

'Which is, I suppose,' added Frau Kästener, 'part of the reason why I have come here in person, to your little Eden.' She looked expectantly at Clarissa, without result. Adeline felt again the strain in the air between these two. After a silence the old woman said heavily, 'For now, though, I will take a little rest, if I may. There will be time to talk later.'

Clarissa got to her feet. 'Of course. We have a small

16

lodging for visitors. It's ready for you. Come, let me show you.'

Adeline stood and watched from the little window as Clarissa helped the ICSA woman across the baked rock to the visitors' cabin. She could see a stiffness in the set of her sister's shoulders and heard her raised voice. A phrase drifted back through the heat: '. . . isn't *ready.*'

The old woman paused and turned before the little door. Did she see the watching girl? The dark eyes seemed to be looking straight at her. Her voice carried clearly, thanks to the accent. 'He must be stopped, my dear. Or this new madness in Briton will plunge us all back into the dark ages.'

When Clarissa returned to the office, Adeline was sitting in silence, well away from the window. No further reference was made to the mysterious Frau Kästener, strange in itself. Instead Clarissa said neutrally, 'A good afternoon's training?'

Adeline thought of the horror of it and tried to sound enthusiastic. 'Yes. Very good. I went as far as the third peak after the Needle. Our names were still there on the rock, as clear as ever.' She paused, undecided. 'You should come with me next time.'

*And if her heart should fail again?*

But Clarissa shook her head ruefully. 'You'd leave me far behind. I'm not in any sort of condition. And there's so much to be done here. Maybe after the rains I'll come walking with you. A gentle day's amble for your poor old sister. Here,' she pulled out one of the desk drawers and handed a covered stone bowl to Adeline, 'you should salve the worst patches when you've washed, or tonight you won't sleep.'

So her sister had noticed the raw, burnt skin, despite the shuttered dimness of the cabin.

*Yes,* Adeline thought sourly, going to the washroom,

*we'd better keep the precious Saviour in good condition, hadn't we?*

But instantly she remembered that such a thing was impossible, and the fear and anger surged again through her aching body. Besides, she thought miserably, the saviour thing was just a muddle, a mistake.

Maybe that was why Clarissa hadn't bothered to tell her.

# DOMINIC
## – day 11 –

Nil points on the looter theory. Perhaps the Newcombe-ites didn't crap in their own shop after all.

By now you're obviously wondering why the first couple of pages of this heroic text are in taped-together pieces.

I'll tell you.

After I met Ruth Beckett, the day before yesterday, I was going over to the canteen block to find stuff for supper. Eight or half past, I should think; I'd been messing around on the Strat for an hour or two. There was a solitary tin of tuna that I'd been saving up, and a few dodgy, sprouting potatoes to boil. Nothing much else fresh by now. I was heading up the side of the sports hall and I heard an engine, right on the other side of the building, moving very slowly back towards Orchard and the other houses.

I thought: An engine! Father at last or someone sent by him to pick me up. Far out! So like an Idiot I raced round, back the way I'd come, to meet him.

The engine was turned off as I was heading round there, and I heard the doors go. More than one, but Father usually has people in attendance. His bodyguard, PA, all that crap. So without thinking (no comment please) I came screaming round the corner and almost ran smack into them, four guys and a girl, standing looking about at the buildings in a shifty way. And I knew at once that they weren't there for me.

We all froze and checked each other out, and one of the guys spat and said, 'A bloody kid' and the girl, probably only twenty herself at the most, looked me up and down in a sneering sort of way and said, 'Is he lost then? Where's Mumsy?'

They made a grab for me before I legged it. What they would have done with me I don't know; is looting with murder the standard deal in the outside world now? But there was no way they were going to catch me round Bede's. I've been here since I was five, for Christ's sake. I sprinted back round the corner of the sports hall then climbed over the wall into the back of Honeysuckle (senior girls' house) using the bin. This is a well-trodden route, by the way. Then, by the time one of the guys was over the wall after me, I'd already gone into the bushes where Angie and I used to have our fags, along with half the school. (Until she showed me how to inhale and when I'd recovered I decided to give up.) Then over the high wooden fence that's hidden at the back there, into the Head's own garden. This is only for complete emergencies and I thought I qualified. Then on, across the painted-on lawns where parents agree to part with their cash, and back to Orchard that way.

(I know I'm talking about the school like any of it still mattered or was going to go on which it doesn't and won't. It takes some getting used to, the fact that Bede's and everything else is out, finished etc. Give me a break.)

The strangers were laughing and shouting and the girl screaming 'Get him, Josh' like it was a game and, just so we're clear, I was shitting myself about this too. At the same time I think I was actually *pleased*, if you can believe that, to be doing something (running away) that was so definite. It was so much better than just sitting round thinking about the world ending. When I got back to the dorm, which is right at the top of Orchard, I had the serious shakes but I was laughing too and dancing about shaking my fists in the air like I'd won the cup. The best thing to happen in days. Or about equal with finding that the Becketts were still around.

It gave me hope.

Who knows, perhaps it was like that for Josh too? Play games, stop worrying etc . . .?

The downside soon clicked in, though. I was starving and I couldn't see the place where they'd parked their heap from any window in Orchard, so I'd have to go back out to see whether they'd left or not. I thought they were just cruising round and would steal something or smash something and piss off soon enough. I opened the window and could hear their voices faintly, somewhere in the school. There was glass breaking and, stupidly, I felt protective towards the old dump. Then there was no sound for ages, more than two hours, but also no car noise. I wasn't sure whether that would carry up here or not. Probably not.

It was dark by now and bloody freezing. The lawns outside were already silver with frost. I lit a candle, but I didn't want to risk the fire, though my own desk was cut up ready to go the way of Kingsley's. Even if they were still hanging about I didn't think they'd bother getting into Orchard when there were so many easier buildings around. And this house is like a maze inside. There are three staircases: they'd need a map to find me. That's what I thought. But it was wrong again.

I'd finally crashed out some time in the early hours. Then, the next thing I knew was that the moonlight was shining in on me and Kingsley's bed, which I'd wedged against the door, was starting to slide over the floorboards, making a hell of a racket. Like a scene from a horror movie.

*Fight valiantly, Bede's.*

The thing is to have a drill, and we've done a night fire-drill in Orchard twice a term since I can remember. I also had a survival kit prepared: a little bag full of stuff I didn't want to lose, plus one desk leg for close combat. I got up and shoved hard against the moving bed, trapping someone's hand between door and frame.

'Shit! You little toerag! I'll cream you when we get in there.'

Then I was up and through the window before they'd even got the door open. From our room it's a railed stone parapet for ten metres to the iron ladder that leads all the way over the roof to the fire escape on the far side. A piece of piss wearing socks in freezing June with looters chasing you and the world ending.

After that I knew what had to be done. It was obvious the strangers weren't leaving for a while. At times like this there's something wretched you can't escape that Father calls 'Doing Your Duty'. Which in my case meant going to spend the night hidden outside the Becketts' cottage in case our uninvited guests decided to go that way.

As a way to spend the night, it stank.

When dawn came at last I went further into the trees – though I could still see the lodge – and consumed my emergency rations: one bottle of water and one tin of (cold) steamed treacle pudding, found on day two in Pinkley's own incredible little store of goodies. I'd been sleeping in my fleece and thermals and jeans but I was phenomenally cold.

I wasn't a hundred per cent sure what to do next. I *was* certain that Miss Ruth-Witchbitch-Beckett would not want me to Do My Duty where it concerned her, and would think I was interfering or being a perv and spying on her, though her old man might understand better. I was also pretty certain that for the same reasons (unclear what they are – suggestions on a postcard please) she wouldn't want to cooperate in keeping an eye out for the intruders. I could just write her a note and stick it under their door, but she's so full of herself that she'd probably reckon she could cope and wouldn't do anything anyway ... or would go and tell the looters to leave, hands on hips. Which only left the option of me staying where I was, hidden, to keep watch.

I decided I needed something to keep me warmer, and more food.

Then the door opened and Ruth herself came out.

It was still early, but the sun was shining. Ruth was wearing an old tracksuit, a tatty maroon thing. She's never made much effort with appearance: the opposite of Jessica Ward. Her hair was loose and looked more red than brown in the sunlight. I decided that if she was going into the school I'd just have to tell her what was going down and take her fit of temper on the chin, but she looked around and stretched and then she started doing yoga of all things. That thing to welcome the rising sun. (Or the new day?) A friend of Mother's used to do it.

Between ourselves, she looked unbelievable and very graceful doing it – peaceful – and I realised I *was* being pervy and spying after all. So, very relieved that she didn't go off towards the main part of the school when she'd finished, but headed down through the Park for a run, letting herself quietly out of the little wicket gate in the fence.

I watched her go, disappearing amongst the trees, like a woodland creature.

Let me tell you about Ruth. I don't know if she was born at Bede's but she was here when I arrived. She doesn't come to the school as a pupil and as far as I know she hasn't ever been to any kind of school. How she gets away with that I don't know. (No problem now, of course! *Fuck it*, sometimes I can even forget for a couple of minutes.) Anyway, Ruth lives at the lodge with her dad because he's the head groundsman and caretaker for the school. No mother ever on the scene since I was here. Her dad's decent enough but he's a drinker and so he does not always Do His Duty. I don't think he's ever violent or anything like that – he's a small, timid sort of guy – but I guess Ruth has to look after him a lot, instead of the other way round. How he's kept the job is another mystery. He has lung trouble

23

from the fags or the paint. When I first came he was a normal, happy sort and must have been about thirty; now he looks sixty, with a spider's web of tiny purple veins over his face and cloudy, wandering eyes.

Confession. Why not?

Even from the first time I saw her I knew Ruth was different, and I felt different about her too, though I was never brainless enough to tell anyone that, especially not her. And then of course, when you're small and everyone else is picking on someone, you find yourself joining in. Either that or you become the next victim yourself. Pathetic, isn't it?

I have one memory, one sparkling memory of showing Ruth that I really liked her, and it kills me.

We were both about ten and for some reason she came with our year on a Saturday trip: a coach trip to London to see some of the sights – the Globe, Tower Bridge engine room, a couple of galleries. The coach was full but Ruth was sitting alone and nobody would sit with her because she was The Witch and everybody was a little afraid of her and used to giving her stick. It never seemed to get to her: she was in her own world, except when she had a go at someone.

Nobody knew that I sometimes kissed my pillow after lights out and pretended that it was Ruth.

That day I'd got a couple of tenners in the post from Father. He's always done that, sent me cash with a sentence or two written on his office notepaper: 'How went Saturday's match?' or 'Reminder: your grandmother's birthday a week on Tuesday. Post your offering latest three days before' or 'Did you see? We've finally bought out the opposition. Get yourself something to celebrate'.

OK, so all the way down the motorway I was mooning to myself about Ruth and playing pontoon with Kingsley and Potts and Harper. I imagined myself sitting in that empty seat next to her, which was obviously impossible. But I was so puppy-lovesick, I suppose I gradually made up my mind that I had to do something to show her how I felt. My heart was thudding with the terrible decision. When we were at the Globe I went into the souvenir shop and bought her a book about the place, with a cut-out model in the back to glue together. Why that I don't know. It had to be something that I might have bought for myself in case I was spotted. As it was, Kingsley (the bane of my life) saw me with the bag and asked what I'd got. I ignored him.

Then later, when we were told to assemble outside again for the bus, I could see that Ruth was coming along last, in a dream, so I hung back and gave her the book, trembling like a leaf. I just pressed the bag in her hand and mumbled, 'I got you this' or something pathetic, and tried to leg it, but she said 'Wait!' and took it out and smiled a perfect smile at me and gave me a kiss on the cheek.

I was over the moon. And bricking it.

We were the last two out onto the pavement, and of course now I had no bag and she did. And I was blushing. And Kingsley was watching in his sly way.

When the bus came and we got back on, Ruth said, 'Will you sit with me?' and there was Kingsley – and the world – watching every move from where we'd been sitting at the back, some of them giggling and murmurs of 'Witch ... Little Angel for The Witch.' So I said to her, 'Sorry. I have to play cards.' And I walked like a robot to sit with the others, whilst everybody jeered.

Ruth didn't look at me properly again and I've never felt such a miserable prick.

Not much else to tell about the intruders.

I risked it and went for the stuff I needed while Ruth was running. A sleeping bag and dehydrated compo rations from the CCF hut, which has/had a flimsy hardboard cavity door. It also occurred to me then that there are all the .22 rifles locked in the strong room at the back there. I'll have to think about that.

I stayed near the lodge, freezing my tits off, until today – but no noise from the school so I finally went to have a look, and the car had gone.

With the whole dump to choose from, the bastards had stayed in our dorm. They'd burned all the wood that I'd cut and the chairs too and trashed all my stuff and broken the window and scrawled their lovely thoughts about me on the walls. Also, they'd ripped up my notebooks.

Worst of all, they've snapped the neck off my Strat. The two pieces are here in front of me. I'll have to mend it. I can't survive without the Strat.

Despite that, I'm going to stay here. It's home.

I'll tidy up tomorrow.

I wish the Scotch wasn't finished. The nights are so difficult.

# ADELINE

There was noise. A murmur or two. The sound of the door.

Adeline woke to find a finger resting lightly on her lips. Clarissa's face was there above her, alert and large-eyed. In the gloom of the flickering night-light it might have been a mirror hanging there, but for the faint lines etched into the skin and the uniform colour of those eyes. Her sister removed the touch. She indicated with a gesture that Adeline should leave her pallet and dress.

The girl could feel the unnatural quiet of Seven and did not argue.

Together they crept the length of the dormitory. Half the beds were already silent and empty, but Eloise was there, smiling to dream lovers in her blonde halo, stick-like Paulette was draped half over the side of her pallet and little Manuela was a hump of blankets, peppered with the mess of stones and birds' feathers she collected. Nearest the door – and the privy – Maman snored and muttered and ground her teeth.

Clarissa lifted the thick wooden catch and they let themselves out onto the moonlit plateau. The undiminished heat and sticky, stifling air told of the rains that would soon come. In the milky brightness, Adeline saw six, seven, eight figures, all recognisable from their individual movement, fanning out from the huddle of buildings and heading towards the southern edge, where the stone stair descended to the precious farmed terraces. She glanced at the lookout for signs of the sentry on watch there but could see nothing, not even the candle lantern.

Her stomach contracted at that and she felt a ripple of fear.

Her sister was following the others, moving as silently as the moonlight. As each shadow drew near to the perimeter, it folded itself down flat and melted into the rocky floor. Adeline could picture them nestling into the rough, camouflaged hollows that had been prepared there.

Who was coming? Who was their enemy?

She wondered, as she always did, if this time it would be soldiers from Briton. Jan Barbieri's men, come to finish what they had begun when she was no more than a toddler. Another sister had been lost to her then, trying to protect her. Only Clarissa had survived, carrying the baby Adeline far up the mountain paths and away from those who would destroy them.

*This new madness in Briton.* That had been Frau Kästener's phrase. What had she meant by it? The New Visions? They were old news surely. Besides, with his mind wholly focussed on his created freaks, Jan Barbieri would not be likely to give her or her sister a thought. That was all in the past. Even the serpent cults – *her* cults! – were dying away to nothing in Briton, so the reports said.

She shook her head slightly in the moonlight, mocking her own fear, half enjoying it. In truth it was as well that Jan didn't look this way. Yet someone *was* giving Seven a thought this night. Adeline heard now the first noise of their arrival; the faintest rattle of a stone disturbed on the winding stair, kissing the rock wall once, twice as it fell to the valley floor. Careless.

At least Clarissa had woken her. At least she was not being shielded from danger, like the sleeping children in the dormitory. It made her feel her old self, from a

year or two ago. She and Clarissa were a team. That
was how it had always been. The greater the challenge
the better. She dropped into her own hollow, pulling the
starchy, scratchy cloth across, and lay listening for more
evidence of the intruders.

What if the pains came? What if she couldn't fight?

Then, already, they were there. A procession of silent,
dark figures, one after another, clambering over the lip
of the rock, spreading out, crouching low, speaking only
with their hands. Adeline had been hasty in her judgement. Despite the dislodged pebble, these were clearly
no rabble of migrants or drifters, amongst the thousands
looking for a place to live, food to steal, easy pickings.
They were organised, methodical. Out of twenty-seven,
six were certainly armed with projectile weapons: long,
lethal shadows cradled in their hands. It was little
wonder that the patrols had not stopped them down
below. The farmers were not here to be slaughtered; *that*
was not in the ARK charter.

The strangers waited a while, checking the lie of the
land, alert for signs of their detection. Two of them
scouted round the silent wooden structure at the stair
top: three more edged towards the eastern lookout.
Adeline lay still and calm and counted four slow minutes
away – twelve full breaths – each one adding to Seven's
advantage. Then the three who had slipped away to the
eastern lip came back, briefly signalling all well, and
the invaders silently rose up and started moving across
the bare land towards the buildings.

Adeline kept two clear in her mind; the nearest to
hold a weapon, who would be the first to fall, and the
figure at the rear, whose progress would determine
the time to act. Unless they took the care to leave a man
behind, of course, to keep the escape open.

They didn't.

The final intruder passed the given point, the first of

three flat boulders, piled untidily together by an ancient rockfall, and Adeline rolled quickly from her hollow and ran low, like a hunting cat, towards the armed man that she had picked out. A little before she reached him, the first shouts were sounding, echoing off the mountain wall, but the man she'd chosen was lying unconscious before his weapon could be fired. Somewhere over to her right, one single silenced shot sounded, like a hand striking a small drum; too far away to make it her business. The other guns stayed mercifully silent, yet there was work enough. Already two other figures had homed in on her, the dull, dirty sheen of unregulated steel in their hands.

Yes, three would be enough.

She laughed aloud now and the endless stale fears and worries fled before the danger and her joy. She could feel how lightly her feet caressed the red dirt, how supple her spine and shoulders were as she shifted balance to meet the first attacker. He came at her with grim purpose, watching her movements, passing his blade easily between hands, not wasting energy on words or shouts. Yet still he came on too hard, and when he lunged, his weight committed to the stroke and her body swinging before it like a door, it needed barely a touch to twist the leg from under him and send him winded to the ground. As he crashed down, grunting, Adeline mirrored his fall, dropping with him, aware of the second thrusting blade, which paused in a moment's confusion before the double figure. In the moonlight she saw without emotion that this one was a woman; perhaps the mate of the first from the tiny gasp that had escaped her lips when the man fell.

She rolled softly away from the man's flailing arms, knocking the sense from him with the narrow bone on the outside of her foot, and was again crouching in liquid readiness when the woman shifted her attack, this time a scything sweep of the knife, followed by a high, roundhouse kick. The knife to steal her attention, the kick to finish it.

Judging the margin by instinct, Adeline drew her stomach wall away from the blade, arching the muscles sharply inwards, but watched instead the deadly foot. She softened the blow to nothing by a twist of her head, then caught the foot and turned the bones sharply, so that the woman had to bend double towards the ground or feel the joint break. With that, her balance was lost and Adeline could send her sprawling. She stooped to rescue the knife as it clattered away and flung it far across the rock, then turned to the woman and shook her head.

'Stay down now. It's over.'

She said it in her three languages, and one – Spanish? – was understood. The woman, snarling, climbing back to her feet, looked round at what remained of her little army, then sank back and put her head in her hands. Adeline stood over her, conscious feeling and thought rushing back unwanted now the brief combat was over.

*Too soon.*

Yet also she could smell the sage and the sweet orange wildfire and sense the warmth hidden in the rock, and like a blow she was aware once more of how little she wished to be taken from this land that she loved. If only she could be always doing, always living through her instinct, never having to pause and accept the heavy, sickly feeling into her imperfect heart.

Then she would stay.

She looked around at the battle scene, concentrating on the mundane. A jumble of bodies were spread over the ground for fifty metres around her, some stirring or muttering, some lying still, as deep in their dreams as little Manuela.

The victory was Seven's.

'Emile!' a voice called. 'Stevie . . . Andoh . . . Elisabeth
. . . Françoise . . .' McCoy's voice, calling out the roll.
Clarissa's name came, and then her own – 'Here, Mac' –
but at the end of the short list there were two who
had not answered; José and Irisz. Adeline felt a tremor
of shock, remembering the silent lookout, but thrust it
away. Nothing was yet certain.

Now there was a hubbub from the stone stair, a
babble of laughter and camaraderie. Twenty or more
men spilled vigorously up over the plateau edge – ARK
farmers from below; one of the night's patrols – roughly
holding two intruders who had tried to fly to freedom
when the trap was sprung. Three or four of them were
telling at once in a patchwork of languages how they
had surprised the men on the treacherous stair, how
they had struggled. A heroic encounter: a great victory!
Adeline laughed to hear it. Their presence seemed to
lighten the tension still hanging over the moonlit scene,
and soon there were ragged yellow torches burning and
the clink of a bottle being passed round.

In due course, McCoy came to Adeline, as to the
others, with cord to bind the attackers, and to remove
their weapons. He was dressed in unfamiliar black and
Adeline realised he must have been amongst the three
who she had seen coming back from the eastern lookout, falsely reporting all well to the other intruders.

McCoy glanced at her as he bound the man who had
carried the gun. 'OK, Beautiful?'

'Yes, Mac. Fine.'

'Three, eh? Some of us could have stayed in bed.'

She smiled, but asked, 'Irisz? José?'

The man looked down. 'Irisz is dead. She was Lookout.
They shot from across the valley, good clean shots, three
or four rounds at once. She wouldn't have known.' He
paused. 'José has a shoulder wound. It's nothing.'

Irisz dead.

'And down below? The farmers?'

He shook his head, finishing the knot and standing back to survey his work. 'This rabble were after equipment, electronics maybe, not food. They were let through when we realised they were so well armed. Too well armed ...' He looked thoughtful in the gloom. 'Anyway, there shouldn't be anyone hurt down there.' He started off with the spool of cord for the next prisoner, but called, over his shoulder, 'So don't go getting morbid on me.'

She grinned, despite herself. Nobody else dared speak to her like that.

Soon, one of the farmers' bottles came her way. The unfamiliar liquid scorched her mouth. After that, the night was a hot, sweaty blur of singing and celebrating with the Arkies, organising the prisoners ready for them to be led (unarmed) far from Seven, and eventually the first tongues of dawn dancing round the eastern summits. All of it pierced by grief. For Irisz or for herself.

At some time or other, Clarissa came and took her hand and led her back to her bed. The two sisters crept once more past the sleeping Maman and the others, fighting like naughty children against a sudden desire to giggle. They embraced before going to their own pallets.

'You make me proud,' her sister whispered, studying her.

'You too.'

But it wasn't enough. The night had only been a dream, a distraction. There would never be enough distraction. When sleep wouldn't come, she lay watching a shield beetle traverse the dry roof timbers and mapped out the school of Bede's in her head, trying to place each building from the hints Dominic gave in his journal. Some she could see clearly, of course, and some were hidden. That was the way it worked. But it felt like a second home, after so many hours spent there in her thoughts. The beetle went this way and that on its errand, lost in the maze of woodwork.

*She came round the corner of the dining block and he was there, tie flapping up over his shoulder as he walked. They were caught uncharacteristically alone and close on the wide Tarmac, two little vessels converging in the mid-Atlantic. He glanced up from under his curls, saw her and almost quailed; she could see the impulse to change direction and dive into the Art building with his pile of books. But he held his course as bravely as any sea captain and an uncertain smile parted his lips. She, too, considered her options while her heart beat strong. She would not melt for him, here under the bare banks of windows, but still she had to look him in the eye. 'Hi,' he said and she replied sharply, 'Hi yourself.' They passed close enough to brush shoulders and when he was gone she had to be stern with herself. Where had she been going? To get a book from the library? She was breathing a little faster than usual.*

But that had been a year or two back, before the journal, Adeline thought vaguely. They'd been only thirteen or fourteen, feeling uncertainly for their adult selves. Then, when you got the key to the garden, you were the wrong size.

She buried herself into her pillow and wept, her head pounding from the farmers' bottle.

It was only well into the next morning, a late, confused morning, that they found Frau Kästener's body. It lay peacefully on the cot in the little visitors' cabin, as if the ICSA diplomat had died naturally asleep. Yet there was a neat line of crimson across her throat and the sheets were blotched with darkening blood. She'd been dead for many hours: the flies were collecting, even at this altitude. The bare room seemed undisturbed, but of the little cloth bag – all her possessions at Seven – there was no sign.

The motiveless murder sent a tremor through all the smaller Seven. At first the night intruders were blamed. One or other of them must have escaped, or perhaps climbed up to the plateau undetected, earlier in the night, before the ambush. But however you told it, this wouldn't fit. The prisoners had been gone since before dawn, first bound tight and guarded at the foot of the stone stair, then roped together and led blindfold down the valley and away from the settlement. Their Arkie escort was led by the taciturn Christophe, who had been a mercenary in the Scorch Belt before he came to Seven to start a different, gentler life. He would be taking them to the very feet of the mountains, on the Spanish side, travelling for three days. The number taken in this group were checked against the first sentry reports from last night, and against what the Seveners had seen themselves in the moonlight. There did not seem any way that one of them could have slipped away. Nor that one had come up before, when the Lookout was still alive. (And if they had, why shoot the Lookout from across the valley? Why not a silent knife between the ribs?)

The answer was simple. Another, undetected killer must be at work in Seven, unless they had already slipped away.

The shock of the killing, its coldness and detachment, touched all. Clarissa, hollow-eyed, blamed herself for the death, yet that made no sense to Adeline. Who could have predicted that a second enemy, an assassin, would strike at the time of the attack? Electronics, radios, equipment and food were the more likely targets. Who bothered with people? Who would want to kill an elderly woman?

Clarissa laid her hand on Adeline's shoulder and looked into her eyes, as if searching for something.

Well, thought Adeline coolly, will you tell me? What is it that Frau Kästener wanted here?

But in a moment her sister took back the hand and said only, 'Come, it's time for the meeting.'

Always after an attack there was the same rumbling argument.

'I say that we need better security arrangements. It's obvious. We need fences, at least across the easier approaches. Proper training for the Arkies. A wider system of lookouts and patrols. A better warning process.'

'And weapons?' Mac said sourly. 'Should we keep their weapons this time? Razor wire? A few mines for good measure, if we can make them, or trade for them?'

Françoise rolled her eyes at him. 'You mock me, when all I wish is to keep Seven – *our* Seven – safe.' She swept her hand around the small hall. 'Look at us. We are too few. The Arkies at least should help more. Last night will not be the last time. You know that. There will be many more people on the move now, running from the waters, from disease and hunger. Look at how many new ones have come to us this month alone! Look at how efficient these last *cochons* were! If the patrols had missed them, what then? Even ready as we were, we lost a friend. And what about the murder of this poor woman who came to us yesterday? Are these events connected? *Where* is our intelligence on this? What information do we gather?'

Many were nodding, amongst them Sebastien, sitting straight-backed and interested, half boy, half man, supporting his mother. Why didn't he think for himself for once, Adeline wondered. Still, she had to admit that Françoise had put the right question. Were the attacks connected? Had Clarissa even told anyone of Frau Kästener's trouble in getting to Seven?

McCoy took a breath – to dampen his impatience, she thought – and then nodded, smiled, opened his palms.

'Yes. You're right, Fran. I admit it. This is only the start. We may well be overrun. Who knows, tomorrow's intruders may have grenades; they may have an army of five thousand terrified, desperate people, looking for a new place to call home. We may lose everything: even our lives. It's true, fear can make people brutal, and there's enough fear out there right now to begin a hundred new wars. But ... *but* ...' his eyes moved across each sweating face in the dim, dusty light, '. . . are we going to join with all the others across Europe, sharpening their knives and digging their bunkers? Are we to become just another armed city, frightened of its own shadow? Because that's not what Seven was designed to do. The ARKs are there to *welcome* people. To take *away* the fear. It's in the Charter, remember? Heck, it *is* the Charter. I didn't start this place to *create* terror.'

He shrugged and sat down, leaving Françoise standing uncomfortably alone until she also chose to sit. Silently, Adeline applauded his timing and performance. It was harder to be sure that his argument was the right one. To do the right thing, to set a goal and stick by it, no matter what. That was hard. Hard to build something and offer it up for destruction. Hard to lose a friend or neighbour every time an attack came.

She thought of those trembling fingers holding the beaker. If only her sister would trust her. But that worked both ways.

Clarissa spoke now, as Adeline had guessed she would, to calm the tensions. 'It's surely already hot enough in here, without us getting hung up on this. I propose that we consider these things and discuss them further during the rains. They'll be here any day, according to the weather data. There'll be time enough then for as much talk as we need, and we all know there's not much chance of another attack until the monsoon is finished. Until then our labour is needed down below, pretty

urgently. Those who have joined us this year are not prepared for the storms. The new ones never believe the
need. We all know what they're like . . . until they've
seen the rains first hand and become converts.'

There were a couple of laughs, sounds of agreement
and relief. The monsoon would keep them safe for now.
The hard decisions could be deferred a while. They must
help the farmers in the few dry days remaining to them.

Adeline shook her head. It was a mistake not to act
clearly, not to decide.

Clarissa's hand had slipped into McCoy's as she talked
and her head now dipped sideways to rest on his shoulder for an instant. It irritated Adeline; this wasn't the
time or place for their private thing. Last night's shared
moment with her twin faded quietly away. Mac said,
'Anyone against deferring this then, as Rissa proposes?
Anyone else want to have their say now?'

No one did. They were thinking of an hour's rest in
the shade, saving energy and moisture for the evening
work.

When the building had emptied and only the four of
them remained, Clarissa said, 'You're right, of course,
Mac. I'll vote with you, when the vote comes. But it's a
tough one. Fran has a point too: our visitors were very
well-organised, don't you think? They smelled of the
city, to me. I know they didn't have city kit, those knives
and everything, but . . .'

He gave no reply and she shrugged. 'Maybe they just
struck it lucky. A clean shot at the Lookout. Finding
the stone stair. It wouldn't do any harm though, would
it, to train more of the wider group?' – she never called
the farmers 'Arkies' – 'Adeline could help me. We can
only train those who wish it of course; there may be
none.'

Surprisingly, Maman nodded savagely and spoke up,
'They *will* wish it. Many, *many* of them are frightened.'

Maman spent as much time on the terraces as up here on the plateau. Adeline knew she felt more comfortable with the farmers than with a daughter not of her own blood. She didn't blame her. The farmers were more fun than anything up here.

Clarissa said, in French, 'No doubt you are right, Yvette. Perhaps then you could go amongst them and list the names of those who wish to learn. If you have the time.'

Maman looked pleased. It would be a better reason than ever to gossip. She gave one more self-important nod. 'I will prepare the list. You can count on me.'

Then the conversation turned to the monsoon, and how the Arkies might be persuaded of the precautions they would need to keep their fragile farms safe from the deluge: the laying of fine netting over precious top soil, the digging of channels to divert water away from the terraces, the dismantling of moisture tunnels. The old hands of eight or nine years had been ready for a week or more, but the newest Arkies always had to be coaxed.

They had the same talk every year, McCoy and her sister. The same last-minute anguish that all might not be well in the settlement they had built together, come the rains. Maman took an armful of the canes she used for her baskets and sat with them, nodding wisely as she threaded the yellow sticks between one another. Adeline felt the need to be alone. Perhaps she would seek out the cool of the pumping house, cut into the rock. She would dream away the afternoon there. She shouldn't have come to the stuffy meeting.

'Hey . . . Beautiful,' McCoy called as she crossed the hall to leave. 'Catch!'

She turned and without thinking plucked the thing he had thrown from the air. A tiny golden square, held tight between her fingers. Suddenly her heart was beating twice as fast. Did they know? Were they offering her knowledge of herself now, after all?

Clarissa suddenly had a face like thunder.

McCoy, seeming not to notice, said, 'That might amuse you. Or not. It's a recording of this new thing they've got going back in your homeland. *Fit To Live*. You know something? That guy Barbieri really wants watching.'

*Calm. Always calm. Let it begin deep inside, in the pit of the stomach, and seep out to all parts of the body.*

No, it was not *the* comcard. This one was much too new, too shiny, still untarnished.

She pocketed the slip of gold, nodding her thanks, but said sharply, 'I've never been there, Mac. *This* is my homeland. The mountains. Seven.'

She didn't think they'd noticed her first reaction, the lovebirds.

'Adeline!' Clarissa called after her, sounding anguished.

She went through the white heat to the pump-house and closed the door.

'What?' Mac asked Clarissa, innocently. 'What?'

# DOMINIC
## – day 16 –

Big changes.

Yesterday, a bus rolled in through the gates. A bus full of kids. To stay, I think.

How likely is that?

Somewhere out there in the mess that used to be Britain, somebody has got it together to fuel up a bus and fill it with kids and send it here.

I thought first of evacuation, like during the Blitz, but this is hardly the same, is it? It's meltdown. Or maybe I'm wrong. Maybe somebody's sorting it all and they just needed a nice quiet spot in the country to park their brats until the right time comes. They haven't sent them alone, after all. There was an army truck with the bus (bus and truck gone now) and it left five adults and a couple of crates of supplies. The adults seem to be there to cook. Nothing else. Everybody's running wild. There have been fights. Nobody's told them to stop or where to sleep or anything. It's just a free-for-all.

Why an army truck, with proper black army plates? Was it nicked? Are the armed forces still holding it together? Are they in charge? When the bus drove in I made sure this time I was well hidden, after what happened before. I didn't get a look at the driver, just the back, so I didn't see whether or not he wore a uniform. The adults who've stayed aren't in uniform and don't look the type.

Luckily, whoever organised all this doesn't have keys, any more than I do, and if Beckett's got any house keys (unlikely) he's not handing them out. Almost all the new-comers have gone for Honeysuckle or Tremayne. There's

41

just one lot here in Orchard, three boys, three of the Kingsley variety: big, loud and ugly. I could hardly tell them to find another place, could I? They eventually found my room and just came in, last night. Stood looking me up and down and ditto the room.

One said, 'What a stinking hole. What died in here?'

We all fell about at this.

Then they left. They're in Pinkley's room, two floors down, so that's something. Good thing I cleaned out all his luxuries before. Think I'll take to hiding my stuff; up on the roof, maybe, as that's still my territory. If I put a lock on the door they'll give me stick and definitely break in for a laugh. I know the way these dickheads operate: I have my finger on the pulse of dickhead-ness. Privacy is out with them. Have to think about warning systems. The last flight of stairs only comes up here, so something might be possible, unless I decide to go ahead and leg it to Tayside.

*I don't know why these people are here*

Wishart said that someone will come for me, and it's true, there is something of Father about a bus full of people coming to Bede's unannounced. It's like how he takes over other papers; usually even the City are surprised. It just hits home with the morning post and some poor sod guzzling his bran flakes finds he's no longer editor of whichever rag it is . . .

Shut up, Dom. Stop rabbiting on about ancient history.

Am I pleased to see other people? Half pleased.

Asked two of the adults about Father and they said they'd never heard of him, though most people have. There are three men, two women. They're pretty seedy, shifty. The first meal they produced, last night, was all warmed up from tins, so no change there. They told me to take a plate and piss off. I almost lost it, after this last couple of weeks. Felt my fists clenching tight, but kept it together. Father's training, or indecision, or a canny waiting game; whatever you like.

Have to get out of the mindset that this is my school and they're intruders. Have to adapt. Grow up.

I asked one more question: what everyone was doing here. They laughed at me. 'Move along, your lordship.'

Didn't tell them the dining hall was a no-smoking area.

Information. How many on a bus? Seventy max, I'd have thought. That bus must have been pretty full; there must be at least that here. They seem to be between fourteen and eighteen, and evenly split between the sexes. (The ones two floors down are sixth-form age I'd say: seventeen-eighteen-ish.) None of them are exactly poor, from what I've seen. All pretty arrogant. All in smart kit, with four-season sleeping bags. (I'm stuck with the grotty CCF one.)

In fact, they could easily be the normal Bede's crowd, but they aren't.

What does any of this tell me?

Could support the Blitz evacuation theory. Privileged families getting a safe option for their offspring. (*Is Bede's a safe option??!!!*)

Undecided whether it's an improvement having this lot here, or not. Not quite so scary, that's true ... harder to panic. But I miss the solitude too. I'd got used to it.

Bloody stupid, Dom.

Realise now that I haven't enjoyed my life at this school much.

Information and analysis. Yes, these are definitely *my* people – i.e. privileged, awkward, snotty, clever, screwed up and all the rest of it. I'm sure now. The dodgy kitchen people get treated with reserve, almost fear: the kids don't know where they are with them as they're not run-of-the-mill serving people. *I* get treated as one of their own – as soon as I speak to them, at least – even if my kit is no longer as smart as theirs. Like recognises like. They seem to assume I came with them on the bus so they can't have known each other before. And Beckett was bustling around this afternoon, looking worried, wearing his overalls, getting on with bits and bobs of maintenance like he still works here. I wouldn't be surprised to see him out rolling the (frozen) cricket pitch. The newcomers are all either ignoring him or patronising him. Like I said, I *know* these people.

Of course I've asked a couple of them about what's going on. Either they don't really know or they're not telling. Almost certainly the first.

Here is a conversation I had earlier. I chose a kid about two years younger than me. The sort that attracts lots of flack and runs away in the Lent term. Thought I could bully gently if necessary. He was sitting by himself on one of the benches outside the sixth-form common room, huddled in Goretex.

I said, 'Hi, are you OK?'

'Yes, thank you.' Shy, polite and well-spoken. Plus shitting himself. (As we all are. These may be my crowd, but there's a current of fear buzzing through all of them. More than me? What have they seen?)

I said, 'Look, I'm probably being incredibly thick, but I'm trying to find out what's going on here. Why we're all here.'

He said, 'Didn't you read the leaflet?'

I said, 'Leaflet? No, I didn't get one. What did it say? Can I see yours?' (Someone is printing leaflets as well as fuelling up buses!)

'They took them back again. Weren't you there?' He was looking puzzled now. Worried by my questions.

'No, I missed the bus. Had to come up here separately. *Who* took them back again? What did they say?'

He said, 'Oh. Oh, I see. God, you didn't miss anything. What a journey.' His eyes filled up.

I wondered what had happened on the journey, but said, 'So what about this leaflet?'

'Yes, well they handed them out and we read them and

then handed them back. It didn't really say anything. Just that we should obey our guardians at all times, and not fraternise with – talk to – any of the general public. And we're going to be looked after and they'll tell us more when we need to know it. It was the same ones that do the meals who gave us them.'

Which means I need to be careful what and who I ask about things. And should have kept my trap shut with the dodgy cooks. Better not to let them think I'm the 'general public'. Shit, perhaps this is all nothing to do with me. (But Ruth said before that the school wasn't closing. Did *she* know this lot were coming? Why didn't she tell me?)

I was pretty desperate to get something else out of the kid though, if I could manage not to worry him more. Just to have the slightest fucking idea what is happening out there.

I said, 'So, what's your name?' Safe ground.

'Nigel.'

'I'm Dominic. What was it like in your bit of the country, Nigel? Before getting the bus.'

He looked down at his feet and then he was howling away, covering his face with his hands. Why? What had I said? Was he remembering? *What* was he remembering?

He told me between tears, 'That's in the leaflet too. We aren't to talk about where we come from.'

I backed off and left him to it. Hope I haven't done any damage, but I think he's too weedy to report me to anyone, even if he is worried.

*Why all the secrets? What's going on?*

Today is the summer solstice, longest day. Bloody freezing.

# – day 17 –

OK, check this out.

Went to the lodge, to ask the Becketts. Ruth and her dad aren't going to have been given leaflets, are they? But Ruth knew the school was going to be used, and her old man was back at work, like I said. They have to know something.

Besides that, I get on OK with Mr Beckett. I helped him mend some stuff and clean up after the looters were here. Cleaning and mending with the world going down the tubes may be evidence of madness.

('Keep busy,' says Father. 'Do your thinking on the hoof.')

I went first thing. I'm in a prehistoric routine now: bed at nightfall and up when it's light. I don't bother with candles any more or a torch. Saving those things for the rest of my life, when it starts. They live up on the roof, hanging down inside one of the old chimneys in a plastic bag. Also decided to knock the fires on the head for the moment – I don't want to draw attention to myself, and it's better to get up than to freeze in bed in the morning. I've cleaned the grate and wedged the board back in.

Nobody at home in the lodge, or nobody answering the door, though a line of smoke from their chimney.

I wandered around, shivering. Had another look at the CCF hut. Still with broken door, as I left it, and the new mob haven't found it yet or bothered with it. It's at the edge of the Bede's complex, quite well hidden and doesn't look like much. Plenty of dried compo food for me there at the moment if I decide to head out of here and don't mind chronic constipation. Not much else useful. Just old combats, boots, jerry cans, all smelling of thirty years of boys. Still no thoughts on the strong room. Sure that Beckett won't have been given the key for that; probably Davis took it. Davis is the teacher who does CCF: *Colonel Davis, Geography and CCF.*

It occurs to me that the bolts for those .22s will be in Davis's own flat, or just possibly in the Geography department. Ammunition probably in the strong room with the guns. None of which gets me any closer to getting past the metal door, even if I wanted to. Maybe the army truck and Nigel's leaflet mean that we are now living under martial law: as a looter of .22s I could be shot.

I went on to the dining hall. I was starving. The seedy cooks were there; looked like they'd just set up their vat of porridge (made with water). Also one or two of the new lot, all girls, none cute. And Ruth.

Ruth was in her tatty maroon – guess she'd already been out running – but she was going mental. Really mental. I could hear the row well before I got in there. I don't know what made it happen, but then they don't know her, do they? Probably someone said something out of order. Probably the guy slopping out the porridge.

She was very focussed, didn't bother speaking. She had to go all the way to the end of the metal food counter to get round, and she did, picking things up as she went and throwing them; trays, serving spoons, plates, anything she passed, all lobbed at this guy. To start with he was laughing at her, telling her to calm down, take her tantrum outside, but she was a good shot and when some of the objects connected he started to swear at her, tell her he'd teach her a lesson.

She just kept on coming. Face flushed, hair wild from running. Our very own Witchbitch. Bloody awesome and beautiful.

She got to the guy and gave him such a shove, back into the doorway from the kitchens, where there were three gas bottles standing – from those crates off the trucks? – and he went flying. Then she just turned round and walked out, cool as you like, no trace of the temper tantrum. She passed me near the door and our eyes met, but she didn't say anything and neither did I.

You know, I almost think she was trying not to laugh. As if it was a game.

I *did* laugh. The girls who were there were shell-shocked, frozen. The guy who'd been pushed was swearing and banging about. He came out from behind the counter, with a cigarette in his mouth and pushed past me out of the dining hall, saying, 'What are *you* looking at, you little pillock?'

I was worried he was going after Ruth. I went to one of the windows and looked out. She was just turning the corner up by the Science block, a hundred metres away, but the guy wasn't following. He lit his fag, and his hands were shaking.

Then he reached into his anorak pocket and took out a gun. He pointed it at where Ruth had been and pretended to fire. Blew the imaginary smoke away from the muzzle like a cowboy. Put it away again.

Nobody was about. Nobody saw, except me.

# ADELINE

Ruth.

Ruth's endless shield of bright-eyed anger. Her games. Her cascades of questions.

Ruth's secret heart beating, unguessed, unrecognised by the Bede's rabble.

Ruth and her poetry, her dreams, her rush towards destruction.

What a performance!

Well, Adeline could match her anger and *she* had good reason. A perfect body that had gone wrong. The truth about herself kept from her by her own sister. A meaningless prophecy that mocked her.

What reason had Ruth got?

Ruth and Dominic.

Ruth and Dom, beautiful Dom whose love had given Adeline her life.

Ruth made her *sick*.

It was one of those days. A day of fury. A day when fate became suffocating. They were still new to her, a surprise, and yet they felt as familiar as the breath in her lungs. Perhaps they'd started when Adeline found the comcard. A wafer of gold where Ruth's shadow lived, and Dominic, and her own strange beginnings. For once Clarissa had been careless and left a gilt line showing where the thing nestled between the roof timbers. How it had shone as the last dusty sunlight of the evening had passed across it! How it had called to her to lift it down from its strange resting place and explore its secrets.

If Adeline could give that day back, she would, a hundred times over.

But then perhaps, in truth, the black moods had come a month later, when she'd had her first, mild attack, climbing the Cobbler. She'd broken two ribs and her wrist in the fall. There'd been enough time trussed up in the sickroom to wonder about the card *and* the pains in her chest.

It didn't matter when the thing had started. What mattered was that she should leave Seven soon, before these days of self pity crushed the song from her life, the laughter from her lips. If only death awaited, then she would face that too, and not let it find her skulking in the mountains, paralysed by her fear.

*And yet* . . . now the monsoon had come to bathe the thirsty rock, to pound on the timber, to make her spirits sing, to draw the fury from her. Truly, even despair was a game you played with yourself, not to be believed too deeply. She took extra Lookout duties and put her chair out on the platform until the sound and smell and touch of the rain was all she knew. She inched through the twelve katas on the slippery planks, hidden by the silver curtain. She scanned the obscurity for enemies and recorded the empty findings diligently. She gloried in the endless weight of water falling.

Inevitably, Paulette came wandering by, listless and downcast by the weather, and they toasted rock-mushrooms that had sprouted overnight in the crevices below the cabin. Adeline climbed recklessly down for them over the drop while her friend hung nervously at the edge, shouting muddled directions.

'I wondered if Sebastien would be here,' Paulette said coyly, later, when they'd eaten. For this she received a beating with a cushion, until both were giggling and sick with the greasy mushrooms.

Then, later, her friend grew bored. She paced round the lookout, unwilling to accept that the sun was gone for these few weeks. She paused and picked up the *other* card, the one from Mac, which Adeline had left unheeded on the table, and said, 'What's this? Let's open it and find out.'

Paulette's unashamed curiosity was fun to watch. It matched her own. Adeline waved a hand from where she rested, brooding on the sill, still half dwelling with the rain. 'Do it.'

The ancient heavy viewer was plugged in to the fat lookout battery and started up, the card fitted into the slot, and presently music filtered tinnily out, crackling. Trumpets and a fast, urgent drumming. Paulette perched herself on the table to watch and started flapping her sandal to the rhythm. Soon, deep, echoing bass sounds were added, whispering behind, giving an impression of vast space and power, the space and power of the oceans, perhaps. Then the mist on the screen cleared and a man stood there, if man he was, at the top of wide steps. Behind him, stretched over a skeleton of pure, regulated steel, stood a tower of glass.

The music was cut short. The man took a step forward and grinned coldly from behind the mask he wore.

'Water's rising,' he said.

Sound thundered out again, louder and more urgent than before, making the heat-cracked old speaker jump and rattle. The man looked at the two girls impassively, eyes glinting in their sockets. Then, for a second time, sudden silence and a step forward, down towards the camera.

'There'll be folks who want what's ours.' He laughed with the terror of it.

Then again, the music, the silence, the step, slow and purposeful.

'There'll be folks who don't know *what* they want.'

And so it went on. Bursts of monstrous sound, startling silences. And the man's threats.

'Rise up now, Briton.

'Be all that you can be.

'Let's see what you got.

'Let's see who's FIT TO LIVE.'

With the last word the music went into a frenzy and there came the sound of many people shouting with joy or fear, though no one could be seen, save for the one masked man. He himself laughed with them, a wild, dangerous sound, and threw himself down the remaining steps in a series of flips and somersaults, the strips of cloth on his tunic whirling around him like a cloud of flies.

The last roll brought him close enough for his covered face suddenly to fill the screen, so that Paulette gave a nervous little jump. Again everything stopped, the rain hissed outside. Softly, the man whispered, 'Hey, are *you* fit to live?'

'Are *you*, creepy-man?'

Adeline laughed at Paulette's screwed-up face, but the other girl said, 'I've changed my mind. I don't want to see this. It's horrible.'

Adeline walked across and froze the image. She could feel the devil rising in her, and could only watch. 'So. What are they trying to do, do you think?' she asked lightly.

'Who?'

'The people who made this. The guy with the mask. The ones who wrote the words he says. What are they doing it for?'

Paulette stopped swinging her leg. She looked cautiously at Adeline. She knew the telltale signs of what she thought of as Adeline's 'questioning mood'. 'Um . . . To get your attention, I guess?' she suggested nervously.

'Yes. OK. To get your attention. What else?'

*Here we go,* Paulette thought.

'Make you think about rising sea levels?'

'OK, why should they do that?'

'They're trying to . . . I don't know, to frighten people or something. To make the broadcast more exciting?'

'First part correct. Second only half there. Try again.'

Paulette said sulkily, 'You sound like McCoy when he's on one. You tell me then, oh great one. What *are* they trying to do?'

Adeline stared at her. When she spoke it was half to herself: 'McCoy, yes . . . remember what Mac said at the meeting? *There's enough fear out there right now to start a hundred new wars.'* She shivered. Dominic's Major floated abruptly into her thoughts, with his bleak, malevolent message. *If a boy or girl falls, you will leave them where they fall. Rations will be withdrawn from those flouting this basic rule.*

'I wasn't at the meeting, remember? I don't know what you're talking about, Addie.'

Adeline was vaguely aware of Paulette watching her, waiting for more, frustrated by her mood, but she was gone, swimming deep in the ocean of thoughts and probabilities now. She stood up, ignoring her friend, and wandered out through the open doorway, onto the platform. At the outer rail the silver sheets of rain hid even the cabin, a few metres behind. The warm water was delicious, cradling her, cooling the sticky heat of her skin, easing her irritation. She floated over the unseen drop and the rain-battered terraces, and was glad that Briton was far away.

When she came back inside, twenty minutes later, the cabin was empty. She towelled the worst of the water off at the little sink and completed the set routine with a slow sweep of the spotting scope, permanently mounted before the wide, glassless window. Again, a pointless formality in this weather, she made a neat note in the log – *14.45, zero visibility (monsoon): nothing to report.* She wandered about the cabin, still dripping slightly, soothed by the steady sound of water on wood. Her feet were bare on the rough, gritty planks. She felt bad about Pauly. She just couldn't help herself.

At the machine, where the masked man still flickered, suspended, she paused, wondering whether to restart the strange communication. Or she could change cards. Clarissa would be down in the valleys. She could run to the office, get the card from the rafters and bring Dominic into her rain-protected island. A smile crept onto her lips as she imagined it. They could surely be happy here together, on such an afternoon, no matter how short the time. They would challenge each other. They would be *aware*, jolted out of themselves.

She shook her head. No. Another day perhaps. There would be many afternoons to spend on Dominic and Tilly and the rest while the monsoon lasted. Besides, Mac would be certain to ask her about the British recordings. She might as well go on watching.

'Make sure you know what tune the Devil's playing,' McCoy always said.

She pressed the button to resume, and the tiny image flickered with renewed life.

After all the fuss at the beginning, 'Fit To Live' was nothing but a game, it seemed. Was this Frau Kästener's 'madness'? Surely not.

'In case you've been in a medical facility having your brain tweaked for the last three months, you can call me "the Ref",' the masked man said icily. 'And now . . . *let's meet the players*!'

A figure appeared from the left, running in to stand beside the Ref: then one from the right, then the left again. They were clothed in white, waving and smiling at Adeline as they ran. Soon there were ten of them, five each side. The hands bobbed back and forth, the teeth showed. And somewhere amongst them was the whiff of fear.

Most of the 'players' were large, young, strongly built. Some were obviously psyched up with whatever was to follow, eyes darting about fiercely. Others, younger even than Adeline and Paulette, were much calmer, faces showing nothing but a faint arrogance, standing unmoving whilst the rules were explained. Three were unmistakeably tired under their smiles: sad and defiant and angry too.

'Are you Fit To Live?' cried the Ref when all ten had been named.

'*Yesss!*' the players shouted.

He looked them up and down, unconvinced. 'Well, we'll see, won't we ... Come, let's play!' He ran back up the steps and into the shining building, and the ten followed.

Then there was a break in the image, a crackling on the speaker, a moment of darkness, and the thing changed. The Ref could no longer be seen, but he became a guide, his voice telling you more about this or that player, and then inviting you to watch them in a game. Perhaps a whole game, perhaps only a few seconds, recording the moment that the player fell or failed the task. Failures, injuries, moments of despair, these were shown in detail, Adeline soon realised. With shock, it gradually dawned on her that death would be welcomed as a premium event in Fit To Live.

The games were randomly chosen by a spinning wheel. Their names were: Combat, Adaptability, Endurance, Logic and Combination. As every game was introduced, an invisible crowd cheered and roared the word.

'*COM-BAT!*'

'*ADAPT-a-BILITY!*'

As if it was exactly what they'd hoped for.

'OK. Welcome to the games. Let's not waste time,' the Ref's voice chuckled. 'And who *can* waste time with the sound of the great, wide seas lapping at our doors and walls? Let's get going right away and take a tiny peek at . . . *Serena*!' An image floated over the screen, a 3-D human revolving to be seen from every angle. Adeline recognised one of the three tired faces from the opening sequence. A girl, perhaps just out of her teens, long fair hair tied tightly back, squaring up to the camera in fighting stance.

'So, what do we know about Serena? Not much, I'm afraid. She's nineteen, or so she says. Unemployed at present. (*That* could change if she wins through today!) Says she swims in the city harbour to keep in shape. (Yeuch, rather her than me, ha ha.) And genetic background . . . unknown.' The Ref paused and then said, in sympathy, real or feigned, 'Well, that's a tough break, Serena. Oh . . . yes, I was almost forgetting – Serena's application score was sixty-two per cent, so she just made it in. That may mean nothing, of course. We've had some *red hot* players with low starting percentages.'

As the voice went on, the same information appeared under the revolving image on the screen, scrolling out in echo of the Ref's words.

'So, this is the moment the wheel span for Serena, and as you can see, she started off with . . . *Endurance*.'

'*EN-DU-RANCE!*'

'Not swimming, I'm afraid. No, Serena's task, randomly generated as ever, was in the gym, on . . . the *climbing wall*!' Cheers again, identical and unconvincing. 'Yes indeed, a simple little game to start her off. What happens is this: Serena will begin at the bottom of our "rockface" wearing a belt on which there is attached, at the back, one end of a loose elastic rope. Now, we've split the climb today into five sections, each ten metres in height, and we've been extra kind and set the hand-holds and gradient to "basic". Serena really shouldn't have too many problems with the climb in itself. A child could do this. The bottom section is static, un-moving, solid as real rock. But, the top four sections are *on the move*. They're going to start well set back from the first section, leaving a ledge between each ascent, and with my starting siren, these mobile sections will begin to roll slowly forward! And, people of Briton, that is *bad* news for our little lady, because on each ledge a word is written, and each time Serena moves to a higher section without shouting the word good and loud, our team below will shorten the elastic rope by one whole metre.'

The screen took the watcher on a simulated trip through the game as the Ref described it. It looked simple: fun even. But to Adeline the amount of materials used – of true 'regulated' steel and plastic, and the build-ing itself, of course – was incredible, almost obscene. All for a game.

'Oh, and people,' murmured the Ref, 'just one more twist. One spicy little nugget. Serena can choose to do this with no safety net, and if she does we'll give her an three extra metres of elastic rope.'

The screen went dark and a tiny line of fire at the centre hurtled out. Two words, revolving, closer and closer, until like the Ref's face earlier, they filled the screen.

*Game on.*

Adeline watched, caught by the drama despite herself, as the rope-carrying belt was strapped onto the girl. Her own muscles tensed in unison with Serena's. She looked at the distances and the length of the rope, shook her head in disbelief.

'So, Serena,' the Ref said genially, 'you understand

the rules? You know the game? Good. Time to choose, then: net or no net?'

The girl was sweating already: her defiance from the opening shot had fled. She had a hand over her stomach as if it ached. She looked round, as if for help with the choice, then up at the fifty-metre climbing wall.

'Net,' she murmured, doubtfully.

'I'm sorry, can we have that a little louder for the viewers at home, Serena?'

'Net!'

'*Net!* She chooses to have a *net*! OK, net it is! Let the fun begin. Three, two, one . . .'

A blast on a siren echoed through the great room and the girl was racing forwards to the base of the wall, the coils of loose elastic straightening behind her. Above her, the four mobile sections of 'rock' began to inch forwards. The theme music restarted in the background, brash and terrifying. One of the cameras floated dizzily up and panned towards the ground so that the viewers could see the four mocking words stencilled on the ledges, still a metre or more from the encroaching chunks of fake granite.

RISK – ALL – GAIN – WORLD

The girl was near the top of the first section now. A little too frantic, not as careful as she might be in finding her hand- and footholds and moving her weight to them, but safe thus far. The slack in the rope she wore was not quite gone, but even the swinging weight of the thing might unbalance her, Adeline thought, if she did not focus more completely on her task. And yet the game was clearly designed just for that; to distract focus, to encourage the heart to beat double time and the hands to grow slippery or careless.

Serena gained the first ledge. The outer edge of the letters was just being nudged by the rolling rockface. She shrieked 'Risk!' Then she was on to section two, her powerful shoulders and thighs working like machines to push her up, up, up. At last a rhythm started to appear in her climbing; the steady, strong rhythm of a swimmer's body, cutting through the incoming tide.

By the time she reached the second ledge, hope had started to grow in Serena. Still no more than a quarter of the letters had been swallowed and the word was shouted confidently out. The rope had begun to make itself felt, but no more than that. Adeline could see her thinking: *Just two more sections. Then the race will be won.*

Hand over hand, the girl struggled upwards. The white tunic stuck to her back and she paused every few seconds to wipe the sweat from her palms and eyes. Muscles and sinews strained. The cameras moved in close to show the taut face, the open mouth, gasping for oxygen.

At the third ledge, the wild hope was crushed.

Serena frantically scanned the slim lower segments of the letters that could still be seen, having to lean forward now against the elastic pull. Thanks to the more recognisable 'G', she managed eventually to scream 'Gain!' But it was clear that the final word would be covered well before she achieved the fourth ledge.

Yet still there was a chance.

There were tears in Adeline's eyes as she saw the muscles work once more, fighting upwards, more slowly now, inch by careful inch, as time need no longer be considered important. The aerial camera, looking down from its dizzy height, showed the last centimetre of the final word disappearing, and in the top right-hand corner of the screen, the Ref's masked face appeared.

'Mmm, things don't look too good now, do they?' he chortled quietly to the audience.

The belt around Serena's waist was being pulled well clear of her body by the straining rope: the front of it was pressing into her stomach. The camera shot panned up to show how each finger had to grip until the nail turned white as the girl laboured upwards. Three metres to go, two . . .

The last ledge was no more than a handspan wide when the girl dragged herself onto it in slow agony, clawing at the rock above to avoid being peeled away from this fragile safety, either by the moving wall or by the straining elastic.

'This is it,' whispered the Ref's floating face. 'All or nothing. Remember, Serena will have to give us a word here.'

It didn't look likely. Serena didn't look like she could remember any words at all. Yet she clung on desperately, with eyes closed, took a deep breath, and gasped, 'Everything!'

A pause – the Ref theatrically slapped his palm to his forehead – then down below, the fat drum winch holding the rope rumbled into action, drawing back a precious metre of elastic. Above, Serena strained at the rock. She was on her toes now, on the disappearing ledge, her pale face crimson with the effort. Then, with sudden force, she was pulled into space, catapulted across the abyss, to drop forty metres into billowing swathes of safety net.

'Now that's just too bad,' the Ref murmured.


Adeline sat alone in the quiet of the cabin and let the sounds of the games die. She'd known from the moment that the girl had chosen to climb with a net that the thing was impossible. The message of the game was clear: Serena was not good enough. She was flawed. A hopeless case.

*If a boy or girl falls you will leave them where they fall.*

But Serena had allowed someone else to choose the rules. A willing lamb to the slaughter. After all, even despair was a game you played with yourself. Your game, your rules.

The rain rattled down and the demons retreated.

*As she walked from the dining hall and her temper cooled, Ruth found herself smiling. Then she was laughing aloud. Ridiculous! She'd been ridiculous. What had Dom thought?*

*You had to laugh.*

# DOMINIC
## – day 20 –

*Se mundumque vince.*

Conquer yourself, conquer the world.

It's all just patterns though, isn't it? Patterns of behaviour. Repetitions. Copy your parents, copy your friends,
do what you're expected to do, what you've been drilled
with since before you could walk. That's the basics of
'se mundumque vince'.

Even language. When I think, I think in English. Not
any old English, but the English Father gave me – that he
brainwashes the nation with by the metre – and Bede's and
Kingsley's and Jessica Ward's English. That's how I solve
problems, that's how I work out what to do. So my answers
are repetitions too. Stale, stinking repetitions.

What answers would I come up with if I could think in
Chinese or Inuit? What language does Ruth think in?!

And then the oceans start to rise and the climate heads
for some kind of ice age and war breaks out, panic, disease
... and you reach for your patterns. A tight ship. All pull
together. It's a bloody joke.

I can't stomach this place or these people. They make
me sick. Doing what they're told like sheep. That leaflet
they were given! Sticking to patterns and nobody *thinking*,
nobody seeing the cracks in it all.

I said before that everyone was running wild, but that's
only half the truth. Sure, they're doing what they think
they can get away with, nicking or breaking stuff for a
laugh, smoking if they've got ciggies, boys and girls getting it on, of course. But at the same time it's business as
usual: they're busy forming cliques and pecking orders and

bossing each other around and even dishing out punishments to the younger ones.

Is that all the patterns are for? Power. Bullying people.

(Answers on a stamped, undressed elephant, Kingsley would say.)

The three idiots two floors down have set themselves up as hard men. They're called Hodges, Barbieri and Loney. They seem to have done some sort of deal with the adults in the kitchens and now they do what they want, even in the dining hall. They came up here again, the bastards. Threw a couple of punches. Went through the things that I haven't hidden. (The two pieces of the Strat are in the roof cache now, luckily.) They had a laugh about my name – I was a fool to have let on.

Hodges said, 'A little angel, then, are you? A sweet little angel?'

Ha ha.

'There's something not right about you, little angel. How come you got up here and made yourself comfortable before any of us?'

I said, 'I don't know. I just liked the view.'

'I don't remember you on the bus.'

'I don't remember you either. I suppose we all had lots to think about.'

A punch on the arm from Barbieri.

'Why such a tatty old sleeping bag? Looks like CCF or something.'

I said, 'It's all I could get, at home. It's one I nicked from my old school. The place was going crazy. But . . . we're not supposed to talk about that, are we?'

Hopefully that did it. They think I got a leaflet too, so I must have been there. The morons.

When they went away, Barbieri said, 'This is *our* House, understand? If you want to stay here, you remember and be a good boy.'

I'm not going to stay here, though. Decided this morning,

when I woke up. I got the maps (another dawn raid) and I'll head for the bothy as soon as I can get some kit together. I'd like to persuade the Becketts to come too, but I can't see them agreeing and old Beckett is hardly fit to travel – he coughs up blood in this cold – so maybe I can leave a message for Father with them.

It'll be a day or two till I'm set, so I've built my alarm anyway, as I can't have those pillocks coming up here without me being ready.

I quite enjoyed thinking it up. (Think on the hoof!) Something they couldn't see or hear – same principle as putting a lock on the door, I'd just get more attention if they knew about it – but enough to wake me up in good time.

What I came up with was this:

At the bottom of the top stairs there's a fire door. I've unscrewed the little screw on the base of the handle a couple of turns – not enough to notice – and filed off one side of the head. Then, underneath the banisters going up, where you wouldn't normally put your hand, there are three or four hooks, nicked from the cloakrooms, bent round into loops, screwed tight into the wood. Another two of these next to each other in the ceiling over the window in our dorm.

I've got a spool of thin twine, and I've tied an old roof tile to one end. That's just about all the weight the twine could deal with. The other end is tied in a loop.

So, imagine ... the loop goes around the filed screw under the door handle, the twine goes up through the hooks under the banisters, through the keyhole of the dorm door (bent the edges inwards so they're not sharp and little friction) and up over the two hooks above the window. Then out of the window, and over the balustrade, with the tile hanging there on the end, ready to fall.

And between the last two hooks on the ceiling, where the twine is taut, I've hung a tea mug by its handle. Kingsley's Spurs mug, to be precise.

Thus: handle turns, twine flies off screw and is instantly pulled v. fast through all hooks as tile falls ... and mug crashes to floor to get my attention.

It was the best I could do. When the alarm is triggered, all anybody will see is a broken mug, unless they're looking hard. When I'm not here, the coiled twine and tile go up the chimney, onto a nail I've wedged into the brickwork.

As long as nobody gets brained by the falling tile.

Supper time. Been to see Ruth. Found her at home this time, and actually got some sense out of her.

She wasn't quite as unfriendly as before, though she always fires prickly questions, gets them in first, if she'll talk at all. No one else makes me think that quickly. It's like an icy shower.

*Have you made some new friends, then?*
*How's the hangover?*
*In clothes today? That's nice.*

She relented and I managed to get a word in. I think she just tests people out with the questions. I said, 'But you knew this lot were coming. You told me the school wasn't closed.'

She shook her head. 'No. No we didn't know. Dad was given some money, that's all, to stay on here and work as normal for a while.'

I was questioner for once. 'Didn't you think that was strange? Who paid him? Why should you stay here when everyone else was leaving?'

She said that here was as good as any place and that the money and instructions had come in his last payslip. Also that they won't come with me when I go.

I said, 'So you're just going to stay here with those loonies in the kitchens and all the other kids running around?'

She said, 'Dad can't leave: I have to stay with him.'

65

I said, 'Do you know one of them has a gun? The one you pushed over?'

I don't know if she believed me. Told her what I'd seen but she was just standing there, looking at me, looking *into* me without being there at all. She goes off to another place when she thinks, like she's listening in to something far away. Then, Mr Beckett came in and she snapped out of it. I could smell the booze on him. God knows where he gets it.

'Oh, hello laddie. Come to chat up our Ruth have you? Put the kettle on, eh, Ruthie?'

'There's no tea left, Dad, remember?' Her face came back to life, reverted to the normal look again, sparks and challenge and scorn; thanks, Father Beckett!

'No tea for young Dominic?' He seemed confused. Just like Mrs McCartney in the village. 'What can we offer him, then?'

'It's OK, Dad, he has to go.'

So I went. It was something, though. The first proper conversation in almost three weeks, and with Ruth too. Only writing this keeps me sane.

There's so much more I want to talk to Ruth about. My Blitz evacuation theory, what made her flip at the serving rail, what's going on outside Bede's, what it was like when everything was normal.

Her performance in the dining hall is generally known about now. Heard a group of girls talking about it.

'Do you think she's a gypsy or something?'

'What's she doing here?'

'She's a mad, gypsy cow.'

'*And* dressed like a tramp.'

'She's a Wild Woman.'

'The Wild Woman of ... what's the name of this dump again?'

I said, 'Bede's.'

They all stopped and looked at me. One said, 'Who asked *you* to earwig?' Then they walked on.

I heard one say, 'The Wild Woman of Bede's.'

And another one, 'He's quite cute, isn't he?'

They can keep it.

# – day 21 –

Three weeks today since the last ordinary people left the school .

Hard to get my head round.

Decided to go up on the hills, first thing, trying to sort my thoughts out. Was going to walk but I came alive and found myself running. It was very special up there today. A real buzz. Deserted, calm, stiff with the frost.

Maybe I've been as bad as any of them. Maybe Ruth's right about me. (She doesn't let herself rest comfortably, nor me neither. Where are *her* patterns?)

*Although blessed with some considerable degree of intelligence, Dominic constantly fails to live up to his potential. This boy needs to start using his brain.*

When Father received that from the Head, last year, he wasn't angry. He doesn't often get angry. He showed it to me, made me read it aloud, then binned it. 'You need to know what others think of you,' he said, 'and then you need to be able to discount those opinions to judge for yourself.'

Some of the kids staying in Tremayne have got colds or flu. Not surprising; but Barry, the guy with the gun, made an 'announcement' at lunch about it. Apparently anybody with symptoms is to get shut on the top floor of Tremayne for the duration, in quarantine. They must be worried about proper flu or TB or something. They should be more worried about cholera. The water has started to taste pretty strange and the pressure's right down. I'm only drinking the tea from their urns from now on (not boiling, but better than nothing). Wonder if they've got purification tablets in the CCF hut – doubtful, but will check.

Of course my two drums of water have long since been swiped.

Personal hygiene is somewhat lacking too. Not so much with the girls of course. Suppose I'm lucky to have Hodges et al in Orchard to scare off anyone else from blocking up our toilets.

Still using the pool for painful, two-minute thrashes as I reckon the chlorine should keep it safe a while longer, whatever people chuck into it. But going murky. Soon just icy showers, or nothing at all if the pressure goes or the pipes freeze.

Water will be the biggest problem, heading across country. I need a camp stove to boil it – or to make fires – and I need to plan a route near waterways.

Funny that the oceans are supposed to be rising and the planet's turning into an oven and in Britain we're freezing to death with nothing to drink. If that's your idea of funny.

Hang on ... can hear more engines. Loud, very loud. Trucks? Going to look.

# ADELINE

What did you do if your heart was swollen and un-reliable? Did you lie in the dark and wait? Did you hide? Did you give up your best moments for fear that they might be taken from you anyway?

Adeline emerged early onto the puddle-strewn plateau and, forgoing breakfast, ran in a cloud of spray across to the stone stair. Within thirty minutes she had slipped and slid past the last few ramshackle buildings at the lower end of the valley and left Seven behind. As she ran, she smiled and dared herself to do it now, to make this the real leaving. *Not yet, not yet*, she thought, *but soon*.

She worked her way to the east along a succession of ridges, taking narrow ways that were crumbling and shifting in the wet. Then north, down the first sodden, unstable descents towards the great lake that lapped the mountains' feet. This was a way she might take when the time came. Who could say where she'd go. It didn't matter, not today. She shrieked as she plunged waist-deep through the new rivers. Gasped as her shoes skated on the treacherous rocks. Tested herself up the shifting banks of scree. She was like a child.

The mountains were almost impassable, her private playground. Only twice did she see other people in the shifting screen of rainfall. First a tattered hunter, all skin and bone, picking his way carefully through a line of low trees, scanning the ground for signs of mountain rabbits. Then a couple bivouacked under an over-hanging rock, nursing a smoky little fire, looking out with pale, bleak faces. None of these three saw her, although she was within twenty metres. The tang of smoke gave the couple away in good time. With the hunter, she dropped swiftly to the mud when his outline swam up out of the weather, and stayed there until he had wandered far enough for her to stand and let the monsoon swallow her again.

It was part of the fun, to stay hidden and free. To be surprised and tested.

She finally broke her fast at a place where, in fine weather, she would see the faint blue of the great lake, shimmering in that other world below. For now it was a window over soft, watery nothingness. She lost herself in it when she'd eaten, humming contentedly. Then, aware that she was due once more in the lookout for the evening watch, she set herself a steeper, more direct route back to Seven.

*Not yet*, she hummed. *But soon.*

She held the thought and gritted her teeth to the savage ascents, half willing the imperfect valves in her chest to fail and spill their blood here, now, at *this* moment; daring the organs of her body as she had dared herself.

There would be no one on these climbs in the rain. She went as a beast now, rather than a child, and her shrieks were more angry than playful as she made her way back to Seven.

Where did the one thing end and the other start?

Yet she was wrong. There *were* others here, on these difficult ways. As she scrabbled carelessly up a streaming escarpment and pulled herself over the lip, she found with shock that she was in the midst of four silent travellers, resting on their packs, passing a flask between them. The four, as startled as she, rose to their feet. Then they laughed.

'Relax. It doesn't look as if it bites. What is it do

you think, Boxer? Not a mountain cat. A drowned rat
perhaps? A fish looking for its river?'

'You don't think it's anything to do with our own business? Isn't there . . . something about her? Look at her.'

'Hardly! Just look at the state of her. Wishful thinking,
mate.'

They spoke, surprisingly, in English. Adeline answered
them, eyes downcast, in thick peasant French. 'Please
sirs, madam, I cannot understand you. I must go. Father
is waiting. I shouldn't have stayed so long away.' She
went to pass them, but the group closed in.

'Can you make head or tail of it? No, nor me. Some
dialect, I expect. Whoa there, young lady.'

'Ryan will know what to do with her.'

'Yes. What do you think, Ryan? Look what we've
found.'

She sensed then, a fifth. Behind her, coming in from
her left. Suddenly the thing smelled of trouble. The
unseen Ryan put a hand on her shoulder.

'Well then, and what have we caught here?'

She reached back and caught the hand, pulled him
down over and round her thigh as she swung it out and
leaned back. As soon as he hit the rock, she was gone,
weaving into the mist of silver droplets, never looking
back.

Shouts followed her but nothing else. In all probability
she had tipped over an honest climber or hunter who
had meant her no harm. But still, she made sure that
no pursuer would catch her. She climbed hard and in
earnest.

What had they meant, though, about their 'business'?
She must mention it at home.

Mercifully, her body stayed deaf to her earlier taunt.
She arrived at Seven whole and safe and in good time
for her duty. Next time she played the game, she'd be
more careful.

She left a note in her sister's office about the climbers and went to get clean.

'Here, this is about right.' McCoy threw down his clumsy armful of tools and wiped the water from his eyes, leaving a trail of fresh mud on his cheek. 'If we dig a new channel here and block the old one, we can maybe keep those three terraces there from being washed right away.' He looked round, then gestured. 'And we can sink a new water tank about fifty metres down, soon as the dry comes, before the ground gets too hard.'

'OK.' Clarissa signalled acknowledgment, trusting his judgement, on this matter at least, absolutely. 'I'll go and explain what we want to do.'

They had to shout to be heard over the relentless rain. She hoped the little, miserable huddle of would-be farmers, standing in the porch of the cabin, watching their long work being crushed and eroded by water, included at least one English or French speaker. She was too tired to spell it all out in sign language. Sleep was rare for her or Mac when the rains came.

Yet the farmers did not speak those languages and she had to make the effort anyway.

Soon they were all toiling in a line, wrestling with the slippery earth, trying to delve the necessary channel and clear the unwanted mud before the deluge undid their work. Where possible, they lined the new streambed with rocks, gravel, scraps of plastic or material; even the precious offcuts of timber from the new dwelling. If this didn't work, they'd be starting again after the rains, levelling ground, digging in topsoil and whatever scant compost their Seven neighbours could spare them, sewing a new crop. Until they saw it for themselves, the migrants who signed the ARK charter would never believe how thoroughly the iron-baked mountains could be transformed in two or three short weeks of rainfall.

The rain was infinitely valuable, infinitely treacherous.

McCoy and Clarissa laboured at the bottom of the line, choosing the path of the proposed channel, knowing the work – and each other – so well that little speech was needed. Next to them, a boy, one of the newcomers, grimly bent his back again and again, frantic in his desire to save the little farm.

'All right?' Clarissa asked him, worried that he might exhaust himself, and he glanced up and nodded mutely, with hardly a stroke missed.

They all soon stood ankle-deep in mire, but at least the rainwater was warm. When the light started to fail, Clarissa raised her eyebrows at Mac and he nodded.

'Sure! We carry on!' he yelled. 'If we don't finish this tonight, we might as well have not bothered.'

She signalled agreement and went to unpack two of the charged work-lights, planting their spiked feet deep into the mud and hauling the resin tubes out of their casings so that the skeletal structures stood crazily over the fresh, glistening trench, cocking their bright heads in seeming cynicism, impervious to the water streaming over their lenses. Seven had twenty-three such lights; when these two were run down, only six would remain charged and available until the sun came again. If only they had a water turbine, the lights and other equipment could be recharged year-round. They must try again, Clarissa thought, to trade some of their produce with one of the city authorities, either in France or Spain.

Yet – the argument went in circles – perhaps it would be unwise to draw too much attention to their existence. Think of the recent raiders! And they were not the first. Everyone was hungry for resources. Food, metal, medicine: it was all growing scarce. If they went looking for machine parts they'd be noticed. Regular troops would come, with a manager, to swallow them up for one of the hungry cities.

*Fool!* A voice said, at the back of her mind. *You've already been noticed. You know it. And so will Jan, by now.*

Since Frau Kästener's arrival Jan Barbieri had never been far from her thoughts. However frail she'd seemed, the old woman had brought a tempest with her. She'd brought the past rushing back. Damn her! Clarissa had built peace here, and something worth striving for. Why should she let it all go?

She shivered, reliving, as she so often did, the savagery of her last meeting with Jan: his wild crusade to eliminate all of her genetic line. There wasn't a day when she didn't mourn her barely-known twin, Mira, and her mother, who was also her twin. Somewhere inside, they soothed her and lent her their strength. It had been their calm voices that had urged her to help McCoy build this place when he'd appeared in the mountains with his ARK charter. A symbol for the frightened world of what *could* be done, a sanctuary for Adeline to grow and thrive, the mountains full of her sparkling child's laughter.

And now, for a long time, God help her, it hadn't been like that. The girl's peace was shattered. Between the better moods, she'd become secretive, angry, depressive. There was an acre of space between them. The bond was damaged. The pain of it was almost impossible to bear.

Was Jan guilty of this too? No! It was Clarissa herself who was to blame.

Sometime in the early hours of morning, the trench was finished and McCoy led the taciturn workers up around the remains of their farmland to break through the final metre into the waterway that the monsoon had dug for itself in only a few days. Immediately a part of the torrent bubbled away into the new bed, and with the reduced pressure they were able to drive upended planks into the mud above the terraces, gradually sealing off the old channel, reinforcing the barrier with earth and stones.

'Sit here!' McCoy shouted at the mute faces. 'Sit here ... all night, all day. Watch the water. Watch!' He pointed at their eyes and the runaway pouring down off the mountain's back. 'Watch!'

They understood. They must watch the stream. They must do the rest for themselves. A man was delegated to take first shift and settled himself miserably under a scrap of plastic, while the others filed exhausted into the little building.

McCoy and Clarissa shouldered their equipment and trudged down the valley towards the winding stone stair. Now the work was done, a coldness settled between them again, so that they hardly spoke. Damn Frau Kästener. Damn Mac, giving Adeline the recordings she'd brought with her. Anyone would think they *believed* in the crazy prophecy. Serpents rising from the flood to save the world!

Damn herself most of all, for not being sure.

It was too *soon* to let her sister go. Back to all that mess, that violence that she'd known as a child. Frau Kästener had been wrong to ask.

Christophe met them at the foot of the stone stair, hidden until they were upon him.

'More newcomers,' he called above the rain. 'Five of them. All men. I was going to see for myself. I do not know how they came here, in this. Will you come with me?'

And so, as it always happened, they were kept from their beds a little longer. They slid and slipped on down the valley with the mild ex-mercenary to see the grim new faces that had sought them out, where they were being held in one of the patrol huts.

'Too big,' Christophe complained, as they went.

'Seven is become too big. We can never be sure. So many arrivals, and in the rains too!'

But Clarissa hardly listened to Mac's reply. She thought: I am become my mother, trying to guide events in secret; trying to keep doorways open for potential. She could hear Tilly's calm, fearless voice, even now, as she had heard it for the last time.

*This strange thing that we are, you and I and the others; maybe this is like the bright coils of the serpent?*

She wouldn't have let Adeline find the comcard but for that voice. She would have left her peace unbroken.

They saw the newcomers. They were northerners from near the ruined bridge to Briton, wishing to escape the austerity measures of the French Families. She took no interest and let the two men debate their fate, not even noticing if, in the end, the strangers were allowed to sign the Charter or not. Gradually she breathed the anger and fear away, and looked more fondly at Mac. In her imagination she could smell his hair and taste his skin.

It was only as they climbed the stone stair, as she watched the steady, solid movement of his back, that they spoke to one another.

McCoy turned. 'Hey,' he called. 'We were fools back there tonight. At the dig, I mean. The boy understood English OK, when you spoke to him. We should have got *him* to translate. Would've saved us a lot of clowning around.'

She smiled up at him wryly. 'But you make such a good clown, Mac.'

'This,' said Tilly Saint, 'is the girl Adeline.' A picture appeared on the screen. A little smiling tot of around two, dusty and unshod, with startling sharp eyes; one green and one brown. Whatever she was smiling at was off to one side, not in view of the camera. Behind her there was a smudge of blue that must be the great lake.

'Adeline is, of course, one of the so-called "spares" which this Family has produced from Stoneywall Fertility Centre for generations. Like all of us – like me – she is a clone, a copy, taken from one original source. By the laws of logic and biology, she should therefore be identical, yet evidently she is not.'

The grimy, sunburnt little girl faded and was replaced by further images: crowds of people chanting in a bleak city square under an iron sky; strange, ragged figures backed by great stone buildings, spreading their hands in welcome or supplication as they addressed the passers-by; a dreamy-eyed, green-clad woman painting a snake onto a sheet of glass and being chased away by an aproned man who came out from behind the glass, shouting in anger; a pillar of corroded green metal that had words running around it in the shape – again – of a snake.

Tilly's calm voice said, 'Concurrent with this "impossible" child, the last spare of the final batch, we have a strong re-emergence of one of the older, more obscure cults or religions that have gripped Briton since the ice came or before. The rhyme or song is well known:

> *Blessed Children,*
> *You are given this sleeping serpent;*
> *Stretched across the years,*
> *Its strong, bright coils buried deep*
> *In the marshes and the floodwaters;*
> *Its mouth closed on its tail.*
>
> *And when the serpent wakes,*
> *And it is full-grown and nourished,*
> *And the beautiful, sleek, knowing head is lifted up,*

*And the two eyes open, one brown, one green:*
*Then, blessed children, you may ride its back*
*To freedom and love.*

*For this serpent is no tempter:*
*She is your truest friend.'*

A pause.

'The different coloured eyes. The mouth closed upon the tail. And the sudden reappearance of this serpent cult. If you, viewing this now, whoever you are, have studied these records carefully from their beginning, you will know how impossible such things must be, and how seemingly empty is this cult. And yet the girl exists and all things seem to concern her. Maybe logic and fact and biology are of no use to us here. Isn't that a wonderful, refreshing thought? Maybe, indeed, we are to be saved, whether we like it or not.'

Tilly's face came back onto the screen, gentle and sad. 'I have therefore taken certain measures to protect this Adeline for the time being. My hope is . . .'

The image flickered once and the sentence remained unfinished. From somewhere nearby there came the noise of an explosion and men shouting. Tilly glanced away from the camera, back over her left shoulder.

She muttered, 'Time to go it seems . . . the girl may take this.'

A slim hand reached towards the screen and the image died, even as new explosions were breaking out. This was the last image, the last piece of information on the whole comcard.

The frozen timing stamp indicated a date thirteen years ago. What had happened on that date was well known to Adeline. Jan Barbieri had taken control in the city and Mira – another 'spare', the same age as Clarissa – had fled to France with a boy called Kay. She had been coming to rescue Adeline, but before she could manage it, she was caught and killed by Barbieri and his troops. At that point Clarissa herself had taken over the quest and spirited the baby Adeline high into the mountains, beyond the reach of the soldiers. There, eventually, amongst the drifters and bandits, she had met the young man from Canada, McCoy, one of the ARK envoys, sent to choose new sites. And so Seven was begun. Her home.

*Time to run ... The girl may take this.*

Adeline assumed that 'the girl' was Mira and that she had carried the comcard until her death. After that, Clarissa must have brought it on. And kept it hidden ever since, except for the day two years ago that she was called suddenly from her desk by a dispute in the valley, leaving the card imperfectly hidden.

*Why* hidden?

Adeline shook herself and looked about the cabin. Night had stolen over the mountains and she hadn't noticed. She should light the lantern, do the necessary checks.

Deliberately she went about these tasks, moving slowly, aching from the morning. She came to turn off the viewer, prising out the slip of gold that must be returned to her sister's office, and thought again, What would my sister fear, in showing this to me?

Was it the violence that the thing had seen? Was it the deaths of Mira and Tilly and no doubt others before them who had carried it? Her twins had saved her life, and yet they were part of a terrible, meaningless story and had died trying to make *her* a part of that story. A serpent with its mouth closed on its tail! As if some dreamer, some witch, had chosen her existence centuries ago.

No. If anyone had 'chosen' her, it was Dominic. Her Dom, whose words were first on the comcard, written in his impatient print.

She closed her eyes, feeling faint, choked by the weight upon her.

*The little line of trucks rumbled in to change everything again and she watched them secretly, still as a deer in the foliage. She thought of Dom hearing them at this same moment from his high room. She thought of his body tensing and his mind tumbling through the possibilities. Was he at his window, fingertips on the cold glass, his breath misting the surface?*

The ghost of a familiar warning ache started up in her chest and despite herself she clenched her muscles in sudden fear, dropping her head between her knees.

Tilly Saint was wrong, she thought bitterly, as the thin, humid air entered and left her body in slow lungfuls. It was not simply her eyes that made her different. She didn't belong in the story at all. They should leave her to her mountains. How dare they push their own stupid ideas and dreams onto her. How dare they talk of serpents and saviours.

But still, perversely, she resented Clarissa for keeping the card hidden from her. She knew it made no sense. It was foolishness and fear.

'Pourquoi si triste, mon chou?' *Why so sad, my cabbage?*

Maman was standing in the doorway, her shawl pulled around her against the rain. How long she'd been there Adeline didn't know. She padded over on her large bare feet and embraced her daughter, pulling the girl's face clumsily against her rough dress, stroking her hair as she had when she was a child.

'There now. There is nothing to fear, my tiny cabbage. It is only your age. At such an age the world seems cruel and without understanding. You need to laugh more, to spend time with your friends. It is bad to mope alone. Go and see Eloise or Paulette. Help them with the meal.' The woman smiled slyly. 'Or Sebastien. A fine boy. No doubt he is in the cabin of the men, waiting for a visit.'

She led Adeline to the door of the lookout, still

chuntering her blunt wisdom, took some weatherproofs down from their peg and fastened them around the girl. 'There now. I will finish your duty here. I will watch for this night. Go. Enjoy yourself a little. All will be well.'

The door was opened and Maman's hand sent her out into the evening and the unending downpour. Then the rectangle of soft light behind was shut away, and she stood alone in the night, the comcard still nestling in her palm.

Ahead of her, shimmering faintly, lay the pale golden lights of the other buildings. Warmth, rest, company. Yet the prickle of water on her skin made her want more. Her sleepy senses swam back out of her core and fastened sharply on the external world, fizzing with its own challenges. She would not go to the women's quarters yet.

She wandered across the rock, undecided. Her steps took her to the stone stair and she started to pick her way down in darkness, not bothering to return to the lookout for a handlight as she should.

As she approached the valley floor, a fragment of music wound its way to her through the night, bright as one of the tiny spring snakes. The Arkies, dancing their month-long welcome to the rains.

Yes, she would be light tonight. She'd forget prophecies and responsibilities. If possible, she would get drunk.

*If anybody is out there, please scream.*

She laughed softly to herself. Dom would approve.

# DOMINIC
## – day 25 –

I'm stuffed.

Seriously stuffed.

I have to leave. I *have* to: this military crap isn't anything to do with me. I can't live like that. But now, shit, I don't know if I'll be able to go. Will they let me? I just don't know. So stupid to have waited, when I could have waltzed out of this dump any time.

I always leave it too late to act. Just like with Ruth.

Need to keep my head down. Need to *keep* my head. Stay cool, stay invisible. Get out soon, at night, with the minimum of kit. Need to keep changing my hiding places until then.

Anybody else who wants to get out will just have to do the same, won't they? I can't *make* anybody come and I'll do better alone. I don't know, maybe this kind of thing is normal now, maybe they're doing it everywhere.

Martial law? God help us.

For the record – if there's anybody out there still in possession of their marbles who can do something about this – four days ago this ex-school turned into an army camp, a prison, I don't know what. Six trucks, all standard army like the other one, but packed with soldiers and equipment. They've put men at the gates, men patrolling the buildings and the Park. They've got dogs. And they're armed. Not like that prat Barry. I'm talking machine guns, automatic rifles, all the standard army shit. Brave, armed men in a school, threatening a bunch of teenagers.

All the main house doors have been opened. By which

I mean *removed*. I guess so nobody can lock themselves away. They did that at once, as soon as they'd jumped off the trucks, screaming orders at each other and lining up. They came stomping round everywhere, looking in every cupboard and under every bed, taking our names, sending us down to the tennis courts. We stood there for over an hour, nobody allowed to get a jacket or a drink or go to the bogs, while they checked the whole place.

More people were sent to the courts in dribs and drabs while we stood there. I saw that Nigel arriving, white as a sheet. I expect I was the same. Everybody looked terrified – even zero cockiness from Hodges et al for once. The army, mind: they can't ask nicely. They have to bully.

Something weird. Standing there in the cold, I suddenly got a whiff of autumn. You know, the change of smell in the plants, the air, the soil. Unless I've gone mad with cabin fever it must still be July, but I got the autumn smell, and it made me remember being here as a kid. The valley turning colour. The cobwebs freezing. The plumes of breath from the girls' mouths.

I just can't bear it.

Finally they brought Ruth and her dad. Must have dug them out from the lodge. Two soldiers hustling them along, with Beckett senior coughing his guts up, not seeming to take much in, and Ruth keeping them away from him, putting herself in the way.

'Keep your hands to yourself! Leave him alone. He's ill; he needs his rest. Who do you think you are? I want your names.'

One of the soldiers grabbed her shoulder to push her into the courts. 'Come on miss, don't be difficult.'

Mistake. She went into her overdrive thing. Launched herself at him and ended up sitting on his chest, shouting at him. 'Difficult? You think this is difficult? *I'll* show you difficult.'

It would have been funny but for the fact that instantly

there were soldiers all around her, five or six, manhandling her into the courts, holding ankles and wrists, waving their guns under her nose, shouting, and old man Beckett bleating along afterwards, unlistened-to. She fought like a crazy thing, wriggling and kicking out. Her fleece got torn so you could see her old vest. Then one soldier hit her – whacked her across the face – and everything stopped, froze like one of the old classic war stills from Vietnam or Cambodia or Iraq. 'Military brutality'. She had blood on her mouth, running onto her chin.

We were all silent on the courts, watching like pillocks. In awe, shocked, useless. Nobody went to help. Somebody murmured, 'The Wild Woman's flipped.' I finally left my place and started to head over there, but a voice came cracking across the courts. *'Pri-vate!'* Then there's this officer coming in through the gate, marching like they do even when there's only one of them. Moustache, pistol, gleaming shoes etc. Tight ship in motion. 'Private! Release the young lady and report to my office!'

The soldiers stood back from Ruth and the one who'd slapped her saluted and said *'Sir!'* and marched off.

'At the *double*, private!'

So he ran.

The officer said to Ruth, 'Please accept my apologies. That should not have happened.' She wiped the blood away, opened her mouth to give him the treatment, but he lifted a hand and said, 'Please. If you would just join the others, all will soon be clear. Then you can get your father out of the cold and tend to your own injury.'

We were all shivering and shell-shocked, but I guess I wasn't the only one to hope that it would all be sorted out now and that the officer would put it right. Whatever 'it' was.

I tried to catch Ruth's eye, but she wasn't there. She was in her own world already, standing next to her old man, oblivious, while the officer spoke. I wonder what she thinks about when she does that. It makes her face very peaceful. I'd like to follow.

One of the soldiers brought a box for the officer to stand on.

'Ladies and gentlemen. Information.' He looked us up and down. I saw him look specifically at Ruth and he seemed fazed to see her in her dreamworld. 'Who am I? You may call me Major. I am to be in command here for the duration of your stay. The next three or four days will mostly be your own, while my men set up and we do a little taking stock of resources and personnel. I suggest you make the most of it, relax as far as you are able.

'Nevertheless, there *will* be basic rules to follow from this time onwards. These will be posted on notice boards around the compound. I would ask you also to show maximum cooperation to my men. Remember that in order to provide adequate food and other necessities, the team that I have brought here need to operate unhindered. It is a question of survival. Simple survival. In plain English, if you are told – or *asked* – to do something, please do that thing with a minimum of delay. This might include a change of current quarters as we assess available billets. Now ... Sergeant?'

One of the soldiers marched out to the Major and saluted. 'Sir!'

'Sergeant, call out the names of those people before us and I will check them against my own list. Ladies and gentlemen, when you hear your name, you will call out, 'Yes, Sergeant' and raise your hand so that we may identify you. You will then be asked to form a new group, over there to my left, your right.'

I realised then what would happen. They'd have all the names of the kids from the buses, but not mine. I was about to be identified as the general public, uninvited.

What could I do?

What would *they* do?

The sergeant called out the names and people answered. Each one was brought out to the front where the Major could look them over, then shunted to the other side of the courts. When it was Loney's name he said, 'Present and correct, sir.' The Major came bowling down off his box.

'When you hear your name, you will answer "Yes, Sergeant" and raise your hand. *Clear?*' Loney nodded. 'So let's try that again. Sergeant, if you please . . .'

Everybody else said what they were meant to and went peeling off to the other side. I knew I was going to be left standing by myself. I like solitude. I don't like being gawped at or locked up by army maniacs.

And then the sergeant read my name out.

The rest was just a dream. I held it together, I didn't let on, but I know now that this is what Father intended. His biggest madness to date.

Here, I've ripped down one of the rule sheets and I'll stick it here, on this page. That will give some idea of what's happening here.

---

## CAMP E – BASIC RULES

1.  **All military personnel are to be obeyed instantly, at all times**
2.  **No attempt is to be made to leave the camp or to contact those outside the camp**
3.  **Any attempt to leave or for civilians to enter or make contact with Camp E recruits shall be reported instantly**
4.  **Each recruit is responsible for maintaining personal cleanliness as well as that of equipment and living quarters**
5.  **Smoking is only permitted a minimum of ten metres from any building**
6.  **No sexual relations are permitted between recruits**

7.   No visiting of billets of the opposite sex is
     permitted
8.   No alcohol or drugs are permitted in the camp
9.   No recruit may leave his or her allotted building
     during the hours of darkness: these will be posted
     each week
10.  Recruits are to attend all meals unless given
     special permission not to do so

**<u>Infringement of any rule will lead to immediate and
severe penalties</u>**

God knows what else they've got in store for us. Father,
what the hell are you playing at?

# – day 28/29 –

The snow has come again. Not as thick as it was in the winter. I don't see that we can be in for more like that, not in July. But then maybe we are. They did warn us, didn't they? It just takes some believing that the weather can go totally down the tubes in only three years.

The Major – none of these bastards have names – has reorganised where everyone sleeps. Girls in Honeysuckle, boys in Orchard. Not that they've let me stay in my own room. Oh no, that's too simple for the army mind. We've got to be two to a room. I'm in one of the fourth year dorms, with Barbieri of all people (first name Frank, apparently). Our 'billet' number is O-17. Isn't that exciting? We're supposed to take joint responsibility for the room and, I think, to spy on each other too.

More notices have been pasted up, inside and out:

> **Please be vigilant at all times and inform military personnel if you know or believe that a rule is being broken. <u>This is for general camp security – *your* security</u>**

Barbieri's a little better away from his mates, but I still don't trust him. Seems very vain and prissy about his smooth skin and fair hair and everything. He's got face-cream and aftershave. Think he'd iron his shirts if we had electricity.

Writing this in my old room btw, by candlelight. Nobody has got put on the top floor. Still got my alarm system if needed. When I go, this will be the way I go, via the roof again to collect my gear and suss out where the sentries are. There are fences now and portable lights on stands. They seem to have brought a lot of fuel for generators, not that they're using any of it to keep us warm or light the rooms or anything useful. But they can't fence the whole school perimeter, can they? And there are only about fifty soldiers, so say twenty or twenty-five at night if they sleep in shifts. Should be able to get past twenty, spread round the whole of Bede's.

The biggest problem will be nerves. I'm shitting myself. It's one thing to talk about it and plan it, but would they be prepared to shoot me? Nothing certain any more – people may do anything.

Maybe this is just Father's idea of a test of character.

What else is new? Well, meals are now at set times. We have to have a room inspection at six-thirty in the morning, then breakfast. Lunch at midday, supper at seven pm, final room check at nine. Barry and co have to jump to it as well, not that the food's improved. Our names are checked off each time we eat, each time they come to the rooms etc. Even the Becketts get the treatment, though they've let them stay in the lodge I think.

Oh yes: they were on the Major's list too. 'Cyril and Ruth Beckett, camp staff.'

Don't know where the soldiers eat. Think they're living in Tremayne. The Major's in the Head's house. Now called Camp Commandant's Quarters or some crap like that.

My usual question. The only question these days; anybody reading this must be used to it.

*What's happening?*

What's happening out there? Is the army in control everywhere? What's happening here at Bede's? Why are these jokers here? What's Father doing; *why* am I on the list?

Why is this bollocks all happening in *my* lifetime?

I sing to myself a lot, but the songs are as painful as the autumn smell. I need new music.

We had another 'parade' (the Major's word) on the tennis courts today.

Now we have to line up in proper ranks. More calling names out. 'Yes, Sergeant. Here, Sergeant.'

Near enough, this is what the Major said:

'Camp Recruits! A lot has been achieved in these first few days. You are to be congratulated. You have adapted quickly. Well done. However, I would warn you not to relax your standards, nor to attempt any action that would jeopardise our continuing smooth operations. Tomorrow at 0500 hours a one-month period of initial training will begin. At that time you will all assemble in sports clothes or whatever you have on the main lawn outside my own quarters. You will be allocated a section and from then on *you* – each recruit – will be responsible for the discipline, obedience and good show-ing of your section. Any disobedience by a single section member will result in punishment for the entire section. But that is *not* to say that you must carry failing members of your section with you through the programme. Quite the reverse. If, for example, your section is on a training run and a boy or girl falls, you will *not* help them: you will leave them where they fall. Rations will be withdrawn from those flouting this basic rule. *Your section is a competing group; not a group of fellows or comrades.* Remember this at all times.'

Assault courses, training, competing sections.

I managed to get to Ruth when we were dismissed. Everyone was buzzing with what the Major had said, mouths flapping. Shock is a permanent feature in the new world order. Ruth turned her head as I approached and I saw she had some bad bruising below her right eye. From that slap I suppose.

Didn't know what to say. Said, 'Are you in on all that too? Sections and everything?'

She shook her head. 'No. We're "camp staff". Cleaners to you.'

I came as close as I could. 'Come away with me when I go.'

She looked at me properly for the first time since I gave her the model of the Globe. I could have fallen into that look. She almost smiled. She said, 'How can I?'

Then realised that my 'billet' companion was watching and shut up. He'd better not end up being another Kingsley.

# ADELINE

Leaving the barn, Adeline had a moment of dizziness. She was flushed and sweating from the crush inside, from the frantic reels. She sat heavily on the wet boards, grinning, and took off her shoes. With the earth churned into syrupy red mud along the pathways, she'd do better with bare feet. She liked bare feet. She liked the touch of the earth on her skin.

Behind her, the Arkies cheered and beat their drums. The porch shook with the pounding. There were peals of laughter, the wild melody of a bouzouki. It was a little island in the storm. A world apart from the ordered quiet that she must return to on the plateau. These people were travellers at heart, refugees. The continent was awash with them. If they didn't manage to make their home here, they would take their music and their stoicism and their rough, soil-blackened hands else-where. They knew they were fortunate in coming to Seven, but how many of them truly believed in the Charter was uncertain, probably better not tested.

Adeline sighed, hauled herself up on one of the porch uprights and stepped out into the night. She meandered reluctantly towards the stone stair, half tempted at each step to turn back. At the lowest point of the valley, the monsoon river roared. Watching half-heartedly from a plank lean-to were two of the night's patrol, playing dice by candlelight. The others in the patrol were prob-ably in the ranks of dancers. They'd take it in turns; everyone knew that floods and water were the only real peril until the rain should cease. Why bother dragging yourself through the dark and the wet to check an empty boundary when you could strip off your shirt and pound the boards with the rest, cocooned by the sweat and the mosquitoes and the yeasty fumes of wheatbeer.

She half admired, half scorned their recklessness. Others worked to keep these men safe; to give them the tools and the land they needed to raise their food and their children. And yet she, too, was tired of being careful. Her head swam. Maman had been right to push her out of the lookout. Whatever she was looking for, it wasn't up there.

Adeline could make no sense of her thoughts. The joy and the despair were so entwined. She wanted so much, had such painful *longing* inside her. It sang through her night and day. All she knew how to do well was to be alone, to let the mountain smell intoxicate her, to feel the soothing rain run over her scalp and the mud ooze comfortably between her toes. And to fight, of course, and to run like the wind.

'Careful' meant dying with the terrible longing for an unknown thing unfulfilled. Didn't it? Her cloned body was flawed. The component atoms would soon break apart and become solids, gases and liquids, that were not her. The Ref was right: a safety net only made you weaker. *That* was why she smiled to see the lazy patrol men.

She walked on. The river roar faded a little. Then, in time, it returned, with a different, harsher note. Her ears were filled with the noise and she realised that in her drunkenness and dreams she had come past the stone stair, past the cabins and terraces and the few lights. Where she stood there was only blackness. From the roaring, she must be at nearly the highest point of the central valley, at the place where the waters spilled from a rift high on South Peak, bouncing down over the rocky slopes, doubling the flow that came more gently along the ancient, natural riverbed.

In a few weeks the cascade would be gone, the bed of the river would be dry once more, the Arkie children would fall on the gifts left there: boughs of bleached wood for tools or fires, flat pebbles for games and, if they were lucky, fragments of rock crystal their mothers and sisters would wear. Silence would again take the mountains: the silence of heat and the careful, precise creatures that had to survive in it. In the mud she thought she could feel with her feet the hard little nubs of the shoots that would burst out at that time for a short, desperate life, throwing their seeds into the last streams, depositing them in the dust to be buried by next year's rains.

She ran her hands across her flat belly and wondered what it would be like to feel a child growing there. She squatted down in the dark and traced her fingers through the mud. Her clothes were sticking to her; she must have left the weatherproofs in the barn. Why not take the clothes off and let the rainwater wash her clean? To *feel*. To *live*, in this moment.

She dropped her shoes and her hands started to unfasten the buttons of her tunic. She turned her face to the dark sky, letting the drops smack against her face.

It was only when she was half uncovered, swaying as she fumbled in the dark with her breeches, that she sensed with a start that she was not alone.

'Adeline?'

Though she could see nothing, the voice in the rain and the dark was familiar. Sebastien.

She fought down a giggle and said, 'What are you doing here? Did you follow me?'

'Yes. You weren't on the plateau. In time I became worried ... The Arkies said you'd passed. I'd given up, but I heard you singing, in the dark.'

'Was I singing?'

There didn't seem much else to say. She should be angry with him, but didn't care enough. Why wouldn't the knot to her breeches come undone, she wondered. The rain must have tightened it.

'Addie . . .'

'What?' she asked impatiently. 'I'm fine, really. What do you want, Sebastien? Go home and sleep.'

Still he stood there, unseen.

'You make it seem . . . so difficult.'

His voice was only a whisper. She sensed him coming closer. Then his reaching hand collided with her cheek, started tentatively stroking as if she was a small animal to be comforted. She felt him shiver.

Now she became angry. Half-drunk and furious.

'Why can't you do it properly? Why? If that is what you want, show me.'

Recklessly she grabbed his arm and pulled him close against her. A cold part of her marvelled at such foolishness. 'Here,' she took the pawing hand off her face and placed it on her breast, 'Is that what you want? Here, hold it, feel it. Kiss me. Make me feel something.' he wrapped her hand around the back of his neck and brought his head down to meet hers. Their mouths crunched together. His was hot, clumsy. His body trembled against her own. Even as she felt unexpected arousal flood through her, he broke away and stood back again.

'No . . . Adeline. Not like that. Please. I don't want . . .'

Then he was gone. The shadow retreated. She heard him sloshing and slipping his way back through the mud, colliding with a building, disappearing into the rain and the night.

She felt dazed. She'd wanted him, actually wanted him and he'd run. From somewhere in her rain-wet belly, a short stifled scream rose up and out into the storm.

A shutter was flung back somewhere below. A hoarse shout came from the night. 'Qu'est-ce qu'il y a? Qu'est-ce qu'il y a?'

How long she spent there, she didn't know. Perhaps no more than a minute. When she moved, she didn't think or feel anything, except the wish to sleep. She wearily pulled the wet clothes back on and turned back towards the settlement. Objects loomed up as she walked. She was back amongst the first buildings, still quite high up. New structures, quickly tacked together from green, sap-rich wood and sheets of resin, perched on giddy terraces of land, crisscrossed with vigorous little streams, coming off the mountains and joining the torrent below. The rattle of the streams and the rain on resin and wood guided her steps in the dark.

In a little while she would be in her bed. Oblivious.

How many hours would be left to her, she wondered. How long until the new day must be broached? She scanned the ridges but saw no sign yet of the light that would creep over there. Just the night and the deeper black of the mountains.

And then, surprisingly, there was noise from above. A crack and a rumble from high up the mountain to her right. She stopped, puzzled, and strained to see something there, without success. It was true that electric storms sometimes drifted in off the warm, southern sea. She waited to see if another clap would follow. She'd seen no lightning, but now as she looked, she could almost imagine a spot or two of light far above. She rubbed her eyes, looked again, and the spots had gone, but sure enough a second rumble sounded. The wheat-beer had addled her wits. It was a storm, far away, with the light and sound reflected on the peaks above her.

But now, building slowly, there was a different noise, and suddenly she felt sheer terror. She knew this noise.

It rolled down off the mountain and swelled towards her in terrible inevitability.

With the sudden need came thought, judgement, understanding. She found her voice and screamed as loud as she could, 'La boue! La boue! Réveillez-vous! Wake up! La boue! The mud!' She cursed the lack of light, groped round the edge of the nearest dwelling, found something, the twisted, broken haft of a hoe or shovel. She swung it against the wooden walls so that they shuddered. 'Réveillez-vous!' And then the next house, and the next. Bang! Bang! Wake up! Danger! But the noise from above was close now, so close, and as she ran, calling, wielding her length of timber, reaching out with her senses to find the hidden, familiar path, the sea of mud and stones came down like a great slow wave behind her, to swallow up life and land.

She was flying, flying from the slide. She foundered in a new-dug channel, the water entering her mouth and nose, then pulled herself out again and ran on. There were voices all around her; screams. They'd woken, they'd understood, they were waking others, bearing out the old and the very young. Would it be enough? Not for everyone. The shouts spread ahead of her down into the midst of Seven. There were lights now, burning torches, a few dancing handlights. By their uncertain glow she stumbled into one of the signal boxes. She cast her stick aside and ripped the little cover off, praying that the flare would be there and dry enough to use. It was. Closing her eyes against the magnesium brightness she held the thing high above her head and pulled the cord. It fizzed sharply into the wet night and broke apart in a shower of stars and a fearsome crack.

There. All would be alerted now. She could afford to rest a moment.

As she leaned there, the first surge of Arkies came along the paths, bearing shovels and picks, making their way towards the carnage. Many were stumbling from the drink, eyes bleary in the light of the torches.

One was going against the tide. A large pale-faced boy, vaguely familiar, expressionless, elbowing his way through the rush of farmers. 'Come and help, come and dig,' she cried to him, and at her voice he turned, looked full at her. He stood there motionless in the press of bodies, then took a step towards her, frowned, stopped. Then he'd gone, swallowed by the crowd and the rain.

But already her attention was on the work that must be done and, staving off the weariness of this long day, she went looking for her own tool with which to dig in the mud.

# DOMINIC
## – *day 33* –

I've just seen a beautiful thing.

I'm too tired to write this, too tired to think, too tired to be up here now. The world has gone down the tubes and we are prisoners here, jumping to the Major's tune, but I'm so excited.

Like a fever. Like the TB patients in the Magic Mountain, or Keats writing his love letters to Fanny. Maybe I have TB?

This is what I saw. The snow is thick outside. The sky is clear. I looked out from the old dorm window, trying to imagine nothing changed from the old Bede's. Kingsley snoring in the corner. Marsh and Webb flitting across the lawns, heads down, for a spliff.

All bollocks of course. The world's been changing every day and we pretended it wasn't.

Anyway, the lawns are snowy, not green, and the Major's assault course is spread out there in a bed of churned-up, frozen slush, waiting for our sweat and blood tomorrow. But I saw someone there. Ignoring the curfew. Doing the course. And it was so beautiful, so graceful, so perfect. Like a ballet in the moonlight.

It was Ruth.

I can't explain why I'm so excited, with existence gone so wrong.

Everything has changed, but maybe there's a way.

# ADELINE

Half of the greater Seven was there, working side by side by the light of a hundred flickering torches. More than a thousand people, labouring in silence. In went the shovels and the rotten half-planks, again and again. In went the hoes and the kitchen spoons. Away went the loads of liquid mud, dragged on pieces of plastic, taken in buckets and barrows, even wrapped in the men's shirts. Some of the women sobbed quietly as they worked. The children, turned out of their beds, were huge-eyed and in thrilled, shivering awe.

Somewhere beneath the mudslide, fourteen farmhouses lay buried.

McCoy murmured 'Christ, oh dear Christ' as he pitched into the molten ground, the sinews of his neck taut with the effort. Next to him, Eloise attacked the mire with a pan snatched from the cooking shed, her blonde hair hanging in limp, mud-streaked clumps; then Françoise, Emile, Elisabeth, Christophe ... By some unspoken agreement, the plateau-dwellers had chosen to dig side by side. The six remaining charged worklights were spiked into a semicircle around them, making the mud glisten white and ghostly. Only Maman and little Manuela were left above, in the lookout. Nobody had seen Sebastien, save Adeline, and she did not tell the others of the meeting in the night.

The first bodies were prised out, eight people who had crowded together to die, or had perhaps been about to leave their shack and run to safety. Clarissa made a small, choking sound. 'It's them, Mac. The ones we helped tonight.'

He grunted, flint-faced. 'Not the boy, though. Maybe he made it.'

It was little consolation. And besides, how *could* anyone have made it away from this great crushing weight of wet earth and boulders?

They dug on. There were more to be found. It was only half an hour later that Adeline paused with her shovel full of wet mud and asked, 'What boy?'

'Huh?'

'What boy made it?'

'Oh, yeah.' Mac shrugged as he worked. 'I don't know. Just some boy. Big kid, your age maybe.'

She cast the load of mud aside, thrust the shovel in again. Now that the drink had been sweated out, her head ached and her stomach burned with bile. It was hard to think clearly.

She cast her mind back to earlier in the night, to when she'd first seen and heard the slide. She thought of that electric storm. The noise of the flare. And then, giddily, she thought of an afternoon, weeks ago, the last time she'd had an attack. The day Frau Kästener had arrived, bruised and tattered. There had been a boy then, too. Huge-shouldered, pale-faced, sharpening a black knife.

They were only fragments chasing round her mind, but she felt suddenly sick. She felt as she had when she had first taken the hidden comcard from the roof beams and sensed, as Dominic's drunken words sprang onto the screen, how her life was about to change for ever. Her shovel fell from her fingers. She gave a cry, clambered away from the workings, pushed past other diggers.

'Adeline?' Clarissa called out to her, '*Addie?*' But the girl was already running away from the light, heading down into the black valley.

'Leave her,' said Mac, tiredly. 'It's just all this. The bodies. She'll be all right.'

But Clarissa stood there, looking after her sister. And feeling the wrongness that Adeline felt, like a shadow in her own mind, impossible to name or take hold of. And she, too, felt the shock of the change to come, and wondered how she might have prevented it.

*Why had the boy been going back down, away from the landslide?*

It would take twenty minutes to get to the stone stair. Then at least twenty more to climb up. Over half an hour until she could even be back on the plateau. And then? She couldn't say. Perhaps nothing.

How she hoped it would be nothing.

She ran and fell and climbed to her feet and ran again. The few lights were all gone from Seven, all taken to the dig. The sounds behind her grew dimmer. A baby cried out somewhere and was still. Her breath came in deafening gasps. Nobody was up and out, unless they were digging. But as she came at last to the sprawl of great stones and smaller shards and flakes that had peeled from the rockface over the millennia, a figure rose up in the dark to meet her.

He said, in English, 'I thought you'd come. Makes *my* job easier.'

She was bent over with her haste. 'Who are you?' she asked, between breaths. 'What are you doing at Seven?' Then the boy hit her, a vicious blow to her jaw, catching her unawares as if she were a defenceless infant. Her legs sagged away from her and the ground rose up.

'I'm the death of you, Spare. New orders, see?'

She gathered herself and looked up from the mud and stones through blurred vision, her head reeling. The boy was staring down at her, as if waiting to see what she would do. She could imagine that a smile played across his lips.

He spat. 'And they said you were dangerous.'

She steadied herself and started to rise. Instantly, he stepped in close again and raised his fists, knocked her back down with a punch like a hammer on her skull.

Her thoughts swam in the unreality of it. 'Why are you doing this?' she whispered, as much to take his attention as for an answer. 'Who *are* you? Who sent you here? *Whose* orders?'

His foot came flying towards her temple, but she saw it or sensed it and threw herself back, scrabbling out of range. Her body wouldn't work. She needed rest. Still he came at her, picking his moments lazily. She was learning the style now, even in her exhaustion. He was fast, fluid. His clear intention was to finish her, and to enjoy the act.

'Did *you* kill Frau Kästener?' She could imagine him doing it, tracing a line with that black knife.

*Yes. Feel his movements, feel their source. Feel for the weakness.*

He stepped in again. 'You won't distract me, Spare.' He kicked out contemptuously and she launched herself not away but up against the blow, taking the power from it before the leg was extended, surprising him. She gasped with the force in her belly, but carried forward, used the leg to pull herself to her feet. Then she let go, stepped back and was at least facing him. Now she had the ghost of a chance.

'You're history, Scroat. You know that, don't you?'

Her limbs were trembling, unreliable. This day seemed to have lasted for ever. She fell uncomfortably into fighting stance, wiped the hair and rain from her eyes, and waited for the boy to come. But even as the shadow of him moved forward, fast as a swooping hawk, she sensed another figure there, heard a shout and saw her attacker turn to deal out fast, telling blows.

It gave her the moment she needed. As the boy turned once more, her foot flew across him from his right, catching his chin. He gasped, paused, and by the time he had shaken off the blow, she had landed three more without mercy and he lay half conscious on the stony ground, trying in his turn to rise to his feet.

She stood over him and his hand groped for a device at his hip, pressed a button there.

'Too late,' the boy said, even as her foot struck again, silencing him.

The other figure lying there was Sebastien.

Dawn must be close: she could see his face, turned cheek-down to the wet stones where he'd fallen. She checked for a pulse. Yes, he would live. She lay her palm on his face for a second, then turned toward the stone stair and entered the cleft, hauling herself up through the gap to the first footholds.

The thoughts swirled and collided like the driftwood in the monsoon river. Should she have bound the boy? Should she have waited for other help? Who else was with the assassin? For sure he was not alone.

Twice her exhausted limbs failed her on the slick rock, and she went crashing down the way she had come. Both times she caught herself within a few metres, spreading her limbs like a spider against the flinty walls. She ignored the blood coming from forearm and knee, could hardly feel the hurt.

At the top of the climb, she gripped the wooden rail set there and flung herself up with a cry, not knowing what she would see. But there was only the rain and the open expanse of rock, ghostly in the first wan glow of a new day. She went to the lookout, burst open the door, and saw Maman, unmoving, peaceful, helpless.

Crying, cursing, she fell out into the rain once more,

sprinted across the open ground towards the main buildings. She went first to the women's quarters, flung
wide the door and stepped inside, but it was empty, still
in disarray from the occupants leaving so suddenly in
answer to her flare. She took a half-charged handlight
from its hook by the door and went on to the men's
dormitory, then the cooking hut. In each place she called
out softly, 'Manuela? Manuela, come out!'

Now she was into the worksheds. First the radio shack,
tiny but vital to Seven, sprouting its maze of antennae.
Next the repair shop, Emile's domain, where he kept
their hotchpotch of equipment functioning and reliable,
despite the dearth of parts or materials. Here, at last, she
found the child, crouched hugging her knees under the
solder-scarred workbench.

'Where are they?' Adeline asked, lifting her out. 'How
many?' But the girl only shook her head mutely, and
hid her smeared face at Adeline's breast. 'Quick then,
little one. Run to the pumping house. The *pumping
house*, you understand? Pull the iron door shut and slide
the bolt.'

Once more she blundered out into the wet, set the
child down and pushed her towards the safety of
the rock. 'Quick now! As fast as you can!' She watched
Manuela run off, then splashed her way heavily to
the much larger power generation building, where all
the precious solar dishes, batteries and lengths of cable
were stored; even more vital than the radios. And still
she found nothing.

*Think.*

Nothing had been taken, no damage done, and yet
they had emptied the plateau with their mudslide. For
what purpose?

'Makes *my* job easier,' the boy had said. What was that
job? To kill her? If so, why draw the Seveners away?
The boy could not have done that alone. He had to have

accomplices and another purpose. *Who* had he warned when he pressed his button? What did they wish here?

Suddenly, she looked round at the shack where she stood with icy dread. *Oh, dear spirits.* She burst out again. She was running, away from the buildings, away from her home. She could see figures in the dawn light, wearing packs, disappearing over the lip of the stone stair. Were there five of them, or only four?

The blast, when it came, splintered the smaller Seven as if with a giant fist. The hot wave plucked her up and spat her back down onto the rock as if she were made of straw. The air filled with singing, burning fragments of wood, machinery, pottery.

Then there was quiet. Only an empty plateau and the figure of a girl stretched out in the morning light.

# ADELINE

*Everything has changed, but maybe there's a way.*

The moonlight shone bright in her eyes, reflected by the snow.

No, that was wrong. The light was warm. Her lids glowed pink with it. The snow couldn't be there now.

Adeline lay unconscious for only a bare minute or two, but when she opened her eyes she almost laughed. The rain had thinned. A few rays of pale sunlight were struggling over South Peak. The monsoon was breaking.

She knew with strange clarity what she must do. In a little while the plateau would be swarming with people. She thought she could hear faintly their hubbub. But she would not stay to answer their questions, to be put somewhere safe and quiet, fussed over, protected.

She rose and went dizzily to the stone stair for the last time, sent her love silently to the hidden child and the dead woman she had called mother. She descended carefully, came out at the bottom to find, without surprise, that the boy was gone. Sebastien was still there, stirring now himself, squinting up at her in confusion through swollen eyes. She held him a moment.

'Tell my sister that the hunted is turning hunter. Tell her . . . tell her that the serpent is raising its head.'

He started to speak but she didn't hear. She was already away, away from the people running from higher up the valley. She jogged down through the empty farm strips and shacks and wondered to see that even now one or two figures were out, dismantling rain defences, checking the precious soil, hefting sacks of seed.

In truth, life went on. What did these brave people care or know what had passed on the plateau? What time could they spend mourning those lost to the mud? The rains were ending, the soil had to be drained and worked, the seeds had to be got into the ground. It was a race. Around them, clinging to the valley sides, an abundance of fresh white and green would have sprouted by the end of tomorrow. Nature was equally eager to renew itself before the sun had the mountains in its tight, choking grip.

'Missy!' the farmers called to her, not seeming to notice her ragged appearance, 'Hello, missy.'

'What a day! The beautiful sun, eh, missy? She has come back to us.'

'Come by tomorrow and there will be new bread.'

'No more dancing now, missy. The dancing is for the rains.'

Gradually their cries fell behind her as she worked her way down the valley, and then into the next, and down again, and again.

She saw them before long. A little knot of figures, well ahead of her. And, as if this was finally too much for her sick heart, she felt the universe recede in the same moment. The pain came, the uselessness, the jarring fall, the unknowing.

Once more she crossed the divide.

*Everything has changed.*

*She laughed as her body played. She made it into a dance. The life force was in every part of her: feet, hands, throat, belly. The touch of frosted wood, the scent of the cedars, the mist of her breath: everything was perfect and thrilling.*

*Round the course she went. And again, like a cat sharpening its claws.*

\*

Then it was another night and her quarry far ahead.

It didn't matter. She knew where they were heading and could follow. It was time to stop fighting what must be. It was time to go home.

*Yes. Now.*

She was kinder to herself and went peacefully. The fear had melted from her, for a while. Down she went, through the mountains that were all she had known, until at last she reached the place where the valleys were filled with tongues of blue water and the air was thick and heavy, making her dizzy.

And the new sun was like fire on the water.

# PART TWO

'I recommend biting off more than you
can chew to anyone'
Alanis Morissette: *Jagged Little Pill*

# CRANE

School was out. The gong sounded discreetly behind the Instructor's voice, through the whispering fabric of the learning-enhancement tape and, as one, the class rose, took off their headsets, tidied their equipment away. Then they filed silently to the door.

'Thirty minutes warm-down in the gym,' the Instructor reminded them, frowning. 'Healthy body, healthy mind.'

Crane felt Anton touch his elbow, a touch full of meaning. Yes, the man was a bore, a prick, worthy of contempt. Nobody gave him a glance as they left. Outside, across the dividing fences, in the main building, the buzzer had also sounded and the ordinary Vision children were spilling out; chattering, skipping, shoving each other. Some of them hung on the fence to watch or call out, but nobody from Crane's side paid them any attention. They walked on, a silent, unsmiling procession, through the gusts of winter rain. Crane fastened his jacket and considered in detail the body of the girl who sat across the aisle and one row forward from him. Netta. She was a step or two ahead, tall and fierce as an Amazon. He ran his eyes from her heels to her nape and Anton touched his elbow again.

'Want her?'

'I don't know. Maybe not.'

Netta, hearing them, half turned her head and said, 'That's lucky, Crane. It really is.'

Crane blew her a kiss. Anton smiled to himself. The group came to the gym but passed it by as one. At the

main gate they palm-printed their way out and deliberately muscled aside the sad little group of protesters,
though there were acres of space to go around.

'We don't blame *you*,' a man said; 'none of it's *your*
fault, of course we know that. But the world should
know. They should.'

'Shut up,' said Crane. 'They'll know all right.' He
pushed the man over and even Netta laughed.

'Scroat hunt?' Lily asked, coming up with them.

'Scroat hunt?' Anton asked Crane.

'Scroat hunt,' Crane nodded. 'Healthy body. Healthy
mind. Let's do it.' And he set off running, powerfully,
through the rain, down the maze of streets towards the
docks, with Anton and Lily and a couple of others following. It felt good to run, to see the Vision faces loom
up gaping and then be left behind, to cut in front of
the buzzing orange Caplink carriages at the last possible
second. Once, seeing a security transport, they paused to
say 'Good day' to the police officers in their smart grey.

'Boys. Young lady.' The sergeant nodded at them
approvingly. 'Off for a bit of exercise are we?'

'Yes sir.'

'Down the docks?'

'That's right, sir.'

The sergeant winked and nodded once more – 'Enjoy
yourselves then' – but one of the ordinary security men
was scowling in distaste, shaking his head in disbelief
that his superior would condone their behaviour. Crane
made a mental note of his serial number. They'd get
him removed later. A man with such dubious loyalties
shouldn't be allowed to wear the Pax uniform. Why
he hadn't already been spotted was a puzzle. As he ran
on, Crane felt warm and satisfied to be going to put the
error right. It was like storing equipment in the correct
facility, like removing pus from a wound.

Ahead of them the land fell away steeply and the

grey-green waters filled the horizon, doing their own job of cauterising, welcome in their mercilessness. In the city harbour the sprawl of shipping moved steadily back and forth, or rolled listlessly at anchor, waiting for cargo. The lowest buildings stood half in and half out of the water, crumbling and slimy with green weed. Gaunt, rusted struts of ancient dockside cranes poked through the surface. A scummy mess of plastic and effluent sucked at these shapes, protected from the cleansing sea by the great tidal barrier.

Scroatland. Hunting land.

Crane shivered at the mess and decay, but he knew that the barrier wouldn't protect this rotten level of the city for much longer. They'd worked on the new figures for sea-level rise only two days ago. Yes, it was time for Briton to clean up and choose a new, leaner destiny. *Rise up now, Briton. Be all that you can be.* In the meantime Crane and the others would help the sea do its job by getting rid of the rats and other vermin.

The pack ran on, silently, into the slum between the piles of rubble, and started searching the broken buildings, pounding open rotten doors, breaking what could be broken, kicking apart the pathetic possessions they found in Scroat sleeping holes – boxes of scraps, old clothes, bottles – working up a good sweat.

The first live one they found was a good one. Good value. A woman in her prime, probably in her late twenties. Filthy, of course – they all were, it was the mark of their inferiority – but strong enough and pretending defiance and pride. She had large breasts and sharp challenging eyes. When Crane ripped the sheet of resin out of the doorway where she was hiding, she took the time to spit and swear at them before disappearing further back into the gloom of the old house. Crane prepared to leap after her, but Lily pushed up next to him in the doorway and put her hot, muscly hand on his head to turn it, forcefully. They kissed hard, teeth clashing, and grinned at each other – 'Lightspeed!' – then went after the Scroat, Crane howling like a wolf. He always howled. It amused him to pretend to be a beast when he was so much more.

The woman was quick, quick as a rat in its hole. She went from room to room, squeezing through gaps in the old brickwork, dropping between loose planks into the half-flooded cellars, working down the row of buildings, pulling herself free of the mire and into the upper storeys again. Fast as he was himself, Crane only ever caught a glimpse of her heels as he wormed through the same holes and between the same piles of junk. But he could hear her breathing and smell her sweat hanging in the air and that was enough. He was delighted.

'Got one coming! Got one coming through!' someone yelled from further along the row. Marco, it sounded like. Yes, they'd get her now, the pack were a well-practised machine.

'Leave a piece for me,' Crane bellowed, and again he heard the Scroat cursing him as she scrabbled somewhere ahead in the dusty gloom. Then a cry and a thud and a whimper.

'Someone get her? Who got her?' he called.

'Not me.'

'I haven't got her. She hasn't been through here yet!'

And then, swinging through a crooked doorway, over a break in the floor, he saw her, a dark shape sprawled out below in the rubble, unmoving. She'd fallen trying to make the gap, hit her head or something. Lily was up with him, glowing with the chase, her pale blue eyes glinting in the shadow.

'We've got her!' she called. 'Scroat down and out.'

Crane was lowering himself through the gap, while she stood and watched. He jumped the last three metres, landing crouched and balanced amongst the pieces of broken brick and timber. Lily saw him bend over the shape of the Scroat and prepare to haul her up. And then there was a grunt and he was rolling over in the dust, while the woman scuttled away again.

'Live one. She's going again!' Lily shouted, and the other three repeated the call from other buildings, starting once more to close the net.

Crane rocked to his feet, holding his groin. He didn't know whether to laugh or tear out the Scroat woman's throat. She'd got him, neat and quick, while he was still bent over her, getting ready to haul the body up and to his fellows. A moment's anticipation of touching her: that was his mistake, one he wouldn't make again. He was pleased to be getting such a good workout, though. He'd never get this in the gym. Now he went up a gear and after her like a bullet, powerful arms and legs levering through the confined spaces, ears peeled for the sounds of flight ahead, breath coming easily into his big chest.

And then suddenly he was through an outer wall, into the grey light of the afternoon again, dropping knee-deep into the scummy harbour water. Ahead of him the Scroat splashed frantically away into deeper parts, heading out towards the shipping lanes. Then she put her head down and swam. He could hear her gasps and see the effort of her limbs. He shook his head in disgust: the hole she'd been living in was bad enough, but the harbour water was just too filthy. It would be washing into her mouth as she took in breath, and all over her body, oily and rank. *He* certainly wouldn't go after this one any more, however much he'd enjoyed the hunt.

He watched her until she was just a slow-moving shadow in the murky water, making sure she didn't try to double back to dry land. The others lined up on the shore nearby and watched with him.

'Exhausted,' Anton said.

'Yeah, she won't make it.'

'Look, there she goes now.'

Five pairs of eyes looked calmly on as the bulk of a seagoing cargo boat, fully laden and just in, converged like a steel whale with the football of the woman's bobbing head.

'Look at you,' Lily said to Crane. 'You're filthy. Dirty. At least she had a bath first.'

Crane blushed. He didn't like to be dirty, but if this was where the Scroats were, what could he do?

'You're not much better. None of you,' Crane growled. 'Come on. I want to do one more before the new FTL loop.'

He waded from the harbour and they set off again on the hunt, leaving the wind-whipped water behind them. But after another thirty minutes, all they'd found was an ancient old Scroat male in a cellar, sitting on his pallet, clutching a woman's metal hairbrush, dirty and tarnished. He must have been ninety years old by the look of him, shrivelled and rheumy. When they burst in he didn't even bother to try and run. He kissed the old brush and smiled and closed his faded eyes while they had their sport. Really he was hardly worth the effort. It left Crane feeling several points below par when he got home.

'Good day, love?' his Vision mum asked him nervously, not looking at the cobwebs and dust and grime on his kit. 'Supper's all ready, when you've cleansed yourself.'

He looked at her and registered the fear in her eyes. The same fear as in the Instructor's eyes and the housing marshal, and everyone else he knew. It had even been in that sergeant's eyes earlier, despite the man's support. He wondered, like a dog toying with a cauliflower, what it would be like not to see that fear. Then it occurred to him that the Scroat woman had not looked at him like

that. Hatred, yes, but not fear. And she was the lowest of
the low, nothing more than the product of natural childbirth by some ill-assorted, random-gened couple. He
frowned. It must have been because she had nothing
worthwhile to lose; or insufficient brain to understand
the risk.

He went to his own cleansing room and scrubbed his
skin until it stung. That was better. His body felt good
after the hunt. He sat in his robe, tapped into the Pax
network, reported the security man from earlier and saw
his citizenship points cruise up to over a thousand for
the first time. His father only had three hundred and
two, not that it mattered; his parents were guaranteed
good privileges through him.

Now came the best part, the thing at the back of his
mind all through the day. He rationed himself. Only
watched once in the day – the fresh broadcast – though
he could have watched repeats or kept the live-streaming on in his rooms twenty-four/seven if he chose. He
pulled on a clean tunic and went to take the dish of hot
food from his mother.

'The set's on,' she wittered. 'All waiting for you, love.'

He settled himself in the best chair and took a mouth-
ful of food.

'Water's rising!' said the Ref.

Crane smiled as he chewed. Let it rise. Let it come.

The credit sequence rolled as usual, Crane's clean bulk
relaxing with the music and the exciting words. Then,
with the same satisfaction he'd had reporting the Pax
man, he watched the ten new contestants trot out. Even
before they were introduced, he could tell which ones
would be history before the end of the show. He was
never wrong. He went along the line, ticking them off.
Yes, the first two were OK – they were his own – and
the second to last, ditto. There were four Visions there,
but three at least were poor stuff, the clumsy (though

well-intentioned) filtering of sperm and egg not producing the best goods in these cases. The three others were Scroats, ready to be made examples of to the nation, to people like that cretin earlier who didn't get the message yet, the message of survival. Almost, Crane disapproved of giving them, the Scroats, *any* kind of publicity – they should properly be flushed away into the sewers, cast outside the city walls, forgotten and ignored – but he had to acknowledge that this was the clever way. Give them a chance. Show everybody that survival wouldn't include this lot.

He studied the three, like a panther eyeing a pig. The first was a fierce-looking, stocky character in his thirties (too old, much too old) with a streak of iron grey down the centre of his hair; the second a boy about Crane's own age or a little older, with bright, clever eyes but nowhere near enough presence or muscle – in fact, nearly pissing himself already; and then there was a girl, the same sort of age, her head shaved bare, her face neutral. Crane paused at the girl and enhanced the image. She was pretty and in good shape, but didn't have the look of a Vision. Her clothes, her expression, something. He was seventy-five per cent sure she was wearing contacts: the deep blue of her eyes was too pure. If he found one like this in the waterside slums, he might be tempted to have some extra fun. But she wasn't tall enough or broad enough. Again, not enough muscle; and her gaze was detached, focussed some-where else. A dreamer. She wouldn't last. Her name was given as Friend, which was stupid, typical Scroat: a made-up name, not in the proper records. Probably she used drugs. They wouldn't help her, though.

'And are *you* Fit To Live?' the Ref shouted.

'*Yes!*' the players roared back, except for the bare-headed girl in her dreams.

Then up the steps into the FTL Tower, once the Saint

building, where the corrupt old Family that had brought
the country to its recent weakness had hidden, until Jan
Barbieri had hunted *them* out and brought some order,
and some focus. It was very fitting, thought Crane for
the hundredth time, that FTL should be housed there
now.

'OK. Welcome to the games. Let's not waste time,' the
Ref said, as he always did, but a little grimly tonight,
Crane would have said. 'First up, this evening, is ...
Ivan.'

Ivan was the grizzled Scroat. They gave him Combat,
predictably enough. Despite the claim of random selec-
tion, the games were obviously always chosen with some
care for these types, showing their supposed strengths
to be nothing but pitiful weakness. So, for the fierce,
pugnacious Ivan, it would be humiliation by combat.
Crane watched in mild amusement as the man was oiled
up like a wrestler, given a thick canvas belt packed with
bits of unregulated steel and wood and rubber hose and
then led to a spotlit area where a sparse forest of perhaps
fifty thick ropes hung down from the shadowed upper
levels, swaying gently.

The Ref explained things to him, man to man.
'Somewhere up those ropes, my friend, two opponents
are waiting. All you have to do is get past them, to the
top platform, using whatever means you wish, including
the objects in your belt. I can tell you that both opponents are women, both volunteers from Pax, and both
unarmed. You may, if you wish, ask for the lights to
be turned up in the upper sections, in which case the
first time you touch the floor you will be eliminated
from the game ... *or* we can leave the lights as they are,
hiding our two young ladies for the moment, unless
they choose to descend. In that scenario you would be
allowed two ten-second rests on the mats.'

It was beautiful. Crane laughed his big, boyish,

growling laugh so that his mother peered in to see if he was all right or needed dessert yet. Ivan was pale, shaking his head, protesting to the Ref: 'I won't fight girls, man. Find me some proper opponents. Anyone. Men.' Someone in the research department had done their homework well. The man was a dinosaur, weak and unfit to survive. He had his belt of weapons and his strength and yet he wouldn't use them against unarmed female opponents. Crane knew with a warm glow that he himself wouldn't hesitate to stove in the skull of anyone – man, woman or child – who came up against him, if it meant precious survival.

The Ref's eyes glinted from the mask. He placed a gentle, threatening hand on the older man's shoulder. 'Please. Don't let's waste time, Ivan. You may forfeit the game immediately or play it as we have set it. Now, what's it to be?'

Poor, weak Ivan chose to play, he chose to leave the lighting unaltered, perhaps out of some archaic code of conduct towards his female opponents, and inevitably he lasted only seconds. He was no more than twenty metres up one of the ropes, straining and grunting, his biceps knotted into half-moons, when the forest of cords gave a flutter and the first woman slid smoothly down to his level, just out of his reach. The dinosaur groped half-heartedly in his belt, chose a piece of rubber hose and waved it ineffectually at the woman, his blows only occasionally connecting. Then the second woman appeared, coming down the same rope as Ivan, *fast*. He grunted with surprise as her feet met his face and then slowly peeled off backwards, grabbing hopelessly for other ropes, before hitting the mats below with life-extinguishing force. The ten-second count was given, then the medics arrived to carry away the body.

In his wide chair, Crane watched unblinking, the light from the viewing set reflecting from his eyes.

Next it was one of his own New Visions (no problems) then one of the poorer Visions (out but not hurt too badly), then the bright-eyed rabbit boy, given Logic but fumbling the task hopelessly.

Where was the girl, Crane wondered. Where was Friend with her bare scalp and strange look? Surely she would be one of the showcase games.

Eventually her turn came, but he was a little disappointed when her task was one of those only briefly referred to. She also drew Logic, in mocking deference to her slight physique and apparent need to think deeply, even when the nation was watching her. The task was to build a kind of igloo from the inside, using blocks that had one design on the inner face that she would see and a totally different but related one on the outside. She wasn't allowed to turn the blocks after the first minute of becoming acquainted with the two designs. At the end, the object was for Friend to have chosen the right blocks in the right order to build the correct pattern on the outside of the igloo, where she couldn't see it.

'We gave our sweet little Friend a time limit of four minutes for this one,' the Ref's voice said, as the image showed the girl standing waiting in the igloo frame, apparently in a daze, head up, mouth slightly open. 'Though we wondered for a while if she'd be able to tear herself away from the land of the fairies and get back to reality in time, ha ha.'

Then, abruptly, the image changed to the girl being led out of the finished igloo, looking about her coolly. 'As it happens, the task was successfully completed,' the Ref said, without emotion, 'so Friend goes on to the next phase.'

And that was it. The little Scroat, incredibly, was through. And they didn't even say how long she'd taken.

Crane called for his dessert and wolfed it down. Tonight was a double edition, with an update on Brown. He settled back happily to watch. Here in Brown, in the floodlands, things got challenging. Here, Mother Nature was as likely to find whether you were FTL as the games themselves.

But when he went to his bed he couldn't get the shaven-headed girl out of his mind. In his dreams she spat at him before swimming smoothly away across the waters, a figure always out of reach, whilst the shrivelled old man stood watching next to him, humming and smiling and holding his brush.

# DOMINIC
## – day 45 –

I ache.

My body aches and my heart. That's about it.

I feel like a piece of steel in the forge, being beaten and reheated, beaten and reheated, changing shape, changing nature.

What will I become?

We're into the routine now. The daily schedule, all the inspections and reporting in and crap, and between that, we get tested, drilled, sent to run round the Park endlessly, shoved over the cold metal, splintered sleepers and barbed wire of the assault course. My body knows every painful bit of that course in its sleep. We wear identical blue boiler suits, like convicts. We get set problems, building bridges over pretend gorges with string and bits of plank, map-reading, mathematics, putting together equipment with no instructions – bits of engine or guns or washing machines, whatever they can find – judging distances and spaces by eye. Then more physical stuff, nonstop until we eat and drop into bed.

We don't get a moment to think. We eat mostly bulky carbohydrates, rice and pasta – the girls shovelling it down as fast as the boys. Everybody looks good, everybody's grown, everybody's getting muscle, clear eyes, attitude. Maybe it's the not thinking that is the real heat of the forge; not thinking but being pummelled into some sort of tough grunt. Sometimes I have a real taste for it too. I'm growing to like something that I would always have hated before.

When you feel so strong, shame flutters away.

Barbieri and I have a laugh after lights out, talking about the girls' tits or comparing people in our sections.

'You're OK, after all,' he said to me. So I'm in with his clique now: Loney and Hodges and that bunch. Under the soldiers, they're still top of the pile and now I'm becoming one of them. I'm in a place I never was in the old Bede's. We give a hundred and ten per cent in all the tests and workouts, we shout the loudest, we eat the most in the canteen. The Major has come round inspecting billets and said he was very pleased with 0-17. I've had two offers of sex, from the tougher, full-on girls, the kind that usually leave me alone. One was the girl who told me not to 'earwig', Siobhan. She's in my section. We were walking back to the buildings, exhausted, two days ago, to clean up for supper, and she pulled me back against a wall and ground her body against mine. I mean *ground.*

'What about missing the meal?' she said.

'What for?'

'What do you think? A shag, Romeo, not a frigging game of I-spy.'

I didn't do it, but you know, she was exciting me, doing that, pushing her warmth against me with the freezing cold on my face, and she knew it. My body no longer my own, after the forge. Christ, no wonder soldiers are able to fight bloody battles.

*Fuck.*

We're in a hothouse, an ant-farm, a laboratory. Everything looking inwards. Rarely a thought given to Britain, the world, the end of it all, Father, anything. Maybe that's the attraction. Not thinking, as I said.

BUT, then the nights ... Every night I manage to wake myself up, I don't know how, and then I drag myself up here, amongst the ghosts of my old, normal life, and I imagine those first days when I was left alone in this adventure, like looking at a virtual stranger, a happy child. I read the first pages of this diary. It's like a candy comic book, laced with the stench of fear.

And then most nights, Ruth comes.

She's changed too, the few glimpses I've got, when our routines collide. Her face is thinner, she's jumpy, less openly defiant in the way she looks at people, if she looks at all. She gets worked just as hard as any of us I'd say, scrubbing and cleaning and all that. Half the school to do. A section of one; or two, when her father makes his appearance. I guess she does his share too, most of the time.

I leave food for her before evening billet inspection, stolen from the canteen, stowed just inside the muddy tunnel that you have to worm through on the course. It's a risk but I haven't been caught yet.

The beauty of how she moves always reaches me across the frozen air, although some nights are too dark to see properly. And then the ant-farm goes away and I remember things. Like who I am. I don't know what it is ... the economy of her movement, the simplicity, the grace, the determination that gets her out there when she's so knackered? Sometimes I'm in unstoppable tears, standing inside my window. These tears cool the forge, like scissors-paper-stone.

I couldn't work out why she isn't seen. None of us is allowed outside after dark, and there're always soldiers about. She stands out against the snow and the frost pretty clearly when there's a moon. But now I know, because tonight while I watched, the Major appeared. I almost had a heart attack when I saw him crossing the lawns with his stupid military walk and peaked cap. That's it, I thought, she's in deep shit with that maniac. But she dropped down neatly from the rope-traverse in front of him and they started talking. No summoning of men to take her away to be locked up or anything, no whistles blowing and boots running. It looked like they knew each other. I saw the Major reach in his pocket and offer her something, but she shook her head, wouldn't take it. Then he tried to touch her face, but she stepped back. I could hear voices raised now, mostly hers. *He* looked around, and I would have said he looked guilty. Then he said something to her, jabbing his finger at her face, and he left.

Then, strangest of all the strange things, she stood there alone and looked straight up at me, at my window. She couldn't have seen me, in the dark behind the glass, but ... And I was shaking from seeing the Major and wanting to run down there and kick his brains out, but also I felt angry with her, and betrayed.

I stepped back into the room for a minute or two and when I looked again she'd gone.

# – day 47 –

In trouble.

This a.m., up and washed, inspected, breakfasted as usual. Fell in in our sections on the tennis courts ready for instructions for the day. But my section – Silver Section – was two down.

The seven sections all have nine or ten people usually. They're all named after colours. Silver is nine. Today it was only seven. I whispered to my section, asking if they knew where the others were, were they ill or something? I think they didn't know, but Siobhan and her friend Kelly laughed at me for asking.

Siobhan is quite spiteful now. 'And poor Dominic thought the nice gentlemen would look after us all.'

The sergeant came over – still no names, just Sergeant, Major, Corporal, Soldier – to bollock us for the noise when we were meant to be silent.

'What's going on here, Silver Section?'

'Sorry Sergeant.' Siobhan looked the model of seriousness now, eyes savagely front, diligent soldier, quite impressive. '*He* asked why there weren't so many of us today.' She gestured at me with a tiny movement of her head.

'Oh, he did, did he?'

*Your section is a competing group: not a group of fellows or comrades. Remember this at all times.*

My mouth opened by reflex to tell the sergeant about Siobhan's plan for missing supper: Rules 6 and 10 flouted. That would teach her.

The sergeant was watching me. 'Yes?' he said, 'Something to say?' I think he guessed that I was going to land her in it too, and wanted me to. Everybody to throw shit at all times.

'No, Sergeant. Nothing to say.'

He fumed. I was made to fall out. I was taken to the Head's old study. It was surreal. I had a flash of being in there on my first day, with Father. A glorious early September day with the sun shining off the Head's syrupy walnut desk and the bowling-green lawns like glass under their sprinklers outside, bordered by huge feathery cedars and sycamores. Stifling in my tiny suit, I still hadn't sussed that Father was proposing to leave me here with this man and his school.

Today can't be that far off the start of September, but I've lost track. We crunched over the snow and squelched through the slush on the path, and entered the hall.

'Sit here and wait.'

There was a man on guard outside the Head's study, lounging with a semi-automatic rifle. The ordinary soldiers don't talk to you unless you're doing something wrong or they're leading your section in a training exercise. It was gloomy and freezing, like everywhere here except the dining hall at meal times. I sat to wait and the sergeant departed. A long, *long* time later the Major let me in. He had a gas fire in there, the bastard, running off a propane cylinder. Hopefully choking on the carbon monoxide. The room was like an oven. The walnut desk was bare except for three stacks of plastic-covered files. One was open on the top of the stacks. The Major made a show of going to close it. He'd left it until my entrance to do that; Father's taught me to notice such things.

He said aggressively, 'I understand that you have been spreading dissent.'

'No, sir.'

I was doing the Siobhan act now. Eyes sharp front, chin up, not meeting his gaze, the grunt they wanted. It felt good. I felt how strong my body was getting. The heat was almost too much for me, now I was used to cold. I thought of this man poncing across the snow to talk to Ruth in the night and I determined to be ice for him.

The Major said sarcastically, 'You can cut the soldier act for a few minutes. I don't like you and I dare say you don't like me either. Nevertheless, we are stuck with each other, and while that situation continues you will obey me and my staff to the letter and you will *not* in any way undermine this project. Stuck with you I may be but, if necessary, I will have you locked in separate quarters for the duration. Is that clear?'

'*Sir!*' As it came out and I stamped my foot I realised how much it sounded like I was taking the piss. And I was.

He came close to me, flushed maroon. I thought he would hit me. 'Get out of my sight, you little shit,' he said. 'The sergeant will find you some unpleasant task for today. Tomorrow you will rejoin your section as usual. Next time you come in here, your warning will have expired.'

The unpleasant task was scrubbing filthy boiler suits behind the kitchens, with luke-warm water boiled up by Barry and chums. They all had a good laugh in their fag breaks.

So many questions to think about, though. Sudden stark questions. (*Why have I asked so few questions recently?*) Like:

1. *Why did the Major assume I didn't like him and why (more important) doesn't he like me? He doesn't know me, we've never really spoken.*
2. *Why is he 'stuck' with me?*
3. *What's the thing with Ruth?*
4. *Where are the two who have gone from Silver Section?*

In bed, in O-17, Frank Barbieri said, 'What happened to you today?'

'I was scrubbing kit.'

He chuckled. 'Lucky you. Why was that? Naughty boy were you?'

Alarm bells there. I'm in with him now but I need to wake up: he's not to be trusted, is he? I said neutrally, 'Oh, I just asked about the kids gone from our section.'

'You prize idiot. They can't keep us all, can they?'

I was silent, not going to be led down any garden paths.

'I mean, they've been weeding out the duds for a while, haven't they?'

I grunted, sleepily, from my sleeping bag. It could have meant anything. 'Night,' I whispered.

But what he'd said exploded in my brain. *Weeding out the duds.* Nigel, I thought suddenly! Where is poor homesick Nigel, that I talked to when the buses arrived? I've never seen him in any section that I can remember.

Just where is he?

Got to keep all my shit up together. Got to keep recording this stuff, however tired.

'Hey, Angel-boy,' Barbieri whispered. I could hear the grin in his voice. 'A couple of looters tried to get into the grounds a few nights back. They shot *them,* clean as a whistle.'

How do you know that, Frank? How, Frank? Are you making it up?

I snored and murmured and heard my roommate chuckle to himself.

Now he's asleep and no Ruth tonight. She hasn't come.

Has the Major frightened her off?

# – day 50 –

At least I think it's day 50.

Does it matter to be exact? Only as a symptom of the 'tight ship', I suppose. Not that this particular ship is tight any longer. Limping along on its jib alone.

I wish I could fix the strat.

Mains water has finally gone and I'm truly amazed it's lasted so long. But what does it mean for Britain? Imagine the disease, the thirst in the cities, people drinking the Thames.

These are night-time thoughts, while I wait for Ruth to delight me again with her grace. (She's still missing.) Daytime is for shouting and sweating and working and being tempered in the forge. In the day the ship is tight but in pirate hands. The water went but something came instead. A message painted on the side of the sports hall, yellow letters, half a metre high.

LIGHTEN UP. LET GO. BE BLOWN AWAY.

Is it her? It made me smile.

Dozing. Desperate tonight. Where's my magic girl to give me hope?

Water. Yeah, today no usual tests and workouts. All sections worked to run a pipe down to the beck that runs through the end of the Park. The soldiers have got a pump that we bunged on the end, in the James Marchant memorial arbour. James Marchant was a boy who died on a canoe trip, ten years ago. Now our camp water comes to the spot his distraught parents built: a tiny courtyard with a bench and tree. Every second day we will have allocated washing times there, by billet. A scrub-down under the freezing trickle.

Of course now all drinking water has to

# THE REF

'Evening meal, sir.'

The man came in without invitation through the unlockable door and looked around for somewhere to put the tray of food. He eventually settled for one of the precious musical instruments, sweeping scrawled pages of notes aside to make room. Watching, the Ref felt his uncomfortable muscles tighten with disproportionate desire to rip the man's head off.

Broken peace. Despoiled instruments.

The man stood up straight and tried a smile. He looked uncomfortable, pitying. He was one of the better ones, despite his manners. He stepped over to the thick oval of Plexiglas and looked out at the darkened city.

'Fair blowing a gale tonight, sir. Sleet too.'

The Ref wished savagely he were out in that wind and sleet, feeling it on his skin. Anonymous in the foul winter weather; perhaps taking a walk by the rolling, clanking ships. Not that it would help him. His muscles were twitching fiercely, his heart going like one of his own drum pieces, his eyes itching. All somehow to be hidden from the man loitering by the window.

Just go, he thought. Go before I lose control and squeeze the bland, useless comments from your throat.

But aloud he said, 'Yes, windy tonight.'

Finally the man turned, gave him a last fascinated, awkward glance, and left. 'Back in an hour sir, to see you're all right and take the tray.'

The Ref stumbled over to push the heavy door shut after him, leaned on it, half crying, could feel his hands shaking, his legs hardly able to bear him. He was awash with sweat, but still a minute more of control was required. A minute for icy detachment to triumph over the craving of his pain-wracked body.

He lurched over to the tray, willing his wavering, clenching hand not to spill the whole thing and leave him ferreting over the floor for his supper like a dog. He stirred up the steaming muck on the plate and scraped half of it onto the small, damp hand-towel, wrapped it up into a squashy sphere. This he took into the bathroom, to drop into the toilet facility and be sucked away. There, now it would end up in the unnatural fishes that swam in the harbour.

Poor fishes.

On the way back to the tray, he collapsed. His eyes blinded with tears of frustration he went on all fours, panted back to the music room. Just like the dog, after all. Only he mustn't be seen with so little control.

With a scream of relief from every cell in his body, he fell on the remains of the meal, shovelled it in, burning his mouth, swallowing and gulping it down, sobbing and grunting. In thirty seconds it was gone: main course, drink, dessert. Now at last he could prop himself against the wall – some music and a pencil next to him in case he was discovered – and close his eyes. Soon the pain would lessen, his limbs would cease their thrashing and twitching, his brain would start to clear, his body would gradually become his own.

For a while.

When he was sufficiently recovered, he'd wash all traces from the hand-towel. But first, he'd enjoy the peace that crept over him, soothing the tremors and fears.

Later, much later, when the city slept – save for security patrols, the pockets of smart young Visions haunting the late clubs, and the occasional furtive Scroat moving

136

through shadows that the cameras did not pierce – the Ref got up from his bed and started to train.

It wasn't as difficult as the business with the food. Nothing was. But still, leaving the merciful, empty depths of his dreams and the soft embrace of the covers was hard. Drug hard. By now the first pangs of deprivation were again clicking in.

*So soon.*

A tremor in his left leg, a line of electricity along his jaw. A tiny muddying of thought and purpose.

With a grunt, he folded the bed away into its wall cavity to make a space, and took out weights, soft shoes, half a dozen socks stuffed with dirt and grit that he would hang on cords from the metal substructure of the ceiling. Then, before he had time to sag back into nothingness, he started to jog around the perimeter of the little room. Ten laps one way, ten laps the other way; then stop and do fifty sit-ups, fifty press-ups, fifty weighted arm-loops, two minutes of shadow-combat with the hanging socks. And so back to the jogging.

During the day, under endless scrutiny, he had the run of the huge FTL gymnasia a few levels below. He even had his own coach for movement, choreography and presence in front of the cameras. They worked together on the tumbling routines he sometimes used. But this extra work would give him more edge, more muscle for the day that he needed it. And better than that, it was his *own*, totally private. It was confirmation to himself that he retained the power of will, the possibility of shaping a future.

The night had always been his time, away from all their plans for him. Why, after all, would anyone bother to check on him during the hours of sleep, when the food that contained his precious fix of Ambrosia (others called it Loop-the-loop, or the Lady) was also, in the evening, laced with sleeping drugs?

Nobody had ever beaten the Lady. That was their guarantee. Nobody had ever shrugged off her embraces and few had even bothered to try. So he'd be safe for the night, they thought, intoxicated and helpless, getting his beauty sleep to serve his master and his master's great show in the morning.

Even when he was on location, in the Brown and Black FTL camps, they trusted him, a dog firmly tethered on a regulated steel leash of addiction. And one day they would regret that. One day he would not return from the camps.

A little before the sun rose, and long after the smart Visions were in their beds and the Scroats had crept to their holes for another miserable day, the Ref towelled the film of sweat from his strong, emaciated body and replaced the room to normality. The best thing of all was that he was so spent that, even pierced anew by the terrible craving for the Lady, even with the fire in his legs and arms and the buzz in his brain, he fell sound asleep until breakfast.

'Not beaten yet, Jan,' he murmured into the pillow, as consciousness flipped away. 'Not yet, my friend.'

Breakfast time was a tougher prospect even than supper for the Ref. He felt like a ghost with so little sleep.

He was managing now to take about a quarter of the morning food off his tray, again to be sucked down to the Docks; but as this meal was composed of two or three or four small choice dishes, plus two drinks, he could never be sure where the Lady lay waiting for him. Would she be spread between syrup and water? In the fish? The waffles? The rice-cake? Doing without the morning fix entirely would be a disaster. He'd be a gibbering wreck within the hour, and then his minders would know what he'd done. Too little of the drug in his veins and he'd be unable to function properly for the cameras, with the same effect. Twice in the last week he'd lost concentration whilst filming, almost fluffed his lines. Yet if he accidentally threw away unlaced food and took the whole dose, his tiny movement forward would be sabotaged, the addiction flowering back to full strength in a single meal. He couldn't allow that. Better too little than too much. Somehow, he'd hold himself together.

As best he could, he mixed up each portion and took away a quarter of every dish and glass. Again, sweating and crying and twitching to the toilet before he could give himself relief.

Then twenty minutes in the bath, letting the drug caress him into what passed for normality in her peaceful, scented arms, before donning his costume and going to fulfil his role: the hideous, undignified part created for him by Barbieri.

*The Ref.*

'The Ref's coming!'

'Watch out, the Ref's on one today!'

'Don't tangle with the Ref, mate, if you know what's good for you!'

'The guy gives me the creeps. Those eyes, staring at you in that mask!'

'I saw him demolish some bloke once. Awesome.'

'Just who *is* he anyway?'

The Ref, that's all that I am, he thought, as he caught fragments of these comments, fearfully whispered around him every day of his working life. A masked, suited figure in the black and silver Jan loves. The front man to Fit To Live. Dangerous and sarcastic and witty. Keeping the contestants on their toes. A god, tanked up with Ambrosia, blessed by the Lady who chains me tight to her wrist. And now, Jan, I've made the role mine, haven't I? I've become important in your little propaganda machine. I have a reputation. I have become truly *dangerous*. Not your figure of fun, your jester, any more. You didn't expect that, did you, great Leader? I'm a survivor, and your show makes a hero of a survivor.

Oh yes, when the Loop goes round, washed through my blood like a shark accelerating to a kill, I'm ten feet tall, quick as a snake, merciless to the weak, devoid of pain. There's *nothing* I can't do.

'Keep your heads down fellas: the Ref's here.'

You didn't expect that, Jan. And now, what will you do with me?

Game on.

Today was routine. Tedious. A White day. The Ref was more interested in the Brown and the Black.

Today ten little newbies would trot nervously out, having been rehearsed so often that even the dimmest should know when to wave, when to shout, when to shut their stupid mouths. He'd gee them up, introduce them, go through the responses, keep them off balance.

'Are *you* Fit To Live?' he'd ask them witheringly.

'YES!'

'Well, we'll see, won't we?'

Ten players in white. All running before the cameras so that Jan could showcase his New Visions, Briton's young saviours. As for the rest, they were here for nothing but injury, or perhaps death. Didn't they *know* that? Why did they enter? Why? Survival was the name of the game, and the Ref had made FTL his, and *he* survived, but he hated every second of it.

So here we go, the intros, the lovely swelling chords that he'd written himself, the corny, threatening lines as he came down the steps, to scare the shit out of anyone that hadn't been nurtured in some laboratory by the madmen in the Fertility Board. Then the newbies running out to the slaughter, waving.

*Who have we got today then?*

The Ref tried to concentrate as the tiniest twitch pulled at his calf muscle. There were three New Visions in the line, three teenage superfreaks, who'd lick their leader's arse if he asked them to. Amongst them, four of the plain, old-fashioned model, yesterday's human being. And last, speeding to destruction, three *real* dinosaurs: untampered-with, hundred-per-cent-guaranteed human beings, here to escape the persecution in their slums, or to win accceptance in the jaundiced public eye, or to give themselves sclf-respect, to prove themselves . . . Who could say why they'd signed the contract? Perhaps one or two really thought they could get to Black and win a major prize. Luxury housing, wealth, a posting in the Pax elite, a guarantee of dry land to build on, when more was acquired abroad.

Madness. Did they think the persecution would end there? Did they imagine Jan would cven let them get that far?

Today it was Ivan, a raging bull with a thick neck and bulging arms, full of a sense of injustice, 'to be castrated in shameful combat'. (The Ref's aide had run through it this morning.) Then Kris, a boy who should never have made it though the pre-show tests; indeed, he'd only sneaked in by a whisker, but maybe somebody in admin had decided that those bright rabbit eyes and girl's lashes were too good to waste. Kris was down 'to be tied in knots in a test of the mind'. He'd probably burst into tears.

Finally, a shaven-headed girl.

A shaven-headed girl.

Friend.

For the first time in months, the Ref completely fluffed his intros and needed a second take. The twitch in his calf was a pinprick of fire now. He thought: I messed up at breakfast. I tipped too much away. The wrong piece of rice cake. The wrong slice of fish.

He saw a sound man nudging his fellow, having a laugh.

'You, over here, *now*!' he called.

There was instant hush amongst the FTL team. *Watch out for the Ref, mates!* The man looked around for support, somewhere to hide, and didn't find either of those things. Slowly, he put down his equipment and walked over.

'You're history,' the Ref said clearly. 'You can't even mike-up the newbies right. Look at that one, with the cable showing. You can leave immediately. Don't come back.'

The man couldn't take it in, flapped his mouth like a fish. 'But ... my family. Where will I work, sir? You can't ... you just *can't*. Not for that, a bit of poxy wire showing. They'll edit it out if they need to.'

The Ref put a hand on the sound man's throat and squeezed. 'Can't?' he whispered. In the background he saw the infinitesimal movement of his Pax minder talking into a wristcom, loosening a weapon. They wouldn't let him do serious harm to the man, but only he knew that. For now he had the attention firmly where he wanted it: on the famed temper of the Ref. With luck, Jan's little flunkies and spies would forget his slip a moment before. It was unfortunate that this harmless technician must lose his job for that end, but the thing was done now: lose it he must.

In due course they went for the second take, and this time the Ref was ready. When the shaven-headed girl appeared in the line and he introduced her, he managed to keep his giddy feelings in check, just enough to get the thing right.

*

The girl, Friend, was down (like the rabbit boy) to face Logic. Admin had again looked at the eyes and made an assumption about her abilities and audience reaction. They couldn't, after all, have the slender, pretty thing beaten to a pulp by mercenaries, or forced to adapt to extremes of heat or cold. Endurance? Yes, that might have been a possible. On her stats the girl had claimed that she did a little running around the waterside streets. (They'd grinned in admin: running to save her sweet little hide from the attentions of the New Vision boys no doubt.) Nevertheless, someone had ticked the box for Logic.

Of course, when she did so well, they held an editing meeting and rapidly opted not to show the full sequence. They even considered wiping the recording and starting again with a replacement, but for the Ref pitching in.

'What kind of cowards are you?' he sneered. 'A Scroat gets through Stage One once in a while, and you want to pretend she doesn't exist? What would they say in the city? Someone will hear if you wipe the tapes; someone will mention it to a friend, whatever their contract says. What would that do to FTL?' He laughed coldly, flapped his hand. 'She'll be out of the game soon enough. Stop pissing yourselves.'

The editors didn't know about the Lady. Poor Jan couldn't tell them, could he? The Ref was listened to. He was nobody's fool. Inch by inch he'd become the driving force of the show. He understood how it worked. So the shaven-headed girl was *not* out. They screened a tiny summary of her task, and that was it ... and it was enough. Like the Ref she was *in*, a screen presence.

When the show went out, a tremor of excited, revolted disbelief went through the Vision viewers. A hopeful rumour or two started weaving its way through the waterfront holes where the Scroats lurked. The New

Visions, like Crane, saw an aberration and went, slightly puzzled, to their beds.

And the Ref himself, bathed in sweat, fighting the evening onset of deprivation, praying for the man to bring the meal soon, before he lost control, played the unedited recording of Friend's task over and over. He watched as she walked slowly and wonderingly to the game equipment. He watched as she hummed and circled the blocks, while the clock ticked away. And he watched as she laid her hands gently on the building pieces of the igloo puzzle, hauling heavy blocks into position with fluidity and grace, humming all the while.

Still in her own world, she slowly fitted the last segment as the clock showed three seconds remaining – she hadn't looked at it once – and stepped back, looking unemotionally at the completed shape.

And the Ref's drug-altered mind knew that an answer was there, somewhere in his billions of tired grey cells. A reason for this girl and his own turmoil.

For now the answer stayed a jump away; but whatever it was, she was *in*.

# ADELINE

'Not permitted out? How can that be?'

'I'm sorry, miss. You're designated as a Brown now, ain't you? Brown's 'ave got to stay in the official accommodation provided until being shipped to the next phase of the show. It's in the paper you signed. Nice enough rooms, too, eh?'

Nice enough for a Scroat, he meant. Better than anything she could possibly be used to.

She said, vaguely, 'Oh. The contract. I'd like to walk a little, that's all. To . . .' she shrugged '. . . just to walk.'

He nodded gleefully. 'Well, there's three ways out miss, there's always three ways out. There's public resignation, that's number one. *To wit*, recording a statement that you're beat or frightened or ill and can't play no more. Now, that would be screened at the end of a show. We don't get too many of those, mind, on account of the other two ways, which are number two, failing a task, or number three, death and severe injury. I can let you out for any of those, miss, any time.'

It was obviously his set joke and she made herself smile, despite the frustration. A smile wouldn't cost her anything. Keep in the man's favour.

'That's *funny*. I'll ask again when I'm dead.'

They smiled some more. 'Dead, that's it', the man chortled happily. And then, 'Oh but miss, I should also say; those designated Brown is permitted to use the gymnasia on floors seven through nine. The elevator from your corridor goes directly there. If it's exercise you're after.'

'Seven through nine. OK, maybe I'll have a look. Some time. Thank you.'

She sauntered away from the man's doorway post and back into the contestants' area, the cameras smoothly tracking her progress. At the next intersection, she took a wrong turning and tried the wrong door handle. When she did finally make it to the right room – the bare little cell she'd been allocated, with its thick porthole of glass overlooking the city – she sprawled untidily on the bed and opened the slim FTL information pack, spreading out the glossy sheets. The fact that she'd read and absorbed the unhelpful information only an hour or two ago was unimportant.

It was all like a dream. She was constantly surprised at the choices she could make, the paths she could tread since coming to this place. A part of her had stayed in Seven. It must have been a heavy, constricting part because now she felt she could move more easily, breathe more deeply. It wasn't just the change in altitude, the rich oxygen that made her physical body so efficient. As Friend, Scroat though she was, she could etch any design across her surprising days.

Her short life in the city had been filled with designs, with deceit, with risk too. She was still learning the part, still making dangerous mistakes. A voice had been un-expectedly easy to find, different voices even, according to her company; but the correct grammatical corrup-tions, the appropriate cultural references, what to say and how to say it in this grey, frightened place, they were more challenging tasks. And then add on what she was to wear, how she should move and gesture, where she should walk or not walk.

It was fun as well as dangerous. It made her wonder what mask she'd worn in Seven, what game she'd played there. Yet she'd never dreamed that life here would be so complex, so fraught with endless observation and checking and paranoia. Neighbour watching neighbour, friend watching friend, Pax and their cameras watching everybody. And everybody blaming the Scroats, hunting them out, driving them one way or another from the city and into the arms of the floods.

So much fear, as Mac had said.

The Visions and the New Visions and the Scroats hated each other, but you couldn't ever really be sure who was who. It depended on such a mixture of things; your face, your voice, your ideas. Most of all, it depended on your birth and identity records. On her face and voice alone she'd managed to pass for Vision, and for Scroat at different times. Yet on her first day in the city she'd seen a crowd outside a dockside bar, surrounding a tired little man, throwing stones and rotten fish at him, jeering, while he pleaded with them, 'I'm Vision. I'm Vision. 3973 Indigo Heights, that's my address. Go and look. Ask my wife. Just because I'm a little short . . .'

The people in this city had a madness about them. The seas were rising, lapping at their filthy, stifling buildings and streets, and the terrified populace were turning into animals, blaming each other for looming destruction, looking to Jan Barbieri to lead them to a better place with his New Visions.

The madness suited Jan well, Adeline thought. He whipped it up, nurtured it, coaxed it to greater strength.

She shivered as she flipped unseeingly through the information pack. She thought of the three strange, pale half-children who'd stood in the line with her before today's tasks. One had nudged another, gestured carelessly at her. 'Not bad for a Scroat,' he'd said, and they'd both looked her up and down as if she were an animal, a milk-goat for their farm. The third was a girl, just as tall as the others, almost as muscular. She'd looked Adeline over too, for all of two seconds, with open contempt. Even though the oldest of the New Visions were only fourteen or so, they were bulky, arrogant, seemingly fearless. People stood aside for them, people stared at them, people called out praise or abuse (the latter from a safe distance) as they passed. Nobody was unaffected.

Somewhere in these corridors the three from today were also housed, designated Brown as she was. The four of them had been shown down here together, after the tasks. From what she could make out, they were the only ones who'd survived the day. Of Ivan and Kris and the four others there was no sign.

Adeline knew she'd need to watch her fellow contestants if they should meet away from the cameras and supervisors. She could sense their desire to hunt, to victimise. She'd seen the packs of them down by the water; the ruthlessness, the fear they sent before them. It was already spreading in ripples through the Visions of the city. A taint of suspicion and violence.

'Is it drugs, do you think?' one of the Fit To Live interviewers had asked a colleague, looking Adeline over curiously, during the registration process.

'No,' the second had replied, acidly, 'I think it's just stupidity, Crystal. From natural childbirth. Which is what got Briton into the mess it's in now. The sooner her kind are shown up and kicked out the better. A tight ship, the leader says we need. Tight and lean. Got to prove ourselves worthy, ain't we? Go on, put *Logic*. That'll do for her, good and proper.'

She got up from the bed, wandered to the porthole to look out at the raging, gloomy weather. In her imagination, Dom looked on from the shadows, enjoying the game, watching to see if she could walk the tightrope between the hunters and the ignorant and the perils of FTL itself. She looked forward to showing him what she could do.

And then?

Then, if she were still alive, she'd take Jan on.

Four days later, at daybreak, an FTL assistant came to Adeline's door. She held a brown tunic, leggings and heavy boots.

'The transport will be leaving to take you on to the Marsh in twenty minutes. Please be ready in ten. Wear these. You may take nothing with you. You will be searched before leaving and any unpermitted objects removed.'

'My old clothes? The things I came with?'

The woman rolled her eyes impatiently. 'Please put on the correct clothes and report to the entrance desk immediately.'

Adeline felt like a snake, sloughing skin after skin. The girl from Seven was becoming make-believe. Only the twinge in her chest reminded her why she'd left in the first place. In a few moments she had changed the white novice clothes for the muddy brown and was at the desk. The guard with his jokes was there again and a small silent knot of players in the same brown tunics. Of course there were more of them now; nine more contestants who'd passed the White phase in the time she'd been here. Seven more of the New Visions, two of the old kind. No Scroats, save her.

The transport, a battered, mud-streaked vehicle, was backed up to a side entrance of the great tower and the players were frisked and issued in, passing first through a metal-detecting device, to sit on aluminium benches in the gloomy rear section. Last came four armed Pax personnel, perched just inside the double doors.

'Here we go,' one moaned quietly, 'sick bags at the ready.'

'Two sodding days away from the civilised world,' agreed another.

The transport doors slammed shut and they started rumbling and rattling down the hill streets. They went, not towards the docks, but into the smartest Vision districts and then, lower down still, to the darker places, the semi-slums, where the bleak floodwalls stood, tall and grey, licked by the rank waters. Adeline followed their progress through one of the tiny window slits, but the moment that they left the inland gate and took the stiltway north was obvious to all. Immediately, the spray drummed under the floor. The sound filled the old transport like the monsoon on the lookout roof.

Sitting in a line, swaying and jumping in unison with the vehicle's movement, the ten NVs took no interest in what was happening outside. They sat straight and aggressive, their eyes on Adeline and the two Visions, further along her own metal seat. It would be difficult to pick out the three from her own day of tasks, Adeline thought, running her idiot's gaze idly along their line. It was not that they were physically identical, like her own sisters, but more that they had an identical vacancy about them, a mixture of intelligence and emptiness in the eyes, a sense of self-belief devoid of imagination.

In comparison the two Visions seemed very human. 'Strange to be Outside,' one muttered.

'Yes,' the other agreed, shivering. 'I went half a mile down the western stiltway when I was a boy, for a dare, but . . .'

If they heard, the NVs didn't even bother to comment; their scorn was always there, lurking behind the pale eyes. 'You,' one said to Adeline, 'Scroat girl. Why did you shave your head like that?'

She shrugged, looked down at the metal floor. 'For the lice. Someone I knew told me.'

The NVs exchanged looks. 'What do you know? She tries to keep herself clean.'

'Better and better. I want a piece of that.'

'Cool it,' said the Pax corporal, 'save it for the Marsh. We've got a long trip.'

'What about your lenses? Why do you wear those, Scroat girl? To keep the flies out of your eyes?'

'I don't know,' she answered vaguely, 'I thought I'd try . . .'

'How d'you afford lenses? You steal them?'

'Someone gave them to me.'

'A boy?'

She nodded shyly.

'A boy!' The NV asking the questions wrinkled his face in disgust, though he was younger than she was. 'She's been with a boy! A little Scroat runt, I bet. Count me out after all.'

Pigs, Adeline thought; ignorant pigs. Yet the NVs were only what they had been made to be.

The corporal said again, 'Cool it,' and for a long while they travelled in silence, the spray from the flooded road buffeting the transport, running down the sides. Gradually, as the water deepened, they slowed. Twice during the day the security men handed out food and water from a locker. Once they stopped and the passengers were allowed to relieve themselves, climbing down under an elevated section of the stiltway onto a muddy island of driftwood and silt. Apart from that, there were plastic pails to use as they went along. All of the NVs did this, boys and girls alike, unbothered by the lack of privacy.

'Cleaner than that heap of shit under the road,' one of the girls said disdainfully, reaching for an unused pail. 'How many people have gone *there*?'

'That's why we're Browns,' joked one of the Visions.

She didn't even look at him.

Finally, with the water above the wheels, the vehicle slowed to a walking pace. The sound of their progress was strangely deadened. In a few minutes they stopped completely and a panel in the front wall snapped open.

'Aspen Sinclair,' a bored voice said, 'you get down here.'

One of the NVs rose and went purposefully to the back of the transport.

'Here,' said the corporal, opening a locker, 'map, light, camera with integral mike, distress button.' He took out a dog-eared sheet of paper and read quickly and tonelessly: 'The camera will stay mounted above your ear at all times, waking and sleeping; the FTL or Pax representative – that's me – will fix it for you now. Any attempt to release the clip will set off an alarm in our control centre and will disqualify you from the game. The distress button, imprinted with your game code, is single use only and similarly signifies resignation from the game. You should wear it around your neck, inside your tunic – to activate, just flip away the cover and press. The rules of the game state that you may not leave the Marsh, signified by the illuminated red tubing that you will cross in a moment. Your Tasks will be assigned to you on the day concerned. You may not participate in combat with another player more than once every three days. FTL Tasks have precedence over individual combat. All else is permissible. Thumbprint here, to show you understand.'

The NV boy thumbprinted the paper and the corporal hauled back the transport doors. With the engine shut off, the only sound outside was of lapping water and the call of a night bird, somewhere off in the gloom.

'There you are. The red tubing is there, directly to our right. You should be able to wade here. Once you cross, this phase of the game is started and you will be monitored.'

The NV took a single blank look back into the dimly-lit transport and stepped outside, splashing heavily away.

Then they were off again, rumbling forward through the floods for a further half-hour.

Next time they stopped it was for Lewis Spacey, another NV. Then one of the Visions, looking worried but determined, then another NV. Each time, the corporal read out the instructions and took their thumbprint. Adeline thought that they were pulling slightly to the right, driving in what might be a huge circle, around the Marsh area, but it was hard to be sure at this low speed, with the water rippling around them.

'Gally Fripp.'

'Katya Steward.'

One by one the passengers were given their equipment and sent into the dark. Finally, with only three of them left in the transport, the voice said: 'Friend . . . Friend whatever-your-name-is. Baldy girl. This is you, much good may it do you.'

She rose and listened and offered her own thumb, and then stepped through the open door into a metre of freezing water.

# DOMINIC
## – *day 54* –

Listen up. Great tidings. Father came . . . and went again.

I hardly recognised him.

'Next time you come in here, your warning will have expired.' That's what the Major said when he bollocked me before, wasn't it? Not true, Major.

When they suddenly came charging up to the old dorm the other night I thought I'd had it. The alarm worked sweetly, but was hardly necessary the way they thundered up those stairs in their boots. Almost broke my neck getting out onto the parapet with my notebook. Slid the window down after me as the door was opening. Heard them rattle it up again as I was on the iron ladder.

Silent and fast over the lead of the roof, round the maze of chimney stacks and I was properly awake and starting to enjoy it, just like with the guys in the car, in my previous, solitary life. Father's right about that: action is best.

*Catch me then, you bastards.*

There's no doubting that I'm much fitter now. And the roof is still *my* territory, such as it is. I went part way down the proper escape on the far side, then in at the second floor. Catch left undone on the window there on purpose. Then back to 0-17 via the toilets. Well planned, Dom. Except . . .

Frank Barbieri was wide awake, grinning in the moonlight.

'Where've you been?' he said.

'The bogs.'

'Oh yeah? You're steaming. Was it hot in the bogs?'

'Boiling.'

So it was him, not bad luck. It must have been him. *Look upstairs Major, sir. He seems to like it up there. Have a look one night.* I can just picture it.

I said 'boiling' and then I couldn't stop myself, I went to his bed and punched him in the face.

'Right,' he said, spitting blood, getting up.

Next day, nothing. Normal day, though bloody painful. The one after, was told at lunch that the Major wanted me again. For the second time, sat outside the Head's study, freezing, and the guy with the gun saying, 'What happened to you? Get hit by a bus?' Tee hee. Inside there was a lot of shouting: the Major in a foul mood giving someone a hard time.

Bits drifted out.

*'You're a disgrace! Useless. And I will not give space to spare parts in this camp; is that clear? Either you smarten up your ideas, or you will be out.'*

*Mumble mumble mumble.*

*'It's much too late for that, you old fool. Can't you even see that? What would you do? Who would you tell? God, man, you're lucky to have this chance to do something worthwhile for a little longer. You make me sick.'*

*Mumble mumble.*

Again felt so aggressive. A sickness I didn't know I'd caught. Wanted to march in there and save the poor sod getting it in the neck. Very conscious of my body and its power, though it didn't do me so much good with Barbieri. I think I'm full of internal switches, switches that Father or Bede's or someone has left 'off'; on purpose? I've deceived myself about my abilities, about coping, about my tight ship. But the switches are being turned 'on' in this mess, and something's going to break out.

Or maybe it never will.

Someone else did the marching and the saving. Ruth. Old black parka and copper scarf, big boots. Coming into the hall, straight through into the study without knocking, hauling her father out (tottering, useless) and back into the cold. Neither she nor the Major said a word. (Why didn't she lose it this time?)

The Major came to stand in the doorway, looking after them. He didn't seem properly angry either. Just thoughtful. He turned and said, disdainful, 'Ah yes, it's *you*. Come through. Sit there.'

Sat in his boiling office getting drowsy and sweaty for forty minutes. On the desk, next to the plastic folders, was a broken roof tile attached to some twine. Neither of us mentioned it. He was filling in papers, I was thinking of Ruth.

Then the sound of powerful engines coming quickly. The sound of engines is terrifying now, rare as it is. Engines bring trouble, change. Not a car or bus or truck this time, though. A helicopter, coming in low, hovering, landing. I'm used to these surprises, now.

'There we are. Come along, Dominic.'

The Major led me to the games pitches. Soldiers were already there, ringing in the helicopter. Men in gleaming Saville Row suits getting out, putting on dark overcoats. Suits! Bloody haircuts, briefcases! Coming here from the wasteland that Britain has become in my mind. Others after them, ten or so men and women, with bags and cases, I don't know. And there's Father at the head of the whole bunch, looking unchanged.

How to explain?

I cried, furious. I was overcome with BEFORE. It rose up in my throat and choked me. How can I explain that? I didn't know how to move or stand, like a castaway coming back to civilisation and not understanding how to hold a fork. I was trembling with anger at him for not being ravaged and thin or something. Anything but normal.

He saw me and came over. We shook hands. We would shake hands if we met in a black hole.

'Dominic.'

'Father.'

'You look well. A little grubby around the edges. And rather battered. A just cause, I hope.' He looked amused by my bruises.

I couldn't take it in. I didn't know him after all. He *wasn't* normal, was he? He'd looked the same from twenty metres away but now, who *was* this? I was shaking hard.

'Let's walk a little,' he said. 'I can spare half an hour or so.'

It was too much. I was dealing with the new life at Bede's until this. I didn't want the door thrown wide unless I was going through it.

'What am I doing here, Father?' I said. 'Where have you been?'

'Here and there. Lots to do.'

'I'm coming with you, when you go, right?'

'Not possible, I'm afraid. Not this time.'

But you know, I didn't expect him to say yes, and it was a relief that he didn't. God knows why. Fear of Outside? Fear of finding the rotten remains of Wildman Wishart, starved of fuel and food at the roadside, in a line of wasting wrecks? Wanting to be done with Father and his kind for good? I realised as we walked that I was as tall as him. Must have grown again. I could have knocked him down.

'Things are changing very rapidly,' he said. 'In a nutshell, this country, like so many others, has been left without government. Without direction. The cold is here to stay, of course. It's going to get much worse. Sea rise too, flooding, disease, starvation. All the problems that are here right now, getting steadily worse. Do you see? And we're so badly prepared. We need leaders. We need people who will keep something safe. Culture. Civilisation. Order.'

His words were fading in and out of my head. I was picturing Ruth again, with the copper scarf nestled against and overlapped by the darker red tint of her hair.

'I made sure that you were here, Dominic. You're going to be part of it, I'm sure, part of this new undertaking. It's a great privilege and a responsibility. Give it everything. Heavens, boy, you're intelligent, fit, resourceful. You're just the kind of thing my colleagues and I need.'

We circled the field. The helicopter sat stark and brooding, under guard. I said, 'I'd better go, Father, my section will need me.'

He looked put out.

*He* did!

We stood without speaking, assessing each other. In a way, nothing has changed – his visit could have been one when the school was still a school, sports day, perhaps – except that I'm here in the forge and I don't want anything from him now, or to be part of his plans.

Culture. Civilisation. Order.

Did he know what the Major's 'camp' was like?


I've realised that I'm in love. Enough switches have been thrown to see it. Enough crap stripped away. It's all there is, like a powerful, raw beast crouching under all the games.

# CRANE

New Visions didn't have a problem with tolerating pain, or hardship or danger. Nothing like that. But nobody had thought about boredom, and Crane was certainly bored.

He gave his instructors one hundred and ten per cent of his attention while they instructed, however rapidly and disdainfully he dismissed them afterwards. What they taught enhanced his potential and might give him the edge one day.

But when would that day be?

Apart from 'warm-down' and 'warm-up', neither of which he needed, he trained with ferocity and determination for his physical coaches. He could run the hundred metres in under ten seconds, was a Slam Master, and could hold his breath for over two minutes underwater. But the city was crowded, space for running diminishing, pools becoming choked by the swelling ranks of NVs. Only in Tactical Roleplay and Field Logic did Crane score less than maximum. Not often, but now and then, an exercise left him puzzled in the same way that he'd been puzzled by the lack of fear in the Scroat woman they'd hunted a few days back. Younger NVs outscored him in Tactical Roleplay and Field Logic. He knew this but didn't feel fear because of it. He admired talent.

Crane was proud of what he could do, proud of Briton, and bored. When would the leader set him and his friends some task that would challenge them and help the country he loved? Everyone knew that there would be war before long, and the search for new lands. But, for now, Fit To Live was all there was, and so he'd put his name forward weekly, fifty-three times, without luck. It wasn't a problem with the entrance tests: he could do them with his eyes shut. It was that every NV wanted to be involved, to win honour and extra privileges.

This morning, thanks to his deep boredom and frustration, for the first time ever he decided to change the main part of his day's schedule and miss school.

He got up early and did some private training in his room: weights, reflexes, stretches. He worked methodically at his skin in the steam-suite and dressed in a clean, pressed tunic and his weatherproofs. He was a little shocked at his decision, but realised that there was a wider perspective. He was not, after all, going to waste the time or contribute less to his own future or the future of Briton. He would order his day as with any other. It was not real rebellion.

He ate the breakfast his Vision mother prepared, silent while she hovered behind his chair, ready with the second and third plates.

'Eat up, Love, that's right.'

Crane wondered how these particular parents had come to be selected for him. There must have been potential there somewhere, as well as solid citizenship.

'They're going to demolish the old eastern docks next restday. Your father thought we could all go. Make a day of it. That'll be nice, won't it?'

'It's good that the old areas are being renovated,' he said automatically. He thought suddenly about all the extra prey there'd be along the rest of the waterfront and grinned.

His mother smiled too and repeated, 'A family day of it,' with faint relief. Crane anticipated and detested the little lack of understanding before it even arrived. It made him more eager than ever to be out. He shook his head at the next plate, looked his mother coolly in the eye to say his goodbye, and left.

Outside, the uncharacteristically dry wind buffeted his bulk and whipped road dust into his face and he felt satisfied, invincible, like the commander of one of the large ships on the ocean. One of the massive new black hulks, perhaps, that were being built just outside the tidal barrier from expensive, rationed steel.

He paused at the Caplink stop, but decided after all to jog across the city. In the orange carriages he'd be back inside too soon, breathing the moist air of other passengers, clogged up by their nervousness and surplus, buzzing emotions. He lazily changed gear on his vessel and moved off along the walkways at twice walking speed, stared at (of course) by Visions going to work, by the schoolchildren drifting towards their own instruction facilities, and even noticed today by his own kind, who might well raise their eyebrows at his direction or demeanour. A small irregular puzzle for them to work on during their studies. He wouldn't meet Marco or Anton or the others from his FB cell on this route, though, and really there was no logical reason not to enjoy setting the puzzle and observing how his change of schedule sent out its tiny, neat ripples.

Of course there were Vision girls who gave Crane the sex look. Vision boys who measured themselves against his strength and stuck out their chests. (Neither were interesting, this morning.) There were police who saw a running figure with suspicion, which changed to respect as their minds caught up and their eyes sharpened. There were people catching his eye and looking away. Frightened people. Hardly anyone who showed what he would have shown in their position.

It occurred to Crane that he was not often out without the pack. It occurred to him again when, jogging through the dingy market complex called Portable Road, an old woman stepped in front of him, looking over her shoulder at something in a shop window, and he knocked her down, so that she rolled on the dirty walkway, a bundle of flapping garments. It was not his fault and he even stopped to help the woman up and collected her dropped things but, despite that, several people gathered round and started abusing him.

Portable Road had already been 'cleaned'. Until recently the network of lanes and small squares had been choked with Scroats and illegal incomers to the city: drug users, beggars, wasters, sheer dirt. They'd clustered in like sodden termites, adding their own taint to the aroma of hot wraps and spiced drink. The Leader, Jan Barbieri, had made it one of the first targets in his cleaning of the city, clearing the decks ready for the game of survival. The lanes had been flushed out, the defiled stones steam-blasted, the camera presence increased. Crane had been too young to come here before the change, but he wondered now if the Leader had done the job adequately, or whether the whole place needed to be demolished and started again, like the old eastern docks. The little crowd that closed in on him because of the accident with the old woman had an unsavoury look. They came out from behind the stalls and from within the little shops.

'Clumsy great ape!'

'Freak boy.'

'What about apologising, eh, Woodenhead?'

Crane looked assessingly at their numbers and realised that brawn alone would not set him free from the knot. Nor would superior intellect. It wouldn't make any difference: nothing he did would make any difference, they'd already made up their illogical minds about him. The thought gave him a moment of anger and frustration. He loved his country and was even on his way to try and increase his personal contribution to their own futures. And these insects deserved it so little, understood the threat so poorly.

But also he felt something unknown to him; a tongue of something that was not exactly fear, more an uncomfortable tremor of impotence.

Resentfully he did what the crowd required. He said to the old woman, 'I'm sorry. It was my fault. Can I offer any further help? I could take you to a medic, for example.' The meaningless words sickened him. Jumping through hoops. Yet it was survival too, there was that: his mind – his computer – was assessing probabilities correctly.

The old baggage was flustered by the attention, frightened by his size perhaps. She just wanted to be about her business, shuffling off with her bits and pieces gripped tight. Good, the idiots would leave him alone. And then he felt his legs kicked out from under him and there were quick blows to his kidneys and jaw sending him down heavily onto the paving stones.

'Don't be so damned cocky, you little runt,' said a voice. 'Learn some respect.'

His mouth was full of blood. He thought he could pick out which ones were responsible for the attack. All of them were drifting away, losing interest, laughing at him. The rain, never away for long, started suddenly: heavy, icy drops, matting his hair to his scalp. He realised there was nothing he could do, unless he wanted a greater beating. And he felt frustrated and awkward and puzzled, sitting bloody in the rain.

The officer at the Pax recruiting building was another surprise. A greying, tired man, with a chiselled jaw. Crane had started to despair of him within a few minutes.

'Didn't you think to go home and clean yourself up before calling on us, sonny?'

'Sir. I explained to you. When I left my parents' home I was entirely clean and presentable. That is my habitual and preferred state. It was the unprovoked attack by a mob in Portable Road that left me in this condition.'

'Young man, it is not any surprise to me that you got yourself into trouble in Portable Road. The question was why you didn't come back another time when you were "clean and presentable" once more.'

Crane blinked, shoulders bunched under his weatherproofs. 'That wouldn't have made sense, sir. I would have had to miss another day of instruction.'

'Yes,' the officer flicked him a sharp glance, 'that was my next question. How you managed to get the time off to come here. Answer: you just took it, without asking. Frankly, that surprises me in . . . one of your kind. So, let's see: so far we've got a tally of disobedience, slovenliness, and brawling in the street. Not a very impressive start if you want to join the force, is it?'

Crane stood up, eye-to-eye with the man, dangerous. 'Sir, I can pass any of your tests!'

The man returned his gaze. 'Maybe this is one of them, son. You think I just want performers in my unit? High scorers? I want people I can rely on. People who can handle themselves.' He raised a hand, stemming any reply from Crane. 'However, since you're here this morning, I'll have someone do the paperwork with you and put you through the first induction stage. Good enough?'

A test. This had been a test too. He hadn't realised. Crane relaxed, obliterated the officer's number from his memory. 'Yes sir. Good enough.' And then, as an afterthought, 'Thank you.'

That was twice today he'd had to speak unfamiliar words.

# ADELINE

Browns were granted eighty hectares of floodland and bog, bleak and windswept. Here they ate, slept and played the game of Fit To Live. Here, quite often, they died.

There was ninety per cent water cover in the Marsh, ten per cent land, if you could call it land. With an average water temperature of 4–7°C on average, if you wanted to survive for any length of time you had to *find* the land and cling to it, or climb the stunted, rotting trees that sprouted from the shallows. Some of the trees, a handful, had been provided with bare platforms amongst the branches. Then, most desirable of all, there was Paradise: a village, a stockaded enclosure of rough shelters built on stilts. Paradise was the easiest place to survive the elements for the handful of contestants – usually thirty or so of them – marooned in the Marsh. The only question was whether the current inhabitants would let you in and share their space. That was one of the unknown factors, the unguessable quantities of the Brown phase of FTL. It all added to the fun and it deliberately mirrored the predicament of the world at large.

As the sound of the transport's struggling engine faded away along the drowned road, Adeline crossed the dimly-glowing red tubing and heard a tiny click above her ear as the camera there came to life. From now on everything she saw and experienced became the property of the Fit To Live editors to use as they wished. Hundreds of other cameras and microphones were concealed throughout the Marsh to catch every second of the excitement.

For the time being the ragged wind had died. She stood quite still in the lull, listening, shivering, trying to get some sense of the terrain around her, whilst the water lapped at her hips. Despite the cold, something inside purred with pleasure. She'd left the city and its confinement, its terrified, manic inhabitants. And yet, she found the sounds here were not the sounds she knew. The smells, the feel of the place. It wasn't clean, solid, reliable, as the mountains were.

It occurred to her, not for the first time, that when the end did come, her sisters would die too, in her. Cloning was no more; it had been overtaken by Jan's tinkering at the Fertility Board. The Saints had been scattered and destroyed, save Clarissa. Her twins had lived their times, well or badly, and each had passed on the trust, the purpose, to the next – but now there was nowhere for it to go. In their complacence they had assumed that someone would come afterwards to do whatever had to be done, to finish the story.

How *did* the story finish?

It was laughable. *She* was the someone, by her own will shivering in this wasteland. She regretted now choosing Friend as her FTL name. It had been a moment of humour. A taunting of the prophecy. But the joke was on her, standing waist-deep in this freezing water simply because she was too scared to die in her home in the mountains.

Consciousness flickered, snagging like material on a nail.

*How would Dom come through the Major's regime? How would he face the pressures? She feared for him. Would he lose that openness, that vulnerability that pulled at her heart? There was nothing she could do to change it. She had her own story. That was the first truth. You could only trust absolutely in others to live their own tales. You could only love them for that.*

There was a short cry somewhere in the dusk, human or animal, the echoes bouncing off the black water. Adeline shook herself and took a step. She should think – how did Dom say it? – 'on the hoof'. The demons should not come and find her here, immobile with fear.

Slowly she waded into the Marsh, away from the glowing boundary, feeling her path forward in the silt. The water had a sharp tang of salt about it. Seawater, spilling up over the land. Soon the salt would kill all the plants here, and the creatures that lived in them and around them. Indeed, at the eastern end, along a narrow collar of the boundary, the Marsh game area dropped away to become real sea, and many of the Tasks were set there. There was even some tidal effect to bear in mind when you chose a tree to rest in.

By Adeline's reckoning she had been left on the northern border, facing back towards the distant city as she waded, and with the sea on her left. The question now was where to head for rest, for food and water. When she was needed for a Task, she would be found at once by the cameras: the hidden speakers would blare her name, summoning her. But that wouldn't be for a day or two; they'd allow time to acclimatise. Until then her only duty was to survive.

A meagre quantity of food and water was distributed daily on the platforms and in Paradise. Apart from that, there were a few poor fish in the water, if one could catch them, and all the other living things, birds especially, that still clung hopelessly to this drowning piece of land. Statistics showed that those establishing themselves in Paradise early on had the best chance of lasting out. But these statistics weren't referring to Scroats.

Still shivering, Adeline made her way through the

flood until she found what she wanted: a gathering of low thorn bushes on a strip of mud. A suitable hiding place. There she forced a way between the plants and, stripping off her tunic, reached over between her shoulder blades to where the band of tape lay flat on her skin, imprisoning a sliver of fish from her last meal in the city. As she'd hoped, the tape had passed unnoticed in the searching process. Next, the awkward boots came off, and with relief she sank her bare feet onto the mud.

There. Each lace would make a line, the scrap of fish would do for bait, and for the hooks? She unscrewed the tiny handlight they'd given her and, discarding the rechargeable power unit, levered out the tiny spring inside. Yes ... with a little careful work that would make two fine hooks. She'd do well enough without the light.

As she worked she kept her head up, and her eyes focussed on the next shadowy clump of bushes, a few metres off. It made the job slow and a little clumsy, but she had practised dismantling and reassembling the wall lamp and the toilet flush system without light each night in the FTL building (for want of something better). With the camera above her ear echoing her own gaze, rule-breaking was a dicey business. She had a feeling that it wouldn't occur to the New Visions at all, in their enthusiasm for the game.

When she was done, her teeth were chattering and her lower body and legs were numb. She fumbled her tunic back over her head, rolled the improvised fishing lines into two tiny parcels tucked into the waistband of her leggings, and waded out once more into the salty black flood.

'What's the silly little bint up to?' murmured the FTL monitor detailed to keep tabs on this particular player. 'Bad toilet trip? Period pains? Just plain petrified now she's out there? Doesn't she realise she'll *die* in that water?'

'Hell, Chaney,' said the next monitor, grinning from his own observation station, 'isn't that the idea? Why draw it out? I'd pay the penalty and move on as quickly as you can, if I were you.' His own charge, four-teen-year-old Aspen Sinclair, had already closed in on Paradise, moving stealthily and powerfully through the marsh water in textbook fashion. Now he was safely ensconced on one of the nearest tree platforms for the night, waiting for daylight to make his assessment of when and how to enter the wooden village. His monitor, Van-Quentin, had every reason to suppose that this solid little performer would earn him yet another sweepstake bonus from the monthly pot by getting to the mountains, to Black. Poor Chaney had already drawn two standard Visions in her last four players and hadn't dined out for three months. If your player didn't make it through Brown phase you put twenty credits into the sweepstake. If they died or were eliminated within the first week, that rose to forty credits. A death in the first twenty-four hours cost half a month's pay.

Chaney said, 'Shut up, smart arse. You watch your guy, I'll watch mine.' But she shook her head again, puzzled. Not for the first time she wondered why Friend's tapes for the opening phase hadn't been shown. Just get out of that water, you strange, bald little Scroat, she thought. Stay alive till seven o'clock tomorrow night and you'll have done fine by me.

Chaney might have saved her breath. Having wasted precious time apparently fiddling about in the bushes near her drop-off point, Adeline did indeed find a tree to climb. Not one with a platform, just one with con-venient low branches and a leaning trunk to support her for a while. There she closed her eyes and regulated her breathing into a slow, steady tide, building up a core of heat, stilling the trembling of her limbs. Her infra-red camera showed an unwavering shot of bare black twigs against a dark background.

'Well, she's either sleeping or gone hypothermal on me,' Chaney told Van-Quentin.

But ninety minutes later (to Chaney's frustration, just as she was clocking off) a squall of fresh rain skittered down, the wind started to whip the twigs back and forth, and the girl's eyes flicked back open. She climbed easily back down into the water and felt for her two lines where they swam limp and fishless at the base of the trunk. No matter. Head tilted up to the rain, she untied and re-coiled them and started moving towards the eastern centre of the Marsh: towards Paradise. The map in her tunic pocket was useless without her light, but the luminous hands of the compass guided her, and there had been a map of the Marsh to study and learn in the information pack at the FTL building.

As she went, mostly swimming now as the tide and the slope of the land brought the water up to her chest, she remembered a time as a tiny child – it must have been before Clarissa and Mira and Jan had come looking for her – when she had been at a place in the mountains where there was a spring, clear and icy cold. It had been the spring that had fed her old lakeside village, Le Porge, with drinking water. Maman had taken her up the hill for a picnic and she had wandered off to watch the water spill from the rock into a cascade of pools, heading down the sharp slope.

How she had *felt* things in those days: the smells, the tastes, the touches on her skin of soil or rock or water. When she had watched the hypnotic, miraculous manifestation of water from sun-blasted rock for a time, it had seemed only natural to step into the freezing flow. At first there had been a shock that was at once delicious

170

and painful. The day had been so hot. Then, soon, she had discovered real deep cold for the first time in her life. Her teeth had rattled in her head. It was fascinating. She'd made herself stand very still and closed her eyes, determined to explore the secrets of this new feeling. And then, after a longer while again, the cold had become part of her and as natural and reassuring as Maman's breast. When she was pulled from the water an hour later, her little body stiff and blue, she'd opened her eyes and smiled.

'Do you know, I turned into the spring, Maman,' she'd said. 'I could feel deep down into the ground. And how happy the water is to come out here and skip down to the lake.'

In those days each new experience had made her ever more sure of her own immortality.

Adeline took the best part of an hour to reach Paradise, slipping through the Marsh like a watersnake, only the nub of her head breaking the flood's surface. She embraced the cold as she had as a child. The rain puckered the water and the reeds and branches flapped restlessly, but in her mind other memories cartwheeled gently, some familiar, some strange, unlocked perhaps by that other memory. Pristine, icy landscapes where your breath hung ghost-like in the air and spirits danced amongst the trees. Great buildings thronged with ugly, power-hungry people gorging themselves on rich foods. A lonely view from a high window, stretching across a clutter of buildings to a clear strip of grey water – that one was familiar. And suddenly, Dominic was there, back with her again, close, so close. His soft surprised laugh sounded close to her ear and his fingers brushed her belly, like a fire in the cold and the darkness.

She knew what she needed. Another player, an NV, somewhere alone and asleep. As luck would have it the player she found was Aspen Sinclair, lying across his platform, breathing the deep sleep of the fearless. She waited as still as rock to be sure, then wormed up the trunk to his platform, checked the camera angles, took what she needed, and dropped down again.

By the time she got back to a suitable place to lie up for the day, she was exhausted and numb. She had strength enough to warm herself again – just – and to reset her fishing lines with face averted, but no more. As the light spread over the Marsh, she wriggled further into her chosen cluster of reeds, within sight again of the red tubing, and fell asleep. And so she was oblivious to the shouts echoing from deeper in the zone as new players sought equal status with old, and as a handful of NVs from yesterday's transport went whooping and crashing through the floodland in search of the little shaven-headed Scroat.

# THE REF

Jan Barbieri came often to the rooms high in the FTL tower. Why? To jerk off? To gloat? To reassure himself that the Lady still held on tight to her little prisoner?

Yes, for all of those reasons.

The Ref and Jan had always known each other. They'd come through the nursery together. In a way, the game they played now was the game they'd played as infants and ever since. At least, that's how it seemed to the Ref. The tiny, surprising, steel core of determination not to be completely broken was one of his earliest memories, and one of the only ones remaining to him intact: a memory of a sense, a feeling, rather than an event. With Jan he'd always been ragged, bloodied, shamed . . . but never quite beaten.

Perhaps that was the greatest reason for the visits. To see if the final defeat had occurred.

Today's visit was different from the start. Today's visit crackled with disquiet, though much of it ran to the usual formula.

'Good morning, Creature. You're looking tired,' Jan said, stalking in unannounced and standing before him, hands on hips. 'You're not coming down with something I hope? Maybe we should get the medics to check you over. I can't pull the show, you know. Not even for a sick Creature.'

'I'm fine, you gutless bastard. Don't worry about me.'

Jan liked that and smiled. He liked his prisoner to rail at him and insult him. It proved all was right with the world, the natural order of things undisturbed. 'So, you're fine. Good. Very good.' He was glancing about the room, restlessly. 'And you're off to the Marsh again this morning?'

'You know I am.'

'Hmm.' Jan went to the little travel-bag standing open on the table and started idly to poke around inside. He pulled out the packet that contained the teasing, impregnated masks and glanced up to meet the Ref's eyes. 'You know, don't you, that if you ever tried to betray me, I'd order the drug withheld. You'd be mad within a day or two. Dead in under a week. In terrible pain.'

Breakfast – the usual struggle, the usual relief – had been only an hour ago. The Ref's body was relaxed; his unreliable mind was for the moment purring and flexing, travelling simultaneously along many routes, like the orange Caplink wagons on their interweaving metal paths. He sharpened at once on the threat and tried to see the reason for it. Jan didn't usually bother with threats in his case: what would be the point? He wondered, strangely calm, if his attempts to wean himself from the Lady had been discovered. It was a delicate situation. He felt in his mind and heart for the right response, and said aggressively, 'Do it, then. Just bloody do it. You think I care?'

Jan laughed again. 'Bravely spoken! But you're full of it now, aren't you? Ambrosia! I can hear it singing round your veins. An hour or two late with your dose, though, and you'd be begging me like a dog. Woof woof.'

The Ref relaxed. He hadn't been discovered. And yet still he *was* being threatened. What, he wondered, had disturbed Jan's peace of mind? What was he poking around for?

The searching of the bag stopped and the Ref went to repack it, smoothing and folding the disturbed clothing under Jan's watchful, mocking gaze. From the cupboard he took two of his suits for the show and folded them in on top, dropping the packet of masks in last. Then he fastened the bag and looked around to check he had everything. And still the other man loitered, watching him.

Jan said absently, as if talking to himself, 'I had a piece of news from France, the other day. From the mountains. Do you remember France, Kay? Do you remember the hot, hot mountains there? What a place!'

This was it. *This* was the reason for the visit. A Caplink wagon slid comfortably into its station. The Ref struggled to remember anything about France. Anything important. He felt that there *was* something about that place, something painful and strange, if only he could dredge it up from his drowned, fuzzy memory. But things leaked from his mind now, without constant reminders.

Jan clapped him on the shoulder. 'Your face! What a study. You couldn't act that, could you? Not that great hole where your life used to be. No, you've answered me: there's nothing there. Is it the drug or the shame, I wonder, that's wiped your memories away?'

'Drop dead.' The white anger flared in the Ref and he took a step towards the hated waxy features, muscles tensing. So near to Jan. So near to snapping that neck. The guards at the door took out their weapons as Jan skipped back a pace, still mocking.

'Oh, not for many years yet, Kay. And you won't know anything about it – you'll be long gone. Have a fun trip now.'

It was strange the way even his emotions separated out these days. When the Ref was alone again he was boiling with fury and impotence and hatred – Jan always sparked off those old, familiar feelings – and yet another part of him was elated. It was as if he was a bystander watching the scenes of his own life. Yes, putting the rage aside, he was quite excited. Another puzzle had arrived and touched him, so soon after the shaven-headed girl. It vibrated in his core. Something was bothering Jan. Something about France. With a little effort he should be able to hang on to this too, as he was hanging on to the fact of the girl. It would be food for him for the days to come. An unknown block of substance to chip away at. The gods knew that he needed *something* to latch on to.

A man put his head around the door – one of his own, familiar minders. 'Twenty minutes, sir. Shall I take your bag up ready?'

'Yes, thank you.'

Twenty minutes. Just enough time to soothe himself with a little music. He went into the room with the oval window, running as usual with streamlets of water, and took his place behind the bank of instruments.

And became himself.

This was the deepest memory of all, another one that needed no events to define it. The memory of his soul journeying through sound. His fingers flashed over the keys and pads and switches, his face slack and peaceful. He was Jan's Creature no more. And somewhere hovering in the chords and harmonies, a taste that was France and mountains and something else revolved slowly, just beyond his reach.

No matter. He was beyond caring for the moment.

It would come, or it wouldn't. That was the nature of life.

Interestingly, the girl, the Scroat girl, had kept mostly out of sight for her first three days in the Marsh.

A few hours and a short hop later, the Ref sat at his little desk in the mobile control centre, leafing through the progress reports for surviving Brown players, while the make-up people smeared fleshy goo on the tiny patches of skin visible around his costume and adjusted and brushed spotless the tasselled black-and-silver clothing. He'd be prompted on background again if necessary and could easily add voiceovers at the end of each day of action, even reading from a script if he wished; but with the diminished dose of Ambrosia – the fire was already rippling up his calves and forearms – he'd do well to use every chance to take necessary information on board. One bad slip and Jan would be back in his rooms, carrying out the terrible threats for real.

The Fit To Live lackeys, tiptoeing round him, thought him every inch the professional.

He found little to surprise him in the paperwork ... except for the girl. Usually the no-hopers, the old-line Visions, the occasional Scroats, would by the second or third day have been forced to seek the shelter and the food offered by Paradise, or at least by one of the tree platforms. By then they would be weakened by cold and hunger, perhaps feverish, and in poor shape to 'convince' other stronger players to cede thcm supplies. It was a metaphor for the world to come. These weak latecomers would be challenged to individual combat or simply chased away, pushed back down into the cold black water. Players that did not establish themselves in the better spots early, when their strength was intact, were a poor bet. Everyone knew that.

Jan's promise to Briton was to be established *first* in the new world order as the land was eaten away by the oceans.

In Friend's case, however, according to the notes made by her monitor, Petra Chaney, no attempt had been made to access any of the hotly-contested daily supplies, or to enter Paradise. On her first night she had set off, swimming towards these benefits, but had apparently changed her mind on finding a well-placed tree platform already occupied by an NV. Her nerve seemingly broken, she'd swum all the way back to the periphery of the game area, cold and foodless. Why she hadn't died of exposure that first night was a mystery. Since then she'd mostly stayed hidden, day and night. Especially during the day, when certain of the NVs were out hunting her in their predictable lumbering way.

Chaney's growing sympathy for the girl came through in the sparse report, but that could be put down to the money she'd saved by Friend not dying yet. (The Ref knew all about the sweepstake.) The girl's low profile might be because her will to continue had drained away, or that she was too ill to compete further.

According to the edits log, few of Chaney's suggested selections of footage had been included in the short update shows that ran throughout the day. They'd been judged too dull, despite the fascination that was generated by a Scroat reaching this phase of the competition. Her lengthy night swim had made it onto screen, in brief highlighted form, but otherwise she hardly got a mention. Only the real FTL-heads, with an exorbitant subscription for continuous live-streaming, would see more.

The Ref was disappointed. He'd felt that Friend had the potential to become a screen presence. She could easily have won some sympathy and support with her striking looks, her strangeness. If only she could add some *fight* to the overall picture. Nothing caught the audience like grit in the face of terrible challenges. They weren't so interested in a dreamy, limp dish-rag.

What would those sadistic animals in the producers' office, back in the city, have planned for today, he wondered. He never knew until the last minute. Would they let Friend rot a little longer on her mudbank, waiting for her to push her surrender button? Or would they try and eliminate her quickly? A warning to those tempted to side with the weak, that the future would be a harsh one. There was no proof for it, but the Ref was fairly sure that certain formidable Scroats who made it to White were softened up before their set tasks. Something in the food perhaps, or threats: he didn't know. But here, the cameras saw all, heard all. That small, crazy, live-stream audience never slept. Here, the harsh environment and the games themselves had to make the producers' point.

He got his answer soon enough. He felt empty when he heard it. They'd decided to finish the girl.

The network of Tannoys strapped to the trees crackled with the names of those required for today's tasks, eight of them in all. A handful of small boats puttered off into the wind-lashed Marsh to retrieve these players, six of them from the sanctuary of Paradise, one from a tree platform, Friend from her bed of reeds. The Ref himself was ushered into his larger vessel, handed a waterproof itinerary for the day, and taken with his crew across the red boundary and through the flooded land to the deeper water on the eastern fringes of the playzone. There he saw lifting apparatus rearranging the great network of submerged cages that sometimes featured in the Tasks, whilst set designers with heated suits and oxygen cylinders plunged and bobbed like ducks around the maze of resin mesh, testing the Task, placing and adjusting underwater cameras, completing the trap.

Nearby, a bare Combat platform had been set up, slick with saltwater, and further out, where the swamp merged with white-topped waves, a series of floating marking points were being dropped for an Endurance task.

The Ref had eyes only for the cages and tunnels, disappearing grimly into the deeps. Item Three on his Itinerary, the last of the day's filming, read: *Underwater Combination event, comprising Endurance, Adaptability and Logic features. A maze survival race, with progress by one player impeding the other player. Duration: four minutes.* A print-out diagram was attached showing how the game worked. A note at the bottom said: *Participants – Asha and Friend.*

Why should he care? He was the Ref, his muscles burning, his mind savage from the Lady's caress. The rain, equally savage, blew into his eyes, stinging them.

'You!' he shouted at a woman placing a camera. 'Higher! The spray – think of the *spray*! Are you up to this job?'

His minions scurried, his lurking minders watched him from a distance – ready to slip on the leash – and gradually the boats arrived, bringing the filthy, brown-suited players, depositing them on one of the anchored platforms. There they were: five NVs, four of them looking well-fed, confident, unnatural, the fifth badly marked by a personal combat challenge some days ago; two old-line Visions, one of them white and pinched with fever; and Friend, who was . . . unchanged.

Three days in the freezing Marsh, without food, and although she was streaked with mud, barefoot, her scalp stained with a faint shadow where the hair had started to grow back, she was her old self. She sat upright and dry and detached in the stern of the boat that had picked her up. She stepped onto the platform, amongst the wolves, with easy balance and grace.

The Ref's anger and bitterness drained away. His gaze was fastened on the girl. He felt like a child, on the verge of some wonderful discovery.

'Sir? Sir? Are you feeling unwell? May I assist? Sir?'

He realised he was gripping the rail, breathing hard. He could not remember what he had been thinking. He straightened himself, turned to the fretting aide with a cold look, forced his consciousness down into the murky depths.

*Anger. Anger was his friend when the mind failed.*

'If everything is ready at last,' he said icily to the crew, 'let's start the fun.'

'OK, listen up,' a man near him shouted through a bullhorn. 'Item One – the Combat. Twenty minutes to the Combat. Let's hustle, people.' And then, cautiously, to the Ref himself: 'If you could come over to the Combat area to introduce this first event, sir? I have the detailed notes here . . .'

He did as the man asked. He pushed Friend far away from the blurred shapes and surging white fire of his mind, made his mocking introduction, his assessment of the players destined to confront one another with long-handled knives on the swaying, slippery surface. He blew the whistle for the Task to begin and saw the stronger of the two old-line Visions fight fiercely and uselessly until his thigh was opened by his NV opponent's blade, so that he collapsed screaming, fumbling frantically at the sur-render button at his throat before the next, fatal blow could come.

'*Attention! Attention!*' the automatic recording blared. '*All Brown players to stay where they are and desist any contact or action until further notice. Repeat. No Brown player to move, on pain of disqualification.*'

Then the system was shut off, the injured Vision treated under the hungry, intrusive eye of the camera, and taken away; and the announcement given over the Tannoy to resume normal activity.

Then a break. Forty scurrying minutes to get every-thing in position for the next event. The gale picked up still further, twirling the ridiculous clown's tassels on the Ref's suit, sending waves smacking viciously against the struts of the lifting gear and the scaffolding camera points. From the contestants' platform the four players down for the Endurance event watched the wild power of the swell mount. Two of the marking points were no longer visible behind the spray.

The Ref watched the waves too and thought of how easily he might lose his minders in that sea, when the time came . . . and then, with sudden, sticky longing, he imagined how soundly he might sleep in the water's caress. As he had once before, so long ago. Down, down, he'd gone, beyond the dappled sunlight. Unable to scream.

'OK sir, we're ready for you again.'

Once more the introduction. A mocking reference to the ugly cuts and bruises of the injured NV girl, a casual patronising dismissal of the white-faced Vision; a brief description of the course, the objects that had to be collected at each point. And a few short minutes later, blending just the right amount of respect and scorn, the confirmation that the two flawed players had been lost to the current, although searches were (of course) being carried out.

The Ref clung to his anger, to his desperation, so that the horror of it all did not overwhelm him, and the minions again nudged each other and murmured that he was inhuman, a machine, the perfect FTL presenter. They half envied, half despised him.

When he allowed himself to notice her again, he saw that Friend was also staring out at the waves. He could almost fancy that she had caught his own longing for oblivion. And such sadness. Such frail beauty.

'How long to the last event?' he asked, taking food from the box the crew had provided for him. No Loop-the-loop, just something to occupy his hands, his mouth. 'This place is a sorry shit-hole. I want to get this done quickly.'

'Sorry sir, we're still making adjustments for the next one. Them that designed it don't know what it's like, sir, laying on these underwater Tasks. Really they don't.'

'Hurry then.'

He wanted now to get it over, to extinguish Friend's little light and go back to normal. He wanted to be in his temporary quarters, alone, to fight the withdrawal pain. He didn't want to be encumbered by hope, or any emotion of the heart. It shook the tight line he walked so dangerously. The Lady demanded all of your heart.

In due course Friend and the NV girl, Asha, were brought forward for the cameras. Friend was no longer looking at the waves. She was holding the diagram of the task, given to her and her opponent, frowning. Asha, a head taller, striking in the contemptuous, rugged beauty of her features, had seen all she wanted to see in a quick, intelligent glance and stood arms folded, waiting.

And still Friend looked at the paper, blankly.

'So, here we are, folks, back at the Marsh. Testing our best and bravest. Applauding their efforts. Laughing at their failures.' The Ref laughed his own cold, wild stage laugh, chilling the future viewers where they marvelled at the harshness of existence in the comfort of their living spaces. 'Which brings me back to our next game, and especially to a mention of Friend, one of our big surprises from the White phase. Gutsy? Lucky? Just plain mad? Opinion is divided on this one. I can only tell you one thing for sure. They didn't allow the poor girl to bring her razor in here: another week and we'll have to send a stylist up. But hey, another week? Maybe we shouldn't count her chickens just yet, because our little Friend is coming up against an old favourite here. Asha – yes, you all know her! – veteran of twenty-three whole days in the Marsh and looking in awesome shape. And *this* will be her last Task before progressing to Black, if she makes it.

'These two girls have drawn one *hell* of a Combination event. Let me explain how it works . . .'

How it worked was simple. Each player had four minutes to pass through an underwater system of cages and reach the finish. The cages were bolted together into a simple maze. No lights or masks were to be provided, so the task would be 'blind'. No breathing apparatus was available. Each cage had a sprung gate leading into the next – you had to haul them back by means of a handle – and the gates could not be re-opened once you had passed through, so that there was no turning back. But most importantly, your own progress affected that of your opponent: as you opened your own gates, other, new gates would close in the parallel course, lengthening it, or changing the shape, or simply causing the other player to waste precious oxygen in surmounting the extra obstacles. If you went neck-and-neck it would be a matter of brute force: a question of who could manage to make the levers work for them, player against player.

The game had been tested, by riggers in diving suits. The initial, straight course, without any interference from an opponent, took only a minute. At its worst, against a strong opponent, it could become up to three and a half times the length. Endless, if you lost track and panicked in the gloom.

Four minutes' physical activity was drowning time. The Ref knew that any 'rescue' would be drawn out for a minute or two beyond that. Without doubt, Friend's pretty, slender corpse would be hauled dripping from the cages only quarter of an hour from now, pale as a mermaid. It was a clever touch. The watchers at home would sigh and shake their heads, moved by her effort and her beauty, despairing of her foolhardiness. They would not blame the producers as they might if she were cut by the wicked, long-handled knives. This way, she'd have been given a chance and found wanting. Who would be surprised?

The Ref groped for his starting whistle, numb with the inevitability of the girl's death. Still the waves called to him. The camera zoomed in on his face to catch the moment the game began; he was grateful for his uncomfortable, stifling mask, teasing his skin with its chemicals. As he raised the whistle to blow he vaguely saw Friend turn and murmur something to the NV called Asha. The taller girl, poised ready to dive into the opening to the maze, looked sharply round at her opponent. Her face was surprised, suspicious, angry, and then puzzled.

'Three, two, one . . .' He gave the starting signal and Asha, taking one last look at Friend, sprang vigorously forward, headfirst, down into the mouth of the initial cage. The other girl, the Scroat, in her dream world again, loitered on the platform, swung her arms in wide circles a few times, stretched up high, arching her spine, looking at the low, grey, skies. Then she too dived.

'Switch to underwater,' murmured a woman monitoring the different camera angles.

The main viewing monitor became abruptly murky green, disturbed by a thrashing of limbs, seen through the imprisoning mesh. The Ref found himself reaching for the microphone, if only to keep occupied. 'A strange start to this one, people of Briton. Our Friend didn't seem to want to go in at all. And who could blame her? It's icy in that water, I can promise you. Icy . . .' He halted, trying to make out the vague shapes in the cages. 'But Asha seems to have got off well. Powerful, coordinated, fearless, that's Asha. She seems to be in the third, no the fourth cage now. Moving well. Not too fast, just steady, pacing it nicely. And Friend? Where is she? Ah yes, Friend is . . .' He swore quietly, then covered the mike to ask, 'Am I seeing this right?' The woman by the little screens nodded, wide-eyed – 'Friend is *not* taking the straight course. I mean, she's not even *trying* those gates. She's taken one of the deviations and seems to know exactly which gates to take – which will be open, which locked against her. As soon as Asha triggers a change,

Friend is there, heading in the right direction. She's moving well, too, as steady as Asha, but then she'll have quite a lot further to go. At least twice as far. Will she make it? Despite her speed, she's not impeding her opponent. Of course she's triggering changes too, as she moves on – that's the game – but all the gates she's closing on Asha's course are just a little behind our NV. Hey, has this girl got a relative in the design team? Questions are going to have to be asked about this. It's so easy, so elegant, it's like a ballet.'

'That's one minute,' one of the crew whispered, timing the event.

'First contestant due out any time,' said the monitor woman. 'She's entering the last but one cage.'

The Ref suddenly made a decision. 'Start this thing up. Take me over there,' he said. 'I want to get a few words when they come out.'

The crew looked at each other uneasily. Interviews with Brown or Black players were rare, frowned on by the controllers in the city. Loquaciousness was not one of the talents that the programme showcased. 'We usually discuss this first,' someone said, 'don't we?'

'Are you questioning my judgement?'

'No, sir. No.'

The little electric engine was started and the vessel began to ease over to the finish. The Ref activated the mike again, signalling the mobile camera with him to track their progress.

'So what we're doing here is heading on down to see who comes out of this game, and just how they did it. I should make it absolutely clear that what I said just now was a joke. There is *no* possibility of cheating in these conditions. The contestants live night and day in this hostile environment, which you all know so well, and have no communication with the outside – except for when we pay them a visit, to make their little lives hell, of course. And as for the games, not even *I* know what they will be until just before the event.'

They'd reached the exits to the two submerged mazes now, the dark mesh squares showing just proud of the water. 'Bring us in close,' the Ref snapped, eyes flashing. 'Get that camera covering me *and* the water they're going to come out of.'

The rain was pounding into the restless seawater as the Ref squatted down in his boat near to where the players would emerge. Somewhere in the depths something was moving, strongly. The mesh shuddered and a few bubbles rose to the surface of one of the cages.

'Sir,' murmured the monitor woman, nervously, 'the potential for edits will be *severely* limited if we go at it like this, with you in shot and speaking as they actually come out.'

The Ref ignored her. He knew what he was doing. The two minders in the background slouched and watched, unconcerned by game business. He flicked the switch on his mike. 'Here we are. Are you getting this at home, viewers? There's something happening here, someone coming out. After – ' he checked the time-board – 'one minute and twenty-three seconds without oxygen or light, in icy water. Yes, here she comes, Asha is definitely coming . . . and *here she is*!'

The water frothed and erupted in the top cage as the big NV girl broke the surface, scrabbling for a handhold, gasping in breath, grinning, shivering.

The Ref signalled people forward. 'Here, we're going to help her out. You there, give her a hand. Asha Ryan, who will now go on to face the perils of the mountains. She's already done herself, and her family, proud. Extra privileges, credits, accommodation, they'll want for nothing. And a career in Special Forces could be hers if she wants it. All at the age of only fourteen. There we go – up you come, Asha. Get your breath back . . . and then tell us, tell the people at home, just what did little Friend say to you before you dived?'

Alarm was registered on the faces of his minions now. This was getting worse, more and more irregular. One player being asked about another. Jobs would be lost. The cameraman shot a look at the monitor woman but she simply shrugged. They had to have an ending to the event, on film. This was not like the White phase, where control was absolute.

Asha was still breathing hard, wrapped in a blanket, but alive with vigour and aggression. She shook her head and panted her response. 'I don't know. I didn't understand. She said I could start first, and to count ten seconds between each gate. I ...' She looked down, puzzled, thinking about it, 'I didn't want to do what she said. I thought: Little Scroat, shouldn't be here, trying to tell *me* how to play the game, I was angry with her, was gonna smash her, underwater maybe. But she said, "What have you got to lose?" And I thought about that when I dived and she didn't and it was right. I knew I was faster, stronger. There's no way she could have messed it up for me. But I was interested to see ... I counted, yeah.' She shook her head again. 'I don't know.' She grinned her big animal grin. 'But hey, I'm through!'

The Ref had stayed silent, hunched over, holding the mike for her to speak into. Now he turned to the camera, swaying a little with the motion of the boat.

He said softly, eyes glittering in their sockets, 'Isn't that strange, though? An NV taking advice from a Scroat?' A great shudder passed up his spine. He lost track of what he'd been about to say, but recovered well, sticking out a dramatic pointing arm to the mouth of the second maze. 'There!' he shouted. '*That's* where we'll see the answer. A corpse or a live human being. A winner or a loser. Which is what this game is all about.'

'Here she comes,' squeaked the monitor woman in his earpiece.

'Just keep the camera on that spot and keep me in shot,' the Ref replied shortly, his mike turned off now.

Silence fell. The Ref looked at the timeboard and saw that the game had continued for just over two minutes, though it seemed like twenty. He found himself willing the Scroat girl on, trying to lend her his own energy. The gods knew, her life was worth ten of his own miserable existence.

At last there were more bubbles on the water. Two or three fragile spheres resting briefly on the dark liquid: nothing like the turbulence of Asha's passing from the maze. Gradually, painfully slowly, a shape came into view below. A pale shape, bobbing upwards.

And then Friend was there, thin as a child, blue-white with cold, but with her eyes open and calm. She lay back on the water, breathing deeply, ignoring the cluster of people and equipment around her.

Not even the Ref could think what to say. His planned moment of drama slipped away.

Friend closed her eyes for a moment, her chest rose and fell in the clinging brown tunic and a little colour returned to her. Then she looked around, rolled over slowly in the water, smiled her brief faraway smile to the Ref and his minions, and swam at a snail's pace back to the contestant's platform, through the swell.

Wrapped in her blanket, Asha said distinctly, 'Shit. Look at that.'

'Cut,' said the monitor woman, 'and lose that last piece of audio.'

Adeline lay drenched on the platform, feeling it roll and shudder with the water. The hot blood pushed at the leaking valves inside her. In her weakness, the two worlds touched.

*We're playing their games together. You there and me here. En effet, it doesn't really matter where you engage with the universe, does it?*

Then she passed out.

# DOMINIC
## – day 57 –

I'm no longer interested in getting away from here. Father's done that much for me. This is as good a place as any for my life to be played out. Doesn't matter really, does it, where you are, where you engage with the universe? Could be a city, a prison, a hospital, a desert village, walking miles for clean water. What would I find out there that's better?

*Se mundumque vince.*

This hothouse (–3°C today) has got me hooked, if you like. Frank Barbieri punches me, on the arm or in the guts, where it won't show, twenty times a day, gets me in shit with the soldiers by messing my kit up, gets his mates to do the same, stops me sleeping, watches me like a weasel. The Major has a special eye on me too. His men squeeze every last drop of energy from us and then he asks a little more. Extra duties, polishing kit, stuff like that. He's never mentioned the roof tile.

Now I must just lie and imagine her grace in the moonlight.

Between him (the Major) and Frank I'm pretty much a wreck. My face has changed shape, my eyes are not familiar to me: they're hollow, empty. One by one, the ranks get whittled away, God knows where to. The larking about, the cockiness, the sex and everything, that's all been burned away from anyone who's left. (You wouldn't recognise the noisy coach-load who arrived a month ago.) I wouldn't be one of them, one of these survivors, if it weren't for Father, would I? I hope that's right anyway, but perhaps I'm fooling myself. The survivors are tough, uncompassionate, focussed on themselves. A lot of snakes, all with a certain background, aeons of families who've got themselves preferment at court, watched their friends die on battlefields, defended the establishment and the rotten, poisonous old order that's sailed Britain into this shit.

Look at me, writing this. You think I'm better?

Ruth moves on her quiet, contained path amongst us. Like everything's been reversed from the ancient history of school life, where she was wild Witchbitch and we were the quiet, sober ones. Now we're savages and she's ... what?

She's the only kind of masthead I can nail my colours to now, beyond just making it through the days. She plays with the rules, makes fun of them. She gets as much shit as ever, though. The ones who are left are exactly the ones – the sort, I mean – who always hated her at Bede's. That old stock. She does nothing to provoke them, but she is herself. They close in on her in their cowardly little knots when they have the chance. Frank – damn him – has sensed that she means something to me – and talks about her in disgusting terms, endlessly, what he'd like to do to her etc. The girls are worse. Like she shows them something they don't want to see.

No, I'm talking crap. There's been no reversal. Things are as they've always been.

Wake up, Dominic.

Do you know, I have moments now when I am happier than I'd ever thought possible. Somehow this all connects together.

Some facts then. Seven more people came when Father came, and have stayed here. They're not soldiers. They're human beings. They keep themselves to themselves, except often one of them will come and watch a section training or doing one of our puzzles. Three at least are American (or Canadian?), one is from eastern Europe. Czech, I think. The others are British, two with Scottish accents. They don't just watch, they take notes, with clipboards or notebooks.

Today, for example, the Czech woman came to see Silver Section. We're down to five in Silver now. Siobhan's still there, of course, prowling like an underfed puma, claws always out, though her friend Kelly is history. We were inside for once. In the new concert hall, recent jewel in the school crown, product of lottery money plus parents' cheques, now a dusty, empty great shed, curtains torn down, broken glass underfoot, a good spattering of bird shit. The Wonderbras played there in last year's Christmas entertainment. We wore silver foil suits and green wigs. We were drunk.

This morning we started with a reflex thing. The grunt had a whistle and we had to do a set movement, depending on the signal he blew. Beat our chests, hit the deck, freeze for ten seconds (cut short and superseded if another signal got blown) etc. There were eight signals, eight responses, and we did them again and again for about forty minutes. The Czech woman sat on the stage watching, muffled up in her great furry coat and pink bobble hat, swinging her legs, scribbling in her notebook. She thought it was a great game.

Then the grunt brought out some mouldy old P.E. mats and taught us three judo throws. You never know what's on the menu, never question it. We spent another hour learning these, practising on each other. They had to be perfect for the grunt, done by the book.

I think everyone's just one finger's breadth from madness. The rage that went into those judo throws. The smell of our unwashed bodies locking together, grappling, swearing. The desperation of it all.

'No. Do it again!' the grunt said, over and over. 'Putting your heart into it's all right, but if you let anger tense up your muscles, you won't manage the throw.' Again, we practised until it was automatic. One throw to use against

a person coming at you from behind, one from in front, one
for the side.

'Now ... two mile run, at the double, through the woods
and back, to the perimeter guard house. Get checked off
there. Back here outside this building in fourteen minutes.
Anyone longer misses lunch.'

And then what? When we got back, just about ready to
die, they'd fixed boards across the windows (must have had
them ready somewhere) and the hall was in total darkness,
except for a tiny light, a torch or something, down where
the stage must have been.

'Now,' said the grunt's voice, when the door had shut
behind us and we were blind, 'each of you will cross the
darkened hall towards the light, retrieve the object you
find there and return to me here. You will be timed doing
this. On your way you will find various obstacles, which you
should deal with as you see fit. At random moments I will
be using my whistle to signal a response, as we practised
earlier. You will respond immediately and correctly to this.
You will also encounter opponents as you cross the room
who will attempt to impede you. Selecting the correct
throw, according to the origin of these attacks, you will
disable the opponents in the manner we have practised
this morning, and resume the activity. You will be ob-
served throughout the activity by means of night-sights,
and marked on all aspects. Your opponents will also have
night-vision. Any questions?'

What could you possibly ask?

We were sent back outside so our eyes wouldn't adapt,
and waited as they called people through the test, one at a
time. I was third. I kept my eyes shut while I waited to
keep the pupils large, but it didn't help much.

The grunt held me by the shoulders in total darkness in
the inner doorway. 'Ready ...' the torch at the other end
blinked twice, '... go!'

Ran forward and almost crippled myself on some large

object made of metal bars, climbed over, whistle went as I got down – windmill with my arms – set off again but there's someone pounding in from the side, crashing into me, just manage to throw them round over my hip, but fall myself in the process and have to scrabble up, whistle again, twice in succession – five press-ups, cut down to two, and sing Happy Birthday – then taut strands of barbed wire in my path, cutting me, to crawl under and immediately there's another attacker coming for me, from the front, better throw this time, dipping and twisting to let him go over my shoulder, then sprinting to the torch, slipping horribly on oil or something on the floor, crashing into stage, knocking my head, trying to stand and feeling dizzy and shagged out, taking the object – a china cup and a foreign voice says 'Don't break it, for more marks' – and setting off back, oil first, remember, careful, but whistle goes again and I slip anyway, cup OK, signal to do what? ... beat my chest like an ape I think, then off to the wire, under it, another three signals – march on the spot, can't remember number two and freeze for ten seconds – then on seven seconds a flurry of activity from behind, attacker number three, who lets out a little sound at the last second, a sound of anticipation of pleasure, and I know from that that it's Frank, and I can't help it, I sidestep all his brutal force and hear him go into the metal bars, and then over and out.

Penalty ... missing lunch. Ruth won't be getting any extras from me today. And the Czech woman comes up to me outside and says, 'Why did you do that? You're not an animal. You hurt that other boy very much. He is quite bruised and a little cut. '

She seemed upset by it. (Why?) I didn't know how to answer. So many reasons I could give but her stupid naivety left me without any words. I just shook my head at her, 'I'd do it again,' and she walked off in her bundle of fur, thinking me beyond hope.

Braced now for the Barbieri regime to double its horror.

And here's a thing. I was standing outside the Geography department over lunch for my punishment. Supposed to stay there in the cold until told I could move. But I climbed in. I've always liked the Geography room: the maps in their different projections, the rock samples, the smell of chalk. Anyway, I thought I'd poke around for five minutes.

The furniture was gone. Burned I guess, in the soldiers' quarters or the Major's fireplace. The storeroom at the back was broken open but they'd left it pretty much untouched, thinking it didn't have anything interesting inside. Just textbooks, slide projector, crap like that ... and a locked metal filing cabinet.

How could they have known? They couldn't, but *I* did. I just knew.

Davis is a methodical sort. Dry and dusty as the room he teaches in, but with a twinkle of humour. Takes his CCF very seriously. I scoured his storeroom, felt behind and under everything, but finally the keys were in a box of rubber bands, on one of the shelves. And inside the cabinet? Rifle bolts, oiled and wrapped lovingly in cloth, laid out in compartments next to their serial numbers.

The keys are now in a new place.

I was back outside, cold and bored, when the grunt came to tell me to rejoin Silver for the afternoon's torture.

# – day 61 –

I'm properly alive, awake for the first time.

I laugh at their tests and their soldier games.

Nothing can touch me now. Ruth's taste is on my lips. One of her hairs is on my filthy shoulder.

I want to dance. I've remembered who I am. My life was only waiting for this.

After supper tonight I wandered around, going back to Orchard, taking my time, putting off the evening session with Frank Barbieri I guess. Cutting it fine with the curfew.

And suddenly there was shouting. Mr Beckett, outside the Head's entrance, pissed as a fart, staggering round, screaming at the windows.

*'Yer great overblown ponce. I'll have yer! I'll bloody cut your liver out if yer keep bothering my Ruthie. Call yourself a man? Come out here, yer bastard, just come out here ...'*

Much more like this, all slurred and tearful. Poor guy.

I ran up to him. I pulled him away. I talked to him. Soldiers were coming running, but I told them it was OK, I'd get him home. Somehow I convinced them. I think they pitied him too. 'Just get 'im to keep 'is trap buttoned,' the sergeant said, 'an' not start something as he can't finish, however good 'is reasons.' 'Drunken old pillock,' said another, 'going to get his head blown off.'

I got him moving, got him back to the lodge. He was crying. 'You're the only one, lad. The only bloody one here with any decency. Why you bothering with their crap, eh? Why you getting into all that muck? Unnatural muck

197

and tinkering. What kind o' future will that be, eh? Get out while you can, that's what you should do.'

'What are you talking about?' I asked. 'What else could I do? And where do you get your booze?'

'Where? *Where?* That's a bloody good one, that is. Where do I get it? From bloody *him,* o' course, him who calls himself Major. Major, my arse!'

Where was the mild little groundsman? I wondered if he was like this at home, when he drank. Poor Ruth.

I said, 'Why would he give you drink?'

He looked at me in disbelief, spat on the ground. 'Time to grow up, eh, Dominic? You can't be that wet behind the ears.'

We were back at his cottage now. The neat little fence had gone, so we could walk right up to the door. I got him in. It was dark, cold, damp, he started a coughing fit, I looked for anything to make a fire, but there was nothing. None of Ruth's chopped wood. She came in while I was on all fours, ferreting by the grate in the gloom.

'Don't bother. They took it all.'

She was a soft shadow, outlined in the doorway by the evening light. Part of me.

Her dad was slumped in a tatty armchair, wheezing, muttering.

I said, 'He was making a racket, outside the Head's office. Shouting at the Major. I don't know if he heard ... The soldiers did.'

'Someone will tell him.'

I stood up. 'Is there anything I can do?'

She said, 'Come outside a moment.'

'Yes yes ... you young uns enjoy yerselves,' old Beckett warbled.

I went out behind her, crunching on the snow, into the tree shadows beyond, where the fence had run. She stopped and turned back to face me. I stopped too and waited.

'Come here.'

I went.

She opened her arms and I opened mine and we held each other. Softly, experimentally. It was like coming home. Everything about her was perfect, magical. We didn't speak. We held on to each other, not tightly and smothering but like cradling a pillar of wafer-thin glass or a trembling wild animal. I was amazed by her shape and smell, how thin she was, how warm, how alive.

After a while we drew apart far enough to look at each other.

We did that for a long time.

I said, 'I watched you from over there, early one morning, doing your exercises. I wanted to keep you safe.'

She was nodding, 'Yes.'

'And on the assault course.'

'Yes.'

We kissed then.

Her mouth was soft as a snowflake. As rich and warm as cream.

'You should go. You'll miss your curfew.'

I ran back, crying, laughing, taking the night paths of Bede's. I knew no soldier could catch me. I let myself into Orchard.

Frank was there, in 0-17, lying back with his hands behind his head. He knew at once, but I didn't care. I couldn't hide the light in me.

He said, 'Oh, I see. Like that, was it?'

I said, 'Come on Frank. Let's forget all the shit. Let's try and get something good going. We could get on OK. We did before.'

He said, 'I don't think so.'

He got off his bed and came and hit me in the guts, twice. I was gasping and doubled up. 'I don't think so,' he said again.

But I didn't respond. He didn't draw me in. I realised it didn't matter. Nothing matters but Ruth.

# CRANE

'Hey,' said Anton. 'So you went for Pax recruitment. Lightspeed. What was it like?'

'Yeah, I went for it. The tests were easy. The officer in charge was a bit screwed, though. Too old, I guess. You know how some people are weird about things, can't think logically, don't react the right way?'

'Yeah. Tainted blood maybe.'

Crane nodded, pleased that Anton understood so easily. 'Yeah. Tainted blood. Something like that. But think . . . this was an officer in Pax!'

Anton shrugged. 'Give it time, dude. Even the Leader says it'll take time, to flush the impurities through.' He nodded towards the work going on on the rotten old quayside. 'It all helps. Think how many this will bring out. We could come back down here tonight.'

Crane's father shivered and said hastily, 'Look boys, they're signalling for the first demolition.'

A horn sounded down below and men and women were seen to be scurrying away, sheltering behind blast screens. A ripple of anticipation went round the hillside, the crowds crammed into the sloping streets overlooking the water. Then there was a puff of white, a cloud that had materialised in the blink of an eye at the base of three or four blocks of buildings, and a crack like thunder.

Slowly, majestically, the ancient stonework tottered and crumpled in on itself, leaving a sprawl of rubble, an occasional strut still pushing skywards in the midst of it. Dust rose and was whipped away to the north and east by the savage wind. Those that stood in its path – not the NVs or their families; they'd chosen more wisely – screwed their eyes shut, bent their heads against the sudden abrasive storm. And then in only a minute it was over, and the engineers were moving in once more to fix new explosives to the dock structures, the cranes and wagons and warehouses that sagged into the black tide.

A great cheer went up for the first explosion. People waved their flags. The waters were rising but the Leader was taking real action. Freeing valuable space. Nobody had dared knock buildings down for many years in the city. It had been argued that every structure was an asset, a resource not to be squandered. But only the Scroats had benefited here, teeming into the decaying stonework as they arrived from their flooded farms, clustered like rats in the incoming ships, or driven down to the waterside by the neighbours that they had known from their unfortunate birth. The random jumble of useless buildings, and the random jumble of useless genes they housed, were overdue for removal.

Briton was to be a tight ship, as the Leader called it, and suitably enough, a large proportion of the space being cleared today was to be used for docking facilities for the smart, new black ships that lurked for the moment outside the tidal barrier. Part of the Leader's plan for the future. The product of ten painful years of metal rationing and reclamation by the state.

Following the first blast, there were cries and screams, curses and shouts from the demolition site. Figures began flitting away from the debris; some limping, or clutching their ears, or simply dragging themselves up the streets a little way, to collapse before the crowds.

'How about that Friend, though?' said Anton cheerfully. 'She could give us a chase, couldn't she? And she'd be worth the catching, that one.'

Crane had known that Anton would bring up the girl. She was the talk of the city, the talk, even, of the NV cells. Debate raged over whether Asha had done correctly in following Friend's request to wait ten seconds between each submerged gate. Was it cheating? Was it logical behaviour? Had Asha been pitying of Friend because the other girl was clearly so unfit for the competition? Generally the NV females were less forgiving of Asha than the males. *They* would not have made such a mistake, they said.

Crane himself was deeply confused by what had happened in the underwater game. He would have preferred not to have to talk about it because, for the first time in his life, he did not have a clear view.

'Yeah.' He tried to summon a smile, to give a semblance of his usual hunger for the hunt. 'Yeah, she'd be something. Give us quite a chase.'

Anton clapped him on the arm, laughing his big laugh. 'You'd find a way to deal with her though, Crane, eh?'

'Yes. Yes, I would. Lightspeed.'

He'd imagined it, of course, imagined doing sex to her or doing violence to her. Yet there wasn't enough of her to grab onto in his mind to make these images work. No weakness or bravado or pleading or rage. No explanation to what she did or how she behaved. It left a hole in his mind when he considered it. It was horrible how many people seemed to be a little like that – the Pax officer and the people at Portable Road and the other woman Scroat they'd hunted not long ago – but Friend was the worst by far.

And then he ended up *pretending* feelings. Politeness for the old lady, desire to hunt for Anton. Where was the sense in it? Why should he pretend?

'She's been lucky, up to now,' someone said, near where they were standing.

'I didn't think much of that last Task,' said another. 'You couldn't make out *what* was happening under the water.'

'You're not saying there was a fix?'

'No! No, of course not! But *she* could have been up to something: you know her kind.'

The topic was taken up by more and more people as they waited for the next blast. FTL always stirred strong feelings.

Crane's mother said faintly in the midst of the hubbub, 'Maybe she's just good at things like that. That's all right, isn't it? No need to find some horrible reason for it.'

Her son heard and looked at her. He thought, *Is it all right?* No it wasn't, it definitely wasn't, but he couldn't say quite why. His mother quailed under his hard, thoughtful gaze but did not look away. Her bravery surprised him too.

Soon, the next wave of explosions were signalled and let off. The ancient, rusting cranes toppled half into the harbour, sending up a plume of surf. Then a third and smaller blast was rigged, for anything that was left. When the dust had again been harried away by the wind, the watchers were facing a huge expanse of rubble, sloping away gently to the water, and a view right across the harbour to the flood walls on the far side, beyond which there was drowned wasteland and the last few stretches of the stiltway that had once led all the way to France.

'Well,' said Crane's mother, 'that was nice, wasn't it? Nice to be all out together, as a family. Are you hungry now, boys? We've got sandwiches.'

'What are yours?' Anton's mother said, holding up her own packet.

'Krill paste and sea leaf. What are yours?'

'*Mackerel* paste and sea leaf.'

The women laughed.

Anton said, 'Well, you can take the sea leaf out of mine. It's inedible.' And then, 'Hey, Crane, let's go and eat down there. We might get some idea of where the survivors have headed.'

'I'm not sure it's permitted,' said Crane's father.

The boys took the food and pushed their way through the crowds, down to the demolition site. Crane felt a little better at once. He did not like being out with his parents. The experts were packing up their tools, winding in reels of cable. They gave the two NVs a brief glance but nobody challenged their right to be there. Indeed, other NVs were also detaching from family groups and picking their way down to the blasted waste-land, perhaps lured by the stench of Scroat, perhaps equally uncomfortable with their Vision parents.

'They'll bring the 'dozers and the gangs into this mess today or tomorrow,' Anton said. 'Wipe it clean for the new facilities. I expect the stone can be used in new flood defences.'

'Yes.'

They went, chewing the food, amongst the toppled cranes and twisted tracks, right to where the water lapped at the debris. From time to time one or other would say, 'One caught under there I think . . . there's a piece of clothing.' Or: 'Blood in the dust there. Look.' Or: 'Two on the move down there. They're going to try and hole up next to the Barrier, I bet.'

'Or get through it and leave the city altogether.'

Anton gave Crane a pitying glance. 'Leave the city? Where would they go? They wouldn't last two minutes.'

'That girl did. Friend.'

'Oh . . . *her* again.' He grinned. 'You getting hot under the collar, dude?'

Crane ignored him. 'Look. What's that?'

'Don't know. It's made of copper, from the corrosion.

A statue, maybe? Looks old. Just part of the junk, now: it'll be gone in the morning.'

Crane went closer to the rotted, little green pillar, jutting out of the water's edge. 'Look. Writing on it. A spiral, stretching round.' He squatted down to look better. '*Strong* ... something ... *buried deep* ... Then it goes behind, I'm not wading into *that* filth. Then ... *mouth closed on* ... That's all I can make out.'

'*"Blessed Children, You are given this sleeping serpent,"*' Anton recited, disgustedly. 'Prophecy song or poem of one of the superstitious serpent cults or religions, first appeared soon after the great climate changes. Finally wiped out by our Leader in the purges twelve years ago.'

'Yes,' Crane nodded, 'I remember now.'

'Piece of junk. They'll wipe it all clean, don't worry.'

They wandered a little further down towards the smudge in the distance that was the massive tidal barrier, and next to it the shadow of the black ships, then turned and walked back up the hill.

'Hey!' said Anton, and threw a few punches at Crane.

'Hey!' said Crane, parrying easily, powerfully, and lazily sweeping Anton's legs from under him with his foot.

Their parents were all laughing at something, looking more animated than usual, Crane noted, the two fathers sharing a bottle of beer. He disapproved. 'We ought to go,' he said, 'I need to shower.'

'Later?' Anton asked him.

'Yeah, sure, later. I'll call Lily and the others.'

He hooked up his terminal when he got home and mailed some other NVs. Then he found that he had a message waiting. From Pax.

*Dear Applicant*, it said, *We require your presence for a second interview. This will be held on Tuesday next at 10am. Your school instructors have been notified and have approved your absence. You need bring nothing with you.*

'All *right*,' said Crane to himself, heading for the shower. 'So I'm in. They got that right, at least.' He wondered if he would get the black-and-silver uniform immediately. He supposed that he wouldn't be allowed to wear it on the hunts. But then, he'd have a more important contribution to make as a Pax recruit. All the more reason to enjoy tonight, though. Yeah, he'd really go for it tonight.

He raised his head in the hot spray and howled like a wolf.

When he set off for his interview, proud now to have a disruption to his routine, a formidable machine of flesh and bone and intelligence moving fast along the streets, Crane's mind was full of Friend. The word had gone through his FB cell late the night before: *Live-streaming ... check out live-streaming for Fit To Live. Do it now. Check it out.* And so he'd checked it out and seen the ultimate Scroat hunt. Rough, inhospitable terrain; tough, angry NVs; nonstop action. Plus a surprising conclusion, that he didn't quite understand. School would be buzzing with it this morning, as Crane's mind was.

So it almost seemed normal when, instead of asking him further questions about his loyalty, his aptitudes, or the arm of Pax in which he wished to serve, the big, weathered, greying man who interviewed him said instead, 'I understand you've applied to compete in FTL fifty-four times, without success thus far.'

'Sir?'

'Have you or have you not applied to compete in the show Fit To Live fifty-four times, without success?'

'No, sir. Only fifty-three times, sir.'

'Fifty-three times.'

'Yes, sir.'

'You must want to do the show very badly.'

'Sir. I want to show what I can do, sir. I want to bring

glory to the Leader and to Briton. I want to be tested, sir.' Crane couldn't understand why the man was going on about FTL when a more important future was being considered for him. Yet there was something about the interviewer that suggested caution. As a dangerous person himself, Crane could recognise danger in others.

'Glory to Briton. To be tested. Hmmph. Well, Crane, I have an opportunity for you to achieve these goals.' The man looked him in the eyes, considering him. 'You'll be glad to know that here on this desk is an acceptance form for Fit To Live. Upon leaving this interview, you will proceed directly to the FTL building, where you will be accommodated until the next White phase transmission, in which you will participate. Then, upon achieving Brown status and having been shipped to the so-called Marsh, you will in due course find yourself involved in a Task or challenge that will include a certain person who is guilty of treason against the Leader and the country. Someone who is a danger to our city and our society.'

Crane was standing to attention, his muscles under tight control, but his mind racing to assess what he was being told. It was all so very different to what he had expected. 'Sir,' he said, again. 'What should I do then, sir?'

'Then? Then, Crane, you will kill this person, in the course of the game. And if you cannot do it at that time, you will find another way to kill them at an alternative time. And in this way, you will have rendered the country you love a huge service. The Leader himself will show his gratitude personally.'

Crane did not ask the question that many Visions or Scroats would have asked – 'Why me?' – but instead, after a short silence he said, 'Sir, I understand. Thank you for choosing me, sir. I have two questions, if permitted, sir. One: am I officially to be a Pax operative for this mission, sir? Two: how will I recognise the person who I am to kill?'

The big man shook his head. 'A Pax operative? Well, of course you *will* be, Crane, but the nature of the ... er, mission, and of the show of course, is such that we will be unable to provide you with any insignia, documents and so forth. You must be entirely undercover. A *sleeper* we would say, in intelligence jargon. On your return to base you will of course become a fully-fledged Pax recruit, and I think I can promise that your passage to first promotion will be unusually short.'

Crane nodded, understanding, proud. 'Sir. Thank you, sir.'

'Yes. And as for your second question, who you are to kill ... I have a picture here. Study it: you may not take it with you.'

Crane looked at the image being shown to him and saw the girl, Friend.

Even though everything had been explained to him so carefully, logically, he felt shocked. His erect stance wobbled briefly, before he recovered himself.

The man, watching him, said, 'Don't be fooled. Remember what I told you. A danger to our city, and our country.'

Crane didn't dare to question further, but still he did not understand.

# ADELINE

It was on the evening of the third night after the underwater cage Task that they came for her. She'd had time over those days to rest, to eat her fish, to drink the rainwater, to dream her dreams in the muddy reeds. Yet still she was weak.

They were new players, just shipped in from the city, their brown tunics still fresh. An exuberant knot of NVs who somehow managed to find her hiding place when the old-timers of the Marsh had failed. The night was her wakeful time. She'd slept away the day and was resetting her lines after a few mouthfuls of breakfast when the noise of their approach came from quite nearby, muffled by the heavy rain on the swamp. Low voices calling to each other softly, the sound of vegetation being disturbed, of movement in the water. This was another difference. These were coming stealthily, whereas the others had shouted and whooped and crashed through the Marsh, hoping that she would be frightened into showing herself.

She knew at once that the rules of the game had just changed and she was glad for it. She'd come to Briton, to this savage land, to die. To test her body and mind and spirit and then to face the inevitable. But also she'd come to taunt Jan, to keep his gaze from Seven, to challenge his ideas: wasn't that what Frau Kästener had been intending to ask? Now . . . now that she had sensed first hand the cold, malevolent intelligence that stirred Briton and drove the people towards fear and violence, her wish to defy it, to harm it, had grown. But the noises of the hunt told her that the intelligence had sensed her too, sooner than she'd thought it might.

Truly now, the game was starting. She would play it for as long as strength remained to her.

She laughed softly, gave a sob.

With flowing, stealthy movements, she lowered herself into the reeds, lay full length, and then squirmed into the water. Full night was still an hour away, but if she could find the right place, she should be able to stay hidden until then. She breathed in, twice, then let the cold, salty floodwater close over her head and started to swim away, south-west along the edge of the game zone. In a little while she would head east again, to the denser vegetation speckling the inner Marsh. Then, when she was far enough away from the hunt, she would find a place to lie up.

But that was not to be. When she surfaced for the next breath, some fifty metres away, she was seen at once. They had not, after all, come from only one side: two had been edging in from the other direction, to corner her. One of them, a boy/man, a typical example of these strange beings, was only ten metres from her surfacing point. His eyes met hers as she came up, and then he was splashing towards her, stealth abandoned, calling out in his big, hungry voice for his fellow hunters to close the net; the prey was caught, pitifully easily. What they planned next was unclear. They wouldn't be allowed to kill her outright, not in the Marsh. More likely they planned a challenge to individual combat and would ensure, by their rough treatment, that she was in no shape to win. The intelligence that had guided them here so surely would have planted some sort of endgame in their sharp, clumsy minds; that was beyond doubt.

The boy splashed right to her, came at her like a boar, and there was nothing for it; she had to measure his momentum and guide him into the rotted stump of a tree that poked forlornly through the tide. The others, five of them it seemed, were too many to face safely at once, but they were still far enough to show them a clean pair of heels. Or would have been in the mountains.

With another breath, Adeline slid back into the brine, swam swiftly underwater for another thirty or so metres, then resurfaced amongst the trees and set off as fast as she could, deeper into the Marsh, sometimes running awkwardly through the mud and sand, sometimes swimming, sometimes climbing through the thickets of thorn and willow.

Behind her, the hunters shouted their pleasure and came in fast, deadly pursuit.

'Hey Chaney. Get your arse over here: you're missing some serious action.'

'Yeah, Chaney, looks like you might get a new one sooner than you thought, after all.'

Chaney put out her cigarette, deliberately slowly, screwing it down into the ashtray, and took her time crossing the control room. Outside, light was failing over the sad, grey streets.

'Action, huh? OK, let's take a look.' She didn't think she'd stay in this job much longer, with these jerks. They were too blood hungry, too obsessed with the betting. It was all turning sour for her. She glanced at the screens of her colleagues as she walked along the row. They showed, from all their different angles, a small group of NVs moving in on a corner of the Marsh. She said, 'A hunt?'

'You better believe it, girl. And guess who's on the menu.'

Chaney half shrugged, her good humour suddenly deserting her completely. She'd known that this time would come. Stupid to give a damn.

She said, 'The new bunch, huh?' And then, thought-fully, 'How did *they* get so lucky all of a sudden?' She went to her own terminal and sat down before it. Friend was there, just visible on one of the tree cameras, plus her own head-shot of course. Chaney could see that the girl had just become aware of the enemy moving in. She'd paused, her camera view was swinging towards the line of pursuit.

The sound came, faintly, of the girl laughing. Then she also cried. The hairs rose on Chaney's neck.

'Hey, any of you morons getting this out on live-stream? And we're submitting it for the show proper, yeah?'

'No,' someone replied. 'Upstairs weren't much interested. There are two big Combat challenges going on in Paradise.'

'Yeah,' said another, from further down the bank of terminals, 'hands off my Combat, Chaney. My guy's gonna slaughter that poor sucker.'

'You hope!' retorted the woman assigned to the 'poor sucker'.

'Just watch Aspen take this newcomer apart,' said Van-Quentin, happily.

It was a normal control-room conversation. The long room was buzzing to have so much action at once. But as Friend slipped down into the water, Chaney closed her eyes a moment in rapid thought, then quietly, worriedly, leaned in and flipped two orange switches on her console. As she did so, a tiny string of red lights came on.

She sat back, reached for another cigarette. It was only as Friend surfaced for the first time and was con-fronted with the NV boy, crashing through the Marsh towards her, that a fellow operative noticed what she'd done.

'Hey . . . *hey*! You putting this out, Chaney? You gone live on the hunt?'

'Yep.'

'Woooah . . . you poor *bitch*. They're going to chew you up and spit you into the sea, Chaney. Going against Control.'

This sentiment was excitedly echoed along the line of consoles. Quickly the on-screen action took back seat to this new development. Chuckles could be heard, bets were placed on how long Chaney herself could last after this subversion of a directive. But she ignored them, went back to get the ashtray and lit her new smoke, brought it back to her console, drawing deep with trembling fingers.

She said to the world in general, 'It's good viewing. It's important. I'm doing the right thing. Just watch.'

Even as she spoke, the NV boy thudded heavily into the piece of dead wood and sagged back in the water. Nobody questioned Chaney after that.

'Shit! How did she do that?' said Van-Quentin, his precious Aspen forgotten as he craned to see her bank of screens.

'Game on!' said another, in delight.

Friend swam softly away, then surfaced and fled. The NVs howled after her like wolves. And Chaney, smoking the bitter filter of her cigarette, wondered properly for the first time who Friend was; and more importantly, why did the controllers of FTL want her finished? She found herself willing the girl to win, to go all the way. Only of course *she* wouldn't be there to see it, not now, not unless it made it to the public screens.

Adeline knew that the Marsh had taken its toll on her. The fish had not been plentiful, although adequate for survival, along with the roots, the insects, the burrowing worms, whatever she could find. Energy had to be used to counter the sapping effect of the elements, even though she'd slept and meditated for much of the time.

Despite that, after a week she *knew* this place; knew its smells and tastes, its feel, its dangers and its possibilities. She missed the mountains, of course, but for the moment she was a thing of the Marsh herself. Part amphibian. Part briny mollusc. Part wind rattling the trees.

Sweat prickled her as she fled. Thought retreated.

*She doubted that any one thing was itself for more than a moment. The cascades of changes flowing around her and in her were so rapid that they left her breathless. She didn't know who Dominic was, half hidden in the shadows of the cold room. She didn't know who or what it was that she held. She didn't recognise its scent or its heartbeat against her, any more than she recognised herself. But the voyage of discovery was sweet. Finding out together. Riding the rapids of change in unison for a while. Recognising a fellow journeyer.*

*She gave herself.*

Time passed, measured by breaths.

Yes, the Marsh had taken its toll but for a long while she evaded the fresh, hungry NVs. They had their strength and agility, yet their bodies were still acclimatising to the cold and wet. And they moved heavily, they became fouled in the mud, caught in the brambles, whipped by branches. Gradually, Adeline lengthened the distance between herself and the pursuers. She steered them towards Paradise, but then veered south and then again east, towards the open sea. For twenty minutes the rain stopped and the wind fell and the sounds of the chase echoed through the darkening wasteland; but then the downpour started again twice as heavily, churning the water, obscuring Adeline's passage from the NVs.

She would be OK now. She would extend her lead, reach the sea, and stay invisible far out in the black tide against the darker eastern sky, however many handlights they shone on the waves.

Just one more effort. Then rest, and the steady fight against cold, until they should lose interest and return to their precious Paradise.

And yet, the unexpected always arose when you thought it would not.

The lull in the weather had brought the noise of the hunt to those inside the stockade, despite the two bouts of Personal Combat that were taking place. Three more NVs, three that had arrived with Friend, excited by the possibility of catching the bald little Scroat they had ogled in the transport, set off across the game area and bolstered the pursuit just as Adeline was drawing away and vanishing into the gloom. Also, they came *across* the line of her retreat, so that they appeared thirty metres away to her left, at the moment that she had hoped to make her decisive move.

It might not have mattered, but that her heart, steady throughout the pursuit until now, suddenly began to race, to hiccup, to ache and then to be a spreading terrible pain that poured the resolve and the careful, economical energy out of her, like blood from a wound.

For fifty more metres she struggled and splashed on, dizzily, deeper and deeper into the tide, feeling the first little waves slap against her numb chest. And behind her the two groups of chasers, converging as one, came with renewed hunger for the kill. Then she stumbled, and disappeared below the black surface.

*She gave herself and thrilled with it, pulled him closer.*

'She's history,' one of the NVs panted to another, as they converged on the spot and cast around.

'Yeah, she'd had it. Did you see how weak she was?'

'Not surprising after that. She gave us a good chase, for a Scroat. Lightspeed.'

'Yeah, lightspeed. No rules broken if she drowns, are there?'

'Of course not. Where would the logic be in that?'

'Hey,' said one of the old hands, 'this female is tricky. Above average for a Scroat. Didn't you hear about the last challenge? We should make sure.'

'OK, spread out . . . feel under the water.'

They began to use their feet and hands to probe the flood, and then a familiar signal came blaring over the Tannoys, running with rain in the trees.

'*Attention! Attention!*' the automatic recording blared. '*All Brown players to stay where they are and desist any contact or action until further notice. Repeat. No Brown player to move, on pain of disqualification.*'

'Oh shit! Someone's pressed their panic button. Who's pressed their button?'

'Could be the Scroat, if she's alive?'

'Yeah, must be.'

They stayed frozen, as required by the game rules, for ten long minutes, until the all-clear was given, signalling that whoever had resigned from the game had been collected by operatives from a perimeter station. By that time the cold of the sea had stiffened their muscles and soured the joy of the hunt.

'Can't have been the girl, then. They didn't come out here.'

'No. But she's dead anyway. We haven't seen a thing since they sounded the siren. She'll have been washed out to sea in that current.'

'Yeah. Let's head back.'


In the city control room, Van-Quentin was almost jumping up and down in frustration and anger. 'My kid, press the button? Never. Gods above, he was doing all right in that fight. Better than all right.'

'Look at the name on the read-out, Van-Quentin. Each button is personalised, remember? There's no mistake. That's your kid's button and it's been pushed. Anyway, you were watching the hunt with the rest of us. You didn't *see* what happened. Come on, admit it.'

'So, what does that prove? Use your brains, there must be some mistake. Aspen Sinclair is a top of the line NV. A cert for Black.'

'Aspen Sinclair is out of the game,' Chaney said lightly. 'Come on, cough up for the fund.'

He turned on her angrily, 'What about you? You can bloody cough up too. Your precious little Scroat is dead meat.'

'If she is, if it's confirmed, then of course I'll cough up too.'

But later, Friend's mike relayed faint sounds of movement, her camera seemed also to be on the move in the darkness, and in the morning it showed a new hiding place. When the tree cameras homed in on the spot, the girl was pale as death, but breathing.

Outside the control room, the city held its breath to see how much longer she could go on, and one or two wondered, with Chaney, how those new NVs had come on her so quickly.

# THE REF

This moment was mealtime, the pain, the sweat, the scraping of the food into the waste.

This moment was worktime, laughter time, anger time, gee-them-up time, knock-them-down time; half tassled jester, half vengeful devil.

*This* was an end to dear sleep, to struggle round the room on aching legs.

*This* was sanity, barely kept. It was control. It was an inch towards freedom. An inch away from sweet poison.

Wait for the day.

The *day*.

Coming back from the Marsh was bittersweet for the Ref. He must leave the wide expanse of freedom behind, must admit that he was not ready, not yet, not for weeks or months even. He must re-enter the prison of his own accord, just as Jan had ordained. And yet, when he came back, he came back to his instruments, to his own familiar lair and scent, to a routine he knew and could work with. The Marsh air was in his nostrils, the sea on his tongue. He came back determined to work his miracle.

Friend had somehow survived and so he could not forget her. He only forgot when there was no reminder but with her survival, Friend buzzed through his blood like a drug herself, and he soon found that the buzz was out there too, in the city, however faintly it reached him.

'It's obvious, mate. Use your noodle. What she did

was . . . Aye aye, watch out, here comes his nibs. Heads down all.'

'Did you see the faces of them newbies when they clocked that she was . . .'

'. . . and then, in the morning, there she is, as pretty as a picture, on the . . .'

'. . . working for an unfriendly power, that's what I heard . . .'

'Look out!'

They fell silent with his passing as they always did, but he could arrive very softly when he chose, softly and smoothly as a dancer. He heard enough, and realised with gradual delight that the city was captivated. Everybody had a theory. Everybody was scandalised or excited or secretly in shocking love or lust with the girl. Below that, they were puzzled, they were asking questions and, despite themselves, they found a tiny hope growing in their hearts that Friend, with her third-class genes, would survive still longer.

Why, the Ref wondered to himself, in his dreams. Why should they care? Did her unlikely success mean that the oceans would also defy probability and lie down meekly in their beds? Did the old-line Visions, in danger of becoming the next lower class, take comfort from her bravery? Whatever the reason, the grey days over the city, waiting for annihilation by the water, or deliverance at the hands of the Leader, became tinged with pink, with the ghost of warmth.

Even the New Visions, lining up for the White phase, were buzzing like drones with the illogical, unexplainable fact of Friend.

'If she's still around when I get to Brown phase, I'll be challenging her. Taking her out of the picture. Don't worry about that.'

'Yeah, certainly won't be as sloppy as those guys out there right now. Making us look foolish.'

'She's got to have inside help, though. Too many coincidences in her favour. Look at that panic button stuff last week.'

'What about you, Crane? What do you think? She gonna last long enough for us to get a piece of her?'

The others stopped to hear Crane's reply. Despite their size, he still stood taller, broader. His bulk sizzled with raw power.

He looked reluctant to answer. The Ref, overhearing their talk whilst they waited for make-up to finish, was surprised that an NV should need so long to formulate an answer. 'She might,' Crane said at last, 'but I guess we can do something about that, can't we?'

'All right!'

'The big guy speaks! The girl's history!'

'Light*speed*, dude.'

But Pax operative Crane didn't seem to want to talk more. He drifted away from the knot and looked out from the FTL building steps over the besieged city.

Inside help?

Working for an unfriendly power?

The Ref laughed at these suggestions, as far as he'd ever really laughed at anything, for many years, back into the murk of his captivity. First the girl was supposed to be a useless nothing, a dreamy piece of insubstantial genetic fluff, fortunate to have made it through to the game at all, doubly fortunate to have made Brown. Now she was a *spy*? An *agent*?

Only thirty-six hours after eluding the NVs at the sea portion of the Marsh, Friend had been selected for another Task. Had they forgotten that?

Three and a half million of the five million people in Briton had not forgotten. How could they? Someone had put the night-hunt out live on the public screens. The Ref knew that heads had rolled over that. Yet when the live-stream images had been pulled off again in favour of edited reruns, the crowds around the screens had growled in dissatisfaction. Missiles had been thrown at some screens. Without further explanation, the word had come from Control and live-stream had been restored, in time for Friend's next Task. A straight Endurance event. Another punishing chase through the mud and floods that seemed an almost deliberate copy of what had happened before. Five volunteer Pax soldiers, pursuing her and a couple of others over a course of two kilometres. All the contestants had to do was stay ahead of the soldiers to the finish. Simple.

When the Ref had seen the girl beforehand – white, pinched and hopeless, rubbing her chest with her palm in slow circles – he'd known it was the end . . .

And yet it was not. She'd sat on a branch, closed her eyes for ten minutes, motionless in the wind, a fuzz of deep red-brown stubble staining her scalp. And then, at the starting whistle, she'd run, swum and climbed with a silent, strained determination that the Ref recognised in himself: the determination of the condemned.

They had not caught her. Not quite.

Back in the capital, the Ref's painful, self-warring existence went on as it always did, day after terrible day, moment by moment. But now, the fact of Friend and the ripples of her wake in the game of Fit To Live filled his mind as often as the Lady did, however cruelly *her* barbs cut at his muscle and heart.

He looked outwards from his oval window. He looked out onto the teeming, frightened city. He felt he saw it with fresh eyes, as something he knew well from long ago. And the girl too; he recognised her. Something about her.

As for the suggestions about spies and conspiracies against the State, they were much easier to place. They had the stench of Jan in them. The Leader, too, was feeling the ripples. This week he paid no crowing visit to his prisoner. Nor the week after.

A single terse note came with his breakfast the first day back in the city: 'No tricks. No ideas. No Lady this morning to remind you.'

Half mad with pain, beating the walls through a day of torment and deprivation, unable to work, the Ref felt Jan's anger and fear in this most of all, and he smiled and sobbed through his pain.

What 'tricks' did Jan have in mind? Help for the girl? She didn't need it.

Except, perhaps, to get out alive.

# DOMINIC
## *– day 64 –*

There are two opposing poles, two forces, in my life. There's the Major and Frank Barbieri and the grinding iron wheel we must run round endlessly in our cage; and then there is Ruth. I wish I could say truthfully that Ruth was more powerful. But sometimes I catch myself acting or thinking like a prick, like the ones I despise. Sometimes I get caught up in the games.

I have started to think again about escape.

The people who arrived with Father are scientists. They've set up an office or laboratory or something in Sandley, the junior boarding house. They are now in charge of the activities we are made to do: they introduce them, they monitor our scores, they note down reams of information on their charts, and they interview us. The muscle and the threats are still provided by the soldiers, of course. The regime is the same: same timetable, same diet, same punishments and rules. Same caveman existence and bitter cold. But the scientists are there, studying us. Also, many of the tasks (a quarter? a third?) are now on paper. Like Bede's is coming back to shaky life. 'You have ninety minutes to complete this test. There will be no talking or collaboration. You may now turn over the papers.' If the rooms we used were heated it would be something. You freeze sitting still.

What kind of thing are we tested on? Well, sometimes it's stuff like IQ tests, or the kind of personality questions you get at the back of magazines: *You see an old man in a shop stealing a tin of beans ... nobody else has seen ...*

*what do you do?* Crap like that. Or it could be an elaborate map-reading exercise, plotting courses, or mathematics, or hypothetical emergency situations. A plane crashes in the mountains, different surviving passengers have different needs, different ages; there are various possibilities of where you head and with whom and who you leave behind and how you maximise your chance of survival.

But, like a lowest common denominator, we always come back to the squalid grind of the assault course (warms you up again), to the self-defence they've started teaching us, to freezing and starving and having to wash every third day in ice-cold water pumped from the beck.

Every day ends in exhaustion, a numb body, Frank Barbieri's violence, an occasional trip to the bogs to write this if I can be bothered.

I've given most of it to Ruth, just for a while.

She said, 'I don't know you. I want to know everything. Tell me.' She said it violently, defiantly, like her old self. But her eyes were very bright, spearing me like a happy fish. She won't sit back comfortably to let life come to her, she rises to taste it, goes out to meet it.

I suggested this journal, although scared of what she might think, because I didn't know what else to give her. And I want to give her everything. To be naked like in those first days. If she reads it and hates me, then we will have deceived ourselves. Better to know?! I must face who I am.

She says she will find something for me too.

What else? Can't think.

Oh yes, I had an interview with the Czech woman. Her name is Eve.

'So Dominic. Tell me all about yourself.' Two women wanting to know my secrets at the same time. (I'll put her on the waiting list for the journal.) Then questions about health, allergies etc. Then, suddenly: *What do you see for the future?*

How do you answer that? I said recklessly, half-facetiously, 'I'm hoping for love and to touch a certain girl's soul in the way she touches mine.'

Eve raised her eyebrows. She put down her clipboard and went to look out of the window at the gloom of slush and snow. Again she was in furry, shaggy clothes and great boots, suitably cavewoman, but designer. She said: 'Do you know, that is a very charming answer, Dominic. It gives me great hope. And yet it is not at all what I was asking. I was asking about your country, about the world, about' – she waved her arm to indicate everything outside – 'all *this*. What do you see for the *world*, Dominic?'

The mood was on me now. 'I see people like my father keeping a piece of the action, keeping whatever wealth there is, hanging on like limpets to their bloody empires. And everyone else being properly, comprehensively shafted.'

A pause.

Was she smiling, or looking stern, or what? I couldn't tell. Suddenly I panicked that I'd said the wrong thing and I'd be out, one of the ones that disappeared, Father or not.

I said: 'I'm sorry. Maybe that was . . . rude.'

But she went to the door and opened it. 'Thank you. I have learned quite a lot. Quite enough. Please, ask the sergeant to send the next to me?'

So it was back to the iron wheel.

# – day 70 –

I sit with Ruth at supper, when she comes. Often she doesn't. She shakes off the rules that bind the rest of us, and what can they do?

Supper's our only proper time together, then and for twenty minutes afterwards, before I must be in 0-17 for evening inspection. There are waves of hatred and scorn that we sit together. From the other inmates, from the seedy kitchen mob – they dish us out less food – and from the soldiers.

Ruth rides the waves. She is unconcerned.

Twice the Major has come into the dining hall and seen us and darkened with his own fury.

Tonight she brought the thing she promised – something about her. It was a shoe box, a large one, for boots.

'To open later,' she said. She was half smiling, blushing, hesitant for once.

'OK.'

She took my journal out of a bag. 'And I've read this.'

'Oh.'

'And I think you should know that you're a Grade A lunatic, Dominic. A real nutcase.'

'Thank you . . . is that good?'

'I don't know. Is it?'

Frank passed by our table with his tray. 'Is this asshole bothering you?'

'He's bothering me and I'm bothering him.'

Like I said before, spiky, wild Witchbitch Ruth is now the most civilised, the most gentle, the most perfect . . .

We embrace when we are alone. It's a slow ritual, not

to be rushed. We face each other and come together by centimetres and become aware of each other.

Sometimes I grow hard. Standing together like that. She must feel it and I worry that she'll think it's wrong, because whatever it is that we share is so different from ... I don't know, *sex*. But she doesn't say anything.

When I opened her shoe box, do you know what I found? The model of the Globe theatre, made carefully and perfectly, fading now with time.

More tears.

So many futures stupidly abandoned. But I wouldn't choose to be anyone or anywhere else at this time of my life.

Under the model was a black and white photo, Ruth as a child of four or five, great round, surprised eyes, hair roughly and lopsidedly cut, legs like little sticks coming out from her dress. Then a John Donne poem, written out by her:

The Good-Morrow

*I wonder by my troth, what thou and I*
*Did, till we loved? Were we not wean'd till then?*
*But sucked on countrey pleasures, childishly?*
*Or snorted we i' the seaven sleepers den?*
*'Twas so; But this, all pleasures fancies bee.*
*If ever any beauty I did see,*
*Which I desir'd and got, 'twas but a dreame of thee.*

*And now good morrow to our waking soules,*
*Which watch not one another out of feare;*
*For love, all love of other sights controules,*
*And makes one little roome, an every where.*
*Let sea discoverers to new worlds have gone,*
*Let Maps to others, worlds on worlds have showne,*
*Let us possesse our world, each hath one and is one.*

*My face in thine eye, thine in mine appears,*
*And true plaine hearts doe in the faces rest,*
*Where can we finde two better hemispheares*
*Without sharpe North, without declining West?*
*Whatever dyes, was not mixt equally;*
*If our two loves be one, or, thou and I*
*Love so alike, that none doe slacken, none can die*

And another one, which must be by Ruth herself:

Song (without music)

*There is no standing still*
*In this high, weathered place.*

*The sweet gale tugs,*
*Like infant fingers, at the cloth*
*Where your body hides;*
*Hurries you along;*
*Beheads the flowers so that they*
*Brush your cheek;*
*Brings bitter brine*
*To blind you, and*
*Gritty, scented loam*
*To choke you.*

*Let go.*
*Be blown away.*
*Be free.*

Finally, at the bottom of the box, three or four leaves that she must have recently collected in the snow, tinged with their out-of-season autumn colours. Perfect veiny shapes, already growing limp.

# – day 71 –

This morning in the frozen dark of our waking I reached for the box and it was gone.

Harder to hide than sheets of paper, and I haven't had the chance and the energy to go up on the roof for a while.

'Missing something?' Frank said, as we struggled into our cruddy boiler suits.

'It's only a box of things,' Ruth said, at lunch.

'But your photo. The model. Your poem.'

She shook her head. 'It doesn't matter.'

I said, 'I loved it. Everything. I don't know how to tell you . . .'

She said, 'Am I enough of a nutter too?'

'Definitely.'

Then she said, 'Tell me about these tests they make you do.'

'Oh God. I don't know. It's just all a load of crap. Games. Hoops. I could bring you copies of the written stuff if you want. You'll see.'

She nodded. 'Bring me copies. It'd be fun. I could do with a diversion.'

I brought her the first written task at supper, from the afternoon, but it was a night when she didn't come.

# CRANE

Crane's life had changed so quickly, it was lucky that he was designed to adapt.

The instructors and the FB cell had been left behind. His weak, frightened parents would now face life without him, though they'd keep their extra privileges. The frustrated, unchallenged NV children, terrorising the docklands to scrape away the gangrene of Scroats, would have to hunt away from his big shadow. Crane was, at last, to have a proper role.

He was a Pax operative. He would help to mould the better future that the Leader had promised. He would be in the first wave of NVs – perhaps he *was* actually the first one, that was a thrilling thought! – to take up the challenge. Now the fight had really begun and the world was going to see some amazing things. Soon, Crane might be on one of the new, black ships, searching out better, drier, warmer lands for his people.

Briton could be proud.

Yet, secretly, Crane felt unready. Not unready for the change of terrain; of course he didn't mind that. He rode the battered, tinny transport to the Marsh as Adeline had done, noticed the water level outside, impeding the transport, and felt nothing for it. He knew how hostile was the drowning land outside and gave it less than a thought.

He looked around at the other Browns. When they met his gaze it was with the respect due. They were no more to him than the water.

He ran through the conversation with the ageing,

dangerous Pax officer, when he had received his mission. Since then, nobody had communicated with him about that mission. He had passed easily through White, he had dwelt quietly for some days in the FTL tower, awaiting the next shipment north; he had practised in the gymnasia . . . and *nothing* unusual had passed, nothing had marked him out from the ordinary players.

He realised when the transport came, that he was alone. The mission was only his. The conversation that morning a week ago might never have happened. It was like a bald, stark, ugly piece of bone that he had to crunch up and swallow in private. A lonely truth that almost made him long for the frightened parents, the FB cell, the childhood he had left behind.

(Gods above, he thought, wasn't he Crane? Wasn't he truly lightspeed?)

No, it was not the Marsh, the danger, the change in circumstances that disturbed him. They held no fear at all. It was Friend, the reality of Friend.

There were niggles, illogicalities that he could not resolve no matter how he turned them round in his mind. These were: the fact of a Scroat (and a female) being seen as an actual threat to the State; and the fact of the noble game of Fit To Live being *used* to bring about her demise. Since his interview with the big Pax officer it had become blindingly plain to him that other attempts had been made on the girl's life and had failed. He was no fool. The difficult underwater-cage Task against one of the game's top performers, the newbie NVs finding Friend so easily . . . and perhaps, extrapolating, there had been other things, further attempts, that he did not know about. It seemed that the game was no longer about testing yourself, achieving glory by your efforts, showing the people of Briton what resources lay waiting to build them their dry future. Instead it was about ensuring the end of the unusual Scroat female.

Crane cared nothing for fair play. If this person was a danger to Briton, the Leader should say so openly and she should be eliminated at once. To give the Scroats the chance to pit themselves against the best and so show the world their shortcomings was one thing. To allow a spy or anarchist to enter the game was another.

One of his companions in the rattling transport turned to him. 'Hey dude, this should be something.'

'Yeah.' He tried to summon enthusiasm, the killer instinct he was known for at home. 'Should be something.'

There, look at that. The Leader had not been open, and now neither could he be. He had to pretend. He could not be himself. It was ... what word could he give it, what taste did it have? Yes, it was ... *shameful*.

He grasped for something solid, thrust away the tainted word, thrust even deeper the feelings the bald girl stirred in his belly.

He could not resent Pax. They were the future, *his* future. The fault *must* lie after all with his target. A Scroat female. A nothing. The *dirt* of those half-people (he thought with disgusted relief) that permeated everywhere and dragged the whole of the country down into the floods! Even corrupting FTL.

He sat up straighter and gazed out of one of the slit windows, at the drowning world of Briton. So ... He would carry out his mission cleanly and quickly and then he would be on solid ground again.

But then, when the transport door opened for him and he splashed heavily out into the icy water and crossed the floating red perimeter, Crane was careless. His new determination made him so. He moved massively through the Marsh, thrusting aside vegetation, consulting his map, taking the straightest possible course to Paradise, confident that his power and speed and quick, assessing mind made him the biggest predator on the land.

When the crooked stilts that held the rough collection of dwellings clear of the tidal flood came into view in his torchlight, he worked his way round the stockade to the entrance to Paradise and impatiently climbed the wide, heavy ladder that led up to it, hand over hand.

(In the capital, and in the four other cities of Briton, the viewers sat up in their chairs and delayed visits to the toilet or to fetch refreshments. Such a bold, reckless approach to the Marsh was rare. Arrogant or foolish, it promised excitement. Now that live-streaming went out in public, Fit To Live was attracting a record audience. Productivity levels were down. Vision restaurants were half empty. Even around the street screens where the watchers were certain to be soaked and blown, the crowds never thinned, except in the dead of night. These days, who could predict *what* might happen in the show?)

At the top of the ladder lay the gates, not yet shut for the night by the current Paradise inhabitants. And just inside the gates, in the gloom, sat three other players, sprawled on the planks. They were almost invisible in their stained brown tunics, and did not move as Crane played his light over their faces.

'Hey,' he said, standing before them, his clothes dripping.

They looked him up and down, glanced at each other. They stood up.

One said, 'Come back in the morning. In the light, so we can get a proper look at you.'

None was quite as big or as broad as Crane, yet there were three of them, and he knew at once that they intended to pitch him back down into the water. Of course they did. There was a certain etiquette to FTL, or rather an exhibition of survival skills, that he had broken in coming straight here in the dark. How could they trust or welcome a new player with such an illogical start to his Brown phase?

Crane did not want to be pitched back into the swamp. He did what he would ordinarily not have done and took on unfavourable odds in the shape of fellow NVs. Before they could drive him back, he span sideways, weighed down by his wet clothing but fresh from a day's travel, and tackled the left-hand one of the three about the hips, grunting as he picked him up bodily and pivoted him back over his shoulder, and down the drop behind him.

(As Crane's victim splashed and flailed into brine and mud, the city audience gasped, rubbed their hands, cheered. Only the largest, most foolhardy old-line Vision ever made such a statement of their presence on the first night in the Marsh. More excitement was guaranteed . . .)

'Do you want to take me on?' Crane asked the two remaining players, his genetic brothers. 'Do you fancy your chances *now*?'

They watched him carefully, but made no other move. His irrationality was sickening to them. He must be ill.

'I'm hungry,' said Crane, and indeed, his big stomach was rattling.

'There's no more food until the morning. Don't you watch the show?'

'Except for Stringer.' (The audience breathed in through their teeth. They whistled low and long.) 'He has a little, I expect. Keeps it to eat afterwards, to rile us.'

Stringer.

Crane tried to remember Stringer, but he hadn't actually *seen* the game for ten days. For some reason it was not shown to those Browns awaiting shipment. He seemed to recall a mention of this Stringer passing through White phase. Then, had there been a Combat the night that Friend was hunted? Two Combats, one with Stringer involved, he thought, but nobody had talked about anything but the hunt. He didn't trust the two NVs before him – he'd thrown trust down into the mud with their companion – but he had clearly shown them his superiority and established himself in Paradise. All he wanted now was to eat and sleep, and then get on with the business of killing the Scroat female.

*Then* everything would resolve itself. The future path he'd always expected for himself would come back into focus.

He'd be a hero.

There'd be time for trust.

'Where's Stringer?' he asked, bluntly.

'Stringer is in possession of the last dwelling on the left.'

There was definitely an atmosphere of deceit about the two. Crane ignored it and walked across the boards. It was a tiny distance to the last low building to the left of the central space, nestling inside the stockade.

'Stringer?' he said, playing his handlight into the dark interior. 'I'm Crane. I've just arrived. I need some food. They said you would have some.'

No reply came.

'Stringer?'

Nothing.

Crane ducked down and entered the single-room dwelling, shining his light around, picking out a simple (filthy) mattress, a pair of Brown phase boots, a tunic wrapped into a ball.

Before he could straighten once more there was a sound, and a heavy blow at the base of his spine sent him tumbling against the wall, cluttered up in the stinking boots. The handlight skittered off across the planks. He'd not been ready for the attack, yet he was back on his feet in an instant, swinging round to the doorway, facing into his own light, which had been retrieved by his attacker.

'*I'm* Stringer,' growled the shape beyond the light. 'Now, *what* was it you wanted?'

Crane, smarting from being caught unawares, measured the distance to his attacker, planning how to cross it to maximum effect. He said, 'I just need some food, Stringer.'

'Sure,' the voice was sarcastic. 'Course you do.'

Crane threw himself forward, rolling twice, and came back to his feet poised to deliver a heavy blow. He found only empty air.

He could not help admiring the speed and anticipation of this Stringer.

'That's enough buggering about,' said the voice, from his left now. 'You're obviously trouble, Crane. Guess that's why those jokers sent you over here. So . . .' there was a sigh, 'let's get it done with . . . I now challenge you to Personal Combat according to the rules of Fit To Live. Here, catch.'

The light snapped on again and came flipping through the air towards Crane. He caught it and shone the narrow little beam back on the other. The face that came starkly out of the shadows was that of a man of perhaps ten or fifteen years older than he was – much too old for an NV – and was covered in a web of fine white scars and newer, uglier cuts and bruises. That face was at the same level as his own and attached to a large bulk, stripped to the waist. The meaty fists were crossed, one over the other, showing to all that a challenge was being issued.

(A shiver of delight went through the viewers, seeing Stringer's blunt, damaged face picked out on Crane's camera. The day that Crane had gone into lodging in the FTL building was the day that Stringer had had his first Combat challenge with an NV in the Marsh, a terrible, brutal bout lasting forty minutes. Friend had been hiding in the black waves when he'd finally stepped away from the body of his opponent. Since then he'd fought again, once more in answer to an NV challenge, this time for only twenty-two savage minutes before the NV realised that he, too, would die if he fought on, and had pressed his panic button.)

'A Scroat,' Crane said to himself, disgustedly.

'No Crane. I'm Vision.' The voice slid high in mockery. 'Save me Crane, save the poor Vision!'

Crane stared at the man, unbelieving.

'So?' Stringer grinned, showing broken teeth. 'They slipped up! Big beast of a body, but a troublemaker. At least, that's what it says in my files. *Violent and disrespectful where he should be diligent and malleable*. That's me, Crane old mate. My parents got eight thousand credits in compensation. Then they dumped me. What's *your* story?'

Crane spoke his first thought. 'They shouldn't have let you in.'

'No. *I* was surprised too. Things are slipping round here in Paradise, aren't they? I mean, look at your little entrance just now! Here we go then, let's not waste time: you *do* know the rules of FTL Personal Combat, do you?'

Crane could see that other people had gathered, murmuring in the shadows. Other NVs, like himself, coming from their huts, powerless to involve themselves now challenge had been issued. It was clear that he'd been manoeuvred by those at the gates into taking on this unlikely old-liner, and that stung his pride. It was like rejection by his own kind. Like being made unclean.

Also, he realised that Stringer was right. How careless he'd been! All he'd wanted was to get back on the right path. A clear and logical path. An honourable path.

He sighed, breathed in once, swung his arms in great

circles, warming the muscles, and said, 'Yes. I know the rules.'

The Visions at home should have despised Stringer, of course. Wrong sperm, wrong egg, a troublemaker, a disgrace.

Openly, they did despise him.

In private, in their Vision hearts?

In private, it was not all bad, seeing the NVs given a bloody nose by one of their own.

'Go, Stringer,' they mouthed silently.

# JAN

In his quarters, with no one to see, Jan Barbieri went hastily and imperfectly through the fifth kata, one of the 'grounding' katas that a child would learn to understand balance, patience, awareness. Then he did it again, more slowly, then again, slower still. Gradually, he reined in his temper, gradually his focus returned to him. After forty minutes on the mats, the movements were precise and perfect and he felt safe to consider his problems. His icy fury was not diminished, but it was at least in check.

He signalled for Hunter and the hungry young Cooper-Smyth to be sent up to him. Before them he laid the images of Friend's thumbprint, as taken in the Brown transport and, next to them, images of prints sent to him some time ago by the boy in France.

'Well?' he said, when they were seated. '*Well*?'

The men examined the prints, nodded, unsurprised. They'd all known.

'Assessment?'

Cooper-Smyth, sharp-nosed, full of himself, said, 'We should finish it quickly, sir. Who hasn't heard of Friend, out there, on the streets? And of those, what percentage has failed to realise that there have been positive interventions against the girl? We're letting strength and control slip away from your leadership in the public eye. We've let the thing go live so the people see that she must fail. So . . . let her fail. Now – as soon as possible. A single foolproof Task: Combat . . . or an impossible Endurance perhaps. Now, while she is comparatively weak from hunger. A single Task to eliminate her, and even if the public guess what we are about, we will seem strong again. In a month she'll be forgotten. We can restore the broadcasts to normal.'

Jan poured himself a glass of pure water, brought from the north. 'And you, Hunter? Do you agree with this assessment?'

The big, grizzled old bodyguard shook his head slowly. 'No sir, I do not. If the game means nothing, then go in there with troops. Arrest her. Shoot her down. Whatever you wish. Make it thorough: the public will not think you weak, whatever else they do think. But if you wish the ideal of the game preserved, let the girl be taken out of the picture naturally by competition, by hunger or cold, and if not by those, then by my operative.'

'Your operative!' sneered Cooper-Smyth. 'Your so-called operative is a fool. Not worthy of his NV blood. Look at his clumsy entrance to Paradise. His heavy-handed attempt to obtain food!'

Hunter smiled without humour, and the younger man felt a little afraid. 'He is what he is. He is NV. A formidable specimen, though not without failings. His entrance to the game was everything I expected and more. The public will have marked him out, will have already formed opinions about him as you have. He will capture their attention. When he completes his mission, it will seem like nothing other than a continuation of his clumsiness, his reliance on the physical, his genetic snobbery ... We will then dispense with him, punish him in the public eye. The girl will be forgotten and we will be seen to be just and strong-handed.'

There was silence.

Jan said softly, 'You want one of my New Visions to be publicly punished for killing a Scroat?'

'Sir. At the moment nobody knows who the girl is. And nobody can be entirely sure that we have any agenda towards her. If you wish to retain those two advantages, I recommend sacrificing the boy. Call it a fault of his genetic programming if you like.' He waited for a response. 'Remember, I am a soldier, sir. I was never in favour of this game.'

More silence. Hunter wondered idly when *he* would finally be judged dispensable. Part of him ached for that day.

'So be it,' the Leader murmured, at last. 'We will let the game run on a little, without further intervention. We will let suspicion die. We will let your operative make his mark in front of the crowds. This . . . this . . . *Stringer* should be a good first test. But Hunter, make no mistake; if the NV boy fails, we must strike heavily. This girl is . . . well, we both know, you and I, *what* this girl is. All her stock are the same. Trouble.'

The cold blue eyes flashed dangerously. A film of perspiration had appeared on the waxy, pale face. So much for the fifth kata. Almost, Jan wished that the ICSA bitch hadn't led him to Ark Seven. He should have had the woman killed with the rest of her party, but for his damned curiosity. He should have wiped their little settlement out, man, woman and child. The girl had slipped through his fingers, and now – he wouldn't tell these two idiots yet – the other viper, the one that he knew from long ago, had disappeared as well, from under the boy's nose . . .

By God, he might have left it too late, but he'd flatten their little Seven when his ships sailed. That would be their first target. The hot mountains would fly the flag of Briton. And if that other viper unwisely came back to his city . . . *if* she came back, then she'd join her fool brother in the arms of the Lady.

Hunter watched him impassively.

Damn the man.

'Dismiss,' Jan said.

241

# ADELINE

Adeline saw Crane's bold arrival in Paradise from a hiding place in a stand of broken yew trees that lay nearby, the berries white with mould. She saw the other NV thrown surprisingly down. And then, a little later, she heard the Tannoy announcement of hand-to-hand Combat. There were cheers, shouts. Soon the screeching tone to start the fight came from the trees.

Cooper-Smyth had been right about Adeline. She was exhausted, hungry, weak. One of her fishing lines had been trodden down by the boots of the hunting NVs. The constant cold was starting to eat away at her self-control. And since the terrible seconds she had spent spinning in the freezing current, surrounded by those who wished her death, trying to make numb fingers press the stolen panic button, Ruth's shadow had lain heavily upon her. Sometimes she did not know which story she was living.

> *Let go*
> *Be blown away.*
> *Be free.*

But *not* like that, not helpless and frightened, swallowed by the sea.

Paradise beckoned. She needed breathing space, shelter, food. The time for hiding had passed. She needed a host of cameras, around her like sentries, day and night.

This new NV player was a godsend then. Just the diversion that she needed.

Slipping down into the water that had become a second skin to her, she wormed her way across to the ladder that led up to the settlement. Then, pausing to check that she had not been detected by those within or on the platforms, she climbed swiftly to the gates, now closed tight. Inside, the shouts and cheers for the Combat had died down to the murmur of a crowd watching a gripping spectacle. There was the noise of heavy blows, of someone grunting in pain, someone gasping. When her naked feet were on the slippery top rung, she felt her way up the wood to the lip of the stockade. Then, taking a firm grip between the sharpened spikes, she swung out over the water. Hand over hand, feet dangling, she carefully worked her way along the lengths of sapling that made the fence.

It hurt. The splinters dug deep into her palms, but what was pain? Pain only lay on the surface of things.

A third of the way around, hidden by the night and by the dwellings that lay inside the stockade, she stopped and hung uncomfortably by one hand only, while the other reached down to unfasten her boots where they bounced at her waist, tied together by the remaining lace. Then, straining up again, pulling herself inch by inch with only the one hand, she managed to place first one, then the other boot over two adjacent spikes.

Her arm muscles went into spasm. She dropped back to hang full length once more. Every second watching for the loss of control, the loss of mind and body, the final sudden obliteration of her heartbeat.

When she was ready, she pulled herself up, chin-high, then waist-high with the cruel spikes. From there she leaned forward, onto the two boot soles and pivoted across on her belly, wriggling a little, steadying herself with outstretched hands on the back wall of one of the dwellings. When she was far enough across, her fingers latched onto the roof of that dwelling and pulled, so that her legs slid suddenly over behind her. As her weight came swinging down, she let go and dropped to the plank flooring. She fell awkwardly, yet the Combat noise just the other side of this dwelling was enough to mask the sound.

She was in. In the lion's den.

She sat there a while, legs pulled up to her chin, trembling and sick. Then she moved, put her head round the corner of the building and peeped down the narrow space into the centre of Paradise. She saw there the backs of those watching and, beyond, a pool of blue brightness where many handlights were being shone for the combatants to see by. She saw the tension in those backs, heard the excitement in the murmurs. She was going to pull back, when one of the little crowd turned to address some remark to his neighbour, and for an instant she had a clear view of the roughly-marked-out combat area. There, she could see up close the bulk of the new arrival, running with blood, locked in a struggling, frantic embrace with a great, half-naked bear of a man. The bear was also badly marked but seemed to be grinning as he crushed his flailing opponent against him. Even as the gap closed, she saw the NV shut his eyes, as if summoning some last energy, then give a great shout as he lunged and twisted sideways, unbalancing the bear, bringing his opponent's head crashing against a nearby doorjamb.

The view was lost again and she sat back in her huddle. More blows came. Flesh and bone on wood. The child's gasp of a man hurt badly. Nothing.

'Lightspeed,' said one of the watching NVs, breaking the sudden hush.

'Yes. Lightspeed.'

The word was echoed, passed around, softly at first and then becoming a shout, a chant. *Light-speed, light-*

*speed, light-speed.* There was relief and defiance and danger in the word.

After a moment, the Tannoys crackled. *'Attention. All players to remain as they are for retrieval of a casualty. Player Stringer is judged unfit to continue. He will be collected shortly. Repeat, no player to move until player Stringer has been collected.'*

Adeline shivered in the dark space behind the dwelling. She reached for the strong circular breaths that would provide warmth, yet her teeth were chattering and she could not get the rhythm. When she fell asleep, coiled up on herself, her clothing was still wet, her breath unsteady. She did not hear the men come for Stringer, or the noise of the savages returning to their huts, renewed by the bloodshed.

But in the city, in the great squares, in the crowds around the screens, there were groans for the end of the fight. As Hunter had said, Crane had captured some attention. For a while afterwards the streets screamed and buzzed with adrenaline so that security transports sent the signal to their headquarters for 'possible trouble, back-up required'.

And amongst the throng, a few more thoughtful viewers, the now-unemployed Chaney amongst them, wondered at Friend's entry into Paradise and asked the question of how the exhausted, shivering girl could possibly last out, with those savages all around.

Food and water deliveries always came in the morning, at first light. The little electric boat would chatter quietly through the Marsh with its crew of three: one to operate the motor and handle the provisions and two armed guards to ensure that starving players didn't let hunger or thirst overwhelm their better sense. The boat would stop at the five tree platforms on the way in, to offload half-day rations for one person at each. Finally, it would come to Paradise, with similar supplies for fifteen, the number that the stockaded dwellings were designed to house.

That made lean provisions and water for twenty of the thirty or so players that lived in the Marsh at any one time. Or plentiful rations for about thirteen, if the food was not shared fairly. The meagreness of it was part of Jan's great metaphor. However, as a player could, according to the rules, only enter into Personal Combat challenges once every three days, and as these challenges used up so much valuable energy themselves, those in Paradise tended to share equally: one of the fifteen wrapped packs for each inhabitant.

The Fit To Live rules dictated also that the gates to Paradise must stand wide for at least ten hours each day, in case newcomers wished to attempt entry. The ten hours began when the signal came from the morning boat. Then the heavy bolts would be drawn, and two inhabitants would pull on the handles to open the portal. With the gates pinned back, the guards would ascend to clear a space, then the other man would climb up and leave the ration packs piled in the central area. It was only when the guards had again descended that contestants moved forward to claim the food.

Any players with ideas of entering Paradise with the new day would do well to wait until at least half an hour after this procedure, when the current inhabitants would not feel the need to protect their precious rations.

On the morning after Crane's Combat with Stringer, Adeline stood waiting in the narrow passage between the two dwellings, shielded from the heavy rain, until the man had set down his fifteen packets. Then, as the waiting players moved in to take their supplies, she came stiffly forward herself, into the light and the sight of all, and stooped to pick up one of the packets.

Hearing the sudden shouts of surprise and outrage, the

retreating guards glanced back, slipping off their safety catches, fearing violence. But instead they laughed to see the ring of broad-shouldered, arrogant NVs with their jaws hanging open and their eyes wide, watching pale, stubble-headed Friend as she opened her packet and took out a wafer of rice and fish, which she started calmly to eat. The guards, after all, were old-liners. Like those in the city they had discovered a secret pleasure in seeing the NVs made sport of, for all their fear of the rising seas.

Strong hands reached out to take back the food, to cast her out, faces were set like stone, but Adeline spoke aloud as the little headset cameras advanced hungrily on her.

'I have spent a night in Paradise. The rules state that I cannot now be removed, except by personal challenge.'

They halted. She chewed as they debated. She felt dizzy. The food wouldn't go down easily at first.

Eventually one of the NVs was pushed forward to challenge her. A girl, reluctant and staring, embarrassed by the farce. She was a chunky, belligerent-looking thing with a dark complexion and grey eyes. She muttered, 'You've got some nerve, Scroat.' And then, more loudly, 'I challenge you, whatever-your-name-is, to Personal Combat under the rules of Fit To Live.' So saying, she pointed to Adeline and made the symbol of the crossed fists for the cameras.

The crackle and whine of the Tannoy came at once, twisting through the rain: '*Attention. Attention Paradise. The challenge just issued to Friend by Vaso may not proceed for the moment. Friend will be required today for her next Task. We remind you that this Combat challenge may only proceed in forty-eight hours from the ending of today's Task.*'

Adeline shrugged at the girl. 'Forty-eight hours, then.'

She breathed with inner relief that she had guessed

right. Now that a challenge had been issued, no other player could challenge her until the first Combat was resolved. Nor could they deny her re-entry to Paradise upon return from her Task. She had her sanctuary, her camera sentries, for two days to come.

Providing, of course, that she could survive the Task.

Crane chose that moment to come out from Stringer's dwelling, now taken as his own. He was a mess in the morning light. One eye was fully closed, the other crusted with blood. He moved awkwardly. His hands were raw and swollen from the fight.

'Dude,' someone said, half-heartedly. 'Lightspeed.'

Crane looked down at the empty planks with his one good eye. 'Where's my food?' he croaked.

He looked up at them, around the ring of faces. He stopped when he came to Adeline. 'What's *she* doing here? What's happening?' He held his head, rubbed the prominent brows, winced.

Nobody said anything. Last night's hero was today's lame duck. He would soon be gone, they thought. If he wanted food tomorrow, he'd have to get there before the Scroat. They'd *both* be gone in a day or two. It couldn't be soon enough.

Adeline held out the last of her wafers to Crane. 'Here. Take it. I think that one's apple.'

She looked around. 'Who else?'

The NVs were dispersing, going back into the dwellings to eat. Nobody wanted to give food to a liability who wouldn't last. The weak and damaged were dispensable, NV or not.

Crane watched them go. He squinted down at the wafer Adeline held and swore.

'Viewers. People of Briton. Welcome! Welcome to Paradise!'

Up close, the Ref was every bit as creepy as Paulette

had said, on that monsoon-wrapped day in another lifetime. He moved with power and some grace, yet with awkward half-movements thrown in, as if his muscles were not entirely his own. He was never without his mask and tasselled suit. His temper flared violently and often as the crew were setting up, but there was also something there that was ... what? Sad? Apologetic? Defiant? Adeline couldn't name it. He was a mixture of the dangerous, the ridiculous and the tragic. A caged beast; or a clown.

His voice, when he spoke calmly, snagged at her strangely, pulled her back from the place between worlds.

'People of Briton. We are here to deliver Friend to what may be her last Task. Look at her, where she sits with her back to the wood, exhausted. For once, we will be merciful. For once we will help her to the boats.'

He signalled to his aides and they came forward to pull her up, but she shook her head, rose by herself. The food had made some difference. She had a little warmth within. She rubbed at her arms and legs, stretched her fingertips up high, swaying gently, then walked to the gates.

As she went, she saw the Ref's eyes flicker hungrily after her. They searched her form as if he would devour it to see what secret lay inside. He and the others came down with her, to the boats, and they set off to today's game zone. She let her eyes close again and heard the steady rhythm of the motor, the lapping of the waters. Her fingers trailed over the side.

Nothing was important. The Major and his soldiers marched here and there. Jan pulled feverishly at the strings of the city. Games: they were only games.

In due course they must have arrived. The Ref was speaking again.

'This Task is Combination, Ladies and Gentlemen.

A mixture of Endurance, Logic and Combat. And it's not easy. Take a look at this.'

The main camera swung in an arc, zooming in on an expanse of clear water, fifty metres across, fringed by the salt-poisoned trees and reeds. On one side of the water a small boat bobbed, its oars shipped. It was tied to a white-painted stake where a steel box hung from a strap. Across the water, a second stake could also be seen.

'What the contestant must do is this: within a strict time limit of twelve minutes, he or she must destroy a series of drone warriors that have been placed both under the water and in the vegetation surrounding the course. Six of them in all. Watch closely please.'

The camera zoomed hard in on a patch of empty water. The emptiness suddenly erupted as a bulky human figure rose menacingly from beneath the surface and fired from its weapon a bolt that skimmed just over the little boat's gunwales. Just as suddenly, the figure descended again, leaving a trail of bubbles.

There was a pause. The Ref cleared his throat, put his hand over his earpiece. 'Erm ... now isn't that something? These ... these little beauties are a new thing, borrowed from the Pax training academy and, as I said, there are six of them, all automatic, all programmed by our FTL engineers to fire their bolts randomly at or around a probe hidden in our little ship, just where anybody who wanted to row would sit.

'So ... how to take care of the drones? Simple. In that little box there – quarter inch steel – is a weapon that will do the job. The box has two locking possibilities. One of these – an electronic lock – is already engaged. We have someone waiting on the far side of the water with the combination. But he will only punch in the code if certain other conditions have been met.

One – The box must also arrive padlocked and with the necessary key to open the padlock. Two – The box may only cross the water whilst at least *two* locks are engaged. The electronic lock *and* a padlock. Three – No key may cross the water. For the start of the game there is one padlock with its keys on each of the two stakes . . .'

*His voice.*

She sat and let the words blur into one endless, gentle sound. The camera was on his face now, moving in on its boom as he leaned close to say something dramatic to the viewers. There was pain in his eyes.

'. . . as I say, first up today is Friend. There she is, standing – no, *sitting* – by the boat, ready to go. She's heard the rules. She's heard what she has to do. On my whistle, then. Three, two, one . . . *begin*!'

Begin . . .

She looked about her. They were waiting, expectant. She stood up and realised then, as the world lurched, that she couldn't do it. She looked at the boat, at the stretch of water, the steel box. *What* was she meant to do? She couldn't remember. The food had not been enough to bring her back.

Somewhere in the Marsh, a bird sang. 'No need to stir yourself, no need to stir yourself': that's what it said in its staccato chatter. No need to play the games at all. Let life flow past and rest.

There was a rustle from across the flood and the first bolt came singing in, cutting through the wind. Then another, from the submerged drone that the audience had already seen. Then a third, again from the trees. The big electronic clock face on the camera crew's platform ticked away the seconds: half a minute gone. The Ref and the crew were looking at her. The Ref bowed his head and a dark curl escaped from the back of his mask, lying against his nape in a curiously vulnerable way. It fascinated her.

I can't do it, she thought again.

*I can.*

Had time passed? Everything seemed so still.

The bolts, singing in towards her, hung like dragon-flies over the water. The whole ring of dying trees and bushes lay shimmering, laid out flat on the surface. She stepped forward, into the boat. She padlocked the steel box, hung it from her neck by its strap, returned the key to its hook on the stake, and took the oars.

She had never rowed before, but memories came to her of the little craft that used to ply in and out to the fish farm at Le Porge. To start with, the heavy oars felt clumsy in her hands and she misjudged how deeply she should plunge their blades into the water, so that the boat rocked and stalled. Even as she sought to balance herself and learn the feel of the thing, the next bolt arrived, its movement a blur on the edge of her vision. She twisted and ducked sharply and felt the wind of the passing missile against her cheek.

She cursed her weakness. She had entered Paradise too late.

*Never too late. Lighten up.*

She laughed, and those watching flinched from the sound, as if flinching from a madman or a witch.

Her irregular splashing started to take the craft away from the stake, out into the expanse of water, veering a little left of the correct line. The clock registered almost a minute elapsed. Again she was forced to dive down for a bolt, losing control of the oars, but as she straightened another arrived almost at once from behind, out of her line of vision. It crashed into her shoulder blade, the impact throwing her full length in the crazily bobbing boat. Dizzying pain flashed outwards from her shoulder.

She groped for something to occupy her mind and remembered the fifth kata. She remembered Clarissa teaching her the fifth kata in the morning sun. She smiled to remember it, and started to take her thoughts through the slow, beautiful movements.

*The paths, the choices, the games lay stretched in every direction, but at their centre was stillness, the scent of frost on the cypresses, the stark, playful moon shadow.*

Her breathing steadied.

Six drones, the Ref had said. Six bolts already delivered, each from a different drone ... Between strokes, she nudged the little steel box over her shoulder so that it hung behind her, providing extra protection from the unseen. *Pull. Pull.* Make the strokes fit the pattern of feet and hands in the dance. She felt instinctively now how deep the blades must go, how she must caress the water. Watching the patch of vegetation from which the first bolt had come, she registered the noise of a surfacing drone with shock and again she had to stop and twist away.

So. The bolts did not have a simple pattern.

Agonisingly slowly, she inched on towards the second stake, faltering and drifting each time a bolt arrived. One caught her lower arm as she span away, so that the nerves screamed from her fingertips to the top of her head. One made the steel box shudder and rattle against her back. Stroke, stroke, stroke, dive, stroke, duck, stroke, stroke, twist.

When she reached the second stake the clock face showed almost five minutes elapsed. And she must recross the water twice more even to get to the weapon in the box.

Turning the boat by hand against the stake, she unhooked the second padlock and added it to the first, so that the box was now locked three times. Again she left the keys hanging on their nail as the rules required. Then she was away, moving now with firmer, more graceful strokes, arching her back to it as though she had been brought up on the water. Stroke stroke, twist, duck, stroke stroke. The bolts came fizzing in, but still her progress was better than on the first crossing. Only once was she grazed by one of the shafts, a purple weal appearing along her cheekbone as she turned away.

Two-thirds of the way back to the start, and with the clock showing seven minutes and twenty-two seconds gone, she laughed again.

She rowed on, more powerfully and confidently. Her lips moved soundlessly. The next time a bolt came, she did not pitch forwards or lose grip of the oars. Instead she lifted the handle in her left hand, and the missile thudded harmlessly into the wood, shaking it, but leaving her free to continue her strokes immediately. Again, another bolt, and this time she leaned forward a few degrees and the thing whistled past and skimmed down into the water. Then a third, straight into the box hanging from her neck.

Now she was back at the first stake, all her movements careful, playful. Off came the box, off came the first padlock, unfastened by its own keys still hanging there. Padlock and keys were neatly rehung, the boat turned and for the third time she was setting off, grunting as she pulled. Sweat started to run over her thin face.

The final crossing took only ninety-seven seconds, during which Adeline avoided all seventeen bolts that were fired at her, her mind jumping through the pattern of them, setting it against the rhythm of the oars dipping into water, and below that, against the kata. She reached the second stake with a little over a minute left, unfastened the remaining padlock and handed the box to the waiting assistant for his code.

The man's eyes met hers and his fingers fumbled over

the keypad. There was an angry bleeping from the box. He re-entered the code, while she kept her personal camera on his hands, and at last the box flipped open.

The weapon inside was of the projectile type, sleek and dark, but nothing she recognised. She pushed herself out onto the water again, rowing for three or four strokes to get clear of the trees, then shipped the oars, allowing the boat to drift.

Still the drones sent in their bolts, but none touched her as she unpacked the weapon, slotted in the necessary cartridge and brought the barrel up slowly, at arm's length, aiming it at the blank water. Within seconds, a figure rose up, dripping, from that very spot, and she squeezed the trigger. The results were unexpected. A jagged hole appeared in the centre of the drone's torso, and then a spurt of flame erupted from it, blowing the wire of its frame apart.

Its remains sagged over the water's surface, the gears burned away.

And in her cold little room in the city – cold from lack of credits to heat it – Chaney danced on her bed. As each drone exploded, she shouted aloud. Somebody was banging on the wall, someone was yelling for quiet, but she didn't care. When Adeline finally lay back exhausted in the boat with the task achieved, the clock showing eleven minutes and forty-eight seconds gone, Chaney found tears on her face. She laughed through the tears.

The banging stopped. Yet outside, the shouting continued. She could hear people running. She could hear screams. She could hear the sound of raw energy, pulsing through the city streets.

They lifted her out of the boat and back into Paradise. Her eyes opened as they laid her down and she saw that the Ref had brought her. They looked at one another, she between her worlds, he between doses of his drug.

And in that unguarded moment before she returned to sleep, something strange happened. She became familiar to him. Something he knew from long, long ago.

# THE REF

It was terrifying.

It was like the sun rising as you walked unknowing across a narrow path over a rocky gorge, showing you the peril that had been hidden.

It was like the Ref's most ancient fear: falling into deep water, being sucked down, feeling the cool weight of it pressing on you.

He went back to the game zone to find they were ready to go, with new drones. Somehow he fumbled his way through the introductions for the two remaining players. Somehow he jeered and sneered, reported their limited success with the right degree of scorn. And all the time he felt as if he were standing over a dizzying abyss of memory fragments, swirling below him without meaning or form.

At the end of the game he took the crew boat back to his quarters, sitting silent and hunched in the stern. Once there he collapsed heavily inside, leaning on the flimsy door, yearning for his instruments, for his familiar rooms. His pulse was hammering. His hands shook. He was sick on his shining boots and on the splintered floor. It was not the Lady, though, for all that she twitched his muscle strings as if he were her puppet, and sent his mind from ice-cold clarity to grey fog and back.

It was fear. It was identity. It was the wrenching sense of loss that came skimming across the empty years.

A name came to him in the gloom and the stench of his sick: Clarissa.

A face came too: Friend's face, yet sparkling with

amusement and mockery and self-confidence. A person he'd loved and hated and been in awe of.

*When* had that been?

*When* had Jan wrapped this cocoon around him?

The Ref could not properly remember a time before the Lady, except for the vague sense of long hours shared with Jan in the nursery. There had been a journey, though. A hard, dangerous journey that had ended in deep water. He'd screamed and the water had flooded into his mouth.

When they came with food, he was clean again and quiet. 'Thank you,' he said to his minder. 'Thank you . . . Petrowski. That's right, isn't it?'

'Yes sir. Petrowski *is* my name.' And then, 'Are you feeling quite all right, sir?'

'Yes, Petrowski. I am quite all right. But tell me . . .'

'Sir?'

'Tell me . . . tell me . . .' What could he ask? What could the man tell him? The year? The mood of the people? The future? . . . 'Tell me what the weather is like out there tonight.'

'The weather? Well, sir, as you can probably hear, the wind's right down and it's been dry for an hour or two. But don't expect it to last. Cloud's coming in, thick and low. We'll have a proper storm before bedtime or I miss my guess.'

The Ref nodded. 'Thank you. That's very helpful.'

Petrowski hesitated. 'You quite sure, sir, that there's nothing else I can bring you?'

'Quite sure.'

When the man had gone the Ref carefully measured out the food he must eat, the food he must set aside. But he felt weak, unhungry, and he was sick again when he'd eaten. Crying softly, he forced himself to re-eat his vomit like a cat on the street.

Then he slept the heavy, drugged sleep, dreaming that he was out in the storm, watching the immense, rolling ships, planning escape, warmed through to his core.

Friend did not leave Paradise again for the remainder of the Ref's stint in the Marsh. He caught only occasional glimpses of her as he went about his FTL business, but he was deeply aware of her closeness, and strangely content with that.

He felt like a newborn infant. He had to reach for the skills and the deceptions that he needed for his role, and found that they no longer came easily. He understood the danger he would be in if the mask slipped, but even so, as the drug softened its grip on him he became weaker, less focussed. He wanted to talk to his crew, to find out about their lives. He wanted to walk in the city and breathe in the smells and tastes. He found that his suit itched and irritated him more than ever. And the NVs who played the games he introduced? He wondered for the first time if they were as thoroughly trapped as he was. The sneers came reluctantly to his lips, on camera, as the great apes lumbered through their tricks.

Piece by piece, the fragments of memory crept back to him, adding to the ache. He knew he was finished as the Ref.

'Kay,' the Clarissa creature murmured to him in his dreams, gathering him into a maternal embrace, stroking his hair. 'Darling Kay.' And then she stood back, laughing at him again. 'Are you just going to run and hide? Are you?'

'I don't know,' he whispered back, in the darkness of his hut.

# DOMINIC
## – day 74 –

When something surfaces from before, I come close to losing it. Just little things, a taste on the tongue. Being in a warm room, electricity, light, the TV on in the corner, a proper cup of tea; Kingsley even, snuffling over his porn. A future. Double History in the morning. The distant groan of the buses at Father's London house.

It's so much better not to remember. To pretend that this is all there's ever been. The frozen skeleton of Bede's, with a handful of white-faced animals shuffling around it in boiler suits. Nothing outside, or before.

I'm no fool. I haven't ignored what old Beckett said. Or the night I saw the Major talking to Ruth when she was working out on the assault course. Sometimes I wish Ruth would ask me for protection. I can't really imagine that. At other times I am so angry. This morning I was down on the rota to wash at the pump. It's half pleasure, half agony. Anyway ... the water had actually frozen, frozen all along the pipes from the beck. They'll thaw them out, sure. But that was one time I lost it.

Loney said, 'You'll just have to smell. What'll *she* say?'

I jumped him, went crazy, rolling with him in the snow, pounding at his face, wanting to shut him up, until they pulled me off.

I'm not the only one, of course. This place is set up to push you beyond coping. They've even cut down on food. You have to defend your own portion if you don't want to lose it.

There are only twenty-four of us still here, plus the

soldiers and Eve's bunch. Everybody flips from time to time. Nothing is private.

Frank said to me, 'I hear you're only still around because of your father.'

What about that other thing Mr Beckett said? What about 'tinkering' and 'muck'? I have an idea about that too. A terrible idea. Could *that* be Father's 'culture, civilisation and order'?

Tonight when we embraced, I said to Ruth, 'What is happening with you and the Major?'

She pulled back and looked at me. She said, very clearly, but softly, 'He wants me to have sex with him. He is trying to blackmail me, by using Dad's wellbeing, or my own, as a lever.' She shook her head, eyes wide. 'Is this new to you, Dom?'

Hearing it all so simply was a shock. I don't know if it made things better or worse. I said, 'I want to help.'

She replied, 'If there's something you can do, I'll ask. For the moment I'm handling it. Let's concentrate on us.'

She's right of course. There's only us.

# – day 78 –

I've done two things without Ruth's knowledge.

The first is that I have started to show Eve the test papers that Ruth has completed.

Why do that? Ruth just sees it as a buzz. She has such enthusiasm for things, for all things, such humour. She laughs at the problems we're given to solve, laughs at the thinking behind them. Then she rattles off answers that make my head spin, all running here and there in her tiny writing. Do you know, she's been educating herself since she was five? Since her mum died.

Why take the papers to Eve?

Even Eve was uncomfortable. 'What is this, Dominic? A window into the soul of that "certain girl" you mentioned before? What is the purpose of this?'

'She's as good as anyone here. Take a look at them. That's all.'

I think she could see through me. She leafed through the papers, sighed and said, 'Dear, charming Dominic, the world has become very different very quickly. You must learn new skills. You must learn to adapt. And to accept some not very pleasant things for the meantime.'

I glared at her. She makes me feel like an infant. She doesn't belong here in the Bede skeleton. She glared back, stuck out her Czech chin.

'So. And the other information we are collating? The physical attributes, the problem-solving in situ? I can do nothing with these alone.'

'Are you crazy? This person is a natural athlete. I'll get you information, times, OK?'

I thought she was going to shout at me. She seemed furious. But she looked away, at the floor. 'Nothing can be promised.' And then, 'You may get the information if you wish.'

Ruth is so private . . . what will she say?

The other thing is that I have written to Father. I have explained a little about the situation concerning Ruth. I have asked that if her test scores are high enough, she be included in the programme, or failing that, that he at least manages to get the Major to lay off.

I found my own headed letter paper and envelopes still in my locker in the prep rooms. I took the letter, sealed, to the Major. I tried to be very casual about it. 'If you happen to be in touch, sir. Whenever. No hurry.'

He took the envelope but hardly gave me a glance.

# CRANE

Crane still hurt. That was his excuse for staying in the hut. He needed to recover, to heal.

Besides, he thought, he'd made his mark. He'd got into Paradise earlier in the game than anyone ever had. He'd beaten Stringer. What reason to go out there into the hungry eye of the cameras that laced the trees around the stockade? The old Pax officer had said that he'd be in a Task with his target, sooner or later. It would clearly all be arranged. There was no need to worry about anything until then.

'Here. Food.'

The girl herself put her head in through the doorway, her cheeks and stubble shining with the wet, her face marked by a vivid graze. She regarded him without expression for a few moments, and then tossed down a flapping, open packet of rations. Half a flask of water followed. He glared at her but didn't move, and she shrugged and ducked back out.

*The food!*

What could he do? There were no longer enough ration packets for the inhabitants in the Village. The girl was immune to challenge until she had faced Vaso, her previous challenger. He could challenge a fellow NV to gain a full ration packet, but he could easily lose if he fought like this, at less than full strength. He could tussle over the last packet each morning like a rat at the bins . . .

Besides hunger, irritation and outrage rumbled in his belly. He knew what they were saying out there. He

264

knew how they scorned him and laughed at him for eating the food of a Scroat.

Perhaps the numbers in Paradise would fall. Perhaps a Task would restore the quota to its proper figure of fifteen, and the other NVs decide to keep out further newcomers. But in his heart he had little hope of that. He could feel the distance that had crept in between his genetic brothers and sisters and himself. His violent arrival, his haste to enter: these might have been quickly forgotten. Yet the fact that the Scroat girl had offered a gift of food that she needed herself, the fact that such a situation had ever come about: that would *not* be forgotten. The taint of the gift lay heavy upon him.

What would Anton be thinking at home? Or Lily, with her hot, strong mouth? What would the Leader himself think, to see his model subverted?

Crane clung doggedly to his mission. When the girl was dead and he was a hero, when they all *knew* ... But it was wretched, false consolation. He chewed a wafer and admitted how false it was. They would never let him explain. The mission was secret, his alone. And if he did tell the world, what then? In his empty gut he knew that killing Friend would never make him a hero. Not even removing the mighty Stringer had done that.

Crane had hunted many Scroats of all shapes and sizes, ever since he could remember. This one, this girl, had a scent of desperation about her: a sniff of exhaustion and collapse, barely kept at bay. Yet they said she had laughed in yesterday's Task. And she'd shared her packet of food with him.

What did the state of Briton fear in her, he wondered?

He lay and waited and slept in the dark.

All his questions and doubts were irrelevant.

The following morning Crane felt much better, sharper. He realised when he woke that the problem of

Friend was out of his hands. What would happen to *him* when Vaso eliminated Friend from the game of Fit To Live, he didn't know. Would Pax come for him, with the promised promotion? Would he still be their operative? Would he be left, instead, in the game to win honour, step by step, through the Tasks? He regarded this latter possibility sourly.

Preparations were being made for the Combat. The noises reached him as he lay on his unwholesome mattress. A space of the required size was being marked out. Fragments of discussion drifted through the door. How quickly would the Scroat succumb? Would she still even go ahead with the Combat? She had not fought before: what chance was there that she could face Vaso and not quail?

For two nights and a day the wind had been relentless, and the clouds had scudded across the skies, black and heavy, depositing their millions of litres of water on the Marsh in frequent sudden deluges. This morning was wetter than ever. In the midst of it all the Tannoys buzzed and coughed: *'Attention. Attention the Village. The challenge issued by Vaso to Friend may proceed today at thirteen-twenty-five hours. A reminder will be given at that time.'*

13.25.

Why was everybody up and about with so many hours to wait? He could see them moving outside his doorway, and sensed the excitement and relief that the Combat was finally to take place. Presently, the noise came of the morning food delivery, the water-swollen gates shuddering and scraping open. Crane felt his strength returning to him. He stood up, stretched and practised three or four kicks and punches, satisfied with the power that flooded through the rested muscles. A few aches, but nothing that would hamper him for long. He healed fast, like all his kind. His belly rattled with hunger, though. He could imagine biting into something good and juicy. A big fish. A sea salmon, perhaps, like his mother had prepared for his last birthday.

At the doorway, he paused. The girl was just stooping to pick up the packet of rations. Either he must go and wrest it from her, or stay inside a little longer, away from mocking eyes.

He hesitated and the moment passed. It didn't matter. He knew he would not be given a Task until at least tomorrow. He could survive until then and do well enough with a full ration packet in the morning. In due course the wet, slender head with its fuzz of red-brown appeared and once again he was looking into the un-natural bright blue eyes.

This time, she smiled at him. 'Breakfast's up!' The half-empty packet came skimming over and he caught it.

'Thank you.'

His assessment seemed suddenly wrong again. The desperation had retreated. The girl was thin and gaunt, but she moved with purpose. Her teeth glinted white and sharp when her lips pulled back to smile. The whispers in his belly were not all for food.

Soon after midday he went again and stood in the doorway of his dwelling. He was noticed at once and felt the hesitancy of the other NVs towards him. They did not ignore him: that would be illogical and potentially dangerous to them. They nodded their greetings, they said 'Hey', but he did not share – was not invited to share – the buzz that was going round in anticipation of the fight.

There was something brutish and tedious about their identical reactions. He found himself glaring at them. He'd done nothing wrong. Nothing shameful. He was what he was. If they had a problem, they could take it up with him any time.

The girl, Vaso, was already in the fighting area. He saw that she was broad-shouldered and formidable. She had power in her frame and an aggressive pout to her mouth. She looked bored, shoulders hunched in the soaking tunic, but Crane saw her give a smirk as someone in the little knot of watchers called her name.

In contrast, Friend was standing very upright, feet apart, eyes far away again. She'd stripped off the tunic and stood in only her vest, her belly rising and falling with her breaths. Her feet were still without boots, but she'd bound material around them, perhaps to prevent slipping on the rain-slick planks. She looked like a twig next to the boulder of Vaso.

*'Attention. This is a time update. The time is now one-twenty-five pm precisely. The Combat challenge between Vaso and Friend may now begin.'*

There was a cheer from the NVs. 'Cream the little bitch. Take her apart!' Further cheers came from out in the Marsh, from the nearest platforms, where they would have been following life in Paradise closely.

Friend wiped the rainwater from her eyes, lifted her arms up as if to touch the sky, brought them down in a slow circle. Suddenly she smiled, bright as a new moon, as she had earlier. She gazed calmly around the ring of faces.

'Well then. At last, something I'm good at!'

They laughed at her, but Crane, watching from his own doorway still, felt the first doubt about the outcome of the Combat. It occurred to him in that moment that they had all been wrong about this girl so far. *Why* they'd been wrong was not clear, impossible to fathom. Maybe she was the terrible spy the officer had suggested after all. But Crane could see in this moment with his experienced eye that Friend not only believed she could win . . . she *expected* to.

A whistle blew, the girls came towards one another

and started to circle, Vaso solid and scowling, Friend lighter on her feet. If it had been Crane fighting, he'd have taken a moment to assess his opponent's body language, then attacked as early and savagely as possible. It was a textbook approach. Vaso would have been trained the same way. Crane saw the line of big muscles bunch, within the wet fabric, then she thundered across the space, with murder in her eyes. She too had been tainted, Crane thought in that instant. Tainted by having to challenge an inferior. She'd want to get the thing done and buried as much as he had. He felt sympathy, surprising himself.

The next moment, Vaso was stumbling amongst the crowd of watchers, her knees sagging from a blow to her kidneys. The Scroat girl stood well back, on the other side of the combat area.

There were roars and howls from the NVs. Advice to Vaso, lots of it scathing. Abuse for Friend. Vaso herself was thrust back into the ring by many strong hands. Her face showed fury, shame; a hint, now, of fear. She faced up to her opponent and spat. Once more they circled . . .

Somebody was hammering again. This time it was on Chaney's door.

Chaney wished they'd stop, wished they'd leave her alone, whoever it was. Goddam it, she'd been quiet enough today.

She sat in the cold and the dirt of her room, smoking amongst the jumble of old food containers and bedding, and concentrated on the glow from her terminal, which was illegally wired in for twenty-four-hour live-streaming now, so that she wouldn't have to go out.

The hammering became a kicking. She could hardly hear the sound from the little headset she wore.

'Not now,' she muttered. 'Not bloody now.'

To her satisfaction, the row ceased. The drongo must

have realised at last that it was the wrong address. She'd ordered nothing, contacted nobody in days. She just wanted to be left alone.

'That's it. Sod off,' she said contentedly.

Thirty seconds later the door crashed inwards, the plastic and resin frame splitting, the debris on the floor skittering away with the impact.

Through the gap walked a woman. She smiled at Chaney and Chaney's mouth hung open in shock.

'You're . . . you're . . .'

The woman offered a hand. 'Are you Petra Chaney?'

Chaney nodded, speechless.

'Then I believe you might be able to help me.'

Again Friend waited for her opponent to strike first. The stand-off lasted two full minutes. The NVs grew subdued, strained. In the end, Vaso could wait no longer. She shouted defiantly and leaped into a low aerial kick, flipping around in the air in the last tenth of a second so that the blow would come unexpectedly from the side instead of straight on. It was a good, clean, crisp blow and might have done the job, but Friend, wrong-footed, allowed herself to fall sideways, limply, before its force, and held tight to the booted foot as she went. Once on the planks she rolled over a full turn in the wet and with a gasp of pain Vaso's remaining leg buckled and she too collapsed. In an instant Friend was standing above her, her own fabric-wrapped foot poised to finish it.

'Stay down,' she said, as she had said to the woman at Seven.

Vaso scowled but made no move and her opponent released her, stood back. Amongst the watchers there was shocked, heavy silence. In his doorway, Crane felt suddenly better than he had since riding the transport from the city. Apart from the girl herself, he was the only one here who'd foreseen the possibility of Friend's winning. He was ahead of the game again. He was seeing things clearly.

*He* could take her, though.

He came fully out, into the rain, and made his massive presence known. Nobody looked him in the eye or had anything but respect for him. He found himself smiling. They were on their own learning curve, now, his brothers and sisters: not quite so sure of themselves. His glance moved to Friend and she noticed his smile and raised her eyebrows. He saw again the fatigue and hardness there. She smiled back.

As she did so a short length of wood swung viciously out from the ring of watching NVs and caught her across the side of the head. She saw it at the last instant, or perhaps she saw Crane's smile slip. Again she fell back before the blow, but too late.

Then she was lying in the rain, the red of her blood mixing with the clean water.

Crane gave no thought at all. He gave a shout and pushed forward through the others. He knelt down to examine the girl. There was still a pulse, he saw.

'What are you, a Scroat-lover?' someone growled.

He realised what he was doing, then. He stood up, confused.

But at his feet, Friend's eyes crept open, flickering.

The lenses, he saw, had been knocked out by the force of the blow. And the eyes underneath were of two different colours. One brown and one green. His personal camera lingered on the sight for a full minute.

# ADELINE

The length of timber swung. It blotted out the light. The NV called Crane had been about to warn her. She fell.

*You betrayed me*, she thought, inconsequentially. *You didn't trust enough.*

*She could feel the blow pounding and echoing through the dimming avenues of consciousness. She could vaguely smell and taste the bitter tang of smoke. She struggled up to her knees – or perhaps that was simply what she intended – but found that she was down again, lying awkwardly on the cold floor. Her thoughts blew this way and that, however firmly she tried to marshal them.*

*She stopped fighting. Much better.*

*She lay still. She accepted the situation.*

*After a while, she thought: Stupid. I'm being stupid. You haven't betrayed anyone.*

*She remembered an hour ago: her body still vibrated with it.*

*She smiled and shivered in her half consciousness.*

*Without the fighting, the strength seeped back, as she'd known it would. Soon she could act with urgency. But the flames were crackling, very close. The heat was on her face. She came fully back into her body and opened her eyes.*

She looked up and saw, like a child, the drops of rain spiralling down towards her face, on their individual paths from the heavens. She saw a few ragged leaves clinging to rotten branches. She smelled salt and mud. There were faces looking down at her. One quite close. The big, bruised Crane.

'*Attention,*' came a crackling voice. '*Attention. There has been an infringement of the rules of Personal Combat in Paradise. Rule seven-point-three has been infringed. A third party has become involved in a Combat challenge. Please wait for the judges' assessment.*'

Her head hurt, and she was weak, but she felt suddenly quite absurdly happy. There had been no betrayal. Only a gift. She imagined the warmth of Dominic's limbs wrapped around hers. The pulse in his neck, felt with her lips as she kissed it while he slumbered. The scent of his skin.

She realised that she was ready now, for the end, when it came.

Crane spoke to her, awkwardly, standing back a pace further. 'You can use the hut, if you want to rest in the dry.'

'Thank you. Peut-être. Maybe.' She was light-headed, tempted to giggle.

She pulled herself up to a sitting position and shuffled back on her bottom until she reached the nearest wooden wall, to prop herself and take stock. There was a sombre, unpleasant feeling amongst the savages as they milled around the central space. The elements ruled the Marsh for now, the storm loud where the people were silent. In a little while a boat arrived with armed FTL guards. Amidst shouts and anger, someone was removed from Paradise.

'*Contestant George Immit has been eliminated from the contest. The judges have ruled that he deliberately attempted to alter the course of the Combat between Vaso and Friend. Disqualification is therefore automatic.*'

Adeline could feel the anger of the others. She expected one or other of them to vent that anger on her while she was weak. She saw her opponent of a few minutes ago, Vaso, leaning on the stockade by herself, staring into empty air as the rain coursed down her face.

In the strange code of the savages, Vaso seemed to have joined Crane as outcast, unacceptable. The girl was strong enough to snap Adeline's neck if she wanted to. Why didn't she come to finish it?

Vaso's eyes darted her way as if guessing her thoughts. They were full of hatred, fear, confusion.

Nothing happened. Soon Adeline grew cold. A chill was not the way she wanted to go. She rose unsteadily and walked to Crane's cabin. He was back in there now, sitting on the bedroll, scowling.

He said, 'There's another hut free now if you want to move in there.' He jerked his head to the right.

She turned away, back into the rain, but as she was at the doorway to the dwelling that had been George Immit's, she heard Crane's voice.

'You. Scroat girl. I challenge you to Personal Combat within the rules of Fit To Live.'

She turned and saw the crossed fists, the desperation in his face.

She went inside to sleep.

They were all quite mad.


Jan Barbieri's two advisers sat in the dusky apartments as they had before. They flinched before the Leader's quiet rage and sought suitable words.

'Suspend the broadcasts,' Cooper-Smyth said, violently. 'Turn *off* the screens. Remove and kill the girl in secret. Give the people time to forget. Start the show again in a month or two, with a clean sheet. A new game zone even. A new presenter.'

Hunter looked at his hands and faintly shook his head.

'A new presenter,' Jan snarled. 'The girl dead! Have you been out into the city, Cooper-Smyth? Have you *seen* the crowds at the screens? Cheering for that ... freak, cheering for the old-liners, cheering that an

*NV . . .'* his voice rose dangerously, 'one of *my NVs* has been removed for breaking the rules! There have been *attacks* out there, Cooper-Smyth. Attacks by Visions, on other NVs. Did you *know* that? That's not to mention the *filth* that's started to float up from the docks. Prophets and priestesses; vagrants and rabble-raisers, obsessed with the colour of that girl's eyes. What message will I send my people if I turn off the broadcasts? Answer me that!'

'A message of strength, sir.'

'A message of *fear,* Cooper-Smyth. A message that one freak of a girl can have us all panicking.' He paused. 'Well, Hunter? What have *you* to say?'

'Sir?'

'Your so-called operative has issued a challenge. Can he take her? What plans have you made to be sure?'

Hunter said quietly, 'I don't know if Crane can eliminate the girl, sir. Doubtful, I would have said.'

'Agreed. Obvious. *So?*'

'We'll work on covert ways to sedate the girl.'

'Good. Make it so. I want her *beaten*: beaten in front of this whole, miserable, Scroat-loving country.'

'Sir.'

Cooper-Smyth, who had stayed silent and sulky since his rebuke, spoke up again. 'According to the rules, as she's just *completed* a challenge, Crane will have to wait two days . . . and *then* she'll be due for her next game Task. More delay. It might be five whole days until they fight.'

'So? *We will wait, Cooper-Smyth!* To have it done *right*. And in the meantime, we'll start, quietly, to clear our streets of the flotsam from the waterfront. For which the people will be grateful. The girl will have done us a favour, after all, bringing them into the light of day.'

And, when he was cooler, recovered from the meeting, he thought, *After all, the girl in herself is nothing. What threat does she pose without followers? I will tidy my city, I will bring the new ships in now, I will remind my people of our strength:* my *strength. All will be well.*

Adeline took possession of George Immit's cabin in Paradise, and also possession of his share of rations when they came, and nobody tried to prevent her doing so. Perhaps it was the example of Immit himself, together with Crane's challenge, that kept the NVs at bay. Perhaps it was her combat with Vaso, or respect for the game. For the moment, though, something was broken or lost amongst the New Visions of Paradise. Crane was no longer fully accepted amongst them, nor Vaso. The pack was split and uncertain of itself.

Those that were called to face Tasks did badly. Crane himself survived an Endurance, happy to leave the stockade for a little while and lose himself in the simplicity of physical effort. Others left for good and had their places quickly snapped up by newbies from outside, but they, too, became infected with the loss of morale. Squabbles broke out, without fresh challenges to solve them. Amongst the newcomers to Paradise, two were old-line Visions. On the nearest of the platforms, another lowly Scroat waited his chance, a flint-eyed, flint-jawed young man with a shock of white hair, called Torr. The game had never seen such a mix.

Adeline rested and ate the meagre food and listened to the storm outside. Her ragged heart hiccupped and skipped in protest at all it had borne, but panic had left her and she learned, during these attacks, to *feel* her body into being soft, accepting whatever befell it. Whether in combat or in pain and fear, if you offered no resistance the destructive force would be spent harmlessly. *Just a little longer,* she thought, hugging her knees, humming to herself.

Still Ruth's shadow was upon her, and her light.

Perhaps it had always been there. She should have welcomed that too.

The days slipped past, the rain fell, and the word spread: 'The road to the city is gone. Washed away by the fresh run-off from the hills. A new river! There'll be no more players unless they bring them in by boat or 'copter.'

A shiver of excitement and fear went through the Marsh. It was felt also in the city, where wild reports came from those living closest to the walls: 'The floods are coming, the water is up twenty centimetres! Thirty! Half a metre!'

The Ref arrived out of the storm in his black and silver FTL helicopter, a relic from a distant past. He rode sandwiched uncomfortably between two pallets of rations for the players and crew and brought five new armed soldiers. Four were hand-picked by the Leader himself, an insurance policy. The other was Hunter's choice, an assassin, with his long-range weapon folded neatly away in his pack.

The Ref's presence did not bring with it the crackle of fear and the straightening of backs that it had. He stayed mostly in his quarters, and when he had to come out for filming, he was preoccupied, or talked to his staff eagerly about things that were irrelevant to the show: music and memory, Briton's history, the great migrations taking place elsewhere. Under the mask, the eyes were wide, troubled.

One of his minders transmitted off a short report on this and Jan, who was well aware that his pet was not himself, decided that the Ref would make no more trips after this one, not for a while. Instead there would be a programme of punishment and humiliation. Meanwhile, the first of the new black ships had been brought inside the tidal barrier to its hastily-built berth, to be properly fitted. The people were already murmuring in awe at the extravagance of steel! Wait till he could parade his first thousand NV commandos on the dock! Wait until the British people saw the lines of conquerors filing up into the ships!

Adeline's next Task was, ironically, Combat, but with an Endurance element included. She and her adversary had to take a tortuous path right across the Marsh, moving sometimes between treetops, sometimes in the water, sometimes even under it, stopping four times to fight fierce two-minute bouts. The NVs, in the Marsh and across Briton, held their breath in hope that the wrong could be righted. Old-liners forgot about the new floods long enough to gather at the screens and wish just the opposite. Hot food sellers moved profitably amongst the crowds, priestesses in green appeared to sing their strange keening song, and Jan Barbieri's Pax officers sat in their armoured transports and tried to assess when their troops should move in with their batons and burning gas.

In the event, Adeline laid her NV opponent gently to rest on the slippery fight platform after only a few seconds of the second bout. She finished the course carefully, though not fast, and went once more to Paradise, turning her face up, eyes closed, to the rain, as the boat crawled along. The NVs watched her return in tense, dangerous silence, but Torr, up on his platform, grinned down and chattered like an ape, goading them. Crane stood silent, contemptuous of them all now, and again he saw the expectation of death in the girl's face. He went into his cabin and wondered, for the first time in his life, about his own death. Nobody could know yet, how long his kind would last.

The Ref, the menacing, dangerous Ref, who had once laughed as the players failed and fell, watched Friend cross the game finish and was also silent, though his eyes never left her.

# CLARISSA

They stood pressed in the sodden crowd, warm from the steaming bodies around them and ate their savoury hot wraps. Chaney felt first sick and then ravenous, bolting the food down. She waved a seller over to buy more with the strangers' money. How many days had it been since she had eaten properly?

'It's amazing,' she said with her mouth full, nodding her head at the mass of people surrounding them. 'It was never like this, not since I was a girl.'

Clarissa nodded. 'Not even then,' she murmured. The energy, the danger, the will of the crowd was something she'd never seen or felt before. She had been a fool to think she could keep *this* locked away in the heat of the mountains. She was glad to be here, now.

'Brothers and sisters!' cried a sudden voice, over the throng. 'It is not too late! We have been lured down this path by the Leader Barbieri. We are close to the war he wants. But it is not too late! We can choose another way!'

Clarissa caught Chaney's arm and started steering her through the throng. 'Time to go.' She could see the Pax uniforms quietly deploying. There would be violence here soon. On the giant screen the Ref's eyes were full of yearning as he reported the Task results.

Poor Kay. In love again.

They left the rain-washed square behind as the first blows were exchanged.

'It's time,' Clarissa said. 'We go now.'

Chaney was thinking of more food, then a cigarette.

She was frightened and excited to be with this woman, but too much excitement might not be a good thing.

'There'll never be an easy time, Petra,' Clarissa said, reading her thoughts. 'Soon Jan will realise that he is losing control, that things have moved more quickly than he expected. Who knows what he might do? We should act before that. Every minute we can buy will help the protests to grow.' And every minute the broadcasts continued was a minute extra that her sister might survive.

They hurried along. An electric security transport crawled up level with them, cameras swivelling on their stalks.

Clarissa nodded, smiling enthusiastically, '... and that's when they offered me the job in the records department. Can you imagine? My credits just leaped up! Plus fifty new Citizenship Points. I knew he'd want me then.'

'What?'

The transport moved off.

'Come on, down here.' Clarissa led the other woman, wheezing, down a steeper, narrower street, towards the water. She'd given the signal ten minutes ago. They should be ready by now.

'Have you *seen* the building?' Chaney muttered, apparently unheard. 'They don't hold the door open for you, you know.'

They turned left once more, past a row of filthy tenements and suddenly three figures had drifted from the shadows, falling into step beside them.

'They're with me,' Clarissa reassured the nervous Chaney. And then to the others: 'All set?'

Three nods.

'Chaney? All set?'

'I guess so. But the *building* ...'

'Then let's go.'

They headed on, towards the FTL tower.

Clarissa glanced across at Chaney as they walked. 'I know,' she said; 'I do know. I was born there, remember?'

# DOMINIC
## – day 83 –

We're going! Escaping.

She'd drifted away while I held her: gone to another place. When she came back, her eyes focussed slowly on me like a child's, wondering. 'All right,' she said at last, as if she was surprised by her own decision. 'Let's do it. We'll come with you. In two or three days, when I've sorted stuff out for Dad.'

We hadn't been talking about that at all.

She became a little wild. She took my hand and pulled me into the trees and kissed me like a savage. Her eyes were very bright. She was laughing. She punched me in the stomach, but not seriously. 'Isn't the power of choice wonderful? Do you love me, Dominic, at this moment?'

I said I did.

I do.


I've started to plan. Two days is soon, too soon maybe. I need to organise my maps, try to get one of those guns from the CCF hut, plus the correct bolt from the Geography storeroom. We need to think about food and water.

It's fantastic, though. She loves me; she's going to come away with me.

Where will we go?

# – day 84 –

A 'parade' this morning, before lunch, for the few of us left. Back in the tennis courts, like on the first day.

*Where have they all gone?*

It was cold *then*, but now it's unbelievable. The last nights we've slept in all our kit and everything we can find. The water pump has to be thawed out each time it's used; but the beck, too, is near to freezing. Minus nine according to the thermometer.

The Major arrived and said, 'Well done to you all. You are the face of tomorrow. I am here to tell you that in the next few days, a week at most, we will be finished here. There will then be a few small formalities to go through with our scientific friends, after which you will be restored to your families.'

I couldn't believe it. I thought this was for ever. For a year. I don't know. But they'll just let us walk out of here, after all. It changes everything. Ruth and I can be together without the risk of an escape. I'll go and tell her when I can. It's wonderful: I'm sure she'll be relieved.

It was like the end of term as the parade broke up. People who'd grown to hate or tolerate each other were waking up, trying to remember what normal life is like. It was quite awkward. We'll all need those tools again soon. Pass the sugar. After you. Exceptionally cold for the time of year, isn't it?

Frank came towards me.

He said, 'Not over yet though, is it?'

It will be soon, Frank.

The scientists had been there too, in the courts, lined up

at the side with the soldiers to listen to the Major. I saw
Eve watching, looking very serious, sad even. I went over,
sliding on ice as I went.

'Cheer up.'

She said heavily, 'Oh Dominic. The things that we do.
The way we tell ourselves lies.'

I said, 'Did you hear back, about Ruth coming on the
programme?'

'No.'

'Oh well. Doesn't matter now.'

'But I graded her papers and the information you gave.
She is . . .'

'Yes? She's what?'

'Don't lose her, Dominic. Keep her safe.'

She turned away, walked off for her lunch.

Of course I'll keep Ruth safe.

Oh Christ. She still wants to go.

She was like a white shadow in that dark, freezing, damp
room, just sitting there, with her dad snoring away in a pile
of rugs on the floor.

She stood up to meet me, and kissed me. I explained
about what the Major had said . . . and she went whiter still.
She cried a little.

'I thought we had a plan,' she said.

'But we don't need it any more, do we?'

'Don't we?'

She held out a sheet of paper, dull-eyed. 'Here. Another
poem for you.'

She seemed so lifeless, so helpless. Another trance?
I haven't seen her like this before. Maybe she's just ill.

I said, 'I'll still go with you. If that's what you want.'

She touched my cheek with her hand. 'That's what I want.'

It's all so crazy.

*

284

Oh, here's the poem. I'll stick it in. She's just written 'Song?' at the top. Maybe I can get some music together for it. 'Ruth's Song'.

Song?

*Blessed Children,*
*You are given this sleeping serpent;*
*Stretched across the years,*
*Its strong, bright coils buried deep*
*In the marshes and the floodwaters;*
*Its mouth closed on its tail.*

*And when the serpent wakes,*
*And it is full-grown and nourished,*
*And the beautiful, sleek, knowing head is lifted up,*
*And the two eyes open, one brown, one green:*
*Then, blessed children, you may ride its back*
*To freedom and love.*

*For this serpent is no tempter:*
*She is your truest friend.*

Weird stuff, but she's weird too. We're all nuts here. Perhaps that's what they've been proving with their tests.

# THE REF

Under his mask, Kay was naked. He was terrified.

He knew that this was the time he couldn't go back. *This time.*

Suddenly his long captivity did not seem so bad. He'd had his own comfortable rooms, regular food, people to look after him. He'd been in the city that he'd known from his birth. Even if he wasn't permitted to go wandering as he used to, he could catch a glimpse of the ships moving across the harbour to freedom; he could see the people out and about their business. He'd been allowed his instruments.

It seemed that the price of memory was high indeed. And it was not even a reassuring memory.

Kay Saint. Last of the Saint family. What was Kay Saint? Memory suggested that he was not much. A bundle of contradictory feelings. A love of music and of solitude. An unspent passion. A muddle of guilt and fear. A history of decisions avoided or funked. In mockery, Jan and the Lady had fashioned him into his opposite and made him powerful, master of the game of Fit To Live. Perhaps he'd been unwise to seek escape after all.

And yet, when he had stopped being Kay Saint and had become Jan's creature, he had left many things undone. He'd failed the girl he had been travelling with, Mira, who had captured his heart and provoked him too. He'd failed his family. He had fallen into the deep water at the foot of the hot French mountains and never surfaced.

Apart from the eyes, the girl called Friend might be

the double of Mira, or of his own 'sister', Clarissa, now no doubt long dead at Jan's destructive hand. For the moment, Friend was alive only because she was in FTL, watched by three million pairs of eyes, but Kay knew that it couldn't continue. Every day her hair sprouted and she grew more into Clarissa's and Mira's image, and every day she challenged the state that Jan had built, challenged his precious NVs, challenged his own rule, just by existing. That's how the Leader would see it, Kay knew from long experience. He would make sure that the girl died, one way or another.

Kay looked around him, looked at his crew, the maintenance staff and game builders, and at the soldiers that had come with him, and he wondered whom he might trust. He looked at the old black helicopter, squat and ugly on its concrete platform, the rotors bending down almost to the flood, and thought about sabotage. With the stiltway road washed away for good, the helicopter was his only link to Jan until a boat could come up the dangerous, stormy coastline.

He considered his three minders. Which, he wondered, stood ready to kill him at a word from the city? Which of them would hold the precious supply of Ambrosia?

Like Friend, he was safe enough in front of the cameras, yet their images could be extinguished in the main city control room with the single push of a button. His best chance might, after all, be to take the helicopter, to force the pilot to fly him to safety. In only three days, he was scheduled to take the survivors of Friend's cycle, old hands of twenty-five days in the Marsh, up to the mountains for Black. Not many players made it to the mountains. The FTL crew up there numbered only six, compared to the twenty or so here in the Marsh. There were no Tasks in the mountains, only survival or death.

How many of the soldiers and minders would go with him? He didn't know, couldn't ask.

*This time.*

It might not be too late to go back after all.

'Turn the screens off!' Cooper-Smyth insisted again, desperately. 'Turn the whole broadcast off! The Marsh is cut off, unless you send another chopper, and even then it would have nowhere to land. Your precious Ref is having some kind of a breakdown, the NV contestants are ill . . . or *something*. For all our sakes, turn it off!'

'No!' urged Hunter, equally forcefully. 'Remember what you decided before. That was the correct judgement. This city, *all* the cities, are watching. They've become obsessed. Turn the show off now and you'll have rioting, revolution, anarchy. Let the girl be finished *within* the game and, eventually, she'll be forgotten. For now, let them watch the screens, let them forget the rising waters. Remember, my man is in position, ready to act. We won't even need another Task.'

Jan's face was pale. He stalked over to the window, caught in terrible indecision.The big bodyguard smiled privately to himself, enjoying his Leader's discomfort even if his own future was also in doubt.

Whatever happened, he'd be able to rest soon. A boat, perhaps: a little gentle piracy, a touch of smuggling. He knew the people who could set up such a thing. What better way to spend retirement? He'd be away from the madness of the cities at last, his own master.

Kay shivered and watched the unlikely couple prepare for their bout. The massive, blunt-featured NV, prowling back and forth like a bull elephant. And Friend, slender as a snake, starkly beautiful, pale and pinched.

He pressed the mike switch, describing the scene to try and keep his mind occupied. 'My friends, history is being made. For twenty-two days, the player we know as Friend has survived in the Marsh, despite every tough game we could throw at her, despite the hostility of many of her fellow players, and despite being no more – or less – than a Scroat. A random collection of genes, cobbled together by Mother Nature. Now, today, we are to see one of the final hurdles to her passing to Black phase. But what a hurdle! To fight the contestant who put Stringer out of the game!

'And afterwards? Well, if there *is* an afterwards, if Friend comes through this, only one more Task will remain.'

The NVs milling around Paradise shot disgusted glances at him. Gone for good were the days when he was looked up to and feared as Jan's angel of destruction. 'What are *you* doing here, Freak?' one muttered. 'Since when has the Ref been covering Personal Combat? Or are you a Scroat-lover, too?'

The staff at the portable monitor rolled their eyes at each other, groaned into his earpiece. 'Sir, we caught that. Try to keep away from them, sir. Remember, this is live transmission. We can't screen anything out.'

Kay flicked the mike off and held up a hand to his team in acknowledgement, but he didn't care now. Live transmission was just what he needed. There was nowhere else in Briton under greater scrutiny than Paradise. Besides, the girl was here too, drawing him like a magnet.

'Five minutes,' someone said.

The Scroat called Torr gibbered and danced in his tree, his long wet hair flapping wildly in the wind. Crane started to stretch his big muscles, looking thoughtful. Friend herself had gone into her dreams, her eyes unfocussed. The NVs were growling with impatience. They shouted threats up to Torr and he laughed at them. Further out in the Marsh, other players called out for news. Only Vaso was absent. She had not left her cabin since her own combat with Friend, except to take her share of food.

Kay felt suddenly nervous. 'The tension really is quite something,' he said for the viewers. 'It feels here as if much more is riding on this than simply a continued place in the game. What, I wonder, has this girl come to mean to all of you out there watching? Is she a witch? A heroine? The lowest of the low? A danger to us all? Just plain lucky? I'm sure you all have an opinion of some kind.' He dried up again, devoid of suitable words. The NVs had started their rumbling chant: *Light-speed, light-speed, light-speed.* It sounded more desperate than ever; savage and violent. Kay glanced at his minders and the two soldiers who had accompanied him to Paradise. Were they still reliable? Would they protect him if he needed it? The muscles in his calves and forearms ached and jumped, and he shook himself. One of the crew counted down from ten in his earpiece. He raised his voice over the din.

'I think we're coming up to start time. Yes, *here* we go, viewers of Briton. Single Combat between the NV, Crane, and the Scroat called Friend.'

The starting tone buzzed from the trees, barely heard over the chanting and the rain.

The two fighters came forward, each looking into the eyes of the other. 'What *are* you?' Crane asked softly, and she replied, 'And you? What, I wonder, are *you*?'

A brief smile flickered between them. Then the boy danced lightly forward and struck a blow at her head. It met only empty air. A feint, testing her, lacking real power. Again he came forward. Another feint, to the body. And another. Each time, Crane drained the force from his fist as he struck, keeping his weight on his back foot, to retreat as soon as Friend was moving.

290

'Clever boy,' murmured Hunter at his own screen. And then to Jan, 'He's reading her, sir. Learning which way she goes.'

'I can *see* that!' the Leader snapped.

It was almost elegant, Kay thought, watching. The probing and retreat from the big NV, the ducking and twisting from the girl. Now the Combat had begun, those watching had faded to silence, though the shouts still came from out in the Marsh. Both players stayed light enough on their feet to make almost no noise on the dripping boards. The sound of Friend's breaths as she shifted balance from one position to the next punctuated the dance.

'He's going to take her! He's going to do the little bitch,' an NV said, breaking the hush, and the assessment was echoed around the watchers. 'He's going to wipe her out!' Suddenly the air was alive with renewed malevolence and purpose.

'Take her out, big guy! Punch her face in. Throw her into the Marsh!'

'Get her out of Paradise!'

'Get her away from us, for good. She isn't clean.'

Crane paused in his movements, swept a glance around the hard, eager faces and spat. Then, in a rush, his great powerful body closed once more with the girl. His lump of a fist flashed out. Friend fell back and side-stepped, and he went with her. A second blow, more powerful than the first, thudded into her shoulder.

The noise of the blow and of her body hitting the wooden wall behind echoed out of ten thousand screens.

She rocked forward, sluggishly, back into her balanced posture and said something, impossible to make out. She looked puzzled, and her voice was thick.

Crane, panting hard, saw fear rise in her and he pitied her. Again he exploded across the boards. This time her defensive move was so slow that he went too fast

291

himself and almost missed with the telling follow-up, his foot glancing off her thigh, so that she dropped to one knee and shook herself.

'Finish it! Kill her! Kill!' The NVs were burning with excitement and aggression and relief.

Kay vaguely saw the soldiers fingering their weapons, but his gaze was fixed on Friend. What was wrong? Why did she not surprise them again?

The girl was talking, babbling. 'There is no standing still,' she said, as if from a distance. 'On ne peut jamais rester immobile. Be blown away . . .' She giggled. 'The human heart never stays still, does it?'

The monitors and the screens switched to the view from her own personal camera. Crane's fist came swinging in once more, growing as large as a planet, the blurred face behind it a strange mixture of emotions.

'No . . .' breathed the girl. 'Not yet. I wanted to tell them . . .'

She giggled again and rolled over onto her back in the wet. Her slim feet came up in the air and fastened on Crane's head as he leaned forward and down for his blow.

'Sorry,' she sang like a child. 'Sorry sorry sorry . . .'

The feet turned sharply sideways, twisting the head so that her opponent cried out in pain and crashed down on his left side.

'Egal. We can call it égal. A draw.' Friend rolled clumsily onto her side, got her feet under her, then fell back uselessly.

Crane was up, ready to fight. Why was the girl just lying there? What was wrong? She'd had the advantage.

There was a voice from the Ref's technical crew. 'Hey. *Fuck* it. We've lost transmission. Somebody's pulled the plug, unless it's this weather.'

People looked up and around at the cameras in the trees. They were dead and silent. The players felt the tiny tubes above their ears and they were cold. They looked at each other. Nobody knew what to do.

Suddenly the Ref felt cold terror. The cameras had gone! He was unprotected. Jan was coming for him! What else could it mean? He started edging towards the entrance to Paradise and the little boats that lay there.

At the same time, a low, ugly sound began amongst the NVs. A growling. A stamping. One or two cast hungry glances up at the now silent Torr. Others at the Ref himself. 'The game is over,' a voice shouted. And then, 'The girl! Kill the girl first.'

The Ref looked back at the combat area. Friend was still lying there, face to the sky, eyes open, unknowing. He signalled to his minders and the soldiers. *Clear a way to the gates. Get us out of here.* But it was too late. Even as they brought their weapons up and prepared to move, two of the bodyguards were knocked senseless by quick, savage blows. One of the soldiers backed up against the stockade, waving his gun in a circle at the grim, advancing faces. The crew stayed at their posts, frozen, horrified, useless.

It would be OK. Kay was at the gates now. Two men were still with him. The first jumped down to one of the boats, started the motor. There were splashings out in the flood where other NVs were coming in, alert to the sudden change of circumstances, ready to join their brothers. The man had his weapon ready and fired a warning shot into the water to keep them back.

A hoarse shout came. *'Ref!'*

He looked back into the heart of Paradise, poised to descend. Most of the New Visions there had advanced in a pack on the prostrate form lying on the wet boards, but before them stood the bulk of Crane, still stripped, his great shoulders steaming.

*'Ref! Get this girl out of here!'*

There was a change in the boy. He was more solid,

more dangerous than ever. His teeth were bared. He didn't have time for another shout. They were on him and he was laying about him like a machine.

The Ref stood there. The soldier beside him said, 'We *must* go, sir. This position isn't defensible.' The man pushed him onto the ladder. Below, the remaining bodyguard had the motor running and was still using his sidearm to keep the Marsh dwellers back at a safe distance, although they were closing. The man was desperately waving at Kay to hurry. In a dream he put his foot on the top rung.

'*You! Ref!*'

Again he looked back. Incredibly Crane had the girl over his shoulder now. He was trying to battle through the mob. There was a shot from the trapped soldier and then another. Two NVs fell before him and the others checked for an instant, before a third shot sounded out and the surprised soldier slid down the wall holding his arm.

One of the NVs held a weapon, taken from the Ref's bodyguard. 'Come *on*, sir,' the soldier next to him said.

'Wait,' he heard himself say. 'We wait for the girl.'

Crane was almost through, but he wasn't going to make it. His eyes met the Ref's. Time seemed to be standing still. Everything Kay had ever been or done seemed to be held in the balance. He longed for safety, for music, for the dark. In a dream he took the step up, back into Paradise.

'*Sir!*'

The soldier with him came up too, in exasperation. As they re-entered the stockade, Crane finally lost balance and pitched forward, awkwardly, those around him grabbing his arms and legs, clawing at the girl, trying to rip her from his grasp.

'*Scroat-lover! Filthy scroat-lover. Kill him!*'

Another voice was raised, hysterically, from the woman on the monitor console. 'We're back online. We're filming.'

There was a tiny pause as the information sank in. Enough for Crane to stagger back to his feet, bloodied and determined. But it had gone too far, now. The NVs could not bottle themselves up once more. They could not deny themselves release. The game was a thing of the distant past. They surged forward with renewed determination and hunger. From his hiding place, fifty metres away, Hunter's sniper, waiting vainly for further instructions, decided to take action and let off two shots, yet he only had sedative ammunition with him, it would take a little time to work.

'*Ref!*'

Still Crane called desperately, engulfed by pummelling fists and feet.

And then someone else was there, helping him. The girl, Vaso, had come blinking from her cabin. She'd looked at the knot of struggling players. Like a sleep-walker she'd come forward, shaking her head.

'This is not the future,' she murmured, though nobody heard. 'Not strength and dry land.'

Doubtfully at first, then with more vigour, she stepped into the little mob, and grappled those holding Crane, felling two of them with her solid fists before they realised what was happening.

Still Kay watched, caught between paths. Finally he gave a great shudder and a sob. He came forward. Crossed the last two metres between him and Crane. He struck out, and found flesh and bone. A surprised looking NV went reeling and then turned back to face him. He struck again, and again. He couldn't stop himself now. The anger in him, the guilt, the unknowing years. His body rippled with strength from the lonely nights. Next to him the soldier raised his weapon and fired a shot. Another NV fell. In a rush, Crane broke through to the ladder and turned to descend.

'I've got her! Go!'

Kay and the soldier fell back, but they were now besieged themselves. The man's gun was ripped from his hands and tossed over the stockade into the flood.

'Go!' echoed Vaso. She moved in front of them, thrusting bodies aside, giving them space. Somehow, Kay and the other man stumbled back onto the slippery ladder. They half fell into the boat where Crane sat, waiting, cradling the unconscious Friend. The motor whined and they set off. Above them, in the open gateway, Vaso was fighting like a tigress, trying to contain the others, to give them precious time, but it wasn't for long. With a shout she was swallowed up and there were heavy splashes as the NVs jumped out into the Marsh and started to give chase, bellowing and churning through the water like maddened cattle.

'The 'copter,' Kay gasped. 'Get to the 'copter.'

'Sir, that's what I was intending. The other men should have it secure.'

'Go you bastards, go!' cackled Torr from his platform. Some of the NVs were swarming up to get him. He looked down at them contemptuously, climbed further up, kicking out at the groping hands. 'Go baby!' he shouted again.

The boat was not fast enough. There were eight or nine of the big NV children, coming after them in a rough line. Eight or nine destroyers wrapped in white spray, gaining on them, one firing shots from a stolen weapon. Crane took the sidearm from the man steering, but it was empty, useless. He stroked Friend's unfeeling head with his eyes blazing. Her skin was tinged with blue.

Kay looked at Crane almost timidly, wondering at

the change in him. 'Is she dead?' he asked, dreading the answer.

'No. She's breathing, but not deeply.'

Kay hung his head. He ripped off the mask and let his sweat-soaked curls fall out. It was so good to let the air in that he didn't notice how the soldier and Crane stared at the head they'd never before seen. His mind wouldn't work, he felt so weak.

'Sir, we're too heavy,' the man at the helm said. 'We should throw the girl out. They might give up then.'

'Nobody throws her out,' said Crane calmly.

The soldier looked at him with mixed loathing and respect. The boy knew that they couldn't overpower him without risking the whole boat.

A minute later, the helmsman spoke again. 'Seem to be keeping our distance now, just.'

Sure enough, with the little motor going flat out, the space between them and the pursuers was no longer shrinking, though it was a bare forty metres. Before long, the dark shape of the helicopter came into view, lying well away from the cluster of control huts. As the soldier had predicted, his fellows had heard the commotion and were already there. The pilot was firing up the reluctant old engines. The rotor was skewing round, weakly at first, then with a leap and a roar. As it erupted into violent life a great hollow opened in the water beneath the platform, pushed away by the downward draught.

'It's going to be close,' Crane said grimly.

But the soldiers at the 'copter had their own weapons out. They were not hemmed in as their fellows had been. There was plenty of time and space to aim and fire. By the time the boat was near enough to the platform two more of the NVs lay lifeless in the mire.

'We might not have to go at all,' the man at the helm said. 'Look, I think we can hold them.' Even as he spoke there was a roar of flame and a plume of smoke from the crew's quarters.

'The fuel! The explosives!'

'Go!'

They were under the rotors now, buffeted by the wind, reaching up to the chopper platform.

The soldier from the boat pulled at Kay's arm. 'We can leave the girl now. *And* him!' He gestured at Crane, who was lifting Friend up to the strong arms above.

'We *take* her,' Kay said. 'We have the time and we take her! Clear? We take them *both*. Do you want them murdered, man?' The Ref's old temper flared in his face and the man shrugged and climbed up himself. Bodies crammed into the little cargo space, the doors slid shut, and then they were lifting off, tossed about in the wind and rain. Below them they saw Hunter's sniper desperately sprinting through the Marsh, followed by two other figures.

'Drop down! We can get him,' Kay's bodyguard said to the pilot. But the pilot gestured at the ground. The sniper had already fallen. The pursuers were on him.

Kay's eyes met Crane's, the big NV still holding Friend protectively across him. *And where now?* His expression said, bleakly. *And where now?*

# CLARISSA

The long control room was filled with bitter smoke, half obscuring the bank of screens and the images that flickered there uncertainly. Some, appropriately, were filled with their own smoke: smoke that drifted over the violence of the Marsh. Others showed the battered metal floor of the helicopter, the knees of two men, clothed in mud-spattered grey. This image juddered and jarred as Adeline's head lolled on Crane's lap. Finally, it faded, broke up, and disappeared altogether.

'*What?*' yelled Clarissa, keeping one eye on the door. 'What's *happening*?'

'Signal's breaking up,' Emile shouted back, pressing switches, shrugging. 'They must be getting too far away from the booster transmitter.'

Chaney nodded, puffing nervously on her cigarette, anxious to be gone. 'It's only got a five-mile radius, the one at the Marsh. To prevent the signal getting hijacked.'

'Can't we get it back?'

'Depends where they're headed.'

'Well . . . keep putting the rest out, and see what you can do.'

The ex-mercenary, Christophe, put his head back inside and beckoned. 'Rissa! Come and look at this!'

She followed him out into the stairwell, casting a glance back at the screens that now showed only the Marsh. She hefted her weapon in readiness as she went. Out here, the fumes were still thicker and the walls were splintered and chipped by internal security once their entrance had been detected. This corner of the tower had been designed to be extra secure, though, and the damage was only superficial.

As she descended, Clarissa realised that the harsh chatter of firearms had faded. Christophe was grinning contentedly. He laid a hand on Clarissa's gun. 'Calme-toi. You will have no need, I think.'

'What? Have they given up? Then they'll come again. Jan won't let us go on much longer here.' She wasn't concentrating. She could think of nothing but that picture of the chopper floor. She wanted to be back in the control room, in case.

'*Look*, Rissa,' he insisted. 'Look! Regarde!'

He led her round the corner. Mac was down below, at the next bend, behind their makeshift barricade of chairs and shelving, a rag tied round his head where he'd been grazed. He waved cheerfully up. Beyond him, through the plexiglas that ran in a strip down the out-side of the stairway, Clarissa could see the street below. It surged with pushing bodies and animated faces, a tide of humanity. In the distance, lower down, a derailed, burning Caplink carriage. Broken glass. People cheering and chanting and running like hares. A city in turmoil.

'Look at that,' said the little mercenary again, in his poor English. 'We have done our job very well, I think. The Pax, they are busy with that for long time. Maybe will leave us alone now, n'est ce pas?' He beamed at her but she felt shocked to see the destruction, the savagery, echoing what they'd seen in Paradise.

She laid a hand on Christophe's arm, went back to the control room. 'The city's in chaos. The people are rioting.'

'Yes,' Emile agreed in satisfaction. 'I found a feed from one of the street circuits. Look, I've put it on those screens there, at the end.'

Four images, the same story everywhere, the same chaos. Clarissa felt sick. 'Emile,' she said, 'the helicopter

. . . is there any way to track it? How would I follow it if I wanted to?'

He shrugged again, ever happy if he had a technical problem to solve. 'I'll keep searching the frequencies. Who knows what Barbieri has out there? No promises. As for going after it . . . another 'copter? A boat? The stilt-roads are no good now.'

'OK,' she said. 'Keep the images rolling as long as you can. Keep searching for my sister. Let me know when you have anything. But don't get killed over it.'

He grinned at her. The smoke was clearing now, pulled out by the silent fans. The noise of the crowd outside rumbled faintly through the walls like a beast. 'You too. Don't be dead, Rissa.'

She turned to Chaney, clasped her hand. 'Thank you. Thank you.'

As she went through the door Emile called, 'We never had so much fun at Seven,' and she laughed, despite herself, as she raced down the stairs.

More goodbyes. For Christophe and for dear Mac.

Then out onto the street, into bedlam and destruction: a city that had at last woken up.

As she had.

# PART THREE

'You push me up to . . .

State of emergency
How beautiful to be
State of emergency
Is where I want to be'

Björk: Jóga

# DOMINIC
## – day 85 –

Why go *today*, with only a week left? Isn't that madness? We have food here, at least. Shelter. Some kind of organisation, even if it's not perfect. What do we know about what's out there now? It could be wasteland, war, anything. We'll freeze to death. I can't relax, can't think properly. I've been up to the roof and got my maps. Went to the CCF hut to look it over again. The compo food's all gone, but the metal safety door's intact. How can I shift it? I'll pick up a rifle bolt later while I think.

In trouble after all that, as I was late for morning training with my section (section = three of us now). Siobhan smirked away when I was bollocked.

'You look all of a tizz, poor thing,' she said afterwards.

Oh God.


Bede's is my home, even now.


The plan is to go to her cottage tonight, late. She says she knows a way out. At the edge of the Park, where it gets near the road, we're going to crawl along the beck. It goes down into a tunnel under the road and she says they won't be watching that as it's well hidden. We should be miles away by morning.

But what if they search? Bring the dogs out after us?


NIGHT! OUT!

I'm sitting outside the school grounds. Isn't that amazing? The first time I've been out for almost three months. A white, empty landscape is beyond me. Beautiful, stark, unlimited. The moon is bright enough to write this but I can see a heavy bank of snow clouds moving in from the west. An icy breeze is just stirring. I'm sitting wrapped in blankets that smell of her. I don't know what I've done, but I've done it. There's no going back.

Ruth and her father are late. It's 2.18 already. What a day! *What a day!*

Tonight when I got to the lodge, she came out straight away. Dark shadows under her eyes, very serene, very whole; but battered, if that makes sense. Thin as a branch. She had a bundle of things tied together into a pack.

She said quietly, 'Dad got a bottle from ... somewhere. I thought I'd taken them all ... He's plastered. I'll have to wait a little while he sleeps it off. He'll be fine in an hour or two. It'll be OK.'

'So what do we do?'

She took my hand. She led me between the trees. 'We'll go on through, check it's clear, leave these things there and yours. We'll come back for him later.'

The Park was silent and empty. We wormed through the tunnel without too much trouble, thanks to the training ... enough ice to stay clear of the water, except for one of my elbows. When we were through, Ruth stood clutching her bundle, looking across the icelands. A queen surveying her realm. A pilgrim. She said, 'Oh Dominic.' She held onto me, tight. After a while we unrolled her blankets, and lay down on them. We wrapped ourselves up again, close together. I couldn't stop trembling. She said, 'You're cold,' and I said, 'No, it's not that.'

Her hands worked inside my clothing. Mine inside hers. Somehow we were naked. Her eyes never left mine. They were huge. Terrible. Amazing. Her softness didn't seem possible as she's nothing but sinew and bone these days. I fell into that softness.

And then, I don't know. Asleep together, dozing, like a single body, a single spirit, then she was up and whispering something to me. She went back down the tunnel for her dad.

Eventually the cold woke me up properly.

Where are they?

# ADELINE

The Marsh fell away below them, veiled by rain and smoke, and the little metal box of the 'copter danced giddily in the wind.

'We can't get above that cloud,' the pilot shouted, 'we'll have to stay down here, below it. Strap in. It's going to be rough.' And then, looking over his shoulder, 'Where to? Back to the city?'

'*No!*' Kay shouted back at once, instinctively. The city was no good for him; no good for the girl; no good, either, for Crane: not now. Just for an instant he wondered how much of the bloody chaos in the Marsh had been seen in the capital, and how the viewers there would have taken it. 'No. We head north. The mountains. We're only a day or two ahead of schedule.'

'But sir! Surely the game is ... There's no reason to go north now, sir. We may not even have the fuel. There was no time ...'

Kay's remaining bodyguard looked at him assessingly and spoke up. 'And there is that other thing, sir. The thing you need.'

The thing he needed. Oh gods above, did the man not have it with him? The guard was smirking. Crane was listening without expression.

The Ref, he thought. I am the Ref. *I* am in charge here. As if mere mention of the Lady had woken her, a surge of fire coursed through his limbs, tightening the muscles, pulling them like cords.

'We ... go ... *north*,' he said to the pilot, gritting his teeth against the pain.

The pilot shrugged. 'I'll have to call it in, sir.'

'Then *call* it in, damn you.'

He closed his eyes, rested his head against vibrating metal, trying to see a way out of all this. If only he could *think*. When he opened them again, Crane was still watching him. The bulky NV holding the pale girl as if she were glass. At some time, he'd wrapped a stiff Pax tunic round her vest.

Gods above.

'I can't raise them!' the pilot shouted, a minute later. 'I can't get anybody.'

'Was the radio hit?' the bodyguard called.

'The radio's fine. Just nobody answering. But we're wasting fuel. We have to have a decision.'

'We have one,' Kay said, looking round at the soldiers' faces, summoning the Ref's sneer back to help him. 'This is my show and it will continue. We head north. Keep trying with the radio.'

Miraculously, nobody challenged him, though the bodyguard looked thoughtful. But on Crane's lips there was the ghost of a smile.

*Well done*, his eyes said.

*She smiled down at him in the milky light. His curls above the mass of blankets were clouded by the haze of his sleeping breath. His limp hand was thrown back above his head, almost on the snow. He stirred and sighed and she felt such tenderness for his innocence that she thought her heart would break.*

*She could have danced in the moonlit fields. She could have sung.*

*Dressing carefully, zipping up each layer to her throat, she crept back to the mouth of the tunnel, where a tiny ribbon of the beck still bubbled past between jaws of snow and ice. It was the work of a silent minute to re-enter the Park and then she was flitting between the great, dying trees, each one known and loved since her baby days.*

*Twice she detected the soft crunch of a soldier's feet and altered her path. The awareness flowed around her and she let herself catch it, merge with it. Only at the dark house did she feel a little heaviness in her stomach. She hoped that her father would be over the drink now and able to understand their need.*

*But at the doorway she paused. She turned around.*

*'Hello Ruth.'*

*She took a moment to identify the figure standing in the moonshadow. The idiot that Dom shared his room with.*

*'What do you want?'*

*'Oh, I'm just the lookout boy. Just here to blow the whistle, so to speak. Would you like to give me a kiss first?'*

*For the first time tonight she felt how cold it was. She advanced on him. 'Have you been following me?'*

*'No need, darling. Dominic's sick little diary keeps me pretty well up to date with developments. That's when he isn't writing to his father about you or trying to get you on to the programme, showing everyone your lovely paperwork.'*

*She felt like she'd been smacked. She felt sick. She saw the boy raise his hand to his lips. He held something silver. He blew and there were shouts, dogs barking. She took the last step towards him and threw him to the ground.*

*'Better look behind you,' he gasped. 'Where's Daddy?'*

*She turned round and saw a glow of orange inside her house. She ran to the door, wrenched it open. There was someone inside, about to come out. He swung the butt of a handgun and she fell to the floor.*

*The figure closed the door behind her, trapping her. Outside, her spirit raced through the trees to the sleeping, innocent boy.*

*Where are you?*

When she opened her eyes, Dom was there, and yet it was not him. He'd aged; he was harder. The curls were flecked with grey and there was pain and sorrow in the set of his lovely mouth. His head was resting back against some dark, scratched surface, the eyes closed.

Still the ghost of that innocence hung over him, but there was much more besides.

Her eyes travelled further down and she saw the strange clothes. The Ref's clothes. Why was he dressed like that?

The world shook and plummeted and she felt the bile in her stomach, the throb in her chest.

She struggled to turn her head against some kind of weight there. Other people were here besides the Dominic/not Dominic person. Above her hung the face of the New Vision called Crane. His hand was resting on her head: that was the weight. It made no sense. He looked down at her with some expression she couldn't read and said, 'Hey. She's awake.'

They were all looking at her, then. Some soldiers, dressed in Pax grey and the other two.

'She seems very weak. Look, she can hardly keep her eyes open.'

'I don't like that skin colour. Why's she so blue?'

Dominic/not Dominic was studying her and she saw that it was the Ref after all, the eyes as hungry for her soul as ever. She shuddered. It was true, she could hardly keep her eyes open. There was something she was supposed to do.

It would have to wait.

'Voilà!' said Emile, turning dials, studying the screens. 'A picture. They must have come near another beacon. But ... our signal is not alone, I think. Someone else may be using that beacon. Mon dieu, look at this, my friend. What should we do?'

'Put it out,' said Mac wearily. 'Put it all out. That's why we're here. We can't do anything else for her.'

Next time she woke up there was chaos, panic, shouting, engine noise, the sniff of violence.

311

'What do you think you're doing? Get us up again. You will fly on to the Black phase control centre! I will not have this insubordination!' That was the Ref, with a tinge of panic.

'Wait! I'm getting instructions. Quiet you lot!' Another man somewhere nearby.

Suddenly she felt herself lifted and twisted and there was a blast of cold air as a door slid back.

'*Get her out!*'

She thought she'd heard someone say that before.

Strong hands pushed her out, her face brushed by cobwebby strings. There was the sound of a shot at close quarters.

'Don't try it! *Go!*' A brief run, bouncing on a shoulder. Then, 'Here, I'll take her back. Can you use this? Try for the fuel tank. Don't let them take off again.'

She was slung from one person back to another. Around her was an expanse of snow. Too painful to look at. She shut her eyes. The cold was intense. Her chest must have collapsed or had something dropped on it. They were running and she was on a shoulder again, hearing the gasps of breath that her carrier was taking. The noise of the engine died behind them. There was a lot of shouting, echoing over the snow. Shots, some close, some not.

A curse. 'It's empty . . . What do we do?'

'Keep going! Head for the trees there!'

That was the NV, Crane, carrying her. She moistened her mouth and said something to him.

'What?'

But she had no breath with that shoulder in her guts.

In a while the light grew dimmer and she could see the papery red trunks of conifers around her. 'You take her again,' Crane gasped. 'Keep going, deeper into the trees. Dig a snow hole if you need to sleep. No fire.'

'What about you? Where are you going?' She was

being passed again, banged and battered like an old sack.

'I'll stay here. I'll give you the time you need.'

'But . . .'

'Save the girl, Ref. Do it!'

Crane looked out of the treeline at the handful of men coming up the slope towards him. They'd taken the time to re-arm and put on snow goggles and parkas. He was still in his Brown phase vest and boots, and unarmed. But he understood, now, about being a hero. The shame he'd tasted recently had come from the other NVs, not from inside.

At last he was going to be tested, and to have glory.

He raised his face to the wan sky and howled like a wolf. Then he set off, down the slope, sprinting, weaving from side to side, towards the men. And they saw him come with fear.

As Adeline turned her head from her new position on Kay's shoulder to catch a glimpse of Crane, charging down the hill, there was a lull in the violence of the city squares and street corners. It had taken a few minutes, even for the people nearest the screens to realise that the story was continuing. Soon the message spread, shouted aloud.

'Quiet! Look! Look at the screen! The girl's alive!'

The fires still burned, smaller battles still raged, blood dripped onto concrete and was washed away: but gradually a kind of peace settled on the capital.

Crane howled and ran at the soldiers. And they watched him, reaching lightspeed.

After a moment, those holding down New Vision children released them, stood up, shook themselves.

They settled to wait for what would come next. They all waited.

# DOMINIC

I haven't moved, in all this.

I'm back where I began. At the top of Orchard in my old room. They've bandaged me up, but I don't think they care much, now, what I do.

I don't care either. Only today have I been able to bear reading the previous page in this journal. I don't think I'll ever read it again. It's too painful. It's better not to know, not to remember how it can be.

*I* have been less than I could have been.

I've a fire in the grate again here. (They just don't care.) My burns are smarting and oozing, just looking at it.

She didn't come.

I waited, still drunk on her and on love.

I looked back and there was orange light beyond the Park.

I went back, splashing and slipping through that bastard tunnel, pissing for it through the Park.

The lodge was on fire, burning fiercely. Nobody was there, doing anything about it. How could that be? I put my hand on the door and it was hot. I opened it. Fire rushed out. I tried to get in. I got a metre or two in. My hair was burned off. My clothes were burning. I couldn't see a thing. I fell out again, somehow, and rolled in the snow.

Eventually they came and found me and bandaged me up. It was snowing hard by then.

This is the fifth day since then, I think. Still snowing.

I tottered up onto the roof yesterday, despite the

314

weather, and retrieved the broken pieces of the Strat. Something for my hands to do.

She was everything. I can't bear to be without her.

# ADELINE

She'd worked it out now. Her head was light and she was deathly cold, and nauseous from the motion of being carried, but her mind was half working again and she'd put the pieces together.

She said, faintly, 'You're Kay Saint.'

She was aghast, revolted by the knowledge. Dom – Kay – the Ref. She felt imprisoned against him, rubbing on the silly, scratchy material of his costume, damp with his sweat. It was intimate, indecent, and there was nothing she could do. She'd been horribly betrayed. Like Ruth. She'd been so full of love.

He hardly had breath to answer. She was surprised by the strength in him, heading on and on, up through the endless, white-laced forest. How long had they been going? Hours rather than minutes. 'Yes . . . Kay,' he panted. 'And you . . . the girl . . . the baby . . . France . . .'

From time to time he stopped, bent forward and propped her up against one of the red trunks, amidst the clouds of needles, while he changed carrying shoulder. His face was strained and a little wild as he paused to catch any sound from their pursuers. His muscles seemed to twitch with a life of their own. He shook himself violently as if to shrug off an unpleasant touch.

He was tender with her and that made it even worse, more horrifying.

'Where are we going?' she managed to ask him in one of these moments.

He was already hoisting her back up, forcing his legs up the slope once more. 'Keep . . . you . . . safe . . .'

Safe. She couldn't be safe. It was impossible.

Light was failing, shadows under the trees darkening. She sensed how this land must be at night, the otherness of it, the taste of sap and snow. They came to a place where the trees became thinner, the snow cover thicker, making Kay take great ponderous steps, ploughing forward, sometimes tumbling with her into drifts that wormed into the starchy collar of whatever she was wearing. She felt like she was made of ice herself. Above them lay the flank of a mountain, massive, unforgiving. Still they ascended, and she dozed, shivering, and dreamed and woke again with new fear, disgust, bewilderment.

Her head bounced against him as he went, dizzying her. She'd slipped a little further down and it bounced against something hard and uncomfortable, stinging the weal on her cheek. She saw that it was the little microphone that he used for Fit To Live, fastened to his shining belt.

She remembered then that she'd been going to talk to the people. To tell them the truth. The camera was still clipped above her ear, she could feel the narrow band that circled her head to hold it. She doubted, though, that it was working. So much had happened.

She closed her eyes. There was a buzzing somewhere that became a throbbing engine, powering over the treetops. Kay flung her down and lay still with her in a hollow while a helicopter passed low overhead, spilling down a pool of white light. When it was gone the mountainside seemed twice as dark.

Kay said, 'We must rest.' His eyes were unfocussed and large and he staggered about like a drunk when he rose. 'Snow-hole,' he said to himself, 'build a snow-hole.'

She lay in the cold, part of it, barely conscious, and watched as he clumsily wedged his fingers into the white and started to dig. His limbs jumped like a puppet's. He seemed to have tears on his face. He was mumbling, dribbling. Revolting.

Everything had gone wrong.

At some later time he decided that the excavation was complete. He turned to her and again, with sickening tenderness, pulled and levered her to the edge, then rolled her into the hole.

In the cities of Britain the people watched his digging, the moving of the girl, his shadowy face peering down at her with pain and concern and love. It was a silent story being told in an alien place. Simple and strange. They'd thought they knew the characters but they did not. He clambered down after her into the little shelter, growing to massive proportions in the camera's view until there was only the dusky pink blur of his skin on the lens.

She felt him come in next to her, half across her. She felt his trembling, the thick muscle of his body. He pulled the snow back around them. He held her tight, sharing warmth, and all her senses were filled with his nearness.

It was torture, but sleep soon carried her away to a happier place.

# DOMINIC
## – day 96? –

This is the last time I shall write in this diary. Whatever has been happening here is ending. I feel such a mixture of emotions about it that I shall try to be calm and set out the final chapter as nothing but a sequence of events.

You've had all my emotions. You must be sick of them.

So.

I'm still bandaged and hairless and in pain, but better than I was and now up and about. The daily routine is all ended. I took no part in the last days of training; I'm not sure if I *ever* really took part.

Yesterday, we were to have a final parade, a passing-out ceremony, and after that we were to report to Sandley, the junior boarding house, to give genetic material for the programme. A programme to make clones. A programme to ensure, in Father's words, 'culture, civilisation, order'. I'll let anybody reading this be the judge of whether what I have described might lead to those things.

We lined up for the parade, this time on the lawns in front of the HM's house, though of course they're covered by the snow and frozen solid. The soldiers were there, and the scientists and even the kitchen team, all lined up. As if it was a day of glory. I was pretty much left in a space of my own. Mummyman in my bandages. Suited me fine.

The Major came last and made a speech. Something like:

'Ladies and gentlemen. Well done. I won't pretend that what we have achieved here has been easy. It hasn't been that for any of us. But it has borne fruit of all kinds. I'm sure all of you have discovered things about yourselves that were previously unknown to you, as I have. More importantly, we have made some contribution towards ensuring that this great nation of ours stays great through the challenges that lie ahead.

'This is uncharted territory. There *will* be dangers and problems. But all of you here today are the best we have: you, and those that come after you, thanks to the miracle technology our scientific colleagues have developed. You *will* cope. You *will* find a way. You *will* triumph!

'One last word of warning. This process has been kept private from the eyes of the world and should remain so. It is not always proper that the led know the secrets of those doing the leading. It causes confusion. Misunderstanding. Take a moment to look about you now ... these are the people to trust, to work with in the future. Keep your secret between yourselves.

'So. Good. I know I can rely on you. It only remains for me to say ...'

He stopped at this point.

There was a person at the side of the lawns who had arrived silently while he talked. She walked forward, muffled in hat and scarf. Her grace in moving was un-mistakeable.

She said clearly to the Major, 'Tell us what you have discovered about yourself.'

I've never seen a man so shocked. Without words, or colour in his face. And *my* heart pounding like a hammer, with another chance of life.

She said again, prompting him, 'We've all been on this journey. We've learned these new things. What have *you* learned?'

Silence.

She turned to us, the audience.

'Let's be truthful about how this thing is beginning, this great adventure that this man and others have persuaded you to take. It is beginning with an attempt to hang onto the old. The familiar. To replicate it. Does that sound like an adventure? It's starting with . . .'

The Major took a step forward and reached out to grasp her. His face showed anger, fear, total incomprehension. I think he wanted just to smother the beautiful strange thing that he could never have, nor understand.

She turned and swept her foot and he fell into the snow. His cheeks were purple. She said, 'Don't lay a hand on me. I am not yours. And I am not finished. Let the adventure start with honesty, Major.

'My father died in a fire a few days ago. You were there. You started that fire. You struck me down.'

You could have heard a pin drop in the snow.

She shrugged. 'Isn't that the old and the familiar? Violence, envy, the wish to control. Not a new adventure; an ancient, stale one. But then, when you've seen it and named it, you can laugh and say: *This is not for me*. You can open your hand' – she opened hers, held it up – 'and it gets blown away.'

She stopped talking and came towards us. Her eyes met mine. Large, challenging, adventurous, playful.

And the Major, climbing back to his knees, shot her.

Matter-of-fact events. Am I managing?

I don't know much of what happened immediately after that. There was chaos. I was at Ruth's side. She was dead. Her scarf had fallen away and I saw that she had the burns too, like mine, on part of her face and hands. Some remaining hair spilled out of the hat onto the snow. Her blood stained it. To lose her twice was . . .

I don't know.

When I was aware of anything, everybody had gone. The afternoon light was fading. Somebody was saying my name. Eve. She took me and guided me to Sandley. 'I've waited as long as I can, Dominic. We have to take the material. We're packing up tonight. This place is not safe for ... our next work.'

I didn't care. She could have cut out my heart for her experiments without me feeling it.

In the room they'd got ready in Sandley, guarded by a soldier, there were bright gas lights, and a small, portable, gas-powered fridge-freezer. She took a little of my hair, some of my blood, a swab from in my mouth. 'We take more than we need, to be sure of success. There will be some error to begin with, no doubt. The process is not exact.'

Error. What will that mean for the living things, the people she will make?

The specimens she took went into little labelled jars, tucked into the freezer. I saw the stacked-up jars in there, with the names of the 'lucky ones' who are left here still.

She hugged me and tried to say something about Ruth. I wandered back out, past the guard, into the snow.

Soon, I was back next to Ruth. Where else could I be? She was half covered now by the snowfall, merging with it, her stain of life being absorbed. She was in her own deep freeze.

That's when I thought of it.

I ran back to Sandley, slipping, falling, frantic. I collided with Eve as she came along, wrapped up in all her gear, carrying a rucksack. 'Give me some of those jars!'

'What? I don't understand what you're talking about.'

'The jars. From the freezer. And a swab and some scissors.'

She looked at me. She put down her bag, took my hand. 'I cannot. We are leaving. The jars will be taken any time.'

'Please.'

She stayed there gazing at me.

She said, 'Wait here,' and left me with the bag.

When she came back with the things she hoisted up her pack and said, 'That is all. Anything else must be done by you.' She walked off without a look, into the snow and the evening.

I went back to Ruth, the mound of snow that was Ruth, and took some of the blood, the hair. Opening the mouth that had rested on mine was hard, but I needed to be quick and just did it.

Approaching Sandley I heard voices, sharp and clear in the frozen air. A man's voice and a woman. 'I don't suppose you have a cigarette for a cold girl?' the woman said.

The man said something gruffly and laughed. There was the flare of a match. In it, as I looked round the corner, I could see Eve's face, smiling, looking up into the soldier's eyes as he lit her fag.

'Thank you. Oh, that is so good. I was trying to stop, but ... Thank you so much!' She was really giving him the treatment. They smoked for a while together. Then she said, 'Also, inside, there is a heavy box. I forgot it. I do not know if I can manage it. Would you carry it for me? Just to the picking-up place? They will come for us in ten minutes, I think.'

She touched his arm. More low comments and laughter. She unlocked the external door and they disappeared inside. When they came out he was carrying the box and they walked along, past me, towards wherever she was expecting to be picked up. I was well back, in a doorway round the corner. She turned her head a fraction as they passed and her eyes met mine.

Bless her.

I was in and out of Sandley in half a minute. I opened the freezer and took out the containers marked with Siobhan's name, put her labels on the ones I held, and in they went.

I was watching, five minutes later, when a detail of soldiers came for the containers, bringing them out packed in iceboxes. By then the thrumming chopper noise could be heard, coming to take Eve and her friends.

I went back to Ruth, but she was not there, now. Only

her body. Her spirit was out in the swirling snow somewhere.

*Se mundumque vince.*

It seems quite clear to me that I have not conquered myself. I haven't made the grade. Father came with the chopper and when he goes I will be going with him, to join his new future.

But there is just the slightest chance now that other Dominics will do better, in some future I cannot see. And that one of them will ... I don't know, be what a future Ruth needs.

None of them will be immune to that girl.

I will get ready now and join Father.

Dominic Saint
September 2023

# ADELINE

The light came through the casing of snow, shining blue-white. The chill of the air outside whispered down the little breathing hole. Adeline felt she was entombed. She doubted she would ever move again. She was encased by the snow, and by Kay. The powerlessness of it was terrifying.

In due course he woke up. She felt the speed of his breathing change against her and the thudding of his heart as if it wished to break out of his chest. Her own was a feeble whisper in comparison. He hardly seemed able to talk. He grunted and broke out of the snow-nest and she could see him standing in the light, dreamy-eyed, stiff, stretching and stumbling and looking down at her in surprise as if he'd never seen her before.

'Must get you out,' he mumbled. 'Out and away.'

Those strong, unsteady hands came down the short tunnel to take hold of her, to ease her from the ice like a baby from a womb. He took some of the snow and put it in his mouth and then forced some into her own, which was dry and thick.

'What's wrong with you?' he asked, more clearly.

'My heart. A problem with the growth process after duplication.'

He reached out and touched her cheek, softly, making her flinch. He took his hand back and hoisted her onto his shoulder again, and she gasped, winded. Then it began, just as the previous day, the endless irregular motion, the bone jutting into her guts, the dizziness, the sweat that came through his clothing and soaked into hers, the hoarse sound of his breath. Why is he doing this, she wondered. Why do we not just lie down and die? But at some moment in the morning they heard faint noise behind and below them. Distantly, the noise of men calling to one another. And when she looked back she thought she could see specks working their way out of the treeline, starting to traverse back and forth across the fresh snow, looking for signs.

She longed to have her body back. To be able to run swift across the snow from those men, laughing at their clumsiness.

*Let go.*

But it was so hard to let go, even when she was half frozen to death and her heart was damaged beyond repair. Again, she thought of her intention to speak to the people of Briton. To speak a little truth, as Ruth had done at the Major's parade. She did not know now what she had meant to say.

'Hey,' she murmured, 'if anybody is out there, please scream when you hear the tone.'

Bleep.

Kay lumbered on, seeming not to hear. Who could say what he thought or heard?

'Because I can't hear you . . .'

It was all quite hopeless. They went on and up and she hung like a rag-doll over Kay's shoulder. She could understand Dom's difficulty on that first page now. It struck her that she still felt the same inside, the same sympathy and warmth towards him, the same love; whereas *this* man, this beast that was bearing her the-spirits-knew-where, was loathsome. It didn't make any sense.

'Where does the story start?' she murmured. 'It starts with being alone. Full of possibilities, full of magic.

Beautiful. But having to face yourself, face your fear.'

She started to cry, softly, the tears running down onto her forehead. She was so cold. She'd hoped for so much.

*Let go.*

'You!' she said savagely to Kay. 'Do you even *know* who you are?'

He only groaned as he struggled on. Whether there were words she couldn't tell.

'You're Kay Saint. But you are a clone, just a copy. A copy of a boy called Dominic Saint, who lived centuries ago, when the great freeze was starting and Briton was still full of people. Dominic's father wanted to replicate certain types, to keep the power, to keep order, to stop things from changing during the ice and the wars and the disease. Jan Barbieri is also a clone. His original shared a room with Dominic while they were in the competition to see who would be copied. What do you think of *that*?'

There was definitely a reaction now. A louder groan, a lengthening of his stride. He was like a hunted beast.

'And I am one too,' she said bitterly. 'An accident, though. I wasn't chosen by the tests. Dominic interfered with the programme to include me. Because he *loved* my original. But here I am, with a failing heart, last of my line.'

They had come to the saddle between two peaks, where the wind screamed across, sharp and icy. Kay pitched her down in the snow, wild-eyed. His arms and legs were jumping and twitching rhythmically. They were like one of the little entertainments she'd seen down in the rotten dockland of the capital: a man making his mannequins dance or argue, playing out his simple show on a bit of plank.

Kay was facing the way they'd come, shading his bloodshot eyes with his shaking hand.

'It's a terrible mess, isn't it?' she said to him. 'Dominic's father and Frank Barbieri and now Jan, and you too – *you, Kay, in that monkey suit* – you've all been trying to keep things the same. Stagnant.'

He came back from the lip, hurrying. She saw that there was a stain of white phlegm around the corners of his mouth. His face was wet with tears. Their eyes met as he bent to gather her up from where she shivered on the snow.

'No,' she said, more gently. 'No, that's not it. That's not all. I'm wrong. The story is one of love. That's the important part. The rest is only the scum on the surface.'

They had gone over the saddle. They were charging down towards new, higher woodland, galloping across the white powder in a lopsided rush.

'This is the real story,' she gasped. 'A boy called Dominic found himself alone at his school. The world was going mad. Panic everywhere. He thought he'd been forgotten. But *enfin* he found that he wasn't alone after all . . .'

# LETTING GO

By the time she'd finished with the tale, another night was gathering in the white valleys, creeping up towards them. Her voice was no more than a hoarse murmur. She was beyond cold, icy to her core, numb from the waist down. She could feel with her mountain-dweller's instinct that they were high. Far up in a line of white mountains, glimpsed sometime earlier, but obscured now by freshly falling snow.

The helicopter had been in earshot again during the day, though not close enough to hide from. As for the men behind, tracking them, there had been no further sign. The new snow would surely be enough to drive them back and cover any trail for good.

As she heard her own voice die away, fading into the soft silence of the falling flakes, she realised with surprise that they were no longer moving. Kay was simply standing there, swaying slightly, braced against the slope. With an effort, she swung her stiff arms, and patted feebly at the backs of his legs.

'Hey. Hey! What's happening?' Her throat was dry and cracked, despite the frozen moisture all around. 'Hey! Let me go. Put me down.'

A tremor went through him and slowly, gently, he collapsed onto the snow, taking her down in a mess of limbs as he went. She turned her head and gobbled greedily at the white fluff. It trickled down her throat in an icy thread. Still on her belly, muscles protesting, she wormed her way round to Kay's mouth and turned his head to get the snow into him as well.

She was shocked by how his face was cracked and bleeding from the cold air, pinched with fatigue, frosted around the mouth and eyes. And yet those eyes had lost their wildness, the limbs had ceased to twitch, and when he looked up at her through the swollen slits, he recognised her and smiled a little.

'Safe. Safe . . . now,' he whispered. Then: 'Snowflakes. Beautiful. Like . . . music.'

He closed his eyes and the ragged breathing grew quieter. She realised that they were alone here and would die before the night had passed. She could leave him if she wanted, leave the aberration and find her own spot to let go, but instead she started to dig, feebly at first and then with more vigour. Gradually, as some tiny warmth crept into her muscles, making her cry out with the pain, she widened the hole, lengthened it, piling snow round the edge to stop too much drifting. When it was done she shouted at him and shook him to wake him up, without result, so she braced herself behind him and pushed his back with her feet, rolling him over like a barrel until he was half in the tunnel. From there she managed to work her way next to him and somehow to wriggle them both down into the tiny space.

Again she felt claustrophobic, aware of how they were locked together. She would not think of the feeling of Dom's touch now. She shut it out. She pulled the snow in after them, leaving a little hole for the air. Her work was not as good as his had been the night before and probably the snow would cover the hole and they would be smothered, but she could do no more. She pressed herself to him and gripped at the scratchy fabric.

He murmured something, no more than a breath: 'Mira?'

'No. Adeline.'

She felt him sigh. A long, long sigh. 'Adeline.'
The word had a smile in it.

In the morning when she woke he was dead. She did
not know it until she'd broken back out of the hollow
and looked down at him. The snowclouds had rolled
back off the mountain, down into the lower valleys. The
sunlight was like crystal. It bathed the face that she saw
down in the snow-hole and at first she thought he was
sleeping. But he was not.

She'd seen that face before. She felt such a wave of
tenderness for the innocence there that she thought her
heart would break with it. Still the boy shone through
in the man and she was glad for it.

She cried for him. She cried for them both.

She quenched her thirst with the snow, but she was
horribly cold, ravenously hungry.

The haze continued to retreat down the valleys,
chased away by the sun's fragile warmth, laying out a
splendid landscape of ice and forest and rock below her.
Gradually, to the east, something else was revealed. The
dark glinting mass of an ocean, lapping at the mountains'
feet. She stood on her own two feet, surprised that she
could do so, and looked down at the rocky coast. And
there, far below her, at a place where land met sea, there
was a cluster of buildings, a trail of smoke. Not a Pax
place, she would say: just a village. Fishermen perhaps.

Should she try to get there?

She'd be too weak. And what would be the point in
any case?

*Why* hadn't she died?

It was frightening to have to decide. Worse than anything. Terrifying to be alive. She sat with her head in
her hands for a while, letting the sun ease the stiffness
further.

She had not really achieved anything she came here for. She had made no difference. And she lived.

*Let go. Let go of the past. Let go of death.*

Her mind span fretfully back through all she had known. The people, the tastes of being alive. Seven; Sebastien; her sister; Maman, searching for her when Adeline herself was no more than a dusty tot, worming her way into the cool spaces between the giant herb pots of their baking garden.

The strangeness of it all!

She rose to her feet, parted them slightly on the slope, facing down towards the ocean. Slowly, as lazily as a summer bee, as careful as a spider, she began the fifth kata, the kata for feeling down into the earth and leaving you free to act.

She slid into the final movement, her arms stretched out, palms flat, one ahead, one behind, knees slightly bent, spine vertical. She allowed the last sighing of breath as she moved, trickling from her lips, to empty her.

It was decided. She would head down for the village.

She said a last goodbye to Kay, gave him her thanks for what he had done, and set off. Her muscles were feeble, uncertain, but slowly they warmed and softened as she worked her way down.

In a little while she was jogging.

Then running.

If this day was all she had, still she would live it.

And suddenly, amazingly, she was happy.

*Life is an intoxicating game,* she thought.

'Yes,' a voice agreed, inside her; 'it is a game.'

# EPILOGUE: MEETINGS

'Please. There is a message for you. A person on the radio.'

The little Norwegian beckoned Clarissa to follow him. She swung out of her bunk and up the tiny ladder to the wheelhouse. That was about all there was on the little fishing boat.

Who could be radioing here for her?

She picked up the receiver. 'Yes?'

'Rissa. Sleeping the day away are you?'

'*Mac!*'

'The very same. Emile's been trawling through all the shipping frequencies to find you. I think he enjoyed it. He's one weird guy.'

'What is it, Mac? Is there news?' She tried to take in air, gripped the receiver a little tighter. 'Is it my sister?'

'Relax. She's safe, Rissa. Emile found her too. He's got the run of this place now. Happy as a pig in—'

'Shut up! Where *is* she, Mac?'

'Place called . . . what is it? Um . . . Abafeld.'

She groped through the charts that were spread out on the little wheelhouse table. 'Abafeld? Just a minute, I'm looking for it . . .'

The captain quietly touched her elbow. 'Abafeld? That is the place? Look.' He gestured at the mountains marching beside them to the west, pointed at a film of distant smoke. 'Look. There. Abafeld.'

'Wow! Mac!' She was laughing. 'I'm right next to it. It's right here!'

'Good then.'

'And she's all right?'

'Far as I can tell, Rissa. Better than all right, actually. You should see this place.'

'What? What are you talking about?'

'The city. This fucking city.'

'What about it?'

'People in tears. People embracing. Parties. Music.'

'What?'

'They all watched her. Watched your kid sister being carried through the mountains. She told them a love story. I don't know. They all watched and listened, every last one of them. Emile kept right on feeding it out, like you said. And now . . . Christ, Rissa! You should see it.'

'But what about Jan? What about Pax?'

'That's all finished. The black ships have been sunk. In the morning they were keeled over. Pax are nowhere to be seen. Nor Jan.'

She was trembling.

'What does it mean, Mac? Is it the prophecy? Is it all true?'

'Search me.'

They were silent. Then he said, 'I reckon it was there, anyway. In them. She just gave them a little push.'

She lay down the radio and went outside the wheelhouse, into the sharp, northern chill. The captain joined her.

'So,' he said in his thick accent, 'we will steer in towards the land a little, and I'm thinking you will be at this place in an hour.'

Clarissa hugged him, wetting his face with her tears.

'This is happy news, I'm thinking,' he said. 'That is good. Very good.'

# EPILOGUE: DOMINIC

It was happening again. A ghastly rerun. A day when Bede's was going to be deserted. Everyone bolting to their secret places and their escape routes. The buildings would stand empty. The clues to what had happened here would fade. Dominic was to be one of them, the escapers. Father was here this time, come to take him away. He didn't know where they were to go. He didn't care. This time he'd as soon be the one left behind.

The bus had returned for most of them. It was parked in the main quad. Someone had bolted a snow plough to the front since it had last come and fitted new, chunkier, tyres with chains. Someone was doing these things, keeping to a plan. The bus would have a soldier escort wherever it was going, for the truck was there too, and a Land Rover with a heavy machine gun mounted on the roof. Next to the vehicles, the bags and boxes were piled up. Khaki kit bags for the soldiers. A little mound of coloured rucksacks by the bus wheels for the children.

'We won't go with the others,' Father had said; 'we'll wait here for the helicopter to come back for us.'

The mound that was Ruth's physical self had been tidied away some time in the night. The scientists had all gone with their little specimens, and Dominic supposed the Major had gone with them, as he wasn't to be seen. One of the sergeants was in charge of the loading, and a corporal was going round the buildings with a detail of men, checking that nothing vital or incriminating had been left behind. The atmosphere between soldiers and inmates was changed, quite jovial now, just as if it really was the last day of term. There was a silent wall around the fact of Ruth's death: maybe that wall had driven the different groups closer together.

Dominic didn't want to be part of it all. He took the broken pieces of his guitar to the craft room to see what he could do to join them again. It was really a professional job but he should be able to make some sort of attempt, even with his bandages. It would keep his hands and mind busy.

He assembled the tools he needed on one of the benches. Plane, chisels, a length of dowling, wood glue, sandpaper. If this didn't work he'd try and cut out a metal brace to run along the back of the neck. Maybe when it was done he could write some music to go with Ruth's strange 'Song'. Maybe Father would have electricity wherever they were going. He wouldn't be surprised. He worked calmly and steadily, clamping the instrument in a vice – the jaws wrapped in cloth to protect the finish – and carefully shaving away and smoothing the splintered edges that were to be rejoined. The sun was shining brightly today, falling in great shafts on the bench where he worked.

'Dominic. Dominic Saint.'

He looked slowly up. Frank was there and he hadn't even heard him come in. Frank was looking half uncomfortable and half triumphant. The pretty mouth was twisted between habitual sneer and some other, alien expression.

'Dominic. I wanted to say. I didn't know she would die. I didn't know he'd do that to her. I wouldn't have intended that.'

Dominic stood with his hands frozen on the wood. He could feel the emotion simmering, trying to break out just when he'd soothed it away for now.

'What do you mean,' he said, 'you didn't know, you didn't intend it?'

Frank stuck his jaw out. 'It was you, you fool. Writing it all down. That's not my fault, is it?' He shook his head in disgust. 'Look. I just wanted to say. I didn't mean that to happen, even if she was nuts.'

He left again and Dominic stood motionless, looking after him. His calm was shattered. The pieces of the guitar remained unjoined.

After a few minutes he put down his tools and went out too. He walked unhurriedly to Mr Davis's room in the Geography department. The broken door swung easily inwards. He crunched across crumbs of dust and chalk to the inner sanctum. But he saw at once that the metal cabinet had been forced open. The rifle bolts were no longer there.

Of course they weren't. It made sense now.

He left the little building more quickly, his walk turning into a jog as he headed towards the quad. Engines were running there, he could hear. Warming up for the journey. He himself was more than warm: he was white hot. Anguish, rage, loss, hopelessness ... Whatever it was, he was running, faster and faster. The frosted buildings flashed past. His body was quick, strong, lethal. There were no ideas in his head, just a white haze, an instinct.

The soldiers were already in their truck and in the Land Rover, ready to go. They were waiting only for the inmates from the cloning programme. The coloured rucksacks were being loaded into the baggage hold of the bus. The first couple of girls were mounting the steps. Frank was there, standing alone on one side, his eyes closed as if he was exhausted. For once he didn't have his little clique around him.

Dominic saw him and looked around for what he needed. A length of timber, a knife, anything. If there was nothing, his fists would be enough. He couldn't slow down to look. He must keep on going.

Barry from the kitchen mob loomed up in his path, his grubby leather jacket flapping, his bag over his shoulder, heading for the bus. Dominic saw him and knew what his weapon was to be. Lowering his shoulder he charged into the man, knocking him heavily to the snowy gravel. He ripped the jacket open and plunged his hand inside, and sure enough found heavy, cold metal. He brought it out, cradled it.

People had noticed him. They could see what he was doing, but they just stood there. Even the soldiers. Nobody could hinder the white fire in his mind. Only one of the girls, Siobhan perhaps, let out a shout of fear. Hearing it, Frank opened his eyes and looked to where Dominic was levelling the little pistol at him, clicking off the safety, his arm straight and steady.

The colour drained from the older boy. He knew he was going to die. There was utter silence through the quad, just as there had been at that last parade. Even the engines coughed and died as their drivers turned the keys back to 0.

Dominic stood in the pool of silence. He had become the maker of events. Everybody waited on him.

He didn't pull the trigger.

He pushed the safety back on, then pulled back his arm and threw the thing high over the roofs of the Art block.

He went back to the craft room without another glance at those about to leave. There he drilled holes in the neck and body of the Strat, sawed lengths of dowling to fit inside, carefully coated the two surfaces with thick, yellow glue and fitted clamps over the join until it should set.

His father was fretting when he came out to the field with the guitar and his other things. The chopper had been there thirty minutes. Dominic climbed inside and immediately the thing roared and jumped into the air, so that Bede's lay spread out and shrinking below them, a little paradise nestling in its white valley.

> *And now good morrow to our waking soules,*
> *Which watch not one another out of feare;*
> *For love, all love of other sights controules,*
> *And makes one little roome, an every where.*

His breath misted the glass as he looked down. Ruth terrified him. He hadn't been ready for her adventure, not yet. But given a little time, he might take the first few steps. Anything was possible.

'You're a Grade A lunatic, Dominic. A real nutcase.'

Her challenging laugh ran across the fields below and Dom laughed with her.

## REPORTS ON CAMP E SUBJECTS.
## AUTHOR: PROFESSOR EVE TSULLISOVA

09/ Dominic Saint

Clearly this subject's scores across a range of activities fall well into the desired zone of this programme. His physical potential is good. He is empathetic, imaginative, creative. He is capable of methodical and careful problem-solving and displays great tenacity, both in resolving the task set and, in a wider context, in resisting deleterious influences upon his well-being (human, physical, situational . . .). This tenacity may veer into stubbornness and, in conjunction with the methodical quality, may lead to a certain preponderance for secretiveness. In short, despite a basically conservative nature and an innate stability, he may not always be relied upon to play the team game, nor to take the course expected. The largest unknown, however, rests with his own perception of his abilities, at the moment at quite a low level. No test we have run can confirm this, but it seems likely that increased confidence in himself would result in highly increased potential in all fields.

XXI/ Unknown candidate

This unnamed candidate, a female, has achieved scores (some unverified) across the whole range of activities tested at Camp E that are exceptional, well beyond any other candidate. She is quick-thinking, a natural problem-solver, physically formidable and capable of motivating herself in situations of incredibly adverse circumstances. She is empathetic in the extreme, imaginative, romantic, and entirely unpredictable. Her ability totally to disregard any system of rules or conventions if and when she considers this to be expedient would suggest that for the purposes of this programme she is not ideal material.

# AUTHOR'S NOTE

The climate change in Dominic's world is a realistic scenario for north and western Europe. At present we are kept warm by the ocean currents coming across the Atlantic from Central America. These depend on a certain salt content to make the water sink down at the end of its run and return to the starting point to be warmed once more. The salt content in the relevant zone is dropping, thanks to the release of new fresh water via global warming. Once salinity drops to a critical level, the current fails and our temperatures plunge, more or less overnight. Nobody knows when this might happen, though some forecasts suggest as little as fifteen years from now. Thus whilst the rest of the world would warm up, we would freeze for a while.

As for the other disasters, pandemics of flu and so forth, they are even more certain. Look at the news from the last few years.

What answers will people find to these problems? Will they try the old methods . . . blaming other people, controlling them, maybe a whiff of elitism? Will they rely blindly on technology?

Or will the answers come from the human heart, where we are all joined and equal, and where anything might begin?

PC
7 June 2005

# AND FINALLY ...

Heartfelt thanks go to the usual suspects. Caradoc and Judith at AP Watt. Venetia and team at Simon and Schuster UK. Loved ones at home.

Thanks and 'respect' to anyone at all who bites off more than they can chew and does it joyfully.

And a grudging nod of the head to the huge list of politicians whose belief in the sacred market economy is helping to manifest the world that my poor heroes and heroines have to inhabit. When oil and the burning of it is more important than water or air or compassion, we're all up a certain creek without a certain implement.